Also by M.G. Crisci

Indiscretion
Papa Cado
Rise and Fall of Mary Jackson-Peale
Save the Last Dance
Seven Days in Russia
This Little Piggy

Call Sign, White Lily

The amazing story of a beautiful young woman who became one of the most famous Russian fighter pilots during the Second World War. Based on true events.

M.G. CRISCI

In collaboration with

Yelena Sivolap and Valentina Vaschenko

ORCA PUBLISHING COMPANY
Carlsbad, CA 92011

Cover Design by Good World Media

Editors: Raymond Mancini Sr., Holly Scudero

Cover Art: Good World Media

Manufactured in the United States of America

Library of Congress Control No. 209912007

ISBN 978-0-9663360

Fourth Edition

To the brave Russian and Ukrainian families
who suffered so much. May the world never forget.

Praise for *Call Sign, White Lily*

Call Sign, White Lily does a superb job of poignantly depicting the life and times of an extraordinary young lady, Lilia Litvyak. But, the book does much more. It provides insights into many important Russian customs and traditions, and accurately depicts the extraordinary resolve of the Russian people to seek peace among all the world's communities.

—Russian Cultural Centre,
Washington, D.C.

It continues to amaze the editorial staff of our newspaper that an American with no Russian ancestry could deliver such an insightful literary work. We applaud his vision, tenacity, writing prowess, and desire to break down long-standing barriers of misunderstanding and mistrust.

—Russia Now Newspaper,
Rossiyskaya Gazeta, Moscow

The story is poignant and powerful. The reader will be rewarded with a magnificent tale of patriotic integrity and characters that must be admired, and acts of valor and loyalty that embody the dedication of undying love and devotion to country and countrymen.

—San Francisco Book Review

M.G. Crisci never disappoints. He writes non-fiction so well that it feels like its fiction. I loved all the characters in *Call Sign Lily;* there's not a person I didn't like. I also loved how the book sound likes it was Russian translated into English. It gave the book more authenticity. Crisci makes you feel like you are actually living the story beside Lilia Litvyak. I recommend this book to anyone who just wants to read a great book.

—Goodreads.com

Lilia Litvyak's unflappable patriotism and amazing flying skills are the perfect vehicle to remind today's generations of young people to never forget the unimaginable atrocities our people (i.e., Russia and the Ukraine) experienced at the hands of the Nazi's. Mr. Crisci's sensitive and approachable style brings the substance to life in engaging human terms.

—Ukrainian Embassy to the U.S.
Washington, D.C.

It is amazing that Lilia Litvyak's coming-of-age story took 66 years to assemble. Her courage, her skills and her love of country are terribly relevant today to freedom-loving people around the world. The story's engaging, the writing more so."

—Lakeside International Group
New York, NY

My name is Lilia Litvyak. I died on August 1, 1943, just 17 days before my 22nd birthday when I was shot down near the small Ukrainian village of Dmitrovka.

I never wanted to be a warrior. I did not want to fight and die so very young. Who would? I grew up in Moscow just like any other teenager—lost in thoughts of young love, games and dreams of a bright future. But my world changed when the horrors of war came to my country.

I'm proud of what I accomplished as a fighter. It helped save the country I love and showed that women are just as capable as men.

Yes, my times and my country shaped me. But as you read my story, you'll see that we all have the same hopes and dreams. Understanding what we have in common is a gateway to mutual trust and a better tomorrow for Russians, Americans and everyone—a tomorrow where teenagers don't have to go to war. Please read. Please understand.

Yours always,
Lilia Vladimirovna Litvyak

Preface

Boris V. Sapunov, PhD. (Doctorate in History)
Honorary Doctorate, Oxford University
Head of Scientific Research, Hermitage Museum, St. Petersburg
Above: Dr. Sapunov in the year 2000, next to the signature
he placed on the famous Reichstag Wall on 2 May 1945.

Dear Reader,

As a lifetime historian, I found the book "Call Sign, White Lily" by M. G. Crisci and his collaborators, Yelena Sivolap and Valentina Vaschenko, to be incredibly interesting. This book has a special place in among all the books written and stories told about the World War II. The author and his colleagues brilliantly re-created the image of the main character—Lilia Litvyak—a courageous and brave pilot who, along with other female pilots, brought down multiple enemy planes.

The author did a fantastic job combining Lilia's biography with the everyday life of pre-war and during the World War II

Russia. What is most surprising is that not only is M. G. Crisci not Russian himself, but also the fact that he does not even have any Russian relatives or predecessors. Moreover, Mr. Crisci does not speak Russian. As a war veteran and a former soldier who fought in many battles, including in Berlin, I was amazed at the author's skill and mastery to re-create the events, of what is now considered to be in the distant past, in such an objective manner.

When I read through the pages of this book, the images and the stories truly come alive. Many episodes of the life of Lilia Litvyak are still remembered by the veterans of World War II. Incredibly, the author was able to include many details of the everyday soldier life that could have only been known to those soldiers.

Today, many people have a misconception about what really happened during the War and either purposefully underestimate or are simply unaware of the role of the Soviet people in the victory of the War. This is why it is so important to preserve the truth about what really took place for the future generations.

In conclusion, I can add that a careful read of the text reveals some inaccuracies. This is probably inevitable, since many years have passed since War World II has ended. Many facts have either been distorted or completely forgotten by the people with the passage of time. The inaccuracies, however, do not take away from the value and the significance of this great book. The book of M.G. Crisci plays an extremely important role in what is our duty to history—to preserve the truth about the tragic and heroic chapters of the 20th century for the future generations. Therefore, I highly recommend this book to both Russian and American readers.

Foreword

(l) M.G. Crisci, Author; (c) Valentina Vaschenko, Curator, The Lilia Litvyak Museum; (r) Yelena Sivolap, English Teacher, School No 1

This book began ten years ago in a most unlikely place.

Boris, my gregarious Russian cab driver, was stalled in South Beach's incessant stop-and-go traffic while attempting to reach my Miami Beach office on trendy Lincoln Road. I decided to ask a simple question. The answer would change my life forever.

Boris, a Muscovite with two Ph.D.'s in computer sciences, his two teenage daughters and his wife also a Ph.D. had migrated to America five years prior, like so many others before, wanting a "better life." Trying not to sound like a culturally insensitive idiot, I asked why one so educated was driving a cab. He paused for a moment. "No good English, no good job. But all right, my time come."

For whatever reason, I persisted. "Since arriving, what has been your biggest surprise about America? Bad or good, it doesn't matter."

Boris looked in the rear view mirror then stopped his cab and turned around. "You want to know. Really know?" He stared in the rear view mirror. "Very sad. Thirty million dead and nobody remember!"

Boris explained. We talked. 40 minutes later the ride was over. I promised myself, someday, somehow, I would deliver Boris's message to generations of Americans, and hopefully to the rest of the developed world, about the millions of peace-loving Russian civilians who suffered unfathomable atrocities at the hands of the Nazis during World War II, ordinary men, women and children, like you and me, murdered and mutilated in their homes, in their factories, on their street corners and in their fields, as they defended Rodina (The Motherland).

I was momentarily motivated, then returned to my self-absorbed life. Two years passed. I was now living in San Diego. There was a story in the newspaper about an exhibition at the Air and Space Museum called *World War II through Russian Eyes*. I heard Boris's voice, "Please Go." Four hours later I was moved to tears and embarrassed I had done nothing. Fate had now given my project a kick start.

My first attempt at telling Boris's story was to create a Russian version of Tom Brokaw's book, *The Greatest Generation*. I would call it *28 Million Dead and Nobody Remembers*. It would be family stories about how ordinary Russians put their lives on hold during The Great Patriotic War. As I was to learn, during 1,418 days and nights of unconscionable aggression, the Nazis burned part or all of 1,710 cities and towns, 6 million buildings, 32,000 factories, 65,000 kilometers of railroad track, 98,000 collective farms and left another 25 million people homeless.

Somewhere along the way, I met the spectacularly beautiful Lieutenant Lilia Litvyak through the Internet. There were numerous bits and pieces here and there. The more I researched her story, the more fascinated I became. Eventually my research led me 8,731 miles from my home to the industrial town of Krasny Luch, Ukraine, near what is now the Russian-Ukrainian border. There I met Valentina Vaschenko, the curator of a modest museum dedicated to Lilia, and her friend, our loving translator and editor, an English teacher by the name of Yelena Sivolap. As I was to learn, Valentina had made it her life's work to keep the memory of Lilia alive, as best she could with limited resources and limited government support.

These ladies helped me accomplish something that I don't believe has ever been done. Together, this altruistic, jaded, aging middle-aged American man and two passionate, trusting Russian women, 8,000 miles apart, took a journey back in time to create what began as a work of literary fiction based on a real life and real events but ended as something else.

They taught me about their lives and their culture in ways I never imagined. I hope I did likewise. The face-to-face meetings, the Skype calls, the electronic correspondence, the misunderstandings of words, the humor in colloquialisms, the delicate listening, the respectful sharing, is a story in itself.

During my travels to Russia and the Ukraine I visited Lilia's old neighborhood in Moscow, stopped by her apartment, talked to her last remaining childhood friend, Lyudmila Agafejeva, and then took an incredible journey to visit my new friends and Lilia's gravesite in Dmitrovka, the small town not far from where she was shot down. Those trips and the memories are etched in my mind forever. Maybe one day this book will have a companion volume. But first things first! People around the world need to meet Lilia up close and personal.

To that end, Valentina and Lena gave without reservation: their pictures, their recollections, their memorabilia, their time, their love. To this day in Krasny Luch, as in most Russian towns, reminders of the Great Patriotic War remain everywhere. Stories are passed orally from generation to generation in homes and schools in the hopes that history will not repeat itself. The overwhelming majority of Russian citizens (and its newly created federation of states) have the very same hopes and dreams as the majority of American citizens—a world of peace where hope springs eternal. Perhaps our little collaboration will add to that understanding.

Clearly, Lt. Lilia V. Litvyak was just one brave soul who perished in Hitler's brutal Russian Massacre, the greatest human tragedy this world has ever known. But because Lilia was a woman before her time and lived such a meaningful life in her twenty-two years, I have chosen to use her as the vehicle to tell Boris's story. In the process I feel I've gotten to know and love Lilia as I've gotten to know and love Valentina and Lena. I hope I have done their story justice.

One last comment. I am an ordinary American citizen. My parents emigrated from Italy in the early 1900's. Dad was a butcher; Mom a telephone operator. I have no Russian ancestry, directly or indirectly. I do not speak Russian. I'm just a man who would like to see a better world for his children and grandchildren.

mulld S Cruci

The author and village children at Lilia's gravesite in Marinova

Chapter 1

Three-year-old Lilia at a park not far from the Litvyak apartment on Novoslobodskaya Street near Moscow City Centre.

August 1921
Moscow...

GRAY. THE SKY WAS A DARK, gloomy gray.

The clouds hung low, thick, laden with chilly moisture. The temperature, hovering around fifteen degrees centigrade, was unseasonably low for a late summer day in Moscow. Women wrapped in wool cardigans shuffled briskly as they ventured shop to shop on busy Arbat Street. It was as if October had arrived early.

The architecturally mundane obstetric clinic at the nearby Moscow Centre Maternity Home showed decades of neglect and long, harsh winters. Hairline cracks traveled from the top floor to the worn, rounded street-level entrance steps.

Here on August 18th, in a non-descript ward, a squirming, screaming Lilia Vladimirovna Litvyak announced to her proud parents, Vladimir and Anna, two former peasants from tiny Istra Village—a six hour horse and carriage ride from Moscow—that she had entered the world.

The midwife handed the baby with penetrating blue-gray eyes and curly flaxen blonde hair to her mother and smiled broadly, "Congratulations, Comrade Litvyak, your daughter is an extraordinary beauty."

Anna exuded pride as she held her child for the first time. The baby appeared surprisingly at peace, seemingly content to stare into her mother's eyes. All was right with the world.

Soon it was time for mother and child to leave the clinic. Vladimir had dreamed of this day for months. He greeted his new daughter with a broad smile. "She gets her beauty from her mother."

After wrapping both in a warm blanket to protect them from the cool morning breeze, Vladimir gently placed mother and child on a mattress of soft hay and straw in the rear of his horse-drawn carriage and snapped his whip to begin the ride home. Anna began to sing *Spi, mladenets moi prekrasnyi* (Sleep, My Charming Baby), written by the famous Russian poet M. Lermontov, while Vladimir pensively reminisced about how his family had come to be in this joyful place at this time.

Just four years prior, on the farm of the wealthy, arrogant nobleman Evgeniy Vasiliev, two young peasants, Anna

Tarasova, 16, and Vladimir Litvyak, 19, had been randomly assigned to long days locating, cleaning, and packing a portion of the season's potato harvest.

The handsome, wire-haired Vladimir was a diligent and muscular worker who moved from main tuber to main tuber seeking mature potatoes. He assumed feeder tubers were devoid of mature crops. Anna knew otherwise, and she was not afraid to say something.

"Vladimir, you work too hard for each potato. Why not search the attached tubers?"

Vladimir's response was predictably curt. "How would you know such things?"

"Believe it or not, Vladimir, women sometimes see other things than men do," smiled Anna, twirling her long blonde hair with her fingers.

"Really," said Vladimir, oblivious to the natural beauty standing in front of him. He handed her a spade to dig and a knife to cut. "Show me."

Minutes later she had traversed the same line of tubers that Vladimir had previously harvested and found another twelve perfectly mature potatoes. She stood and smiled proudly. "I believe you will now have a much larger harvest!" And so Vladimir came to realize the subtle determination of the beauty that stood before him.

Other Russian men of that time might have kicked and screamed. Made excuses. Vladimir, in a society dominated by men, was ahead of his time. His broad imposing physique masked a deeply sensitive nature. But cupid's arrow had pierced him deeply, and for all time.

"Maybe you can teach me how you did that?" he flirted.

"Maybe," smiled Anna devilishly. She, too, was smitten.

Some eleven months later, in that same potato field, Vladimir would ask Anna for her hand in marriage. Not long after, they exchanged vows in a peasant ceremony typical of the times. During their first year of marriage, the socially aware Vladimir felt the couple should move to Moscow. Anna was at first reluctant; the farms were all she knew.

"Dear wife, wasn't that what the Revolution was all about?" argued a confident Vladimir. "To create a better life for us. And that of our children."

"Let me think," responded Anna, delaying the inevitable.

After weeks of discussion, Vladimir ran out of rational arguments and attempted a different, more subtle tactic: "My wife," he said lovingly over dinner one evening, "you are the most beautiful woman I have ever seen. I hope our life on the farm never wears that beauty."

Two weeks later, the couple packed their meager belongs, and Anna's vanity, and headed to Moscow.

~

Not long after arriving in Moscow, Vladimir knocked on the door of the manager at a bustling furniture factory on the outskirts of the city, adjacent to the waterway where ships collected the factory's completed product for other ports of call.

The manager wanted experienced help. Vladimir did not fit the bill.

"I can make anything with my hands. Just need to show me how," passionately pleaded Vladimir. "I work hard and long. You will be satisfied. I give my word."

The gray haired manager rubbed his hands across his beard and then smiled. "I take a chance."

"No chance," said Vladimir. "Sure thing."

In time, Vladimir became an accomplished carpenter. For Anna's 20th birthday, Vladimir created a surprise. "My wife, we must go to your birthday present."

"Why can you not give it to me here?" said Anna, reaching for the bag at Vladimir's side.

"There is a good reason," he responded.

"Then, what is that?"

"If I were to tell you, there would be no surprise. Just follow. For one time please, stop all your chatter."

Twenty minutes later they were standing by a pond not far from the factory. Vladimir took a handsome red-and-yellow wooden sailboat from the bag and proudly announced, "I made with my own hands. My tribute to you."

Anna smiled at the handsome boat with her name inscribed on both sides of the bow in bright blue letters. Her heart pounded with pride. It was probably the closest she would ever come to owning a real sailboat.

"This is the most beautiful gift I have ever received."

"We can now imagine sailing to far off places together," said Vladimir.

"And, will we always return home?" teased Anna.

"Most certainly," smiled Vladimir as he pulled a string from his pocket and attached it to a small hook on the front of the boat.

Weekend after weekend, weather permitting, the handsome couple placed their boat on the pond and watched it being carried by the wind.

"Today I say we sail the Volga to the Caspian Sea and taste the breezes of the salt air."

The couple laughed as Vladimir pulled their vessel to shore. He then looked inside the boat.

"I am disappointed to say, it was a poor day at sea."

"It is never a poor day when I sail with my husband," smiled Anna.

~

It was a bitter cold January. The couple had long since placed their boat in storage.

Vladimir, who accepted but did not enjoy winter, look-ed out the window. His mind filled with thoughts of a splendid picnic after one of their imaginary sailing trips. He smiled.

"Why such a smile?" asked Anna." Do you suddenly love winter?"

He rubbed his hand across his stubby beard. "We were having a picnic by the shore. Under the tree, not far from where we went ashore. The picnic basket was so full. The apples and pears were delicious, the lemonade so refreshing. We ate until the basket was empty."

Anna rubbed her stomach. "Not so, the basket is still full."

"Now you are going to tell me about my dreams," laughed Vladimir.

"It is not a dream."

Vladimir looked totally confused. Anna realized she needed to be more explicit.

"Dear husband, I am talking about this basket," said a smiling Anna pointing to her stomach.

And so it was that Vladimir learned he would be a father in the near future. As Vladimir recalled those early days of their relationship, he wondered if his wife's staunch determination and sense of vanity would find its way into baby Lilia.

~

Lilia's first "home" was a small but tidy two-room apartment on Smolenskaya Street. Vladimir, Anna, and Lilia slept in one room, while the other was a combination kitchen, dining room, and place to read and invite friends to discuss matters of the day.

"We will save our rubles and one day give our daughter a better life," declared the optimistic Vladimir, who now worked two jobs—Monday to Saturday during the day at the furniture factory, and Tuesday to Friday evenings as a railway clerk. While neither job was the stuff that dreams were made of, Vladimir received regular wages and still worked less total hours and had better working conditions than the virtual servitude of Vasiliev's farm. Anna and Vladimir were proudly and solidly lower-lower middle class!

~

"I need to shop for dinner," said Anna one day when Vladimir arrived home from work. "Can I trust you with little Lilia?"

"Trust me?" responded a clueless Vladimir.

"You know, make sure nothing happens to our daughter."

"What can happen, my wife? She is but three months old. She simply lies and sleeps."

"She struggles to turn more each day," said Anna.

"With all respect, wife, your imagination runs wild."

~

After Anna left, the politically passionate Vladimir invited his equally passionate neighbor, Boris, to share a drink. Matters quickly turned to a discussion of current affairs, who was doing what to whom.

Within minutes the men were waving their arms and shouting at each other, trying to convince the other of his point of view. "I still do not trust Kamenev [a Bolshevik revolutionary and well-known Soviet politician in the 1920s]. Remember he and Zinovyev were the only two Central Committee members to vote against the October Revolution [the Soviet seizure of power in October 1917]," offered Vladimir. "Did not Lenin write a pro-clamation calling them deserters?"

"That is old news. Times change. People change. Must you always live in the past? Even Lenin had a change of heart!" responded Boris emphatically.

While the men drank and swore, little Lilia, in an adjacent room, was awakened by the commotion and attracted to a dark brown kerchief on a nearby chair. Rather than cry, she determinedly squirmed to the edge of the bed and slid onto the carpet. The startled baby began to cry from the tumble. The increasingly boisterous Vladimir and Boris heard nothing...until Anna came home.

"How has our daughter been?" she asked.

"Quiet as a church-mouse," replied Vladimir. Boris nodded. Anna saw the half empty vodka bottle. She went into their bedroom. Lilia's cheeks were pink from the tears she had shed. She looked at her mother and cooed lovingly, as if to say, thank goodness you have returned.

Anna was furious. "My husband, how could you be so unaware! Thank goodness our daughter fell to the soft carpet."

~

At six months, a surprisingly well-coordinated Lilia began to grasp the legs of the kitchen table in a determined effort to stand erect. By nine months, she had taken her first steps. A month later, she first uttered mama and papa. By the twelfth month, Anna was teaching Lilia the names of animals and letting her smell the flowers she had picked.

Also during this first year, the couple accidentally learned about another of their child's unique gifts. Anna always placed a wide neck jar of fresh wildflowers on the table between Lilia's crib and their bed, preferably red and white to commemorate the day she told Vladimir of Lilia's impending arrival. One evening after Anna sang her daughter to sleep, she and Vladimir returned to the kitchen table to read a few more hours before retiring. Unbeknownst to both, Lilia had awoken, seen the flowers dangled over the side of the crib, grabbed two white wildflowers (her favorite color) from the jar, and then went back to sleep.

Anna turned the light on in the bedroom.

"Husband, look at your daughter."

Lilia lay sound asleep with two wildflowers by her face.

"How could that happen?" wondered Vladimir.

Concerned that the wildflowers might poke their daughter in the eye, Anna quietly removed the flowers and returned them to the jar.

"Perhaps we should move the jar, so our daughter cannot get into any additional trouble," she said.

"That is a good solution," said Vladimir.

Later that evening, Lilia awoke to find the wildflowers had been removed from her direct view. The determined child cried and pointed for a solid hour.

"That little girl has an iron will. Let her have the flowers," whined Vladimir.

"She must learn," responded a determined Anna.

"Learn what?"

"Learn things cannot always be her way."

At 4 AM an exhausted Anna acquiesced. She tore the rough stems off the wildflowers and returned them to the crib. Within moments, Lilia stopped crying and went right back to sleep.

"We lose. I guess the solution was not so good," said Vladimir, covering his head with the blanket.

~

"Congratulations, Comrades," smiled the doctor at the child's first annual medical examination. "Lilia is a perfectly healthy and very well-coordinated little girl."

"But what about her continued temper?" saidVladimir, referring to their sleepless nights.

"I don't understand," responded the doctor.

Vladimir then described his tale of woe. "She will not go to sleep without wildflowers by her side."

"And so?"

"Once asleep, we turn out the lights. We remove the wildflowers from her crib so there is no accident during the night."

"That is good, no?"

"Every night is the same. She awakes, realizes the flowers have been removed, and 'the temper' cries until they are returned to her side."

"I do not believe that means the child has a particul-arly difficult temper," responded the doctor.

"Then what does it mean?"

"Comrades, it means Lilia appears to possess good night vision in addition to her advanced coordination and deter-mined personality."

"Will that remain as she grows?" wondered Anna.

"Comrade," smiled the doctor. "Are we referring to

her vision, her coordination, or her determination?"

Vladimir laughed at the interplay. "Perhaps she will use her gifts to become a night watchman."

"Perhaps she will decide to become a pilot and fly night missions!" imagined the doctor.

Vladimir, Anna, and the doctor laughed. Baby Lilia did not.

~

The couple needed a larger apartment, so all could have their own space. Anna, over Vladimir's protestations, got a part-time job as a store clerk. "We will work as partners to raise our child," declared Anna. "The situation will only be temporary."

Anna was right.

Ten months later, the couple had saved enough to move to a larger, more functionally proportioned apart-ment on Novoslobodskaya Street, a 400-year-old street that had burned to the ground during the Patriotic War of 1812 and had been since rebuilt. In fact, Lilia even had her own room, a rare amenity in Moscow for one so young.

"How did you find such a grand place?" said Vladimir, thinking he had died and gone to heaven.

"While I was stocking the shelves, I heard my manager tell his assistant about the apartment. I told my manager I was feeling sick, and needed to go home. Then I went right over, and here we ar

Chapter 2

*Lilia's father, Vladimir, believed ardently
in Stalin's vision of a better life.*

September 1927
Moscow...

AN AMBITIOUS JOSEPH STALIN warned delegates at the 15th Congress of the Communist Party of the impending "capitalist encirclement" caused by the failure of Lenin's New Economic Policy. His vision: the survival and development of the Soviet Union could only occur by

12

pursuing "state-controlled" development of heavy industry, managed exclusively by him.

Change came swiftly. Stalin had cleverly captured the mood of the day. People, particularly the ordinary proletariat like Vladimir and Anna, embraced these Communist ideals as the way to the better life they were seeking. The State formally laid claim to all the shops, farms, and factories in urban and agri-cultural centers alike.

"I believe we should take advantage," explained Vladimir one evening. "Working for the State will mean regular employment and regular pay." Anna agreed.

After passing a series of detailed security checks (Stalin had become preoccupied with eliminating anyone with dissenting views), Anna became a clerk in a government-run general store in downtown Moscow, not far from their apartment, while Vladimir was appointed to a position of railway switchman for the rapidly expanding Soviet Railway system.

Before long, the highly organized and detail-conscious Anna was promoted to head stock clerk, which allowed her to view all the merchandise shipped to and sold at the store. Occasionally a few out-of-date and heavily edited Western European and American fashion magazines would find their way to her store. Anna would select those of visual interest and place them in a side cabinet; then she would study them on her lunch break and at the end of the day, imagining what the words to the pictures might say. She quickly concluded that "bourgeois culture" underscored the essential, universal, and immutable qualities of all women: the desire to improve one's appearance.

"So you like?" said Olga, her distinctly unfashion-able manager, noting Anna's magazine interests.

Anna's instinct was to say nothing, lest she be accused of anti-state behavior.

"No worry," said the cherubic woman with her black hair in a tight bun. "You are a very good worker. Take one from stack; nobody will say anything."

A few days later Anna arrived home with her first selection, a German edition of *Harper's Weekly* magazine. The chauvinistic Vladimir thumbed through the pages in utter amazement. "Those women are so frail; no wonder the Germans tell their women to stay home and make babies."

"So, my husband, you are saying I'm fat?" teased Anna.

An unsuspecting Vladimir was flustered. "No, I did not mean that."

"Then are you saying I am no longer the beautiful wo-man you married?"

Vladimir realized he was damned if he did and damned if he didn't.

~

Six months later, a few tubes of foreign made lipstick arrived in damaged, unsalable condition. Anna was curious. "Olga, may I try one of the broken color sticks?"

Olga's response was as surprising as it was insightful. "Anna, with your dark complexion and brown hair, I would apply one of the darker shades. Here, let me show you."

Olga selected a bright, glossy, deep red lipstick, applied it, and then dabbed the excess so Anna's lips had a pronounced, almost earthy definition.

"See. Take a look," said Olga pointing proudly.

Anna was pleased with the woman she saw in the mirror. That evening Vladimir was equally pleased to be met at the door by his "fashionable working lady." From that moment, Anna rarely was without her lipstick, a trait her daughter would soon emulate. In fact, by the tender age of seven, Lilia refused to leave the house before Anna applied "her lips," as the girls came to call the process.

The magazines also touted the self-indulgent bath oils and scents used by the ladies of New York, London, and Paris. One day, while picking a wildflower bouquet for the dinner table, Anna came upon a patch of fragrant wild rosemary bushes. She picked some blossoms, brought them home, boiled a few liters of water, and soaked them for 30 minutes. When she deemed the scent of her infusion ready, she strained the sweet-smelling liquid into a bottle she kept in a cabinet. That evening while bathing, she added a liter or so of her homemade infusion. Anna's fragrantly scented body attracted Vladimir like bees to honey. He was driven to a bout of passionate lovemaking. Quite accidentally, she also discovered that infusing her homemade concoctions with certain wildflowers (particularly poppies and daffodils when in season) further enhanced her attractiveness to Vladimir.

Anna made it a practice to bathe in her rosemary water whenever she wanted to communicate to Vladimir that she wanted his love and tenderness.

Lilia also came to enjoy her mother's homemade bathing fragrance, although still too young to understand Anna's ultimate motivation.

"Mummy," asked little Lilia, "you smell wonderful. Might you make some additional liquid for me?"

~

Vladimir was an excellent and obedient employee, who was interested in and quickly absorbed every facet of railroading: conducting, maintenance, scheduling, dispatching. His work ethic was a role model for a disgruntled and increasingly passive workforce. His ability to train new switchman and schedulers permitted him to earn small production bonuses under Stalin's rule that provided material rewards in proportion to contributions, less a withholding for state expenses.

Unfortunately, Vladimir's multiple skills and positive attitude created an unexpected strain on his family because he was summoned away from Moscow far more frequently than he would have liked. One month he was training dispatchers in the Urals, and the next building a maintenance staff along the foothills of the Volga. But Anna never complained and Vladimir never refused a "suggested" assignment.

The question was always the same when Vladimir returned home from a trip.

"Daddy, can we go to the swings?"

Lilia loved the sensation of being airborne, the breeze passing through her hair, from the time she was old enough to discover a park swing. Fortunately, Novoslobodskaya Street was not far from the Central Park of Culture and Rest where there was an abundance of bright red swings and see-saws.

Vladimir looked at Anna. "Go, enjoy your daughter. Dinner will be ready in an hour, give or take," she said.

"How long is 'give or take?'" teased Vladimir.

"Give or take when you two return," smiled Anna, who understood how precious father and daughter time was to both of them.

Their park ritual was always the same. "Have you selected your swing yet, my daughter?"

"I am still deciding," said Lilia, who had narrowed her decision to two swings to her right. "I think this one has two less links, which should make it go higher."

Vladimir was not about to dispute her observation. He had learned Lilia, while never disrespectful, had a mind of her own.

On board, Lilia would say, "faster and faster." Once she attained her desired speed, she would urge her father, "now—higher, higher."

"Daughter, we can only go so fast, so high; otherwise, you can slip and fall."

"Daddy, no worries. I want to touch the sky.

Chapter 3

*The annual May Day celebration in Red Square
was a Litvyak Family Tradition.*

THE FIRST OF MAY WAS considered one of the great-est working-class holidays of the year for millions of Muscovites.

The streets surrounding Red Square were a feast for eyes and ears: hundreds of flags, banners, and slogans were mounted on carts as they rolled past cheering crowds, reaffirming freedom from Tsarist oppression and a better life for all. Laughter, singing, dancing, and sounds of the garmoshka were everywhere.

Vladimir and Anna always enjoyed the festivities, but this year was very special–they were bringing eight year-old Lilia for the first time.

"What do you think?" asked Anna, holding a beautiful white wool coat she had made for Lilia to wear.

"It is almost as beautiful as the wife who made it and the daughter who will wear it," smiled Vladimir.

"The railroad does you well. You have become my silver-tongued husband."

"Truth is truth."

"Time is fast approaching," reminded Anna. "We do not want to miss the people's parade past the reviewing stand or listening to Comrade Stalin's words."

Quickly, the family dressed and headed for the square. Before long, they were surrounded by the masses. Little Lilia in her white coat, brand new black leather shoes, and long blonde hair began to tug on her father's pants.

"What is it, my child?" said Vladimir, looking down.

"Daddy, I cannot see," complained Lilia.

Vladimir knelt down. "Come, get on my shoulders and hold my hands. You will see all."

Lilia noticed the hordes of soldiers passing the Tribune, paying tribute to Comrade Stalin.

"Why do all the soldiers look to the Tribune?" she asked innocently.

"To pay their respect."

Lilia's expression turned blank. Vladimir realized he had assumed too much.

"The man on the Tribune is our leader, Comrade Stalin. He helped Mummy and Daddy get out of the fields, far from our home. If it were not for him, Mummy and Daddy would not have the fine jobs we do. He wants everybody to have the same things we do. And he wants all the people in the world to speak kindly of our motherland. That's why we have such a powerful army with all the soldiers."

Lilia got the general sense of what her father said. Vladimir assumed this explanation would suffice. But, as always, Lilia had questions. "Why do we need soldiers for people to speak kindly? Doesn't everybody have jobs?"

As Lilia got older, she would spend hours discussing such matters with her father *privately*. In fact, Vladimir would become the primary cause of her unshakeable sense of patriotism. But Vladimir also made it abundantly clear to Lilia that political discussions in public, however well-intentioned, had to be avoided for fear of retribution by the authorities.

~

This particular day, the heavens opened, the rains came, and spectators and participants alike got soaked. Still it was a happy time, so the demonstrations continued. Finally, when the festivities concluded, a weary Vladimir removed Lilia from his shoulders as the crowd began to disburse.

Lilia again tugged at her father's pants.

"What is it now, my child?"

"Carry me! My feet hurt so. The shoes are very tight." Vladimir, his back already aching, tried to reason with his daughter. "My child, it is a long trip, please be..."

A determined Lilia interrupted, "Carry me!"

About that moment, a cart with familiar faces stopped next to the Litvyak family. It was Novoslobodskaya Street neighbors Maya and Semyon Demidov, carrying deco-rations from the demonstration.

"Can we offer a ride home?" said Semyon. "There is no room on the bench in front, but you can sit near the flags and banners! It will be comfortable."

Vladimir nodded yes.

As the cart shook and rattled its way home, Lilia soon found herself sitting on the flags and banners in the rear.

Thirty minutes later the group arrived at their apartment. Vladimir, favoring his back, gingerly began walking toward their apartment with Lilia. Anna began to laugh rather hysterically.

"And what is so funny? Your husband, the hunch-back?'

"No, no. Not you," said Anna, pointing at Lilia

The rain-soaked red flags and banners had dyed Lilia's brand new white coat a bright Communist red.

~

Maya Demidov was the perfect neighbor—initially!

She and her husband, Semyon, an office clerk in the local MGB office (the forerunner of Khrushev's feared KGB), and their three children lived down the hall from Vladimir and Anna on Novoslobodskaya Street. While his income was substantially less than the dual income Litvyak household, his position did provide his family certain perks not available to the general public—for example, first-selection foodstuffs and preferential treat-ment at various medical clinics.

To earn some additional rubles, Maya agreed to act as a part-time nanny for Lilia while Anna worked at the store. After all, she rationalized, "When one already had three small ones, what is an additional small one?"

In time, Maya's eight-year-old daughter, Elena, had become steadfast friends with Lilia. After school and homework, they would spend hours playing games together. The girls had become particularly fond of a game called *Words*, in which one child would write down the longest word they knew. The other child then tried to make as many words as she could with letters from the long word. Each word counted ten points. Each child also got chances to write a long word.

Typically, Lilia, who was a more advanced reader then Elena, would write longer words and identify more words with a word, thus winning at least 70% of the time.

"I don't want to play anymore," said a frustrated Elena one day. "You cheat."

"Do not!"

"Do too!"

Anna tried to interrupt. "Girls, girls."

Maya looked at the words and sided with her daughter.

"Let us forgive and forget," said Anna, willing to compromise in order to keep the peace.

"See, your daughter makes a word spelled t-r-a-i-l. There is no such word. Only t-r-i-a-l."

Anna tried to explain the difference between the two words. Maya became incensed and left in a huff. "You cheat like your daughter."

~

Once home, Elena told her father how the neighbors always cheat.

From the Demidovs' standpoint, the Litvyaks now had two strikes against them. First, Anna defended a daughter who cheated in children's games.

Secondly, the Litvyaks had a larger apartment—one more bedroom—despite having fewer children. Sharing one bathroom and toilet in turn, one kitchen with several kerosene cookers, several kettles and pans, or one stove to cook in turn constantly reminded Maya of the inequity.

In time, she also discovered Lilia's room contained a polished ash wood dresser, while her children's furniture was mostly rough timbers that had a tendency to splinter.

Maya asked the building superintendent for a larger apartment. "I believe the size of my family and my husband's position should warrant a larger flat."

"Comrade, I'm sorry," said the building manager. "You will have to wait like the others. The waiting list is several years."

Maya seethed with jealousy

Chapter 4

*Lilia at age nine shows early signs
of inquisitiveness and determination.*

IN 1930, LILIA WAS GRANTED admission to the ad-vanced School No.1 off Tverskoy Bulvar. There she ex-celled in the basics, especially mathematics. According to her teachers, she was also becoming master of the one word sentence... "Why?"

"Comrade Litvyak," said School No.1's principal, middle-aged Yekaterina Solovyeva, during a parent discussion, "my teachers tell me your daughter's sense of order leaves much to be desired."

"She is always respectful at home," offered Anna.

"Here, she needlessly wastes valuable student time during history classes."

"I don't understand."

"As you know," glared Solovyeva sternly, "Comrade Stalin wants *all* Soviet children to understand how and why the State works."

"Yes... and... "

"We tell your daughter about the benefits of the collective farm system, and she wants to know why people can't grow what they want. We tell your daughter about the need for controlled industrialization, and she wants to know why the peasants in the fields are ignored. We tell your daughter why food shortages occasionally occur, and she says how that can be with all the land we have."

"Those sound like reasonable questions," commented Anna, realizing full that Lilia's emerging interest in political debate was inherited from her father.

"Not for a nine-year-old. Comrade Litvyak, our job is to indoctrinate our youth, not debate irrelevant bourgeois issues."

"I believe that to be your opinion. Mine is different."

"I can see why your daughter is so undisciplined," said Solovyeva, the anger burning brightly in her eyes.

"That's not true, Comrade Solovyeva."

"Does she not get the proper orientation at home?"

"I resent the inference. The Litvyaks love the Motherland," said Anna. "We believe everyone should share our country's great riches. Comrade Stalin has the opportunity to transform us into one of the great nations of the twentieth century."

"We are already a great nation."

Anna paused before responding. She decided it was best to placate instead of debate. "Comrade Solovyeva, you're right."

~

Lilia's inquisitiveness with her teachers, and her apparent lack of time studying her lessons at home, led Anna to become concerned about Lilia's grades and future opportunities at the University. She made it her mission to help her study. Two days before each quiz and test, Anna would ask Lilia questions that the teachers might ask. To her amazement, Lilia rarely got a question wrong.

One night, sipping a cup of tea, Anna finally asked what she had been thinking. "Lilia, you realize you do not study as hard as the other children"

"It has been said."

"Then how do you know so many answers?"

"Mummy, I'm really not sure. All I know is I read something once, and I remember virtually all."

Lilia's photographic memory combined with her natural night vision would become significant when war struck.

~

While Lilia's determination gave her teachers fits, her engaging smile and easy going demeanor made her a favorite with classmates. She was fascinated by games that required some thoughtfulness. Lilia would urge classmates to participate in the latest game making the rounds.

"Girls, today I want to explain a new game. It is called *Compositions*."

"Why can't we just play hide-and-seek?" asked the stocky ten-year-old Katya, who would become Lilia's best friend.

"Because I said so," responded Lilia, authoritatively. "Everybody take a piece of paper from the stack. I will ask a question. You write down an answer and pass the paper to the person on your right. When all the questions are finished, we will all read the compositions on the sheet in front of us. Then we vote which is best. The person with the most votes wins."

The six girls nodded. Lilia began. "Write down a boy's name or the name of a famous person or literary character."

Lilia scribbled, then passed her paper.

"Now write a place you know of."

"Good, and now a time.

"Almost done. What were they doing together? Finally, where did they go?"

Lilia looked at the paper in her lap and began to smile.

"I will read my composition aloud first; then everybody must follow."

The girls again nodded, more curious than earlier.

"Natasha and Dubrovsky [the former nobleman from Alexander Pushkin's novel] went in the cellar..."

Girl #1: "in the middle of the night..."

Girl #2: "to play cards..."

Girl #3: "and milk a big cow."

Everybody started to giggle. And, so it went. This day the winning composition was, "Napoleon and Antoinette went swimming in the river at 2 AM so they could boil potatoes."

~

The first tragedy in Lilia's life involved her best friend Katya.

Her geography class had been on a hiking trip deep into the woods outside Moscow. They stopped for a rest by a stream. "I want you children to rest before we return," said teacher Comrade Trofirmova.

Katya decided to ignore the instructions. She wanted to climb a nearby tree to get a better view of the meadows. To Lilia's surprise, Katya quickly scaled five metres, then ten.

"Katya," called a concerned Lilia. "Get down, before Comrade Trofirmova sees you."

Katya laughed. The sound carried. Comrade Trofirmova was furious and horrified.

"Child, get down right now before you hurt yourself. I am responsible." By now the entire class was at the base of the tree. Reluctantly, Katya agreed to come down, but lost her footing and tumbled through the air, wincing in pain as she landed on her back on a rock. There was a crackle, and then she fainted from the pain. The group panicked. Even Comrade Trofirmova was unsure what to do in such a medical emergency. However, Lilia calmly remembered what her father had taught her about camping and hiking.

"Boys, boys," she directed, "go fetch some strong branches, and we will make a stretcher." Then she looked at the oldest boys, Vadim and Yura, and said, "And, you two, please run to the nearest village; fetch a horse and carriage, so we can carry Katya to a hospital as fast as possible."

Within an hour Katya, had been brought to the hospital. Unfortunately, despite the best efforts of the doctor and staff, Katya's backbone had been shattered, her breathing severely limited, and she quickly passed.

Katya was dead at eleven.

Chapter 5

Circa 1930. Lilia, age 9 (top right); with best-friend, Lyudmila Agafejeva, age 8 (lower left). 2009: Lyudmila, age 87 (far right).

EIGHT YEAR-OLD LYUDMILA Agafejeva sat patiently looking out the window of her family's second floor apartment at 19 Novoslobodskaya Street. It was 4:00 P.M. and Lilia had not yet returned from school. For Lyudmila and the other children in the building, Lilia, who lived across the street at number 14, was like their big sister. She taught them all kinds of games and activities.

As Lyudmila would recall some 79 years later, "Lilia was kind and generous and always had a smile on her face. She always made time to teach us younger children something new."

Lilia turned the corner and waved. It was the signal Lyudmila knew well. She grabbed her coat, ran down the hall to tell her two girlfriends, Elena and Vera, that Lilia had arrived. As the girls hopped and skipped down the stairs, they wondered what Lilia had planned for the day. To their surprise, it was something new that Lilia simply invented.

"Would you girls like to play puddles?" asked Lilia, blond hair tucked under her brown wool cap. The three girls shrugged their shoulders. Lilia smiled. "Now tell me you don't know how to play," teased Lilia warmly. "Perhaps I should teach you." The girls nodded like bobble-head dolls.

She then pointed to the small, uneven road filled with dirt potholes that sat between Buildings 14 and 19. It had rained quite heavily earlier in the day, so the potholes were filled with water. "The object of the game is to hop and skip around the puddles. Whoever reaches the fence at the end of the road first wins. But you must avoid the puddles. If you accidentally step in a puddle, you have to go two puddles back and begin again. Does everybody understand?"

Lyudmila raised her hand. "Suppose there is a big puddle. How can we go over without getting wet?" The ever-resourceful Lilia offered a solution in the form of a question. She wanted the younger girls to learn to think for themselves, to solve problems with little or no assistance from others. "Lyudmila, is there another way of getting around the puddle without jumping straight over?"

The little girl thought for a moment, then smiled. "Go around."

Lilia offered a compliment. "Absolutely correct. You're very smart."

The girls lined up, Lilia called out, "Ready-set-go!" The three girls giggled and splashed their way to the corner and back, with Lyudmila in dry socks and shoes almost six metres ahead of the other girls.

~

Despite Moscow's biting cold, winter was Lilia's favorite time of year. She loved everything about snow from the soft, billowy flakes that tumbled from the sky to the cool taste of melted ice on her tongue. Most of all she loved to sleigh ride on her stomach down the little white mounds that dotted her neighborhood after the horse-drawn plows left. By the time she was ten, she was the undisputed neighborhood speedster, consistently winning belly-sliding competitions against all comers—male and female.

"Teach me how to go fast," said Lyudmila.

"There are three secrets. But you must not tell everybody or they won't be secrets anymore. First, you need to find the right spot on top of the mound. Most of the children will look for a spot that seems smooth and goes straight down. You want to find a spot where there is a bump in the slope. When you slide over that slope it will carry you further." Lilia took Lyudmila's hand and walked her to the top of the tall mound that sat between the two apartment buildings. "See the difference?"

Lilia explained the second secret. "When you begin to slide on your belly, lift your head as high as you can. It will increase your downhill speed. But that's not all. You have to wear a coat with the fewest possible buttons. Buttons get stuck in the snow and slow you down."

She placed her brown wool cap with earflaps on and demonstrated her technique.

"I want to be just like you," said Lyudmila. During the next three days, Lilia patiently coached her little friend.

Finally, Lyudmila's time came. Her six-year-old neighbor, Boris, boasted that he was faster than most of the other kids on the downhill. "I'm not sure you can beat Lyudmila; she's very fast," replied Lilia. "Just remember what we practiced," she whispered to the stiffened, unsure young girl.

"Ready, set, go!" Boris and Lyudmila zoomed down the icy, snowy slope. In seconds the race was over. "Lyudmila by one length," crowed Lilia proudly.

"Lilia, time for dinner," called her mother out the window. "Then time for homework." Lilia did as requested, but she had left her brown cap at the base of the snow mound. Lyudmila called up to Lilia's window. "You forgot your cap."

"I'll get it tomorrow." But Lilia never did. She knew Lyudmila did not own a warm cap, and she was fortunate enough to have two.

Chapter 6

The German sewing machine that Anna used to teach Lilia how to make clothes.

May 1932
Moscow...

VLADIMIR LITVYAK'S DREAM OF a better life for his family had come true, despite increasingly troublesome rumors that any dissent with Comrade Stalin's philosophies and policies could bring terrible consequences.

What a busy life it was! Anna had been promoted to general manager at the local department store, Vladimir was now a highly respected railroad supervisor, and Lilia excelled in school.

Anna, a supermom decades before the term entered the vernacular, cooked the meals, tended to the house, sometimes worked overtime shifts, and designed and sewed virtually all the family's clothes–from Vladimir's shirts to Lilia's skirts.

Lilia, now eleven, was fascinated by her mother's creativity with the German *Zinger* machine, as it was called, that sat in the corner of the family's living room. She would watch as Anna would take square pieces of colored fabrics and turn them into useful clothing without the slightest need for a pattern or instructions.

One Saturday Anna was making a new play dress for Lilia to wear after school and on days when the two of them would walk through Moscow Center Park to observe the seasonal flowers.

"Mummy, can I help?"

"Perhaps another time," said the time-pressed Anna, concerned that a famished Vladimir would be home within the hour bellowing about his dinner.

Lilia would not be deterred. She responded like a determined woman, many years older. "Motherrr," she said. "This is my dress. Doesn't it only seem proper with your busy schedule and all that I should help you?"

Experience told Anna debating her steel-willed daughter was a fruitless exercise. When Lilia got something in her mind, she almost always got her way. Anna and Vladimir had learned to save debate and rebuttals for those requests they deemed truly inappropriate for an eleven-year-old.

Anna smiled. "Then let it be."

"What should I do, mummy?"

"Let us select the cloth that we will use to make your skirt," said Anna, pointing to pieces of cloth in a wicker basket in the corner. "I believe we have two choices, gray or red. Do you have a preference?"

Lilia selected the red wool cloth. "This is a happy color. It reminds me of the purpose of the Revolution."

Anna was startled by the response. "And, what do you know of the Revolution?"

"I have learned in school. Besides, Daddy and I have talked. Remember, I also learn more each time we go to the annual celebration in the square."

"Your father and politics. He should work for Comrade Stalin."

"Are we not better off than you and Daddy in the fields?"

"I see your father has taught you well."

"Daddy, is the strongest, bravest, smartest daddy in the whole wide world."

Anna shook her head. Lilia's love for her father was admirable, her command of basic political concepts astounding.

"Give me the fabric, child. I will measure it against your body and then make the necessary cuts."

Lilia did as instructed.

"Now, come sit next to me by the machine; I will show you how to make a hem."

Lilia slowly passed the fabric as Anna put it through the needle working the foot pedal to modify the speed. When she had completed half the hem, she looked at Lilia. "Now it is your turn. We switch seats. I pass the fabric to you, you place it under the needle and I will work the pedal."

Lilia followed Anna's instructions perfectly. It was now time to make another decision. "Lilia, before we go further, we need to decide how wide you wish the skirt. The wider we make the skirt, the more ripples and folds it will have. The narrower we make the skirt, the more it will follow the lines of your body."

Lilia answered without hesitation. "I wish the dress to have more folds, so that when I run through the park, I will feel like a bird in flight."

Anna again smiled. "So you wish one day to be a bird in the sky?"

~

The time flew by.

Mother and daughter were having a great time— sewing and sharing cookies and milk. It was 6:30 P.M. In walked Vladimir.

"Hello, my family. It has been a long, hard day on the tracks."

Anna looked at the empty stove, suddenly realizing dinner had been forgotten. Lilia sensed a certain fear in her mother's eyes and came to the rescue.

"Daddy, today Mummy showed me how to make a skirt today that I must wear tomorrow. Would you like to see?"

Lilia was the apple of Vladimir's eye. There was nothing—within reason and their means—he would not do for his daughter.

"Absolutely," responded a pleased Vladimir.

Minutes later, Lilia with her long blonde hair was twirling around in the living room like a fashion model. Vladimir applauded.

"Daddy, I'm glad you like it. But there is one thing."

Even Anna was curious what Lilia was about to say. "Mummy and I have worked hard on my new dress. It was so much fun learning. But it took a long, long time. Would you mind if we ate leftovers for dinner?"

Anna held her breath.

Vladimir smiled. "Not at all, ladies. Not at all."

Chapter 7

МОРОЗКО

The tale of Morozko was a Litvyak family favorite.

VLADIMIR WAS AS PASSIONATE about fairy tales as he was about politics. He believed Communism provided a better life for all, while fairy tales, passed from generation-to-generation, were the moral compass for everyday life.

On a cold and damp winter evening, Vladimir tucked his little angel under the blanket as he began to retell the tale of *Morozko*:

> "Once there lived an old widower and his
> daughter. In due time, the man remarried to an
> older woman who had a daughter herself from

a previous marriage. The woman doted on her own daughter, praising her at every opportunity, but she despised her stepdaughter. She found fault with everything the girl did and made her work long and hard all day long.

One day the old woman made up her mind to get rid of the stepdaughter once and for all. She ordered her husband,

'Take her somewhere so that my eyes no longer have to see her, so that my ears no longer have to hear her. And don't take her to some relative's house. Take her into the biting cold of the forest and leave her there.'

"Why is the mommy so mean?" interrupted Lilia. "Mommies aren't supposed to be like that."

"You're right my daughter," said Vladimir, surprised by the innocent wisdom. "God has a way of making sure things turn out as they should."

Lilia wasn't sure what that meant. "Daddy, tell me more of *Morozko.*"

"The old man grieved and wept but he knew that he could do nothing else; his wife always had her way. So he took the girl into the forest and left her there. He turned back quickly so that he wouldn't have to see his girl freeze. Oh, the poor thing, sitting there in the snow, with her body shivering and her teeth chattering! Then Morozko, Father Frost, leaping from tree to tree, came upon her. 'Are you warm, my lass?' he asked.

'Welcome, my dear Morozko. Yes, I am quite warm,' she said, even though she was cold through and through.

At first, Morozko had wanted to freeze the
life out of her with his icy grip. But he admired
the young girl's stoicism and showed mercy. He
gave her a warm fur coat and downy quilts
before he left. In a short while,
Morozko returned to check on the girl. 'Are
you warm, my lass?' he asked.
'Welcome again, my dear Morozko. Yes, I am
very warm,' she said. And indeed she was
warmer. So this time Morozko brought a large
box for her to sit on. A little later, Morozko
returned once more to ask how she was doing.
She was doing quite well now, and this time
Morozko gave her silver and gold jewelry to
wear, with enough extra jewels to fill the box on
which she was sitting!"

Vladimir paused. "One day you will tell this same story to
your children because it is important for people to under-stand
that God most rewards those who ask for little."

Lilia looked at her modest surroundings. Her mind was
filled with pictures of noble grand residences she saw in
magazines at school. "Father, why did we ask for so much?"
Vladimir was not certain how to reply. He choose to continue.

"Meanwhile, back at her father's hut, the old
woman told her husband to go back into the
forest to bring back the body of his daughter.
He did as he was ordered. He arrived at the
spot where had left her and was overjoyed
when he saw his daughter alive, wrapped in a
sable coat and adorned with silver and gold.
When he arrived home with his

daughter and the box of jewels, his wife looked
on in amazement.

'Harness the horse, you old goat, and take my
own daughter to that same spot in the forest
and leave her there,' she said. The old man did
as he was told. Like the other girl at first, the
old woman's daughter began to shake and
shiver. In a short while, Morozko came by and
asked her how she was doing.
'Are you blind?' she snapped. 'Can't you see
that my hands and feet are quite numb?
Curse you, you miserable old man!' Dawn had
hardly broken the next day when, back at the
old man's hut, the old woman woke her
husband and told him to bring back her
daughter, adding: 'Be careful with the box of
jewels.' The old man obeyed and went to fetch
the girl. A short while later, the gate to the
yard creaked. The old woman went outside
and saw her husband standing next to the
sleigh.
She rushed forward and pulled aside the
sleigh's cover. To her horror, she saw the body
of her daughter, frozen by an angry Morozko.
She began to scream and berate her husband,
but it was all in vain. Later, the old man's
daughter married a neighbor, had children, and
lived happily. Her father would visit his
grandchildren every now and then and remind
them always to respect Old Man Winter."

Vladimir kissed his daughter on the cheek and turned out
the light. As he left the room, Lilia whispered, "Daddy, when I
am older and have a family of my own, we will come to visit
you and Mummy often. I promise."

Chapter 8

Like mother, like daughter.
Lilia falls in love with wildflowers....forever.

ANNA FILLED HER TEENAGE daughter's heart and mind with a love of wildflowers.

From the time Anna was a shy orphan with no friends of whom to speak, she learned to explore the meadows in search of wildflowers. In time, she realized that no matter what the season, nature had provided its bounty for all to enjoy. She became quite expert at drying and arranging, although the red, white, and purple colors of late spring and early summer remained her favorite.

"Young lady, have you finished your school work?" asked Anna one sunny Friday afternoon in May.

"Yes, Mummy."

"Then let's go for a walk in the meadows; I want to show you something."

They walked hand in hand about two kilometres from Novoslobodskaya Street to a big open meadow at the base of the rolling hills. Anna saw a patch of wild white flowers with dainty yellow tongues. She bent to pick a handful. "These are very unusual. They are called wild irises and are usually purple."

"Like these," said Lilia, picking up a handful of delicate purple flowers. "What are these called?

"They have a complicated botanical name, so Daddy just nicknamed them Dragon's Head because of the shape of the flower. See?"

"What about these?"

"They also have a complicated formal name."

Lilia stared blankly. "Why does every beautiful flower require a complicated name?

"Let me explain it this way. Your full name is Lilia Vladimirovna Litvyak. But most people call you Lilia.

"It's the same thing with flowers. Dragon's Head is short for some long name... Draco something or other [Draco-cephalums Argunense]. It's too hard."

"Why do people make the name of something so beautiful so hard to say?"

"That is a good question," smiled Anna. "Perhaps it is simply human nature."

"What do you mean?"

"Human beings have a tendency to make things more complicated than God perhaps intended."

"Mummy, I don't understand."

Anna looked at the darkening sky.

"Another time, we discuss," smiled her mother. "It's getting late, and our bouquet still needs more."

Anna finished picking the Dracocephalums, added some nearby yellow Angel's Trumpets and a few sprigs of green ferns. She gave the makeshift bouquet to Lilia, who looked like a picture postcard standing in the field with her red dress, flowers, and long blonde hair.

"White," said Anna definitively.

"White?" wondered the teenager.

"Our bouquet can use some white. And, I know just where we should visit."

Anna took Lilia's hand and they walked deeper into the meadow until they came to a field of white flowers drenched in late afternoon sunshine not far from a crystal-clear stream. Anna took a pair of small scissors out of her pocket, carefully picked a few stems of the delicate flowers, and placed them in the middle of the bouquet.

"Mama, they are so beautiful, what are they called?"

"I am not sure, but they are so fragrant."

Lilia reached over to smell. "The smell is so pleasing."

"This field has been here as long as I can remember. Somebody probably planted these flowers a long time ago, and then the flowers made more flowers. I discovered it one day while walking with your father. Let us keep it our little secret."

"Can we have a flowerbed near our home and plant such flowers each spring and summer?"

Anna thought for a moment. "We can grow white lilies. They are easy to care for and also have a fragrant smell."

And so it was that lilies would come to be Lilia's favorite flower.

Lilia nodded and then bent over to smell the flowers one more time. "I wish to remember this scent, until our planting next spring." Her nose touched the tips of the flower. She now had a brown spot on her nose. She tried to rub it off but only smeared the substance more broadly.

Anna laughed.

Lilia, who had become increasingly appearance conscious, wondered what was so funny.

"Ahhh... those little brown buds on the end of the flower," said Anna pointing to the plant pollen. "They are certainly sticky but filled with good food for the bees that make natural pollen, which will keep you strong and healthy."

The buds and natural healing properties were of little interest to Lilia.... at that moment.

They took their bounty home and filled the house with yellow, white, and purple flowers.

From that day forward, Lilia was to have a love affair with lilies. She picked and gathered wildflowers and white lilies in season. Her bedside table, and eventually her combat planes, were rarely without a bouquet of seasonal delights.

~

Vladimir was equally proud of his beautiful daughter.

He very much looked forward to his free time with "his women." His favorite hobby was hiking the trails and hills outside Moscow. His favorite time? Early evening in early fall, when fireflies were most profuse.

"Daughter, see these little lights?"

Lilia nodded.

"They can be captured and placed in a jar." Vladimir's hand gently reached out and gathered a firefly, which he promptly placed the small glass jar with holes in the cap. He did it twice more. "Wish to try? smiled Vladimir.

"Yes, Daddy." Lilia swiped to no avail.

"Gently, my child. The firefly can feel your breeze."

Before long, Lilia had captured two fireflies and placed them in the jar.

That evening, Vladimir placed the jar by her bedside. The fragile fireflies blinked brightly then quickly dimmed. In the morning, Vladimir helped Lilia return them to their rightful place in the natural order.

Chapter 9

Although very much the lady, friends could see the competitive fire in her eyes

DESPITE HER PROWESS AT indoor games, Lilia's first love was sports.

Her compact and well-coordinated body made her a natural in competitive sports. During warm weather, she excelled at the guard position in basketball, outscoring all the girls and most of the boys. When the weather chilled, her extracurricular interests turned to ice skating. She seemed to be impervious to the bitter cold, sometimes skating in weather twenty below zero with little more than a thin wool sweater, wool stockings, and gloves, with a small cap that allowed her hair to proudly flop in the breeze. By the age of ten, she was the fastest skater at School No.1, routinely beating the older girls in the nearby secondary schools.

The faster she skated, the more she believed to imagine one day she might represent her country in a Spartakiada competition in a vast stadium in Cechoslovakia.

"May I borrow your watch?" the now twelve-year-old asked her father.

"For what purpose, my child?"

"I need to record my best time."

He would laugh; then she would take a scrap of paper and pencil and head to the rink. Noticing his daughter's diligence to practice and record, Vladimir became curious. "And what time did we record today?"

"Twenty-six seconds."

"You do well for 40 metres." (Vladimir knew that was a good time for one of her age).

"That was not 40 metres."

"What distance then?"

"Approximately one hundred metres."

"That is not possible. How did you measure?"

"I found two trees a distance from each other next to the pond. I measured using my feet as rulers."

Vladimir was certain his daughter measured wrong because that was a men's speed skating time.

"I would like to go with you tomorrow and watch you skate."

She hugged her father, thanking him for his interest. "That would be wonderful."

The next day, Lilia showed her father the trees. He did an approximate measurement. They were about 102 metres apart. Lilia crouched on her skates as if to imagine a starting line. "Ready, set." She crouched deeper. "Go!"

She sped like the wind. The cold air refreshed her lungs. The breeze blew off her hat, leaving her blond hair to billow like a soft cloud.

In what seemed like a heartbeat, she reached the second tree. Vladimir looked at his watch. He estimated 25 seconds.

~

"Mama, I need your help."

Anna nodded, aware her independent daughter rarely asked for help.

"I would be pleased," replied Anna. "What do you wish to do?"

"Mama, I merely need help making a wool jersey with large numbers."

"Do you not have enough clothes?"

"The sweater is not for school, it is for sports."

"What sport requires a girl to wear a sweater with large numbers?"

"Speed skating."

Anna just smiled and shook her head.

"And, the number, have we decided?"

Lilia paused. She remembered her favorite footballer on the National Football Team, Andrey Starostin, used the number 4. And, the best player on her school team, Dmitriy Stenikov, also carried the number 4.

"Forty-four."

"And, why such a number?"

"It will make me go faster."

The comment made no sense to Anna. But she knew her daughter always had a reason for everything.

From that moment, Lilia's new favorite number became 44.

Initially, in sporting competition, and ultimately in battle.

~

Lev dreamed of one day competing in the Olympics. He believed unequivocally he was the fastest teenage skater in Moscow. To reinforce that point, and prepare him for "the real Olympics," every Saturday during the winter, Lev, which means Lion, would loudly challenge any boys skating on the frozen rink to a race. "Who would like to get their butt kicked by THE LEV today?" he would laugh smugly.

One day, Lilia and her girlfriends cheered in vain as a handsome young skater named Alexei came surprisingly close to beating Lev. Alexei actually led for the first 20 metres, was dead even for the next 50 metres, but then Lev's powerful, muscular legs kicked in as Alexei tired.

"Not bad for a boy," smiled Lev. "Now do we have anyone else today?"

Lilia, attired in her number 44 jersey skated onto the ice.

"You cannot be serious, little girl," mocked Lev. "Where is your daddy?"

Lilia ignored the comments. "Shall we skate from tree to tree?" pointing to the imaginary track.

"Men do not skate little girls. No one on my team would dare. That is foolish."

Lilia's steel blue eyes glared coolly at Lev. He could feel her intensity. "Fine. Fine. It will be your problem, not mine. Do not expect me to help if you slip and fall."

"I do not expect."

~

"Ready, set, go!" The skaters were off. Lev broke to the front rather quickly. By the 40-metre mark, he was confident Lilia was beaten.

But Lilia had a strategy. Let Lev lead, build false confidence, and then speed past him. Having watched him enough times, she felt his final burst would be no match for her continuous speed.

Sure enough, as they reached the 70-metre mark, they were side by side. Lilia accelerated. Her cap again blew off; her hair exploded into the air. From the sidelines it looked as though Lev was standing still. She beat Lev by an astounding 10 metres.

The girls all ran on the ice and hugged Lilia as if she had won a first place medal, while Lev stood fuming at what he deemed an anomaly. There could be only one course of action: a rematch. Little did he know matters would only deteriorate further.

"Little girl, perhaps you would not be too nervous for a rematch?"

Lilia grinned and looked at the girls listening nearby. They were waving no, as if to say, "Take our win and leave!"

"Sure, Lev."

Moments later they were at the start line. The now ultra-determined Lev was grinding his skate into the ice for additional traction at the start.

"Ready, set, go."

Lilia's strategy changed. She just took off like a shot and never looked back. By 50 metres Lev trailed by 10 metres. At the finish, he lagged by 20 metres, and was breathing heavily, like a big black bear who had just chased a wiry red fox.

Lev had met his match. This time he was a surprisingly gracious loser. "Apologize. You can be on my team anytime," said Lev offering his hand in congratulations.

"I am interested in another team," smiled Lilia.

"But we are the best in all of Moscow."

"*Were* the best," responded Lilia wryly.

No one challenged he

Chapter 10

*Father Frost and Granddaughter Snegurochka
were regular holiday guests at the Litvyaks.*

NEW YEAR'S AT THE LITVYAKS was a joyful affair,
even though public celebrations were forbidden, dismissed as
bourgeois remnants by the young Soviet Republic.

Certain rituals were a constant. After a bountiful feast that
filled the stomachs of family and guests, the children would
be greeted by the kind, white bearded Grandfather Frost
(Vladimir) dressed in a long red coat trimmed with white fur,
a cone-shaped hat, and a long hand-painted stick. He would
always carry a big sack of presents to distribute and was
accompanied by his granddaughter, the Snow Maiden
Snegurochka, played by Anna. One particular New Year's Eve,
the precocious Lilia playfully asked Snegurochka
why she always accompanied her grandfather.

"Does he need to be the protection of a woman?"

Snegurochka responded by explaining the legend that had been handed down for centuries. "Hardly, child. Many years ago, I declined to accompany grandfather on a visit to the children of the not-so-fortunate because of the cold weather. However, after thinking about what I had done, I changed my mind. I filled my basket with presents for the children and searched for them. Unfortunately, I was unable to find my grandfather or the children who went without toys that year."

The children, sitting in a circle, felt sad for the children of the legend.

"I was so sorry. I vowed that would never happen again. So each holiday season, I, Snegurochka, make sure to visit the homes of good children with Grandfather Frost to distribute toys and good wishes."

Lilia's little cousin Vanya applauded.

"Vanya," asked Snegurochka, "have you been helpful to Mummy and Daddy this year?"

The child's eyes opened wide, and his head bobbed like a rubber doll.

Snegurochka smiled, took a small dark green biplane from her bag, and gave it to the little boy. She then turned to Lilia and pulled out another toy—a small, colorful stuffed doll. Lilia responded with a monotone "thank you." Privately, she strongly preferred the plane.

When they finished disbursing presents, Father Frost nodded at a friendly neighbor, Uncle Fyodor, who removed a shiny black and silver *Garmoshka* (folk button accordion) given to him by his father and began to play *Lesu Rodilas Yolochka* (A New Year Tree Was Born in the Forest).

As Vladimir saw the joy in the eyes of the children, an idea struck. When the men were finished, Vladimir said, "All please wait here," as he got up and left the room. Moments later, he could be heard rustling around the attic above.

"I have something very old that may have belonged to the house's former owner. I have saved if for just such an occasion."

Father Frost slowly removed the blue velvet cloth cover, as if presenting a collection of rare jewels. There sat a polished wooden Balalaika. Father Frost picked up the instrument and began to play the joyful folk song *Svetit Mesyats* (The Moon Is Shining) while the children all began to dance gleefully.

When he finished, Frost and Snegurochka announced, "We have other children to visit this night," and headed out the door.

Once outside, they doubled back to a small room in the rear of the house, removed their outfits, and again became Vladimir and Anna.

"Where have you been? You missed Father Frost and Snegurochka," said Lilia.

"We are so disappointed," responded Anna smiling at Vladimir.

"Mommy, look, Father Frost gave me this beautiful stuffed doll and Igor [a little friend] this red wooden car. We also sang and danced."

As the evening drew to a close, Vladimir offered his traditional toast to the family's good fortune, wished others the same, and closed with a tribute to his Anna. "To the woman of my dreams who picked more than potatoes in those peasant fields long, long ago."

Anna never tired of hearing the words. She would blush like a teenager, and then Vladimir would accompany her on a very old gypsy guitar decorated with a red ribbon that he found in the marketplace, as she sang another classic folk song, *Dorogoi Dlinnoyu* (Those Were the Days).

> Once upon a time there was a tavern
> Where we used to raise a glass or two
> Remember how we laughed away the hours,
> And dreamed of all the great things we would do
> Those were the days my friend
> We thought they'd never end
> We'd sing and dance forever and a day
> We'd live the life we chose
> We'd fight and never lose
> For we were young and sure to have our way....

~

As Lilia grew to understand the annual presence of Father Frost and Snegurochka was symbolic, she said nothing because the annual tradition was such fun. Until...

Early one morning after the usual New Year's festivities, Lilia, now thirteen, went to retrieve her mother and father's bag of costumes from the other room. Since the bag had already been taken, she assumed her father had already been there.

"Mummy, when did father pick up the New Year's bag?"

"Lilia, whatever do you mean?"

"I merely wished to see if Father Frost left any additional presents, since two of our cousins were not able to attend this year."

"I'm not sure Father Frost would approve."

Lilia smiled, "Mummy, I have known for some time you and father play the parts and change in the room. Promise, I will tell no one; I very much enjoy the legend."

"Thank you, child. That is important. As for the bag, your father probably stored it somewhere for next season. He is in the next room. "

Lilia approached Vladimir. She was surprised by his response.

"Child, I did not retrieve the bag this year. I assumed it was your mother."

Lilia smiled as she looked to the heavens.

~

Despite the early rattling of Hitler, times remained hopeful and spirits high.

For Anna and Vladimir, 1934 was a particularly bountiful year. They decided that Father Frost should give Lilia a very special present: an upright oak veneer piano made in Belarus. "My child, perhaps one day you will study at the Moscow Conservatory [Russia's leading school of music]," smiled Vladimir with pride.

In the end, Lilia never achieved her father's lofty musical aspirations, although she did become quite proficient at playing the piano, often entertaining her girlfriends on Saturday afternoons in the winter. Her particular area of interest was traditional Russian town romance songs from the nineteenth century and earlier. A typical Saturday concert always included three of her personal favorites: *Priznanie* (Words of Love), *Dushechka, Krasna Devitsa* (Soulful, Beautiful Girl), and *Belolitsa, Kruglolitsa* (Nice Face, Round Face).

After academics, sports, and the piano, Lilia's interest

turned to her wardrobe.

"Mummy has taught me to use the sewing machine," said Lilia. "I wish to make my clothes, so you can save money for your old age," said the suddenly practical Lilia.

Vladimir knew his daughter too well. "Mummy and I will be fine. What's the real reason, my daughter?"

"I wish to make dresses and outfits like these ladies are wearing" said Lilia, pointing to photos in several of Anna's foreign magazine collection.

Anna thought her daughter's goal was frivolous, but realized Lilia had inherited some of her mother's playful streak of vanity. Ironically, within a matter of months, Lilia was designing and creating her own outfits. By the time the school year ended, Lilia had made and owned more outfits than any girl in school. She was now aware of her attractiveness and which design styles were the most flattering.

Anna and Vladimir began to notice the local boys flocking around their sweet-smelling daughter with the soft billowy blonde hair and interesting dresses. It seemed a weekend rarely passed without some young man inviting Lilia for a walk.

After ten or fifteen of these informal dates, she developed a distinct preference. When the time came, she would date only broad-shouldered men with dark hair who were significantly taller than she!

Chapter 11

Controversial poet Sergei Yesenin
was a particular favorite of Lilia.

VLADIMIR'S UNFAILING allegiance to Stalin's belief that a modern, industrialized Russia would gain world respect if all contributed to the common cause heightened Lilia's sense of patriotism.

Lilia, a mature fourteen, believed in the new Russia, no dream was too grand to imagine nor impossible to achieve. She concluded the need to document for later this historical period in the form of a personal diary—a letter that unfortunately would never arrive. Each day after school she would retreat into her room, quietly make an entry, and then re-read the words several times to insure it captured her feelings of that precise moment.

Anna thought the goal admirable, while Vladimir dismissed the activity as "typical women's thinking." After nearly sixteen years of marriage to the independent minded Anna, he still didn't get it.

In time, Lilia's diary became more than merely a record. It was Lilia, the young woman.

The diary expressed her love of beauty. She wondered why heaven's canvas remained constant and why its hues constantly changed; why trees touched by the sun reached for the skies; and, why wildflowers were wild. Where were seeds born? How did they germinate? What was the purpose of so many different species and varieties?

The diary articulated her love of the Motherland and her commitment to defend it against aggression. "I wish one day to fly, not as a fleeting fancy, not as a hawk or an eagle, but as a military pilot, a recognized guardian of our skies."

~

Lilia also grew to love poetry during this period.

On many a cold winter's night, her mother sat by her side in the living room, softly reciting the verses of Pushkin, Blok, and Klyuev, until she knew many by heart.

At school, literature was also a favorite subject. Her diary was also dotted with her favorite verses. Some merely recopied from books, others she had heard verbally and memorized in part or all. Lilia's selections included poems of beauty, poems of questioning, and, most prominently, poems by the popular but tragic poet, Sergei Yesenin, who committed suicide at the age of thirty. Despite the beauty of his verse and intensity of purpose, Yesenin lived an erratic, almost self-destructive existence. Lilia was well aware Yesenin's poems were not approved by the State for distribution. She entered from memory and never mentioned them to her mother or father.

One weekend, while Anna and Lilia had gone to visit friends on the other side of Moscow, Vladimir decided to rest in his favorite chair. A cold breeze told him a draft existed somewhere in their apartment. He wandered from room to room, searching. As he moved the chair by Lilia's bedroom window, her diary, hidden under the seat cushion, fell to the floor.

A curious Vladimir casually thumbed through the book, smiling at his daughter's dreams. His hand ultimately came to discover a patriotic but controversial poem by Yesenin, *Goodbye, My Friend, Goodbye.*

> Goodbye, my friend, goodbye. My
> dear one, you are in my breast. A
> predestined parting
> Promises a reunion ahead.
> Good, my friend,
> without a touch of hand, without a word,
> Don't be sad and do not frown,
> Dying is nothing new in this life.
> And, living, of course, isn't any newer.

A concerned Vladimir sat quietly. How had his daughter gathered such a dangerous work? Just then the door opened. Anna and Lilia had returned early.

"Father, what are you doing with my diary?"

Anna was also upset and about to defend her daughter's right to privacy.

"Daughter, you are my pride and joy. I am freedom-loving and wish you the same, but Yesenin? Of all the beautiful verse in literature, why Yesenin?"

"And why not?" replied Lilia.

"He talks only of pain, of suffering, of disappointment. Is our life not better than that?"

Lilia was Lilia. "It may not be your sentiment, but does it make his sentiment any less moving?"

"You mean the sentiment of a man with an uncontrollably rebellious nature, an amoral man with five wives, a coward who hanged himself rather than face life's difficulties. You consider that life worthy of your diary?"

Vladimir's sense of outrage even surprised Anna. She gently tried to intercede before Lilia or Vladimir said something in a fit of anger they would long regret.

"Husband, are his poems not filled with beauty and love of our land?"

Vladimir stared at Anna as he waved his arms. "It does not matter what I think. The State has spoken. What if someone were to find his verse in your daughter's diary? In these times, would we not fear for her?"

Nothing more needed to be said. Anna and Lilia realized Vladimir was correct. The physical page was removed from the diary and burned in their wooden heating stove. But the words never left Lilia's soul.

Chapter 12

*Lilia attends the first approved New Year celebration
in the Column Hall of the Kremlin.*

A AS STALIN CONTINUED to consolidate his
power, he restored certain previously forbidden celebrations.

In December 1935, a candidate for the Political Bureau
of the all-powerful Central Committee, Pavel Postyshev,
proposed a New Year's celebration be reinstated for Soviet
children. The initiative was approved, and in January 1936
the first citizen New Year's party was organized in
Kharkov and other cities, towns, and villages, although the
grandest was, and still is, held in the Column Hall of the
Kremlin.

For that first event in Moscow, tickets were in great
demand. Every child in every school wished to attend.
Vladimir lobbied for tickets from the School No.1

allocation on the basis that Lilia, as the school's leading pupil and best sportsman, deserved to be present.

"We have been awarded tickets," said an excited Vladimir, waving the tickets.

An excited Lilia asked, "Mummy, will you help me make something special to wear?"

For the next two weeks, when Anna came home from work, they cut, sewed and pasted.

"I assume I will provide for myself during the production period," laughed a hungry but understanding Vladimir when he returned home.

Finally, the dress was completed. "I would like to surprise Daddy," said Lilia. Shortly thereafter, Vladimir entered.

Lilia entered as the Queen of Roses, adorned in a fancy and frilly red velvet dress with a billowy base and a top lined with glittering stones. The demure neckline was woven with a dark red ribbon. The colors made a magnificent backdrop for Lilia's delicate facial features, long blonde hair, and steel blue eyes. Lilia walked toward her father, spinning to the right and left.

"Today my precious daughter has become a lady," smiled Vladimir proudly.

~

That first New Year's party was all Lilia had imagined and more. The hall was filled with colorful decorations and lights and a massive, perfectly-shaped pine tree. The evening's festivities had contained dances, games, performances, and competitions. Lilia was at her best, dancing in the folk dance competition, entered by many boys and girls.

Each child was given ninety seconds to do a version of one popular folk dance or another. A handsome young man named Igor, from the Sokolniki region, seemed to be the overwhelming favorite based on the applause from the audience. Finally, it was Lilia's turn. She lifted her skirt slightly, waiting for the music to begin. All eyes in the audience were on her. She could feel the butterflies in her stomach. Suddenly, she was twirling magnificently, her feet moving faster and faster, the steps distinct, theatrical. Her long blonde hair blew in the breeze, like clouds traversing the sky.

Vladimir's heart was filled with immense pride. At that moment he felt like the luckiest man in the world. He looked at Anna lovingly and kissed her hand. Her eyes told him she felt the same way. Nothing more needed to be said.

Lilia executed one final dramatic circle of stage, hands extended. She came to a sudden stop with the music. Anna and Vladimir and the whole audience stood and applauded.

Minutes later, the decision was reached. Lilia's name was announced. Proudly, she walked up to the New Year Tree to receive her prize from Father Frost and Snow Maiden Snegurochka. Anna and Vladimir beamed. Father Frost handed her a small, colorful carved stone statue of himself, holding a red bag, standing in front of a New Year tree.

That evening she put the statue on her dresser and told Frost that he would be her forever companion wherever she went.

Chapter 13

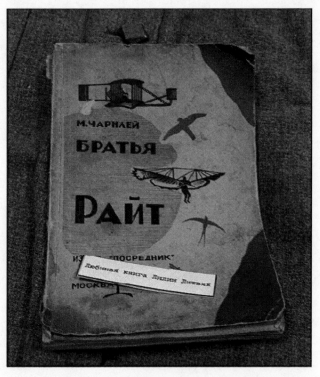

Lilia's favorite book: the life and times of the fathers of modern aviation, Wilbur and Orville Wright.

LILIA'S FIRST TRUE LOVE arrived during high school... airplanes.

The exploits of flyers during World War I had turned the interest of many young men to the skies. Air clubs were formed. All who qualified were provided the opportunity to fly. Lenin, and then Stalin after him, realized the day would come when the use of planes would grow in military importance. Papers and magazines glamorized the exploits of peacetime flyers.

While other young women dreamed of husbands and families, Lilia's spare moments were filled with dreams of traversing the sky, touching the stars and clouds, testing the capabilities of different planes, and captaining flights. She began to read every book about aviation available in the school's library. She also made a scrapbook in which she placed photos and drawing of planes, and whenever she obtained duplicates she brought them to school and glued them inside her desk.

One day her teacher asked, "Why are you so fascinated by planes?"

Lilia smiled. "Someday, I wish to be a pilot."

Her classmates laughed.

"It is a good dream," smiled the teacher, privately convinced that flying was a man's job.

"Why do you smile so broadly?" wondered Lilia.

~

It was now the mid-1930s and the paper was filled with the exploits of distance flyers, particularly a trio of bold, brave woman: Marina Raskova, the first Soviet woman to be certified as an aviation navigator, and her two close friends, pilots Valentina Grizodubova and Polina Osipenko.

The women attempted to break the long-distance records by flying from Moscow to the Soviet Far East, a distance of 9300 kilometres. Some 300 kilometres from their destination they ran out of fuel. A mechanic forgot to top off their tanks after completing a battery of preflight tests. Raskova and Osipenko were ordered to parachute through the workstation in the nose of the plane by Grizodubova, who feared a belly landing in the forest would kill or injure the navigator and her co-pilot. Grizodubova landed by herself and spent the next ten days surviving in the wilderness. After a massive search and rescue effort that kept the nation spellbound, Valentina reunited with her two comrades. On April 11, 1935, Pravda proudly declared, "Our Comrades have been found!" Even with the shortfall, the women had broken the world distance record by an astounding 1000 kilometres. For their efforts, the trio was awarded the Gold Star Medal and the Order of Lenin. Overnight, the highly articulate and charismatic Raskova became a role model for women, particularly the younger generation, as she proudly declared "In Russia, a woman can be whatever she wants to be."

Lilia diligently followed the exploits of the three brave pilots, carrying photos and newspaper articles in her school satchel. In her spare time, she would also go to the library and read all she could about the development of flight, including the biographies of Orville and Wilbur Wright, the American brothers who were known as the fathers of modern aviation.

One blustery cold afternoon, Lilia was on the way to the library when the class bully, Boris Kuznetsov, who had a major crush on Lilia, sneaked up and grabbed her satchel.

"Satchel for a kiss."

"Never. Give me that back!" demanded Lilia with fire in her eyes.

"For me to have and you to retrieve," taunted Boris, who suddenly noticed the satchel's unusually heavy weight. "With bag so heavy with books, no wonder you have no time for boys."

Lilia headed straight toward Boris. The two began a tug-of-war. "Nobody takes my bag." The satchel burst open as a flood of navigation books, flying magazines, and news-papers fell to the ground.

Boris glanced at the contents as he smiled cynically, "Let me guess: the little girl dares to be a pilot."

"Like Raskova and the others," responded Lilia unhesitatingly.

"And, one day I will be the king of angels," mocked Boris.

~

The crush of work and school combined with Anna's increasing management responsibilities at the store meant mother and daughter rarely had free time to spend together.

Finally, one morning at the breakfast table before school, Lilia begged "Mummy, could we make this Saturday our day? It's important."

"Why so?"

"I've made some decisions I would like to share."

"I would like to. However, I must inform the store director."

Fortunately for Anna and Lilia, the director was in a benevolent mood.

It was a warm, sunny Saturday. They decided to hike the woods and pick some wildflowers. Afterward, they sat by a small clear lake. "Mummy, I'm not sure how or when, but some day people will fly planes to visit far-away places."

"From what I have read, that is probably true."

"I want to take them there."

"What do you mean 'take them there'?"

"There will be airports and airdromes. They will need pilots."

Anna's response was predictable. "You dream big dreams, my daughter. This I applaud. But regrettably, I cannot permit such foolishness."

"Why, Mummy?" asked a disappointed Lilia.

"Flying is dangerous."

"That will not happen," retorted Lilia confidently. "I will be a very good pilot, like Osipenko and Grizodubova."

"They are the rare exceptions. Flying is not our destiny. There are rules."

"Who makes these rules?" asked Lilia.

"They are traditions formed by the people's opinion."

"Suppose the rules are a mistake?"

Anna was unprepared for such a question. "That is unlikely."

"Why?"

Anna changed the course of the conversation. She knew Lilia's determination could degenerate into an unpleasant dispute. "Suppose I was to lose you? Then what?"

Anna's guilt trip weighted heavily on Lilia's mind. She would have to dream her dreams privately... at least for the foreseeable future.

But there was also good news that Saturday. The ladies strongly re-bonded.

"I will make you a deal," smiled Anna. "I pledge to take more Saturdays off if you pledge to delay such dreams."

Lilia paused. If was a good offer. But the desire remained. "Mummy, let us ask Daddy." Lilia assumed she would get her way. "I will abide by his decision."

Anna was confident that Vladimir would side with her, and that would be the end of that.

Both were wrong.

"It is a most unusual request. I am both proud of your desire and concerned for your safety," said Vladimir thoughtfully. "I am about to organize a week-long training session for the new recruits. Let me think while I am away. I will give you my decision when I return.

Chapter 14

A Stalin priority: expanding the rail system across Russia into Siberia.

IT WAS LATE SATURDAY EVENING. Vladimir was exhausted. He had spent six straight 16-hour days teaching the latest class of recruits how to operate and maintain the increasingly sophisticated trains that were being manufactured in the country's numerous and growing production facilities.

"Administrator Lazarev wants to see you before you leave," said the Moscow Centre switching facility manager. "The subject?"

"Ask the administrator," glared the man.

Vladimir became concerned. Rumors had started to circulate about a potential attempt by the Germans to invade Russia and take over industrial production facilities and pillage natural resources. Some citizens believed these "secret rumors" were planted by Stalin in a clumsy attempt to further centralize his power and authority. Vocal dissenters mysteriously started to disappear, including two of Vladimir's best friends at the railroad.

While he had done nothing wrong that he knew of, he was still concerned about the precise nature of the Lazarev meeting.

"Comrade Litvyak, as you know, our Trans-Siberian railway system travels great distances (almost 8,200 kilometres) from Moscow to Yaroslavl, Sverdlovsk and, ultimately, Lake Baikal and beyond. Comrade Stalin wishes to build a parallel railway from Baikal to the north as a military precaution and ultimately for civilian use." (BAM, as it would come to be known, would not ultimately be completed until the time of Leonid Brezhnev).

Vladimir wondered what that a railway from Baikal to Amur could possibly have to do with him.

"Because of your unique talents, you have been selected by the party to train a class of switchmen who will dot the railway in the towns and cities along these routes." What Lazarev failed to mention was that these routes were to use forced labor, often suspected but rarely discussed openly. "To make the work as efficient as possible, you will visit each of these cities for three months to complete employee indoctrination and training."

Vladimir made his first blunder. "Comrade Lazarev, wouldn't it be more practical to train them in Moscow, where we have the proper tools and facilities?"

"Frankly speaking, Comrade Litvyak, you may be right," said the smooth talking Lazarev, not wishing to raise suspicion. "But we need someone of your experience to screen for the proper men in Chita (at that time, the main town around

74

Lake Baikal). After your first visit, you can create a report about which is both cheaper and more practical. I will then consider your observations."

Vladimir was still not sure about the approach.

"Comrade Litvyak, do you realize you and your wife earn more than most?"

"Yes, Comrade Lazarev, we do."

"And, we wish to continue those distributions?"

"Yes, Comrade Lazarev."

"Then it has been decided."

Vladimir realized any further discussion could be construed as a challenge to a direct superior.

"When will the project begin?"

"In two weeks."

"How long will I be gone?"

"Including your travel and retraining possible dropouts, about twelve months."

"And, my family? My daughter is so young."

"Don't you realize we know that? Next June, invite your family to spend the summer with you at Lake Baikal. It is beautiful that time of year. They will enjoy it immensely. After all, the Lake is the world's largest, filled with fine fish and surrounded by alpine meadows."

"But my wife works many days a week. She can't take an entire..."

"Thank you for your commitment, Comrade Litvyak," interrupted Lazarev as he walked Vladimir to the door and slammed it in his face.

~

Anna was surprisingly understanding when Vladimir broke the news.

"We have been through worse, my husband. Let us enjoy our next two weeks like they are our last," she joked. "Lilia and I will then look forward to next summer's vacation at the Lake, compliments of Comrade Stalin. I have heard it is a most beautiful and peaceful spot."

"What of my flying request?" asked Lilia.

"I believe that is a selfish question at this moment. I did not raise my daughter to be so brazen."

Guilt overcame Lilia. She bowed her head. Lilia's mind became filled with questions about her by father's assignment.

"Why do *you* have to go?" "Why do *you* have to travel so far?" "Why can't *you* get help to train the new people?"

Vladimir knew the questions would not cease unless he occupied Lilia's inquisitive mind and hands with less philosophical matters.

"Anna," whispered Vladimir loud enough for Lilia to overhear, "I understand the Lake winters are very harsh. I will do my best to stay warm until you are in my arms again."

Anna got her husband's message. "I will be sure to pack your warmest clothes, my husband."

Lilia smiled. She too got the hint. "Perhaps I can help?"

"How so, child?" smiled Vladimir.

"Just give me some time."

Lilia scanned the shelf in the corner of the room where Anna had stored some random pieces of heavy wool cloth to one day make an extra household blanket or two.

"May I have these?" asked Lilia.

"For what purpose?"

"A surprise."

During the next four days after school, Lilia measured, cut and sewed on her mother's machine while her parents retired to the far corner of the room to read the news of the week.

When Vladimir attempted to peek, Lilia smiled and said, "I see you. No looking."

The evening arrived. "It is finished," announced a proud Lilia as she presented her version of a man's brightly colored winter work shirt to her father. Although the seams were a bit uneven in places, it fit surprisingly well.

"Daughter, my new shirt is as beautiful as its maker." "Daddy, look inside the pocket."

Vladimir opened the button on the pocket that sat over his heart. There he found a picture of Anna and Lilia sitting in a field of wildflowers.

"The wool will warm your body; the picture is meant to warm your heart."

Vladimir was deeply touched. A tear formed in the corner of his eye and rolled down his cheek. Anna smiled as she dabbed her husband's cheek.

~

Lilia made Vladimir an additional promise. She would go to the fields, whenever weather permitted, collect some fireflies in a jar and place them by her bedside.

"You will always be by my side at night."

"And no Yesenin," smiled Vladimir.

"And no Yesenin," echoed a smiling Lilia.

Chapter 15

Vladimir Litvyak becomes collateral damage in
Stalin's reign of terror designed to eliminate all enemies of the state.

IT WAS A CHILLY FALL AND a long, cold, lonely winter. Anna looked forward to Vladimir's weekly letter, his handsome money transfer and his thoughts for next sumer's vacation.

She and Lilia would sit by their Burzhuika (a metal stove with a pipe chimney that vented through the window) and read the letters aloud. In one such letter Vladimir observed.....

> "Dear Love of My Life,
> My daily routine is usually nothing exciting. We wake up around 8 AM, do some
> morning exercises, have a bowl of porridge, and then teach class till noon. Lunch is

usually soup. The afternoon is filled with
switchman exercises in the outdoors, where I
try to prepare the men for potential problems
they will encounter. The evenings, until
it gets too cold, are quite pleasant. We make a
huge bonfire and sing traditional folk songs.
When you come with Lilia, I will promise to
take a leave for hikes. This is some of the
most beautiful countryside in the Motherland. But it is quite far, and I'm not sure we
will ever come this way again.
Always and Always,
Your Vladimir"

Another read:

"Dear Lady of the Potato Fields, This Sunday
past was quite an adventure.
A local guide insisted on taking us on a
true Siberian experience. We set off around 10
AM for a hike into a beautiful gorge near the
lake. Some three hours later, we reached
the depth of the gorge and were about to
have lunch when sheets of rain started to
drop. The sky became dark as nightfall. The
lightening crackled. The thunder boomed.
Within half an hour, the gorge had filled with
water up to our knees, and boulders were falling from the cliffs. Six hulking men all held
each other's hands as we slowly and
carefully climbed back.
I'm sure if Lilia had been here, our resourceful
daughter would have found a faster way out!
My cold body to your warm heart,
Vladimir"

And a third contained some of her husband's dry wit she
had come to enjoy.

"It is now spring. There are no showers here, so
I go swimming everyday while the men heat up
the Banya (wooden hut) by the lake. We go in
groups of four, get really hot and sweaty and
then hit each other all over with birch leaves.
When no one can stand it anymore, we race
down to the lake. Hitting the cold water always brings an instant and pleasant rush to my
head. The winner has dinner made to his speci-
fications by the other three. I have eaten well!
These men are hungry for women, so when
you arrive I will make sure we have the
Banya to ourselves.
All love, to my one and only,
Vladimir"

What was to be his *final* letter pictured a return home.

"Dear Forever Love,
More good news. Thanks to everyone's diligent efforts, we have expanded the railway into Siberia, not far from Baikal. Today my
supervisor explained we will be allotted an additional state vacation as a bonus for our good
efforts.
I have decided we should use that reward
to rediscover a 1,000 years of Motherland history by cruising a steamer from
Moscow to Penza, Ufa, Omsk and Barnaul.
Admittedly our accommodations will not be
that of the Czar, but we will be comfortable.
Those days have long since passed.. With Lilia'
s inquisitiveness, we should be answering
questions long into the night!
Sweet dreams,
Vladimir"

Vladimir's upbeat correspondence made no mention of the images he had begun to observe.

Clearly, more trains were running more frequently than when he first arrived. And now there were military equipment, guns and ammunition rather than merely railroad equipment and supplies. The trains also started to carry a sprinkling of soldiers being dispatched to the towns and villages that dotted the railroad route from Central to Eastern Russia.

The trains also carried laborers transported from the Gulags run by the State Department of Camps who were accompanied and overlooked by special warders or soldiers.

On the other hand, the young railway employees who performed most of the physically taxing tasks of track and switch installation remained cheery and enthusiastic for the opportunities in the young Soviet state, particularly those who were Communists or Komsomol Members (young Communists).

And, while Vladimir was strictly forbidden from talking to the "troublesome peasants and proletarians," from time to time there were rumors of difficult living conditions and the ever present threat of torture for imagined crimes to the state.

Vladimir said nothing publicly. Compared to most, he lived in relative comfort despite the harsh climate and difficult working conditions. He was granted his own hut with a cast-iron stove for heating and cooking, a larger oak dresser for his personal belongings and thick timber bed with a comfortable horsehair mattress. Besides, according to the calendar on his wall, it was only 64 days till Anna and Lilia arrived and 124 days till he returned to Moscow permanently

~

During this lonely and difficult period, Anna showed Lilia how to make do should they get stuck in some misadventure in the countryside while hiking, swimming or camping with Vladimir that next summer.

"Should you get chilled, there is one sure way to add warmth," said Anna. "I learned this trick on the farms during the bitter cold winters. It is very important to use scarves to keep the cold breezes away from your neck."

"Why, mummy?"

"Because your neck communicates with the rest of your body. If your neck feels warm, so will the rest of your body. If your neck thinks it is cold, so will the rest of your body. Remember that, wherever your life shall take you"

"I shall," not imagining for a moment that that advice would one day save her life.

"Now, you select from your mother's possessions," said Anna pointing to three colorful scarves she kept in the draw. Lilia giggled as she tried each on and looked in mirror. "Depending on the color you select, you can look like a movie star!" Lilia selected the red and blue scarf.

"Bravo," said Anna.

Lilia paused. In her mind, something was missing. She reached into her pocket and took out her lipstick. After applying the lipstick, she began to playfully bow and swirl in front of her mother.

"Beautiful, my dear. Beautiful. Bravo," applauded Anna.

~

Semyon Demidov had been promoted to chief of local NKVD, and Anna believed they were steadfast friends. The Litvyak apartment was empty a good portion of the day as Anna worked and Lilia attended school. Maya Demidova knew conditions were now perfect.

"We should probably exchange apartment keys in case of emergency, for those days you are working," thoughtfully suggested Maya. Anna readily agreed, not realizing Maya's lust for Anna and Vladimir's larger apartment had reached the point of emotional irrationality.

(As the wife of a NKVD insider, she knew the fastest way to discredit someone was to volunteer troublesome information, which was defined in the increasing paranoid Russian society as anything that could vaguely be misconstrued as anti-Motherland).

The following Monday morning, after Anna headed to work, Maya slipped into the apartment, searching for "shreds of evidence" that she could use to her advantage. She found and read Vladimir's letters. She smiled ghoulishly upon reading the one which lauded "the Czar's way of life."

That evening Maya planted a seed. "Semyon, have you not wondered why Vladimir and Anna live so grandly?"

"Occasionally, but they both work hard."

"I believe there is more to it than that."

"What do you mean?"

"Today I found evidence they are part of an underground movement to restore the policies of the Czar. Look, see. I believe they may receive secret contributions toward that event."

Maya spread the letters in front of Semyon.

"You have stolen from our neighbor?"

"I don't understand," glared Maya. "Is not your job to protect our Motherland?"

During the next 20 minutes, Maya convinced Semyon that Vladimir's references to political matters were a secret directive for Anna to provide information to other members of an unnamed resistance organization about clandestine activities against the state. Semyon took copious notes.

The next day Maya returned the letters while Semyon discussed "the evidence" at headquarters. As part of his investigation, he chatted with Administrator Lazarev of the Railway Ministry, who recalled "attitudinal difficulties" with Vladimir. The investigation was now complete!

~

Sixty days before their planned family reunion Vladimir's letters suddenly ceased.

A concerned Anna went to the Railroad Ministry. They had no record of Vladimir's employment or current status.

"My husband has worked for the past year in the godforsaken east, there must be some mistake. I want to see Comrade Lazarev."

"Comrade, Comrade Lazarev is a very busy man."

Anna would not take no for an answer. "Then I will sit and wait until he has a free moment."

"That could be a very long time!"

"No matter, I will wait forever if I have to."

The clerk could see the passion in her eyes. He got up and walked down the hall.

"Comrade Lazarev will see you now."

"So how can I help you, Comrade..."

"Litvyak... Remember, you sent my husband, Vladimir, a switchman, to Lake Baikal to teach others to route and dispatch trains."

"You must be mistaken, Comrade Litvyak. Lake Baikal is a long way away. Why would I do such a thing?"

Anna was furious. He lied directly to her face. She had proof. "Comrade Lazarev, I don't know why you are lying. I just want my husband."

"Comrade Litvyak, are you calling me a liar? That is a very serious accusation!"

"Damn you! I have proof."

"What do you mean proof?"

"My husband sent me letters every week. I have kept them all as mementos. They are clearly postmarked 'Chita.'"

"And, where are these so called letters of proof?"

"They are sitting in the desk drawer at my apartment."

"I see," said a kinder, gentler Lazarev. "Let me have someone check our records further and get to the bottom of this matter. It will take a few days."

After Anna left, Lazarev called Demidov who authorized him to compose and send a telegram to the Chief of Guards at Lake Baikal.

~

It was 2 AM. There was a thunderous knock on the door. "Militia, open up!"

Anna struggled from her bed, assuming there was some mistake.

"Are you Anna Litvyak?"

"Yes."

"We are here to collect the evidence."

"What are you talking about?"

"We have reason to believe your husband has been discussing secrets of the state. We want the letters."

Anna became irate. "That bastard Lazarev! He is twisting what I said."

"Comrade Litvyak, your remarks about the minister are cause for arrest. We understand you have a child. Just give us the letters, and we will ignore your indiscriminate outburst."

"I will not," she said defiantly.

"Hold her," said one militiaman to the other. He walked over to the desk, and searched the drawers until he found the stack of letters postmarked Chita. The militiaman then stood directly in Anna's face.

"The State thanks you for your cooperation, Comrade Litvyak. At the moment, neither you nor your daughter will be required to visit prison for custodial questioning."
She nodded nervously.

"But that can change at any time... Do we understand each other?"

Lilia had quietly watched the drama from the corner of the room. It was a scene she would never forget.

~

It was 2 AM. There was a thunderous knock on the door.

"Militia, open up!"

Vladimir struggled from his bed, assuming there was some mistake.

"Vladimir Litvyak?"

"Yes."

"You are under arrest!"

"For what?"

"Crimes of the State. We have an order from Comrade Stalin declaring you an Enemy of the People."

Two large militiamen went to tie up Vladimir in front of his roommates.

He pushed them away. "There must be some mistake. I have always been loyal to the Motherland!"

"You can tell that when you will be asked. Either you come with us, or we will shoot you here and now. We have our orders!"

Moments later, a rope bound Vladimir was thrown in the back of the voronok (a cramped, poorly ventilated vehicle used to transport prisoners to prison) in the bitter cold night air, wearing only the winter shirt that Lilia had made and some tattered work pants.

By the time they arrived at the makeshift prison deep in the woods, two toes and three fingers had frostbite. He was put into a concrete room with a thick wood door and a tiny window laced with bars and open to the elements.

The following morning he was dragged into an austere room in a nearby log cabin that housed a table and three chairs.

One said, "The trial of Vladimir Litvyak for crimes against the state commences!"

"The trial" was perfunctory.

"We understand you have been sending the location of our military installations to the Germans through your wife for the past year," said a large burly black haired man with wide eyes and a handlebar mustache, known simply as the citizen investigator.

"That is not true."

"Have you not written to her regularly?"

"That is true."

"And what did they say?"

"Just family matters. Talk of vacation, a typical day at work, and so on. Nothing more. Contact my wife; she will show them to you."

"There is no need. Comrade Lazarev has written of these matters. (Lazarev had never accepted Vladimir's brazen challenge to his authority. Once the letters to Anna were confiscated, he had his staff search for some words, some phrases, some sentences that implied ill intent toward Comrade Stalin and the communist way of life).

"Did these political letters not suggest life was better under the Czar?" continued the investigator, glaring at his assistants. One, with a family of his own, mistakenly stepped forward, believing Vladimir was unjustly accused.

"There does not appear to be irregularities," said one of the assistants.

The investigator became furious. His authority had been challenged in front of all. He began to verbally intimidate the assistant. "Are you that lazy? That stupid? Perhaps you should spend time with these misguided citizens, so you can learn how they create unrest, how they lie against the state!"

The man lowered his head. He said nothing.

"Look here, does not citizen Litvyak's comment about steamship accommodations provide strong 'evidence'?"

"I now see your point; I am so sorry about my lack of attention to detail."

"Apology accepted. Make sure you send your findings to the Chief of Guards at Irkutsk.

"I shall, Citizen Investigator. I shall."

The closed-door discussions among the authorities at Irkutsk declared Vladimir guilty based on the evidence provided.

Vladimir was neither granted anyone to defend him, nor was he allowed to speak.

~

The sunrise peaked through the forest shortly after 6 AM. Clothed in his beloved wool shirt and tattered pants, Vladimir sat frozen and shivering in the corner of the makeshift guardhouse.

"Remove the enemy and bring him to the birch," demanded the slovenly commander of the guards.

Vladimir pleaded one final time as the pictures of Anna and Lilia fell from his pocket.

"Please, I have done nothing wrong. I swear. Mercy, I have a wife, a daughter."

The soldiers dutifully followed orders. They dragged him by the scruff of his neck from his cell, blindfolded him and placed him against a large birch tree. Despite the tragedy about to befall him, his mind was filled with the notes of the Andreyev Waltz, heralding the spectacular beauty of the nearby Amur River. He remembered how Anna loved to dance to the song in the Central Park in Moscow. And how Lilia would listen to the brass band and watch them dance.

Suddenly, his heart became calm. The rapid beats subsided. The six-man death squad pointed their thick barreled rifles at their target.

A determined Vladimir cried out, *"Da Blagoslovi Vas Gospod"* (may God keep you well until we meet again.) The chief of guards barked, "Ready. Aim. Fire."

The soldiers dumped the still mass of humanity that moments before was Vladimir Litvyak into a burlap sack, dragged it a few miles offshore to a hole in the frozen ice pack of Lake Baikal, anchored the bag with a large rock and pushed it down the hole.

~

There was a foreboding knock on the door.

Anna opened to find a messenger holding a letter from the office of the War Ministry.

"Mrs. Litvyak?"

"Yes."

"This is for you."

Anna opened the letter. Moments later her hand was quivering, and she began to scream, "No... No."

Lilia ran to her mother's side. Anna clutched her daughter tightly.

"What's going on?"

"The letter said they have concluded the results of your father's investigation."

"Father's investigation? What investigation?"

"They did not say. They merely said they had documents, proof. See?" Anna paused. Tears streamed down her face.

"Proving what?" stared a horrified Lilia.

"The letter says Vladimir had been judged an 'Enemy of the State.'"

"That is not possible; my daddy loves the Motherland. I will go to the authorities and plead our case. I will not leave daddy's side until he is free to come home."

"It is already too late."

"It's never too late."

Anna looked deep into Lilia's eyes. "The letter said he was tried, found guilty of 'despicable crimes' and executed accordingly." Lilia screamed shrilly. Anna held her quivering body tightly.

"When and where did all this take place?" whispered Lilia. Tears now poured down both their cheeks.

Lilia's sadness turned to bitter confusion. She had been taught to believe in the justice of the state and Comrade Stalin.

"How could they?"

"I do not know."

"I have been taught only our enemies kill good people. Are those teachings all lies?"

"Be careful, my child. Rumors fly that dissenters are being exiled to harsh labor camps in large numbers."

Lilia was genuinely conflicted. It was now clear to even one as young as Lilia that political paranoia was now pervasive. She had seen the newspapers, heard the men at the canteens whispering rumors of those who had disappeared.

Could Vladimir's outspoken preference for Lenin's "visionary" NEP instead of Stalin's "stifling" progressivism been accidentally misconstrued? Had he been nominated by some self- aggrandizing informant? After all, did Stalin not support this self-policing of the citizenry? These were questions to which Lilia would never find the answers.

It never occurred to her, or Anna, that a seemingly close friend, a neighbor such as Maya Demidova, could possibly have been involved.

~

The state moved the Demidov family into Anna and Lilia's apartment, while the two women were granted the Demidovs' smaller apartment. In addition, Anna was told she would be under continuing investigation for political views that were detrimental to the wishes of Secretary General Stalin.

Two weeks later, Maya Demidova had a housewarming party.

The Litvyak women were not invited.

Chapter 16

*Lilia takes her first steps towards flying solo
at the Taganka Flying School.*

WITH THE MYSTERIOUS disappearance and death of
Vladimir, the loss of his income, and the downsizing of their
apartment, life became difficult for the Litvyak women.

Their circumstances created a cautious, almost paranoid,
atmosphere. Former friends were skeptical about visiting or
even being seen with the Litvyaks. Lilia and Anna wondered
if every acquaintance was a disguised member of the secret
militia monitoring their daily activities.

Despite the general gloom and doom of her surroundings, the indefatigable Lilia continued to attend high school and worked part time after school at a local grocery store. She regularly consumed those unsold copies of *Pravda*. Young Russian men were increasingly interested in Lindbergh's highly publicized round-the-world flight and the arrival of three engineering inventions: the gyro horizon, rudder foot pedals, and a more sensitive stick for easier elevator control.

Finally, Lilia decided to find a way to launch her flying career, with or without the approval of Anna.

~

Taganka Flying School, on the outskirts of Moscow, was little more than a bright red shack with a few drafty windows, a collection of stained and scarred wooden desks and chairs, and a large counter that separated the "back office" from the applicant-processing area.

But the facility (the city's only combination ground and flight school) was populated with a variety of vintage aircraft on which to train and fly, and facilities manager Pavel Shereshevsky knew how to cater to the pleasure pilot as well as the potential Air Force recruit. The club maintained a rare men's-only lounge—complete with tea, sweets, pinups, and occasionally vodka—where the pilots exchanged information, experiences, and other pleasantries.

Lilia had made a deal with her mother which she planned to keep. But she also realized that without actual airdrome

experience, she would not be able to live her dream.

Fortunately for Lilia, the hobbyist flying boom made Taganka desperate for clerical help to process the increased flood of applicants, schedule training lessons, and complete the state-approved licensing paperwork. Lilia responded to a small ad in the local paper.

Lilia arrived for her interview conservatively dressed with make-up and her long blonde hair properly tied in a bun, looking years older than 14.

"Young lady, can you type?" asked Shereshevsky during her interview.

"*Tak tochno* [exactly so]," responded Lilia.

"And, you've processed aviation licenses before?"

"Tak tochno."

"And, you've executed flight training plans?"

"Tak tochno."

Shereshevsky wondered how one so young could have done so much.

"You've done all that, and you're just sixteen?"

"Tak tochno," responded Lilia.

"Young lady, I have the feeling that you would say you've flown planes upside down in a thunderstorm if it would permit you the job."

The shapely, petite, 5'1" Lilia smiled. "Tak tochno."

Shereshevsky liked her spunk. "Let's give it a try then. Can you work after school three days a week and all day Saturday?"

"Tak tochno."

"How silly of me to ask such a dumb question!"

A shy smile lighted Lilia's face. Her steel-blue eyes sparkled. "Tak tochno."

~

Lilia decided lying to her mother—for the first and only time—was troublesome but necessary if she was to pursue her passion.

"Mother, I've have secured a part time job assembling parts at the machine factory near the outskirts of town. Working just three afternoons and Saturday, I'll be able to contribute some rubles to our house fund."

"How did you find such a job?"

"My mathematics' teacher's brother is a supervisor at the factory... And I am one of his best students."

"I will miss our reborn Saturday activities."

"As will I. But won't the extra money reduce your work shifts?" asked Lilia, mature beyond her years.

"Yes," said the physically weary but nevertheless disappointed Anna.

"And, is that not a good thing?"

"Yes."

~

Lilia was like a sponge during those first few months at Taganka. She handled every clerical task with excellence, and volunteered numerous ideas on how to improve efficiency, many of which were immediately adopted. For her efforts, facilities manager Shereshevsky promoted Lilia to part-time office supervisor over a number of the other full-time employees in the office.

Eventually, a full-time supervisory job became available. A lazy, jealous co-worker, Irina Ivanova, attempted to discredit Lilia' s work ethic in order to insure she received the supervisory job.

"Comrade Shereshevsky," mocked Ivanova, "the *girl* thinks processing faster and better is important. She strongly resists the communist way that each produce according to her ability. Society is no longer a capitalist marathon."

Shereshevsky, who unbeknownst to Ivanova believed the impending war situation required dedication, not procrastination, took Irina to task in front of her comrades.

"So, you believe one should not overproduce and create abundance?"

"I do."

"Irina, let me ask you a question. Suppose the Germans invade the Motherland, would you still avoid the production of abundant war materials and supplies?"

Irina did not respond.

Lilia was promoted to supervisor two days later.

~

Lilia now had three balls to juggle—her schooling, her full-time job, and her increasing desire to learn to fly. But she remained steadfast to her priorities and promises.

Good school grades and working productively came first. Learning to fly was a work-in-progress since there were no prior rules, no benchmarks. But she knew intuitively, if and when opportunity knocked, she had to be flight-ready.

She decided knowledge was a critical element in becoming a successful pilot. She would privately critique student take-offs and landings until it was too dark to see. She took notes on a small pad. It was obvious the trainees had a difficult time stabilizing the PO-2 's wood and canvas fuselage when they reached an altitude of 609 metres and an even more difficult time landing in the sharp and unpredictable crosswinds at Taganka's bumpy dirt airstrip.

Her inquisitive mind wondered. Why were future pilots of the air force being trained on non-military aircraft? After all, according to newspaper reports Russia's new experimental fighter plane, the Yak-1, was far superior. Should the young pilots be called to battle, wouldn't they fly these new Yaks? And why was the club's airstrip not upgraded? Everyone knew it made training pilots to land even more difficult.

One evening Lilia broached matters with Shereshevsky in hopes that her suggestions might move her closer to a flying opportunity.

"Many of the pilots struggle with proper training," commented Lilia.

"Really," laughed Shereshevsky dismissively. "How would you know that?"

"I have spent hours observing and making notes," said Lilia as she showed him her notepad.

"And there is the matter of the planes. PO-2's were designed for civilian use; they will never go to war, so why practice on such equipment?"

"Let me imagine," said Shereshevsky cynically, "Perhaps I should contact Comrade Stalin and ask him to send new planes!"

Lilia missed the humor. "Perhaps, not Comrade Stalin but..."

Shereshevsky interrupted. "Young lady, and I do mean *young* lady, I appreciate your interests, but return to your clerical duties."

"I wish to do more."

Shereshevsky laughed. "Such as?"

"I wish to fly."

"And once you learn to fly. Then what?"

"I will train others."

Shereshevsky was impressed by her passion, and he had needs at the airdrome.

"I will make you a deal."

"What kind of deal?"

"You clean up oil for two months, and I will try to find a pilot who wishes to train a woman. [Cleaning spilled oil at the hangars was a dirty job, one that no self-respecting male wanted.] In exchange, I will ask the men for training time."

"Agreed."

"But no promises. The men must decide. Their needs take precedent."

"I understand."

As agreed, two months to the day, Shereshevsky asked for volunteers to train Lilia. None was forthcoming.

"But she has desire; she has passion," pitched Shereshevsky to Anatoliy Morozov, a handsome twenty-something pilot with deep black eyes and a flawless olive complexion, long considered the airdrome's unofficial ringleader.

"And she will make your plane more attractive."

"You want me to train that delicate waif instead of others," glared Morozov. "I say no."

"Suppose I give you extra flight time...scheduled at your request."

"I still say no. Anatoliy doesn't not waste his time training little women."

~

"I know we had a deal," said a disappointed Shereshevsky, "but I cannot get anyone to train you."

Lilia was furious and more determined than ever. She thought for a moment. "What about Anatoliy?" Lilia had seen the way Anatoliy looked at her. She knew he found her attractive.

"Anatoliy most of all."

"What does that mean?"

"He said he does not train little women. He was very clear."

Lilia decided to take matters into her own hands. "Let me talk to him."

"Be my guest."

Chapter 17

*The beautiful and personable Lilia, now 16,
had no trouble attracting the opposite sex.*

THE VERY NEXT SATURDAY, Anatoliy, who thought Lilia to be 18 or 19, taxied back to the hangar after his final flight of the day. A smiling, self-confident Lilia with black greasy hands stepped in front of his biplane, hands on hips.

"Get out of my way, woman!" he shouted.

"Not until you promise."

"Promise what?"

"Come down and I'll tell you."

He was intrigued. Lilia's assumption was correct. He had a crush on her from the first day he laid eyes on her.

"This better be good," stared Anatoliy.

"I wish to become a pilot. I need a trainer."

"Why me?"

"You are the best," said Lilia with the proper hint of wistfulness.

Anatoliy's coolness started to melt. "And what do you expect to accomplish?"

"I wish to be a trainer."

Anatoliy shook his head. "I don't know if training pilots is an appropriate job...." He paused.

Lilia smiled warmly. She had heard it all before and didn't need to hear it again. She knew she had to take a risk to capture Anatoliy's attention. She decided to make an offer untypical of the times, and certainly untypical of a fourteen-year-old, no matter how beautiful, no matter how mature. "I'm willing to trade."

"Trade what?" wondered Anatoliy.

"You do for me, and I'll do for you."

"What exactly does that mean?"

"If you help me get a pilot's license, I will teach you how to kiss better."

"What makes you think I need help in that department?"

"I have talked to others," exaggerated Lilia. "Improvements need to be made."

"Really. Who are these others?"

"I cannot break confidences."

"What have they said?"

"Let us just say my proposal will be helpful."

"If my need is so dire, perhaps I should receive my lesson first," smiled Anatoliy. "Yes?"

"No," responded Lilia firmly. "You train first, and then I pay."

"But I will have to take others off the list to train you. How do I know your lessons will be as good as mine?" smiled Anatoliy.

Lilia knew she had Anatoliy right where she wanted him. "As I said, a deal is a deal. You take it or leave it."

"That's your final answer?" said Anatoliy.

"Final answer."

Anatoliy looked into Lilia' s eyes and shook her hand.

"I'll take the deal."

~

"Why so quiet?" said Anna over dinner."You seem exhausted. Are work and school too much?"

Lilia wanted to reveal the deal she had struck. That she was about to take the first step toward realizing her dream. On the other hand, she was afraid Anna would again deposit a burdensome guilt trip. Lilia made her decision. "Mummy, I have something important to say, and I do not wish you to be angry with me."

"Love does not allow time for anger," smiled Anna.

Lilia took a deep breath. She had never openly deceived her mother before, and she was not sure of her reaction, either to the deceit or to her desire to work at the airdrome. "I do not work at the factory."

"Then where do you go after school?"

"I go to the airdrome."

"Lilia, it is not the right place for a woman!"

"Mother, I want to fly, but I must learn how. Working at the airdrome will help me achieve my goal."

"Fly? For what purpose? To be another Osipenko or Raskova? That is important to you?"

"It is my dream."

"And, what do you do at the airdrome?"

"I help the clerks with paperwork. There is much to flying."

Anna noticed her daughter's unpleasant body odor. "I do have another question." Mummy smiled. Lilia's eyes opened wide. She wondered, had Mummy weakened? "Daughter, you smell like a barrel of oil. Do they have you doing paperwork in the fuel pits?"

Lilia decided to act out a little drama. She smelled her clothes and then feigned surprise.

"Sorry, Mummy. I guess one picks up the scent of her surroundings."

~

Lilia took her first flying lesson the next evening at sunset.

"Do you know the five rules of flying?" questioned Anatoliy as they began to ascend.

"No," said a surprised Lilia.

"Number one. Flying isn't dangerous. Crashing is what's

dangerous.

"Number two. The only time you have too much fuel is when you are on fire.

"Number three. The probability of survival is inversely proportional to the angle of arrival. Large angle of arrival, small probability of survival and vice versa.

"Number four. A 'good' landing is one from which you can walk away. A 'great' landing is one after which you can use the plane again.

"Number five. Stay out of the clouds. The silver lining everyone keeps talking about might be another airplane going in the opposite direction. Reliable sources also report that mountains have been known to hang out in clouds."

Lilia laughed heartedly. She was taken by Anatoliy's dry wit and wry smile.

"Tonight I'm just going to familiarize you with the controls." After starting the engine and letting the carburetor warm for a few moments, Anatoliy accelerated down the runway. "Now I'm going to begin lift off by pushing the stick up. See that?"

Lilia nodded.

"But not too fast. You don't want the engine to stall. Also be sensitive to head winds; if you feel the plane pulling hard to one side or the other, don't fight nature. Go with the flow and keep climbing. If you need to turn, employ the rudder controls near your feet. Left rudder turns to the left and right to right. But no sudden foot pressure or the plane will tilt on its side."

Lilia smiled and nodded. Her mind was like a sponge. Anatoliy was quite handsome, she thought.

"The third item you need to be familiar with is the aileron yoke. The yoke," he said, pointing to the steering wheel, "is designed to keep the plane from rolling side to side. If you are caught in a crosswind, the yoke keeps your plane balanced so the wings do not flop side to side."

The impatient Lilia wanted to test all three controls. "Enough instruction, when do I take the controls?"

"Not tonight," said Anatoliy. "Tonight is fam-iliarization only." He then demonstrated the use of each control.

"This will be easy," crowed Lilia.

Anatoliy realized Lilia needed a little humility instruction. He pumped the left rudder pedal and pulled the yoke far left. The plane was now flying sideways. He waited for Lilia's scream before rolling the plane back into balance.

"Yahoo! Absolutely incredible!" screamed the steel-nerved Lilia.

Anatoliy, sensing her excitement, headed straight for the picture perfect yellow sunset and then pulled straight up.

Lilia was breathless from the silent beauty and exhilaration of floating through the heavens. She would never forget that first airborne sunset.

When they landed, an elated Lilia jumped from the plane and waited for Anatoliy to exit the cockpit.

"So that is lesson Number One," smiled Anatoliy as he put his arms around Lilia's waist and gave her a tender kiss. Her lips were soft and moist, just as he imagined.

"And that is my lesson Number One," smiled Lilia.

"Why not an advance on Lesson Two and Three?"

"And break our deal?" teased Lilia.

"Deals are meant to be broken."

"Not my deals," responded Lilia, concerned about maintaining her reputation.

~

Flying lesson two was manuals.

"You read this book. It is an official training manual. I'll ask you ten questions; if you get eight correct, you can co-pilot the rise."

For the next three evenings, Lilia went home after school and devoured every page of the manual. Marking sections, making notations, memorizing key paragraphs. Sunday morning Lilia met Anatoliy at the air club. The place was deserted. They sat on a rock under a big elm tree not far from the hangar. He handed her a pencil and a piece of paper with ten questions. "Let's see what you've learned." Anatoliy looked at his watch. "You have ten minutes beginning right now."

Lilia finished the test in eight minutes and smugly handed him the paper. He checked the answers. She scored 100%.

"I'm impressed," said Anatoliy referring to the exam.

"So am I," said Lilia, referring to Anatoliy's profession-alism and his sense of restraint.

"Do you want to go up?"

"What do you think?" Lilia helped Anatoliy with a few last minute flight checks.

"I'm not sure we have enough fuel," observed Anatoliy. "Maybe we better postpone our lesson until Monday when the fuel tanks are unlocked."

Lilia leaned against the wing of the biplane and waved the fuel pump keys in Anatoliy's face.

He shook his head. "I'm not even going to ask."

A few minutes later they were skyward with the warm summer air blowing through Lilia's flaxen blonde hair. Anatoliy turned, nodded, and pointed to the stick.

Lilia grabbed the stick and slowly but surely ascended the plane through a small puff of white clouds and then leveled off. Anatoliy offered congratulations by raising his hand and waving in the air. Lilia signaled back as if to say she was going to turn right. Anatoliy smiled and stretched his arm out as if to say be my guest. She pressed the rudder pedals and turned to the right. Then she took the yoke and balanced the wings perfectly. They practiced the maneuver a few more times before Anatoliy signaled that it was time to descend.

Lilia nodded and pointed to herself. He shook his head no, but it was already too late. She was rapidly descending at a G force that pressed her and Anatoliy firmly against their seats. Lilia was smiling ear to ear. Anatoliy was concerned. He realized his life was now in the hands of his wet-behind-the-ears protégé.

As they came within a hundred feet of the air club building Lilia sharply turned the plane to the right, circled the airfield one more time, straightened the wings during her approach and landed smoothly on the runway.

"Are you crazy?" screamed a shaking, quivering Anatoliy as the plane touched down. "We could have been killed."

"Did I land correctly?" smiled Lilia.

"Yes, but..."

"Do you really think I'm crazy?' said Lilia taking the brightly colored scarf off her neck.

"No, but..."

Lilia opened her arms. Anatoliy walked over and kissed

her. His quaking and shivering subsided.

"That is lesson number two," laughed Lilia.

~

Anatoliy was deeply concerned about his reputation. Word could not get out about the fear he had just exhibited. But how to approach Lilia without embarrassing himself was the challenge. His father had taught him that he should not show weakness. It was a character flaw, not to be tolerated.

"Perhaps, I can escort you home and share a coffee or tea along the way." Lilia smiled and nodded, her blonde hair swaying in the late afternoon breeze.

As they sat in a small café on Arbat Street, not far from Lilia's apartment, Anatoliy commenced his mission, cautiously but causally. "Tomorrow is an important day in my life. It is my twenty-first birthday." Anatoliy reached into his pocket. "My father has given me these handsome flying gloves."

Lilia held them in her hand. "Why did you not use them today?"

"It seemed more fitting to wear them on the day itself."

"When is your next birthday, and how old will you be?" asked Anatoliy unknowingly. Lilia knew she could not go there. It would be embarrassing. More importantly, if Anatoliy knew her real age, he might refuse to continue the lessons.

"Do you expect an additional present from your mother?"

Anatoliy turned somber. "I have never met her."

"I beg your pardon," said Lilia.

"She died at my birth. I have only seen pictures. She was very beautiful. Like you," said Anatoliy.

Lilia was speechless. Anatoliy, sensing her uneasiness, changed the subject. "What do you really want to be when you grow up?" he teased.

Lilia hesitated. Would Anatoliy be accepting of the real truth? She decided to trust her instincts. "A fighter pilot in the Motherland's Air Force."

Anatoliy was surprised but not shocked. His was quickly learning about his young protégée's dogged determination. "I believe when our lessons are complete you will be a very talented aviator. Perhaps the best I've ever trained. But a fighter pilot? That's an entirely different skill set. I have a question. Do you really believe women have the heart for such matters? Are women not built with kindness and reared to have families and children?"

Lilia responded confidently, matter-of-factly. "That was two questions. The answer to the first is 'yes, some do.' The answer to the second is, 'I wish those too.'"

"So you wish to give birth to one life while practicing to take another life away?"

"My father taught me that we have a duty to protect and defend our Motherland, regardless of potential consequences. The loss of enemy life is merely a by-product of that mission," said Lilia, sounding more mature than her years.

"And you believe society approves?"

"More so than before," responded Lilia confidently. "Comrades Lenin and Stalin seem to agree. Have you not read the stories, seen the posters?"

"Do you believe all you hear and see?"

Lilia realized the conversation could go no further. "Why don't we agree to disagree?"

"Deal," smiled Anatoliy. "I have another question."

Lilia had sensed Anatoliy's growing fondness. The hug on the airstrip was mutual. But she was fourteen, and he was twenty-one. She wondered how she was going to handle the obvious.

"I believe fear is a good thing? What about you?" She stared blankly, wondering why such a question.

Anatoliy offered an oblique reference. "You know, I believe by facing inner fear, one can achieve heights never imagined."

Lilia was mystified and silent. She had no idea where the conversation was headed. Until...

"Let me give you an example," continued Anatoliy. "Today we flew. Your unexpected maneuver challenged me. I was not sure we could fly so low and bank so sharply without causing danger for the others on the ground." Anatoliy paused. "Do you understand what I am saying?"

Lilia smile mischievously. "Now I understand. You don't want anyone to know the maneuver of a little woman in flight caused a big tough man's hand to shake and body to shudder."

Anatoliy put his hand to his chin, smiled sheepishly, and then nodded, "Something like that."

~

Two weeks later, Lilia took and passed her instructor's test with flying colors. She was fourteen years and two months old. She was not only the air club's youngest pilot; she was also the air club's first woman pilot.

~

Summer 1937...

The air force had chosen Taganka as one of three locations to debut Russia's new YAK combat plane that—at a top speed of 560 kilometres an hour—could compete with any plane in the sky.

Anatoliy, now considered the entire area's top flyer, was awarded the honor of piloting this first public flight. He spent the entire week prior to the event familiarizing himself with the YAK.

There were almost 700 employees, pilots, families, and guests present as Anatoliy waved and taxied down the runway. Lilia boldly raced to the middle of the tarmac, causing Anatoliy to stop suddenly.

"What the hell are you doing, woman?"

"I want to give you something to remember me by." She held up a bouquet of freshly picked wildflowers. He smiled and shook his head. Lilia climbed on the right wing near the cockpit, handed him the bouquet. The handsome pilot smiled broadly.

The smiling young man was cleared for takeoff and roared down the runway. He executed two barrel rolls over the airstrip in the shiny green and red plane and then disappeared into the clouds at an altitude of some 4000 metres. "Unbelievable experience, over," said Anatoliy over the flight leader's radio at the airdrome headquarters.

Lilia, who had been permitted to listen, smiled broadly. "Bring on the fascists, over."

Less than two minutes later, trouble struck. "Oil gauge overheating, permission for emergency landing, over." A stunned silence came over the room. Lilia could feel Anatoliy's heart racing. "Cabin on fire. Parachute jammed. Not going to

make it."

There was a loud crackling sound. The dashboard fried in the heat and flames. The last sounds over the radio were that of Anatoliy screaming and gasping.

111

Lilia ran outside and searched the skies, hoping against hope. A shooting star crossed the heavens. There was an explosion on the distant horizon, not far from where the star had dissipated.

Chapter 18

*Mother and daughter grow closer through their
personal tragedies and societal changes.*

ANNA WAS CONCERNED ABOUT Lilia's emotional
well-being. The ebullient, self-confident spirit of her sixteen-year-old
daughter had been shattered by a string of personal tragedies:
best-friend Katya's unfortunate accident, her father's
senseless murder, and heartthrob Anatoliy's unbelievable
ending in front of her eyes.

Dinner was no longer a joyous affair where the women
laughed and shared. It was now a mother walking on eggshells as
she tried to communicate with the contemplative young lady
sitting across the table. One evening in late fall, Moscow was
drenched by an all-day heavy rain. By the time Lilia finished her
classroom training sessions at the airdrome, she was tired,
soaking-wet, and chilled to the bone.

M.G. Crisci

"Child, please get out of those clothes before you catch a terrible cold."

Lilia stared as if to say, "So what?"

Anna smiled, wishing not to upset her daughter further, "I've made one of your favorites, nice hot barley and tomato soup; it will warm your bones. What do you think?"

After dinner, they sat and read quietly in their respective favorite chairs. Anna, an ardent reader of *Pravda*, thanks to her husband's keen interest in current affairs, scanned a front-page article discussing Comrade Stalin's grand vision of transforming Russia from a lowly agrarian society into a respected industrial nation with a modern military complex. It was right on schedule, assuming the mass entry of patriotic women into the workplace, particularly the young, the strong, and the bright. The article also ran a reproduction of a poster popular in big Russian cities that depicted women as an important catalyst in the Motherland's future success.

Anna saw the article as an opportunity to raise her daughter's spirits. "See, Comrade Stalin recognizes the importance you shall play in the coming years." Anna handed her the paper. "See."

As she reached out to show Lilia the article, the paper slipped out of her hand and fell to the floor. "I'll get it, Mummy."

She picked it up with a different page on top. On it was a small story that referenced the disbandment of Zhenotdel ("the women's sector"), a division previously created with much fanfare by Lenin to promote women's rights and issues. This article stated the sector was no longer necessary, and that sector head (and a Lilia role model) Aleksandra Kollontai, the highly-educated, elegantly-mannered, beautiful woman who spoke seven languages and wore stylish clothes, had been assigned "other unspecified duties."

"What would Daddy have said of this?" asked Lilia. "The truth, please."

Anna paused, but her body language spoke volumes. "I imagine he would have said that the beauty and intelligence of Aleksandra intimidated the Party's more conservative elements, causing her to be unceremoniously stripped of government influence."

"Will women ever be truly equal?" thought Lilia.

"I understand your frustration," said a pained Anna, trying to move on despite her own travails. "Daddy was a good man who wished no one ill. And nothing or no one can ever change my opinion."

"Then someone in government permitted Daddy's wrongful death," retorted Lilia, growing aware of the unspoken rumors that Stalin's behavior was becoming increasingly ruthless against contrarian opinions.

Anna knew this conversation was dangerous, even within the confines of their apartment. "I try to believe that his death was not in vain. Perhaps his tragic fate was the accidental by-product of a misguided, secret declaration by some well-meaning citizen to protect the Motherland from dissenters."

"Are you trying to convince me or you?" asked a teary-eyed Lilia, struggling with her own rite of passage.

"I'm not sure," responded Anna honestly. "But we must move on. There is an element of truth in Comrade Stalin's assessment. I do believe, as your father did, that Hitler, despite the Nazi-Soviet Non-Aggression Pact, wishes to eliminate our way of life. And, so, as a woman even with limited rights and free-doms, I must support Rodina."

~

A few days later, Lilia decided it was time to "partially" reveal her activities to Anna. "Mummy, I have something exciting to tell you," said Lilia at the dinner table. "I have passed the test."

"The test for what?"

"I am now the Taganka Air Club's first woman flying instructor."

A stunned Anna was at first silent. Then she shook her head, and began to smile with pride at her daughter's determination to dream big dreams. "You are indeed a 'woman with purpose,' as your father used to describe me when we worked in the fields." Lilia was pleased at her mummy's reaction "What then after high school?"

"I have a plan. I will become a flight instructor. Prepare pilots for the air force. Then one day I, too, will join the military and become a fighter pilot."

"Daughter, it is one thing to have a grand dream, but a fighter pilot?"

"That's exactly what Anatoliy said."

"I can only imagine. I remember how you begged your father for those ice skates until he was finally exhausted, and had no choice but to say yes," said Anna.

"Do not concern yourself, Mummy, I will come home safe and sound," said a cheerful Lilia. "We will defeat Hitler. I will meet the man of my dreams. We will live next door to you. You will watch our children grow... We will live in peace and happiness."

"I am not aware Comrade Stalin has agreed to a women's division in the air force? Has not Raskova been rebuffed on numerous occasions?"

"There is a real need," interrupted Lilia. "Comrade Stalin has said, 'It is the beginning of a new era for women.'"

"I have my doubts," said Anna, eyes raised, yet afraid to express her true skepticism about Stalin's numerous unfulfilled pronouncements, even to her daughter. Anna also sensed Lilia's impenetrable passion. Her emotions raged. She had lost the love of her life and was not willing to risk the physical loss of her daughter. At the same time, as a mother, she could not risk losing her respect and affection. That pain would be more than she could bear. She'd one last attempt to persuade her daughter to pause, to wait. Ardent beliefs became thoughtful questions. "Are there not important roles in the factories to support our men in war should it come to that? Do you believe women are destined to kill during air battles?"

Lilia steel-gray blue eyes twinkled with higher purpose. "Mummy, I understand why you are concerned. Do not be afraid for me. Daddy taught me well. As for destiny, sometimes it must be challenged. I believe I may have been chosen to do more. There is a reason why I have been given the skills to train others to protect our way of life."

Anna hugged her daughter tightly. A tear formed in the eye of each, and slowly ran down their respective cheeks. They smiled at each other. There was one last matter that weighed on Anna's mind.

"Let us assume for the moment, women can enlist in the air force. Then what of the Litvyak name?"

"I do not understand," said Lilia.

Anna's speech raced, "Your father's name was obviously on some secret list. Suppose during recruitment, they cross-check that list, and suppose they identify our family name, and suppose..."

Lilia interrupted. "Are you suggesting I live my entire life in fear?"

"No, but I am suggesting you change your name."

"Change my name? Impossible," said an indignant Lilia. "That would suggest Daddy's life had no meaning."

Anna could not dispute her daughter's wisdom.

"I was born a Litvyak. I will live and die a Litvyak."

Chapter 19

Lilia's training plane, the post World War I Polikarpov Po-2.

TRAINING PILOTS AT TAGANKA Airdrome gave Lilia insights about the challenges that lay ahead.

"Why has no one been assigned?" asked Lilia, who noticed there was no training candidate posted next to her name.

"No one wishes to be trained by a beautiful woman. They are afraid you may be too fragile," responded the manager.

"Who would say such a thing? Shall I become an ugly duckling? Perhaps dressing more like a man, covering my hair, removing my lipstick... I was joking. I am who I am."

"Then you must wait for an enlightened male."

Then assign a woman. I will demonstrate the foolishness of their thinking."

"There are no women."

~

Lilia sat dejected on the plane wing.

A tall, thin young man with black wavy hair and square shoulders and jaw approached. "I have watched you for some time. Can you teach me the things you do with a plane?"

"It depends," said Lilia.

"Depends on what?" responded the man.

"Do you have a fearless heart?"

He smiled into her steel-blue eyes. "I have more heart than you can imagine."

Lilia liked his smile. "My name is Lilia Litvyak," she said, extending her hand.

"I know," smiled the man again. "I am Georgiy Shereshevsky."

"The son of the airdrome manager?"

"I want no special favors."

"None intended," smiled Lilia.

After only a week of lessons (ten in all), Lilia had transformed Georgiy from a green trainee into a relatively accomplished pilot.

"I am ready for the advanced course," said Georgiy. "Those acrobatic rolls and steep drops."

"My job is to train you for a war. Not an air show."

Georgiy persisted. He was like a male version of Lilia. She recognized the trait. Finally, she acquiesced. "But should you get ill, I will not be your nursemaid. Deal?"

He extended his hand. "Deal."

~

"Full throttle up," directed Lilia shortly after they had reached a modest cruising altitude of 2000 metres.

Georgiy raised his thumb as if to say, *understood*. At 3000 metres, she shouted, "Higher!" At 4000, "Higher!" As they approached 5000 metres, the plane started to shudder. Lilia knew her plane had reached its max! Georgiy became animated.

"Now, dive, dive!" shouted Lilia. "Do you want me to take the control?"

Georgiy waved her off. Moments later they were crashing downward through the clouds. As they approached 2000 metres, Lilia shouted, "Level off. Level off!"

To her surprise, Georgiy shook his head no. They fell straight down to 1500 metres, then 1000. Lilia was concerned Georgiy had lost control and they might crash. Suddenly, the plane leveled off, and Georgiy guided the plane to a perfect landing on the airstrip.

Lilia jumped out of the plane. "Suppose the controls failed. You could have killed us!"

"We all die sometime," smiled the unflappable Georgiy.

~

Lilia was not only the airdrome's most skilled pilot, she was also its most experimental, willing to push the envelope whenever the notion struck. In time, she also became legend for her low flying capabilities, her ability to see clearly through the darkest cloud conditions, and for making picture perfect landings on the darkest of nights.

The feedback from the male pilots was also outstanding. She projected the right blend of professionalism and wit. She could push their buttons without intimidating; she could build confidence without the appearance of a sophomoric cheerleader. This combination of pride and practicability led Shereshevsky to contact the Ministry of Propaganda. He urged them to print a story about Lilia's unique flying abilities and to obtain comments and insights from some of the pilots she had trained. "A story such as this will inspire more young people to fly, strengthen the Motherland's air defenses, and let other women see what has been achieved under Comrade Stalin's new programs.

Soon a very complimentary article appeared with the headline, "The Young Pilot Who has it All." Shereshevsky's phone rang off the hook with candidates now wanting to fly.

"What is the meaning of this?" fumed a surprised Lilia. "I do not do what I do for publicity." Shereshevsky tried to respond, but he had incurred the wrath of Lilia. "What will others think?"

"But Lilia... "

"A film actress perhaps?"

"Lilia, please...."

"No, I am merely a woman." She turned her back and walked away. She did not communicate with Shereshevsky-in any fashion-for the next two weeks.

But it did not matter. From the moment the article appeared, Lilia became the airdrome's most requested pilot. During her entire stay at Taganka, she would go on to personally train and successfully license 48 student pilots, which enhanced the prestige of the airdrome and delivered a cadre of first class recruits to the Soviet Air Force.

~

Elena Demidova was an imposing figure at 1.7 metres tall with short black hair, dark brown eyes, oversized lips, and a robust figure that tipped the scales at 72.5 kilograms. She followed Lilia's training exploits as Lilia had followed Raskova's long-distance flight across Russia. Although, there was a difference. Elena, the daughter of the highly decorated MGB operative Semyon Demidov, was jealous about Lilia's newfound notoriety. After all, how could the daughter of an *enemy of the state* receive such pubic accolades, while she, a well-compensated government store manager, toil in relative obscurity?

Elena's plan was simple. She would finish courses at the flying school, sign up to train with Lilia, learn her tricks of the trade, and then surpass her accomplishments. Along the way, she would also take advantage of her father's influence to discredit Lilia's reputation. Or perhaps worse...

"Father, do you think it wise to allow such children to train candidates for the air force in such difficult times?"

Semyon, who had since been promoted to local head of the MGB, concurred. "Daughter, it will be wise for you to befriend our subject, so you can monitor her every activity and write reports. If she is like her father, we will make sure she ends up like her father."

~

Lilia scanned her activity sheet for the day. She saw the name, "Elena Demidova." "Could it be the same one?" she thought.

"I understand I am your first lesson," said Elena, uncertain how Lilia would respond.

Lilia was tempted to pass the young lady to another trainer. But Elena's father, a master of deceit, had taught his daughter to read an intended victim's body language. Elena cleverly took the offensive. "Lilia, I have thought many times about my stupidity as a child. Over a silly game no less. I have heard of your skills. I wish to one day be among the best." Elena reached out her hand.

123

Lilia paused. Much had happened to preoccupy Lilia's mind since the day a spoiled eight year-old huffed out the door of her apartment during a simple game of *Words*. Lilia chose to nod and move on, but she would not go as far as to shake the other woman's hand. "Have you ever flown before?"

"No, but I have taken courses at the flying school and did quite well."

"Why do you wish to fly?"

"Like yourself, I wish one day to train. To help the Motherland in our cause against Hitler."

"An admirable goal."

The conversation turned surprisingly political.

"Do you believe Hitler will invade Russia?" asked Lilia.

"It is a matter of when. Reports suggest that time may be rapidly approaching."

"Reports?"

Elena realized her error. "I meant rumors."

"Do you believe all political rumors?" pressed Lilia.

"That is not my business. I am a store manager."

Lilia's intuition told her something was amiss, but she wasn't sure what.

"Perhaps we should focus on requirements?" offered Elena in a patronizingly friendly tone.

"And what about your mechanical capabilities?"

"I do not understand the question," said Elena.

"When one flies, I believe it wise to know details, should you be forced to land somewhere with no support. I would suggest we do two sessions at the utility shack before we go airborne."

Elena was impressed by Lilia's professionalism but privately wondered what she might put in her first report.

"You're the boss."

Elena quickly became bored and a little impatient. The discussion of yoke to rudder mechanic, tire brackets, and carburetor component seemed overwhelming. "Why do I need to know all this technical stuff?" challenged Elena. "You get the plane in the air, you steer properly, fly safely, then land softly."

"Suppose there is a wind shear as you drop to a low altitude, and your carburetor stalls?" responded Lilia. "You need to know whether to drift with it based on available landing area or perhaps abort and retry."

Elena realized Lilia was right. But Lilia was not finished. She felt everybody she trained should think as she did.

"And, suppose your landing gear jams; how do you most safely land?"

~

Lilia fully expected day one to be a disaster, but things went surprisingly well. The takeoff went without incident. When Lilia reached 2000 metres, she asked Elena to take the throttle. "Steady and at a reasonable speed," directed Lilia. Elena increased altitude exactly as instructed.

"Good," complimented Lilia, "now that we are at 5000 metres, bank ninety degrees west in a slow arching fashion." Elena again obliged perfectly. "See the dark cloud formation ahead?"

Elena nodded.

"Go through the blue opening between the clouds. It should be smoother."

As Elena headed to the hole in the clouds, the plane began to bounce, shake, and shudder from clear air turbulence.

"Let me take over!" shouted Lilia for safety reasons.

"I'm fine. I can handle it," responded the confident Elena. "You have taught me well." Moments later the plane was cruising steadily.

After a few more turns in clear sky, Lilia decided it was time to land. "Do you wish to assist me in landing?" asked Lilia. Elena nodded yes.

"I will drop us to about 500 metres above the landing strip and then briefly turn the wheel over to you. Your job will be to position our plane in line with the dark green patch of flat grass a distance from the utility shack. I'll then take over for the final approach." Again, Elena nodded.

When they got to 500 metres, Elena took over and headed for the patch.

A strong wind shear pushed the plane sideways. Elena knew instantly she was overmatched. "Lilia, take the controls, take the controls!" Moments later the plane landed safely.

"Elena, you did well today, under surprisingly difficult conditions," said Lilia reaching her hand out in congratulations.

During the next few weeks, Elena learned more with each lesson. Lilia was proud of her star student. "You are ready for solo flight," announced Lilia. "I have recommended that you be fully licensed." The girls hugged at the edge of the runway.

~

"Where are the reports?" asked Semyon. "It has been twelve weeks now."

Elena had a change of heart. She realized Lilia was not only an outstanding pilot and teacher, but also a very honorable human being. She wondered about Vladimir. Could the state have made a mistake? It seems unlikely to her that a young woman with such an obvious commitment to the Motherland could be raised by a cynical traitor. "Father, I have gotten to know Lilia quite well these past weeks." She paused. "Does the MGB make mistakes?"

Semyon's eyebrows rose, his face became more stoic than usual. "What are you saying, my daughter?"

"It does not appear to me that Lilia could ever be an enemy of the state. She possesses too much patriotism. Too much honor."

"So there will be no reports."

"No."

"Are you certain?"

"Yes."

"Then the matter is concluded; there will be no investigations."

"There is more. I now believe it would have been impossible for her father to also have been an enemy of the state."

"What are you suggesting?"

"I am saying that Vladimir Litvyak's case should be reconsidered."

"But he is long since executed."

"I know, but perhaps he can be officially absolved posthumously?"

"You know what you are asking is highly unusual, even dangerous?"

"I do."

Semyon leaned back in his chair and thought quietly. Perhaps his daughter was right. But what would others think if he proposed to reopen the case? What would others say about his commitment, his judgment? Could he be perceived as a traitor trying to help another traitor?

Thirty seconds passed. The silence seemed like an eternity. Elena smiled. She assumed. After all, don't daughters always get their way with fathers?

"Daughter, it is impossible; the Party is never mis-taken."

Chapter 20

Lilia's first commanding officer, Major Marina Raskova.

"YOU WISH TO DO WHAT?" questioned the portly, bald, middle-aged officer in his drab olive-green uniform from behind the counter of the bustling recruiting office on Oktyabrskaya Street.

Lilia was on mission! Stalin's public appeals for women to do their fair share merely heightened her strong convictions.

She desperately wanted to defend the Motherland by using the substantial flying skills she had acquired. "Become a fighter pilot," said the diminutive Lilia with her blonde hair draped over her shoulder.

"Things may be bad, but we're not so desperate that we're going to put little girls like you up in the skies. Go home and help your mother!"

Persistent Lilia stood her ground. "I have been training pilots for four years at the Taganka Club," countered Lilia. "See my papers. Over forty men have been licensed and joined the air force under my tutelage. Here are letters of commendation and endorsements from the pilots and club management."

The officer examined the documentation. His tone changed. "I'm impressed. But I still can't help. Comrade Stalin has not approved admission of women into the air force."

"The rule should change," said Lilia.

"Why don't you just call the Kremlin and talk to Comrade Stalin yourself?" he said. "In the meantime, the most important thing you can do for the Motherland is to go back to Taganka and train more pilots. We desperately need them. I'll call you if circumstances change."

~

The athletically-built Marina Raskova was a gregarious, no-nonsense woman with jet black hair and deep olive complexion who commanded attention whenever she spoke. She had no early interest in flying. Ironically, she would come to inspire thousands of young Russian women to fly. Her original goal was to become an opera singer, but financial hardship, the premature death of her father and singing instructor, and a bout with depression caused by self-induced stress forced her to quit music and change careers.

After graduating with honors at the prestigious Lomonosov Moscow State University, she became a chemist, married, had a daughter, Tanya, and eventually became a draftsman in the Aero Navigation Laboratory of the Russian Air Force Academy, thanks to an introduction by her engineer husband, Sergei Raskov. There she was exposed to mechanical engineering, physics, radio theory, and navigation. She subsequently worked at the Leningrad Air Force Research Institute and became the first Soviet woman to be certified as an aviation navigator.

Sergei and Marina subsequently divorced. While Raskova would never discuss her personal life, the general assumption was that, since she never even considered remarriage, her career took precedence over the family.

After setting the world's nonstop distance record in 1938 with two female comrades, the articulate and engaging Raskova became a member of the Communist Party of the Soviet Union in 1940 and went on the lecture circuit, drawing thousands of women to hear praise of the progressive policies of Stalin. These policies, despite the government's wanton disregard for individual civil liberties and people's fear of being labeled an enemy of the state, would cause millions of soldiers to give their lives on the front with a final cry on their lips, "Za Rodinu, Za Stalina!" (for the Motherland, for Stalin).

Hitler's brazen aggression across Europe continued unabated. He annexed Poland and Czechoslovakia, conquered France, Yugoslavia, and the Baltic Countries, and rescued his failing Italian ally, Benito Mussolini, in North Africa and the Balkans. The smugly self-confident Hitler also accelerated reconnaissance missions across the Russian border to gather intelligence firsthand and to terrorize the civilian populace prior to his eventual Nazi invasion.

As Raskova's popularity grew, so did her influence within the highest government circles. She was offered, and accepted, a noncombat position in the Russian Air Force, where her significant skills in military strategy became legend. She was quickly promoted to the rank of major and became a civilian poster child to her female comrades as well as a trusted strategic advisor to numerous military leaders. Still, Raskova felt unfulfilled. She yearned to fly in defense of the Motherland. The closer Hitler came to Russia, the more vocal she became about the deployment of women in the military and her request to establish, recruit, and lead a female air combat battalion.

~

One handsome officer strongly disagreed. "And who are you exactly?" asked Major Raskova during the regular weekly military planning session at Moscow Centre.

"I am Major Gennadiy Alekseyev. I have been assigned to assist by General Shaposhnikov."

"Assist in what way?"

"Perhaps provide some guidance in the planning and deployment of our air force."

"You are a pilot?"

"I have been so honored," said Alekseyev, one of Russia's outstanding pilots, as he pointed boastfully to his medals.

Raskova was not impressed. Her passion for the cause of the Motherland had nothing to do with personal gain. She continued to chair the meeting, eloquently reinforcing the shortage of potential pilots, should Hitler decide to invade. "I suggest we consider female conscription," concluded Raskova.

"With all due respect," interrupted Alekseev, with the typical male bias of the times. "I do not believe that is such a good strategy."

"And your reason?"

"We should accelerate the recruiting and training of other young men. The rigors of air are not for women."

Raskova was incensed. How could this brash man have such a point of view at a first discussion? The presiding officer saw Raskova's body stiffen. He sensed the possibility of a passionate, protracted debate. "Comrades, your discussion will have to wait. We have other pressing matters to decide."

As they left the hall, Alekseyev did the unthinkable. "Major, could you join me for a cup of tea?"

"First you insult me in front of the others; then you want to share a tea?"

Alekseyev's eyes winkled a boyish smile. Raskova felt his warmth and charm. "All right."

The two majors shared many cups of tea after many future meetings. During those sessions, Marina learned Gennadiy's highly motivated mother had become smitten by the flying bug when Gennadiy was only eight. Unfortunately, she crashed and died during a flying lesson.

"How was she accepted to fly?"

"I guess she kept badgering the Comrade Commander until he finally acquiesced," smiled Alekseyev. "But they must have made some agreement not to publicize the matter because my father didn't know my mother was flying till the wreckage was recovered."

"She must have been quite a lady," smiled Marina.

"As is the lady sitting across from me."

~

Marina Raskova and Lilia first met at the Moscow Secondary School No.1 Komsomol, where Marina had been invited to inform young people about the latest developments in Soviet aviation and international affairs. A question and answer session followed the meeting.

"We are honored that Major Raskova, such a prominent member of our military, has chosen to speak to us today. So please be attentive," said the principal to a room filled primarily with boys and a sprinkling of girls.

Marina's speech was designed to boost graduating students' morale at this most difficult time in Russian-German relations. "We are a great country in the midst of a historical transition. The Motherland has been blessed with resources to harvest and gather which, when combined with Comrade Stalin's insightful industrial policies, will insure abundance of all the necessities for a good life. I am also confident, under Comrade Stalin's guidance, we will also one day be a country where all are equal and all share equally, a model for the entire world. We are a proud people who understand that nothing comes easily. Life is a struggle: reward is a struggle." In an indirect reference to Hitler, Raskova continued passionately, "Rest assured, no one shall ever take ownership of our homeland!"

The audience stood and applauded.

"There is time for questions," said Raskova.

"And, how do we plan to deal with Hitler?" asked one.

"When the time comes, and that time is approaching, we will demolish Hitler and his brazen fascists. What happened to Polish families like Zosya, Yanek, and Tomash shall not be repeated!"

The audience sat quietly, wondering who these people were as Marina walked over to her briefcase sitting on the desk, pulled out a recent edition of *Pravda* and held it over her head. "About a week ago, a Polish man named Tomash, under the cover of darkness, left his wife, Zosya, and son, Yanek, to visit his ailing sister, Katarzhina, some villages away. According to the report, on second evening of his absence, a Nazi recon patrol banged on the family door in the middle of the night. They searched the house for spies. When they found nothing, they became further incensed. A witness hiding in the woods said the fascists started to ravage the home. Zosya tried to protect what few belongings they had. A soldier tossed her to the floor, perhaps worse. Apparently, Yanek demanded they stop.

The officer began to scream: "You peasant Slav. How dare you tell a representative of the Fûhrer what to do? The insolence! Take him outside!" The witness could not see what happened next—merely that there was a rustling sound, a long silence, a moan, and then a single shot.

The patrol, led by an obnoxious young officer named Herman Gerdes, dragged Yanek into an adjacent field and taunted him.

"Till the soil with your fingers then eat the dirt, you miserable swine," demanded Gerdes.

The young man resisted.

"Tie him to that tree." The officer walked into the nearby stable and found a branding iron.

"Make a fire."

When the fire was at its peak, Gerdes heated the end of the iron.

"Open his mouth" he directed two members of the patrol. Gerdes then shoved the iron into Yanek's mouth until his tongue was severed.

As the young boy writhed in pain on the ground, Geddes took his pistol from his holster and smiled demonically as he looked at his squad. "Now let me show what happens to those who disrespect a German officer." He then placed his pistol on the boy's forehead, and pulled the trigger once.

When Zosya found the bloody mass of humanity that was once her son, she screamed hysterically.

"After the soldiers finally left, she went outside to search for Yanek. Blood was everywhere. The boy was practically unrecognizable. Zosya screamed so loudly that the nearby neighbors came running.

"According to the witness, Yanek was buried that evening."

Raskova paused. There was moisture in her eyes. She held back the tears. The children sat in stunned silence. Lilia felt as though a sharp arrow had pierced her heart.

"Does the story say what Tomash did upon his return?"

"Tomash never found out. He had a massive heart attack on the trip back and passed immediately."

Lilia could not hold back the tears. She gripped her chair tightly.

"A few days later, a grief-struck Zosya wrote her final message and left it on the kitchen table: "Please place this picture of Leonid with his beloved guitar near his place of rest. It is how I would like all to remember him. Do not try to contact me. By the time you read this letter, I will have joined my husband and son. With Tomash and Yanek gone and life as difficult as it is, there is little to live for."

You could now hear a pin drop in the room.

"Zosya's body was never found," concluded Raskova.

Lilia recomposed herself. She had her own story to tell. She raised her hand.

Raskova acknowledged her. "Comrade Major. I wish to do my part. As perhaps many others in this room, I tried to enlist at school's end. I was rejected not once but twice."

"Are you not well?"

"I am in perfect health."

Raskova assumed it had something to do with women in actual combat. "To those young women in the audience, and I see many: have patience. There is nothing *we* will not be able to accomplish in this century. History will note our contributions to society. Follow my lead."

Lilia wanted to believe Raskova. But....again she raised her hand. This time her question was decidedly blunter. "Comrade Major, why is Comrade Stalin reluctant to permit women in the air force?"

"I do not believe that is the case," said Raskova, assuming Lilia was referring to a ground support position.

"With all respect Major, as I said earlier, I applied twice for combat fighter pilot duty and was refused."

"Ohhh... that is another matter," responded Raskova.

"And, why is that?" persisted Lilia.

"Do you have the appropriate flying qualifications?"

"I have trained more men for combat than anybody at Taganka Air Club during the last three years. I am more qualified than most of them."

"What is your name, young lady?"

"Lilia Litvyak."

"Lilia, why don't we speak after I finish? Any more questions?"

Lilia again raised her hand.

"Yes, Lilia."

"Your flying accomplishments speak for themselves. Why have you not proposed a female flying battalion? Certainly somebody would listen should you speak."

"You would think so," responded a slightly flustered Raskova.

"Then why have you not tried?" challenged Lilia.

Although insulted by Lilia's accusation and the underlying assumption, Raskova could feel the depth of Lilia's passion. "That answer would require more time than we have."

"We have more time," said Lilia looking around the room. The girls in the audience supported Lilia's comment by again applauding.

"Are there more like you?" smiled Raskova.

"Absolutely. Hundreds," said Lilia, having no idea. "And what of those brotherly peoples in Europe who have already perished? Hitler needs to be halted. Now!"

Raskova was concerned the room would shortly be out of her control.

"I am not sure this is a matter for entire group. Perhaps you would like to discuss your particular situation privately?" asked the Major.

"Yes, most definitely," responded Lilia firmly.

Raskova thanked the audience for their attention. True to her statement, she motioned to Lilia to join her in an empty classroom where they stood face to face. Some girls might have been intimidated in a situation like this. Not Lilia. "The story of Zoya took my breath away. I am more deeply committed to defend the Motherland in the air than ever before."

Raskova realized Lilia did not wish to hear the word no. "My child, I will continue to see what we can do," she said solemnly. "But I do not promise miracles."

"I look forward to reading of your progress."

As Raskova sat in the rear of her car on the way to her next speaking engagement, she imagined what it would be like as Lilia's military superior. Little did Raskova know

Chapter 21

The man who approved Raskova's proposal for a women's air regiment.

A FEW WEEKS LATER MARINA Raskova was appointed to the prestigious People's Defense Committee. There she befriended the highly influential Marshall Boris Shaposhnikov, then head of the General Staff of the Red Army.

Shaposhnikov was one of the few Red Army commanders with formal military training, and in 1921 he joined the Army's General Staff where he won Stalin's respect and trust for his insightful military mind. He served Stalin in various military roles. In 1937 he was appointed Chief of the General Staff, and in 1940 was given the title Marshal of the Soviet Union, in recognition of his lifetime military achievements.

"Major, as the newest member of our committee, it is tradition for you to offer a proposal to improve defense of the Motherland, particularly since we live in such perilous times."

"Very good, Comrade Marshall," said Raskova.

"At the next meeting then?"

"I am prepared today." Raskova had probed some committee members prior to her first meeting and knew of the tradition. "I have studied the pattern of Hitler's European invasion strategies," said Raskova, placing a map on the table. "First he dispatches the Luftwaffe, usually a fleet of Messerschmitt 109's, to strafe and disrupt vital ground installations, munitions dumps and so on. These 109's are faster and more powerful than most of the world's aircraft, save perhaps for America's F-1's. This strafing activity creates confusion within opposing forces, thus allowing Nazi ground forces and armored tanks to penetrate with maximum destructive force while incurring a minimum of casualties."

"And your proposal?" asked the Marshall.

"To dramatically increase the size of our air force. Should the Luftwaffe attack, we can quickly respond with numerical superiority."

"This is a familiar refrain, I am told," said the Marshall. "Major, even if I were to agree with your assessment of Hitler's tactics, we simply do not have the qualified pilots. It will take many months to properly train and expand our air force."

"Respectfully Comrade Marshall, we have the pilots now."

The General chuckled playfully. "So Major, do I take that to mean you have been secretly training and hiding pilots from Comrade Stalin?"

"It means I believe I can attract and train many dedicated and able bodied women to become effective combat pilots."

The room full of male officers sat back in their chairs and began to laugh.

"Is it funny that our soldiers and citizens should be victims of the Luftwaffe?' scowled Raskova, "Or placed in concentration camps as the Nazis proceed through the Motherland?"

"Let us assume your assessment is correct," said the Marshall. "There is still the matter of aircraft shortage. No doubt you are aware our factories are producing Yaks at full capacity."

"I am aware of that, Comrade Marshall."

"So what do you propose these brave, highly qualified pilots fly? Magic carpets...Armed of course." The male-dominated room again roared.

"Just make available all the biplanes sitting in mothballs. I will devise a plan."

"Major, be serious. I'm told Messerschmitts can travel 600 kilometres per hour at an altitude of some 5,000 metres, making them all but invisible to those old biplanes. At 600 kilometres per hour, they would have three times the range of those planes."

"Perhaps my father, (Raskova's father was a field general), can discuss the matter with his friend Comrade Stalin?"

Shaposhnikov did not wish to be outmaneuvered by a woman. "I will discuss the matter with Comrade Stalin at an appropriate moment and get back to you."

~

Three days later, Shaposhnikov broached Raskova's proposal with Stalin, who promptly rejected the initiative. He stated that he had time. While he believed Hitler would attempt an invasion at some point in the future, by not stirring the pot, it gave him the opportunity to train more men and produce more planes and defense materials. What he didn't state was that he did not want women flying and failing, thus making him a military laughing stock and weakening his grip on the government.

~

June 21, 1941...

School exams complete, it was time for the graduating children to party in Krasny Luch. As was the custom, most of the boys arrived for the festivities in white shirts and dark trousers, a few in suits, while the girls arrived in beautiful white dresses.

The school director proudly talked about his pupils' successes and their achievements and pointed out the best pupils. He awarded all certificates with their marks, as well as some special certificates of high progress and laudable leaf (good conduct). Most parents wept with joy and light sorrow-they knew their children's innocence was over and their new independent adult life was about to begin.

The teachers also wept. After six or seven years together, the emotional bonds between teachers and students were strong. In many ways, these students were their children also.

The best pupils took the floor. First they thanked the school and the teachers, giving them flowers. Then there was a two-hour concert where the school's best dancers and singers exhibited their talents and recited poems of peace and hope for the future. A number of the more creative students made up their own verses and song lyrics and joked about each other, the teachers and their school life. In the spirit of the party, no one got offended. The boys and girls and teachers danced until about 3:30 AM.

"Children," said the director, "it is time to see the first dawn of your independent adult life." It was also customary to see the sunrise, then walk the streets and squares, and visit favorite places. Some of the children decided to climb the bridge over the railway and paint their names on it. They stood arm in arm and cheered, "Hurray! A new life is beginning! We are free and happy!"

At 4 AM, unbeknownst to the citizens and children of Krasny Luch, the Germans began bombing Brest and Kiev. At noon, Vyacheslav Molotov, the Chairman of the Council of Peoples Commissars, spoke on the radio informing the population of what had happened just hours before. In spite of what had been going on in Europe, Molotov, as the principal signer of the Nazi-Soviet Non-Aggression Pact of 1939 (the Molotov-Ribbentrop Pact), expressed measured concern.

For those without radios in Krasny Luch, people gathered in the streets and listened to his speech via loudspeakers attached to special poles. Many of the schoolchildren, who had partied just the day and night before, learned of the grave situation at the same time as their parents and grandparents. While all were shocked, they hoped and prayed the conflict would only last for several weeks or months.

~

The scope of Hitler's vicious Operation Barbarossa clearly showed that this would be a long, bloody affair that would only end if the Russians surrendered or Hitler was destroyed. There would be no alternatives.

Hitler did all he could to rain terror and fear on the ill-prepared Russians. Hundreds of Soviet planes were destroyed in the first 24 hours of combat. The Germans attacked 66 airfields, where 75 percent of the Russian aircraft strength was based. On the first day of attack, the Soviet government admitted to losses of 1,136 planes, 800 on the ground. By week's end the figure had risen to 4,107 aircraft. Russian aircraft and ground units were decimated.

It became painfully apparent to many brave Soviet airmen that the only way to save the situation, lest the Motherland be completely overrun, was to resort to the ultimate heroic gesture–*taran*, (suicide ramming tactics). One of the first pilots who committed *taran* was Nikolay Gastello, posthumously named Hero of the Soviet Union. On the ground, another hero, Aleksandr Matrosov, covered a German pillbox with his own body, and gave his friends the opportunity to rush to the attack.

Despite these and many other deeds, the Soviet bear reeled under the Blitzkrieg, conceding thousands of miles of territory. Military materiel, tanks, artillery, buildings, plants and factories were obliterated.

As Hitler pushed toward Stalingrad and Moscow, Stalin's confident mood changed. He realized the air force in particular needed immediate reinforcement. If at least 50 qualified women candidates volunteered, Raskova would be given a training budget and the appropriate number of combat ready aircraft.

Stalin's order to allow the regiment met with immediate success. Women volunteered in droves. True to his word, he quickly authorized a female air regiment under the direction of Major Raskova. It was further authorized that all regiment personnel including mechanics, armorers, and ground staff would be women. Shaposhnikov, seizing the moment, directed the propaganda unit to create and place throughout Moscow posters depicting these brave women. To maintain efficiency and avoid the potential embarrassment of no-shows, a single tent was constructed at Gorky Park.

July 7-12, 1941, was selected as recruitment week, and 478 women, including Lilia, made applications. After Raskova or her assistant, Sergeant Tatyana Lazurenko, reviewed each application personally, Raskova deemed 296 qualified for initial training, enough to fully staff not one, but three battalions, even after expected dropouts. At week's end, Raskova held an orientation session to explain the mission, including the risks, in graphic detail.

"The likelihood is high that many of you will not reach your next birthday," stressed Raskova as she walked around the room. "War is not a game, not a flying lesson, not a glamorous escapade. Man does terrible things to man. So I ask you once again, does anyone wish to reconsider?"

The ladies looked at each other. Not one woman recanted. Hence the 586th Fighter Regiment, the first all-women's air combat battalion in the world, was born.

~

The battalion chief's first task was to determine who should be in the first training battalion.

"Comrade Major," said Tatyana, "this applicant's credentials are outstanding for one so young."

"How young?"

"Eighteen."

"Thank goodness, I thought you were going to say fourteen."

"According to the official records, the candidate obtained her instructor's license at fourteen and has qualified over forty men. Her recommendations are quite impressive."

"Such as?"

"The airdrome manager, as well as many of the pilots she trained, all say her flying skills are of the highest order."

"And, what is this woman's name?"

"Litvyak. Lilia Litvyak."

Litvyak, thought Raskova, recalling that Moscow secondary school, the year before. "Ahhh Lilia, so we meet again."

"You know her?"

"She's quite the determined young lady."

"From her picture, I would say quite beautiful also."

"I know. That is what troubles me."

"I don't understand."

"Will she be tough enough? War is a difficult matter. Flying combat planes is a violent profession. Flying combat missions against experienced Nazi pilots is a noble work but even more..."

Tatyana was perplexed by her commanding officer's reluctance. "Comrade Major, based solely on requirements, Comrade Litvyak is our most outstanding recruit. Perhaps officer material!"

"Make an interview."

~

"You understand we will be a laughing stock if we fail?"

"I do" said Lilia.

"There is reluctance at the highest levels."

"Because of our inexperience?"

"Because we are women," said Tatyana.

"But this is 1941."

"No matter, old beliefs die slowly. Most believe that war doesn't have the face of a woman. War is a very rude, pitiless, bloody thing; it is not for women."

Lilia smiled confidently, "No worries."

"But I must worry. My job is to train, to destroy and to worry."

Lilia's intuition, impatience and bluntness appeared front and center. "Comrade Major, why are we having this conversation?"

"I'm concerned."

"About what?"

"Your inner conviction. You have the credentials; you say the right thing; but can you handle the pressures of war? Suppose you are shot behind enemy lines, can you survive? If a comrade is in need during a dogfight, will you come to her rescue? Can others depend upon you for leadership and not merely bravado?"

Lilia was surprised by the Major's litany of concerns. "My actions will speak for me."

"You know lipstick and mirrors on board combat planes are strictly forbidden."

Lilia was incensed by the cheap shot. She stared at the Major. "Do you believe women should not celebrate who they are? What does it matter if I can take down a Messerschmitt and apply my makeup?"

The Major stuck out her hand. "Comrade Litvyak, welcome to the 586th."

Chapter 22

Lilia begins life as a soldier.

July 1941
Engels, Russia...

ENGELS AIR FORCE BASE WAS now home, a ramshackle collection of shanty shacks and crumbling huts within hailing distance of Moscow, replete with a strip of barren rocky earth that was to serve as the primary runway.

One of Raskova's first tasks was to arrange maintenance staff before the recruits arrived.

She knew the men of the squadron were conflicted. On the one hand, leaders like Sr. Sgt. Yevgeniy Mikhailov, a recipient of the Gold Star Medal and the Order of Lenin, publicly chuckled and laughed softly at the concept of women in vicious air combat, while privately admiring these female volunteers and their intentions, so much so that he felt responsible for their safe keeping.

On the opposite end of the spectrum were the more typical males of the period like Sgt. Danilo Lutsenko, who thought the concept of a woman's fighter battalion was "a dangerous exercise for the pilots themselves as well as those men who flew by their side."

Raskova professionally and matter-of-factly laid out her needs in detail in front of the philosophically diverse group.

Mikhailov offered his support through silence. Lutsenko's grousing was more vocal. "Women should remain housewives, cooks, and store clerks. Fighting is a man's job."

"I could have you shot for disobeying orders. Do we understand each other?" said Raskova angrily. The conversation was over!

The July weather cooperated: warm days, cool nights, and billions of mosquitoes. Within four weeks, the barracks were made minimally livable. A quartermaster shed was added with uniforms and personal affects. A shipment of small kerosene heaters arrived, one for the center of each barrack to provide warmth from the bitter winter just around the corner.

Lilia and the other twenty-seven wide-eyed female fighter pilot recruits, from all walks of civilian life, were trucked eleven hours from Moscow City Centre military depot to

Engels Air Base across bumpy, muddy dirt roads in a driving rainstorm. While all were ruggedly determined and diligent individuals, none had ever been involved in projects that required a disciplined team structure. They knew nothing of longstanding military concepts like chain-of-command and rules-of-order.

~

The portly 180 centimetres tall, 23 year-old Galina Petrova had short black curly hair and muscular arms that could break a thick branch in seconds. Most recently, she had been employed as a crop-duster on an enormous collective farm about 60 kilometres south of Moscow. Stalin's agricultural collectivism afforded her the opportunity to fly biplanes to dump prescribed amounts of fertilizer into the poorly cultivated fields below. "The girl is fearless," said the farm manager. "She could dump the proper amount fertilizer on the proper field with her eyes closed in a blinding wind storm."

Despite her supreme confidence in flying planes better than most men, she was deeply insecure about her unattractive appearance. Consequently, she had not dated often and rarely fraternized with the opposite sex, even in a group setting. She believed most men were laughing at her behind her back.

~

Twenty-six year-old Polina Fomicheva was as diplomatic and chatty as Galina was seemingly masculine. At 170 centimetres and half Galina's weight, she possessed a catlike quickness. Her mother was a seamstress and a sprinter in the 1932 Olympics, while her father, a fur trapper, had been one of Russia's first pilots during World War I. So it was not surprising Polina had a strong interest in flying at a relatively early age. What was surprising was her management and organizational skills. By the tender age of 21, she was managing a small clothing factory in the port city of Vladivostok. The factory ran so efficiently that once the war broke out, it was selected by the government to receive new mechanized equipment to produce additional military apparel. As shop manager, she got to negotiate and plan priorities directly with military decision makers many years her elder.

"You start with what you want," said one officer, "but you eventually get what Polina has decided is appropriate, given the Motherland's priorities. When you meet with Comrade Fomicheva, you need to remember you are always negotiating, always compromising."

Somewhere along the way, like so many single women of the day, she decided she wanted to help the Motherland more directly. Since she was bitten by the flying bug, it didn't take her long to determine a logical course of action.

"So you plan to stop work," said her father in amazement. "And what do you plan to do in the middle of a war?"

"I have decided to learn to fly at the local air club until I am granted permission to fly."

"Fly where?"

"In the air force."

Stalin's decision to authorize a women's flying regiment occurred four months later.

~

At 182 centimetres, the resourceful Nina Onilova from Dzerzhinsk, a new city founded in 1930 about 400 kilometres east of Moscow on the Oka River, was a towering presence among the other women. Her mother died while giving birth and her father, Nikolai, moved to Dzerzhinsk and became an "industrial parts" (chemical warfare weapons) assembler in the new State-owned factory. It was there that Onilova demonstrated strong mechanical aptitudes and became a maintenance specialist in the same plant as her father. In time, her proficiency exceeded her father's, but caused difficulties in their relationship.

Nikolai, frustrated by his daughter's lack of respect, impossible streak of independence, and the plant manager's increasing demands for greater productivity no matter what the sacrifice, began to drink heavily. The more depressed Nikolai became, the less parental guidance he was able to provide to Nina, and the more confident she became in her own abilities. When the call came to create a women's air combat battalion, Nina figured she was well-suited to keep the planes in running order. After all, she was the best!

~

A deep raspy male voice shouted sarcastically from the driver's cabin, "Ladies, better do whatever you do to get ready. We'll be at base camp in less than an hour."

Galina's insecurities with the opposite sex rose to the forefront. She defiantly waved her hand in the air, as if to say, don't tell me what to do!

Lilia saw no reason to arrive at Engels with a chip on her shoulder. After all, they had all volunteered to help the Motherland remain free and independent. "Is that really a wise thing to do?" asked Lilia.

"Who's asking?" glared Galina, confident her overpowering presence would intimidate the diminutive Lilia.

Lilia just stared calmly; neutralizing the inflammatory comment seemed the wisest course. After all, the enemy was the Germans, not each other.

Galina mistook Lilia's silence as a sign of weakness. She was about to press on when Polina interrupted with a smile and a handshake.

"I am Polina," she said to Galina, "and your name is?"

"I am Galina Petrova."

"And what is your specialty?"

"I fly planes. I will be a combat commander," she said sternly, trying to get back into Lilia's face.

Polina thought Galina's aspiration was a bit unrealistic, but at least she had discovered an opening.

"I hope to fly also. I bet I will learn much from you. Where did you train?"

"I dusted crops on a collective farm. Rain or shine."

Lilia was bursting at the seams. She thought to herself, a crop-duster is putting down a skilled trainer!

Nina overheard the part about all three of the girls aspiring to be pilots. "Perhaps, you are all lucky. I am the best airplane mechanic."

"And, how did you come to your skills?" asked Polina.

"I repaired the machines in my factory when they broke down. After all, we had government requirements to meet."

"Perhaps we become 'The Four Musketeers,'" smiled Polina. Galina was still not convinced there were Four Musketeers.

"And you?" she said pointing to Lilia.

"I am Lilia. I trained some male pilots for combat at Taganka Air base," she said matter-of-factly.

"And how many is some?" asked Galina.

"Forty-eight."

Prior tensions evaporated then and there. The four girls smiled. There was a chemistry building.

~

Lilia began to rummage through her duffel bag. As she pulled out a brush, mirror, and a tube of red lipstick, her good luck charm, the Father Frost statue she won as a child, stared at her. She gently placed him in her bed. Then she began to brush her long blonde hair and apply her "lips."

"Are we going to war or a bourgeois ball?" said Galina.

"Mummy always made it a point to look her best wherever she was."

"With all due respect to your mummy, I don't think the Luftwaffe gives a damn."

"It's not for the Luftwaffe," said Lilia, "It's for me." Lilia decided to leave the rest of her makeup in her bag. It was obviously not the right time to apply her rouge and a few dabs of the very popular perfume Red Moscow.

~

Major Raskova stood stiffly in the roadway, hand raised skyward. The convoy screeched to a halt. "Out! Out! Everybody out of the trucks!" she barked. "Make three rows! Three! Three! Three!" The recruits hustled to do as they were told. Galina, who was last out, got stuck on a metal brace extending from the truck. As she pulled to get free, she tore the upper portion of her pants. She was so intimidated that she never realized she stood alone in row four.

"Private" screamed Raskova in Galina's face. "Can you not count to three?"

"Yes, Comrade Major," replied Galina nervously.

"Then why do you stand alone in row four?"

The girls began to chuckle, as did the male convoy drivers. Raskova glared at the men. "Comrades, you are now dismissed, back to your unit!"

The major initiated a head count. "When I call your name, respond 'present and accounted for *tovarisch komandir* [comrade commander].'" Raskova wanted to install the concept of blind allegiance right from the outset. "Do we understand each other?"

The group casually responded yes.

"Yes, what?"

"Yes, *tovarisch komandir.*"

Raskova spotted Galina's indifference. She needed to send a message to all present. "Petrova, step forward."

Galina shuffled forward.

"It appears to me, your enthusiasm wanes quickly."

"No, tovarisch komandir."

"I say yes. You have earned your first reprimand. One additional reprimand and you will have a work order for latrine cleanup duty every evening for the next three days after all your other assignments have been completed satisfactorily."

Raskova looked at the frightened faces of her first recruits. She wanted to establish strict discipline but not at the risk of being perceived as a fool. She understood these girls had volunteered to sacrifice their lives, to share a very difficult and dangerous life and fight with men. And she understood that most of them would be killed.

Raskova paced up and down for a few seconds, thinking. For her new recruits, it felt like an eternity. "So we understand each other. I am a major, a woman, and your mother. My job is to teach you how to defend the

Motherland and to keep you safe and well. Nothing will be asked of you that I have not done myself. We are the first. We must set the standard. Eyes are watching, ears are listening. Do we understand each other?"

Raskova's message was clear. The girls all responded proudly and in unison, "Yes, tovarisch komandir." An additional 27 names were called. Each responded robustly.

The roll call complete, Raskova smiled, "Good day, 586th battalion."

"Good day, tovarisch komandir. "

She again demanded, "Is that the best you soldiers can do?"

The recruits shouted at the top of their lungs, "Good day, tovarisch komandir!"

"That's much better."

The major walked down each row, pausing here and there to make mental notes of each individual. "For those of you who don't know me, I am Major Raskova. And, you are now soldiers! From our short time together, it is obvious most of you have no idea what that really means. You will find the transition from civilian life difficult. But everything has a purpose. Most importantly, soldiers do precisely as they are told."

Raskova paused for emphasis. "I said do we understand each other?"

"Yes, tovarisch komandir!"

She turned away and looked skyward as if she was receiving a communiqué from a supreme being.

"At the same time, congratulations are in order. You are now part of Russian history. You are the first women in the world to have been accepted into an air combat battalion. It is a responsibility you carry for not only yourselves, your family, and the Motherland, but also for the ages. Your success will open the door for others to walk through; your failures will be documented and magnified." She sensed her battalion's competitive pride beginning to build.

~

First stop was the quartermaster to get properly outfitted with uniforms, boots, coats, hats, and such.

Galina fit perfectly into a man's extra-large combat uniform and full length winter coat, although she did discover an issue. "Does Comrade Stalin not realize that men and women are different?" she laughed, pointing out the unbuttoned front fly on her newly issued overalls.

Nina cleverly summoned her family tailoring skills. She took a pair of scissors, cut the buttons off the trousers, found a needle and thread among the supplies, and sewed the front closed. "There, now you have the only custom-tailored outfit in the regiment!"

As for the rest of the women, most were not as fortunate as Galina. This was war and they had to make do. Nina wound up with high-boots that were two sizes too large, so she filled the fronts with socks.

Lilia was the smallest in height and size. Her heavy green wool greatcoat touched the floor like a wedding gown.

"Nina, can you help me?"

Lilia's alterations were more complicated than Galina's. "This will require more time. This evening perhaps."

The bell for lunch rang. With Lilia dragging her long coat along the dusty path, the girls hustled to the mess hall in a rather disorganized fashion,.

"Comrades, comrades" ordered the Major. "We are sisters. Make a line. One behind each other. There are adequate provisions for all."

The Major noticed Lilia dragging her coat. "Private Litvyak, are we preparing the road?"

Lilia was unsure how to respond. Was she to say she was the smallest woman in the group? Would such a disclosure be a benefit or a hindrance?

Nina felt compelled to answer. "Tovarisch komandir, some of the uniforms were provided in men's sizes."

"Who are you?"

"*Airman* Onilova."

"And what did you do before the war?"

"I assisted at a clothing factory in Dzerzhinsk," said Nina modestly

"Airman Onilova, the next time you speak, I suggest you provide solutions."

"I understand, tovarisch komandir."

"Then what will you be doing this evening to help your friends?"

"I will help them fit."

"Very good, Onilova. You have learned your first lesson about war! We begin training at 0600 hours tomorrow. I expect by then you will all appear like Airman Petrova and Fomicheva."

Once back in the barracks, Nina was overwhelmed.

Twenty-four girls fought to be first in line behind Nina. Lilia stood to the side. Nina worked until 3:00 A.M., showing the girls how to measure, trim, and sew, as well as doing some of the more difficult adjustments herself.

"I see Mama taught you well," she said to one of the girls. "But dealing with materials of this thickness requires a trick or two. Let me show you."

Two hours later, the girls were abruptly awoken by the sound of an officer walking through the barracks shouting "Wake up time, Comrades. Up and at 'em."

Nina looked to the side of her bed. Each woman in the barracks had placed some of her chocolate rations by her side as a silent thank you. She quickly consumed six pieces for an instant energy boost.

~

Next stop was the hairdresser.

The Russian military had an appearance policy for women recruits.

"Comrades," said the gruff female sergeant inspecting the squadron, "we are making progress. You almost look like soldiers. There is but one matter remaining. Comrade Stalin has decreed no long hair." She paused. "And recruits must begin with hair no longer than ten centimetres."

The pride of virtually every Russian woman of the time was her hair. It was rarely cut during her lifetime and usually braided or placed in a bun when in public.

The girls glanced under each other's cap. The average squad member's hair was about 25 centimetres in length, while Lilia's was perhaps twice that length.

"We have two arrangements. You may use the regiment's barber, Corporal Timur Mustafin," said the sergeant pointing to a handsome, dark-haired young man to her right. "He has never cut women's hair, but there is a first time for everything. Or, you may work in teams to help each other. The regiment owns many scissors, mirrors, and rulers. One can cut and measure, while the other holds the mirror. When finished, you will report to the hut next to the airstrip where the major will hold classes in flight basics this week, prior to the arrival of our equipment next Thursday."

Most of the women were in tears. Cutting their hair made them feel they were being forced to abandon their identity as women. Nevertheless, they obeyed the sergeant's order. Those who thought Corporal Timur cute had him cut their hair. The rest formed teams.

All that is, except Lilia. She had other thoughts.

Lilia's long locks had been part of her persona as long as she could remember. She was determined to let things be. After all, she had learned to fly and train numerous male comrades without incident. What did it matter if she wanted to maintain an important element of her womanhood?

She waited for the teams to form and then quietly retired to the rear of the classroom where she sat with a cap on her head, long hair tucked inside in a tight bun. Lilia's absence went completely unnoticed until Raskova was halfway through the first training class.

"I'm sorry, tovarisch komandir," said Lilia sweetly, hoping against hope the Major would go no further.

Galina, Nina, and Polina, rolled their eyes.

Raskova and Lilia were now old friends in the art of subtle confrontation. "Comrade Litvyak, please come to the front of the room. Remove the cap," said Raskova curtly as she reached in the desk draw and took out a pair of scissors. "I see my order has not been fulfilled!"

"Comrade Petrova, front and center." Raskova handed the scissors to Galina. "Please undo Comrade Litvyak's bun and give me 10 centimetres." Moments later Lilia was ankle high in blonde curly locks.

"Comrade Litvyak, I also wish the floor of my classroom cleaned properly." Wide eyed and disappointed, Lilia scooped her clippings into a wastebasket.

Raskova was not finished. "Now please tell the class why you did not obey my order. Was I not clear?"

"No disrespect, Comrade Major," replied Lilia innocently. "I had no team member. I assumed I could tend to the matter on another day."

"A soldier's worth is measured by passion and integrity. You clearly have but one of the two. We will see how three days in the guardhouse on limited rations affects your passion to fly."

Lilia was placed under what amounted to house arrest and marched to the makeshift guardhouse, a dark, wooden shack with one small window near the top of the rear wall. It was furnished with a single cot, straw mattress, and a small hole which acted as a comfort station. There were no lights and nothing else to distract a soldier from thinking about why she was there.

To pass the three days, Lilia moved the cot to the middle of the room and created an exercise regimen by walking around the perimeter of the small room. Each day ten laps around the room represented a sequence. Each day she did 20 sequences. She kept a record of how many sequences and laps by scratching her nail in the wood wall. When the door was finally open, she had completed 2257 laps.

"It is time for you to return to your squadron to await the arrival the *new* aircraft. They are due today," said Raskova, seemingly towering over Lilia.

"Girl, you look like hell," said Galina, as Lilia arrived at the barracks to shower and change into a clean uniform. She looked at herself in the mirror. She was shocked by what she saw—a woman with a dust-covered face, hair sticking out, and deep, dark rings under her eyes.

Lilia wished to make a statement that her fierce determination could not be broken.

She quickly showered, combed her hair, and found some makeup she had buried in her duffel bag. She then covered the dark rings under eyes and applied bright red lipstick. As she stood with her squadron, the other girls marveled at how well she looked after three days in the guard house.

"If that's the way I'll look after three days in the brig," smiled one soldier to another, "perhaps I should ask the major if I can volunteer."

"The planes will be arriving in fifteen minutes. Everybody to the landing strip," shouted a voice going from barracks to barracks.

~

That evening she wrote to Anna,

"Dear Mummy,
These first days I have made new friends,
applied new skills, and learned much about
military order. Military life is much of a
compromise. There are others to consider.
I realize now, one cannot always have exactly
what she wants, when she wants it, no matter
how much she demands. I know, I know. You
always said such. Now I believe.
Thanks goodness I maintain the sense of
humor given me and the lipstick and pow-der
I had stashed on arrival. (That is a story for
another day. It is late now.)

When I have children of my own, I expect I
will apply some of what I have learned but
perhaps not as sternly. Until we meet again,
you are always in my thoughts.
Love,
Your Lilia"

~

Against all odds, during the next six months Raskova
transformed her rag-tag aviation unit of young girls and
women who had attended air clubs, aviation technical
schools, and institutes, or worked in civil aviation, into a
disciplined military unit. Lilia was recognized by the officers
and peers alike as the 586th battalion's outstanding new
recruit.

Raskova's unit was given a training budget for fifty
qualified candidates and the appropriate number of combat-
ready aircraft.

Chapter 23

Lilia gets a few final tips before heading into the night skies

August, 1941...

AS THE PLANES DROPPED through the clouds, Raskova's face was filled with disappointment. The highly anticipated "new" aircraft were 15 vintage wood-frame, canvas-covered Polikarpov biplanes that had been a staple during World War I. Top speed was a paltry 200 kilometres per hour, with a payload of 227 kilogram bombs rigged to the cockpit in a most rudimentary fashion.

Word spread like wildfire through the 586th. The regiment was clearly unhappy with the hand they had been dealt.

~

Raskova pleaded her case.

"Comrade General," explained Raskova over the radio, "This is suicide!"

"Major, Rodina demands you sacrifice with what is available."

"But Messersmitts against Polikarpovs? That is like men fighting children."

"Every plane is spoken for."

"What, then, is our mission?"

"As you can imagine, Comrade Stalin appreciates your difficulty. So it is for you to develop a mission that best suits your available assets. I expect to discuss your decisions in 24 hours." Stalin and his advisory staff had determined that the deployment of lightly-trained and poorly-qualified women pilots against the Luftwaffe was an "acceptable cost of war"—a delaying tactic to be employed until more qualified male pilots and more modern planes could be added to the Russian Air Force.

Deeply disappointed, Raskova privately spent the evening with a few pots of tea and packs of cigarettes trying to identify a mission that made sense, one that would not put her entire squadron in harm's way.

"We have received our orders," announced Raskova dutifully the following morning. "We will undertake preemptive harassment missions."

The squadron stood silently, staring at the old planes on the runway.

Only Lilia had the courage to speak. "Comrade Major, what is the plan?"

"We will fly directly into the German front line camps when least expected—in the middle of the night—at exceptionally low latitudes, perhaps 450 to 500 metres, drop our payloads, and then retreat. We will change the place of entry and angle of attack with each mission."

The pilots began to grumble aloud. "That is madness. Who would attempt to fly that low? And, what are the odds of ever returning?"

"I understand your concerns. Nevertheless, orders are orders. I want volunteers for the first mission?"

The group remained motionless. Except for one... Lilia. "I have had experience with such maneuvers at the air club."

Raskova had learned enough about Lilia to realize she was truthful. "Comrade Litvyak, you and I will begin training at 1900 hours. Squadron dismissed."

"Lilia," said Galina as they walked to the barracks, "Why would you volunteer for such a mission? It is almost certain death."

Lilia smiled, recalling her escapades at Taganka, "I have substantial low-flying experience."

~

"You do realize the dangers?" said Raskova later to Lilia as they stood by their biplanes.

"What makes you think I do not?"

"Your preoccupation with your appearance," chided Raskova. "Do you think that matters to the enemy?"

"Comrade Major, perhaps they will get distracted," smiled Lilia a touch flippantly.

For the first time in their three face-to-face conversations, Raskova smiled and shook her head. "Lieutenant, I suggest you follow me. I'll teach you all you need to know about low flying maneuvers. Perhaps when your comrades observe success, more will volunteer."

Once air-bound, Raskova started radioing orders. She wanted Lilia's first training flight to be a highly visible success. She slowly rose to 3000 metres. "We will level here, bank sharp left, then right to simulate flak evasion."

"Accepted."

"Good, Comrade Lieutenant, good. Careful, alert, descending to 500 metres," commanded Raskova over the radio. "Excellent. Now level. When I count to three, we practice opening our bomb bays."

"Understood, Comrade Major."

"Commence equipment check."

"All functions normal," smiled Lilia.

Raskova looked to make certain Lilia's bay was open. "Excellent. Now return to the base."

"Roger and out."

~

Now it was Lilia's turn.

"Comrade Major, I have some suggestions that might improve the success of our missions."

"Really. After one lesson?"

"As I said, I have trained pilots at Taganka."

Raskova couldn't imagine this petite teenager had much to contribute, but she didn't want to deflate her ego or drown her passion.

"If we shut down our engines and lights as we drop to a low altitude, the Germans will find it particularly difficult to locate us. Once we drop our payloads, we can restart our engines and return to base. With the confusion and noise, it is unlikely the Germans will recover quickly enough to follow us."

Raskova recognized the plan had merit but required a high degree of skill. "And what makes you think we can accomplish that, Comrade Lieutenant?"

"I taught pilots night gliding at Taganka. I can instruct my comrades."

Raskova was still skeptical.

"Show me."

Moments later, the two women were speeding down the runway. This time Lilia was in front. After a sharp right bank over the air base, Lilia began to climb at a breathtaking 90 degree angle and leveled off at 5000 metres. Raskova was not far behind. Lilia radioed she was about to begin her descent to "gliding altitude." Raskova nodded. Suddenly Lilia dropped through the clouds. Raskova, concerned Lilia's plane had malfunctioned, descended as fast as she reasonably could, searching for the troubled plane! 4000 metres, no Lilia. 3000 metres no Lilia, 2000 metres and still no sign of Lilia.

Just as Raskova was about to declare emergency conditions, she spotted Lilia playfully circling at less than 500 metres.

"Major, I was about to search for you," laughed Lilia over the radio.

As the planes flew closer, Lilia could see the major shaking her head. "The night is very clear. Virtually no turbulence. I believe we can drop to 200 metres without much concern," announced Lilia.

Raskova eyes bulged as if to say, "Are you crazy?"

"*No problem*, Comrade Major. No problem."

Moments later the women were flying so close to the ground that they could clearly see the lights in the structures at Engels. Lilia placed her two fingers in her eyes to signal 'engines off, lights out.'

Raskova followed suit.

The women skillfully glided over the airbase and continued on a path westward. About ten minutes later, Raskova, concerned about stalling, turned her engine on and began to rise.

She signaled Lilia to do likewise. Lilia continued gliding for several more kilometres then banked left and continued for several more. By now, Raskova had landed and was furious that Lilia had ignored her orders.

Lilia was not quite through. She turned her engine back on and rose through the clouds once more. At this point, the entire squadron was at the edge of the runway looking skyward. Lilia decided to end the exhibition with a dramatic plummet and one last loop over the airfield at such a low altitude that the reverberations rattled the generators and shut down the barrack lights.

Lilia exited her plane to a round of applause. She smiled and bowed.

"Comrade Litvyak,' said Raskova storming down the runway. "Have you no respect for the chain of command?"

"Comrade Major, I apologize. Although I am unsure what I have done," said Lilia sweetly.

"Did you not receive my command to return?"

"I am sorry, Comrade Commander, my radio malfunctioned. I heard nothing clearly."

Raskova thought Lilia's excuse was imaginary but wasn't certain. Could she afford to make an incorrect example in front of the entire regiment?

She paused. "Starting tomorrow evening, you are in charge of night training. Do we have any volunteers?"

The entire group stepped forward.

"One more thing, Comrade Litvyak," said Raskova. "Make sure all the radios are checked and function before flight."

For the next two weeks, Lilia pushed the squadron hard. She began by having each pilot shut engines at 1000 metres and glide. When that milestone was reached, she reduced the glide ceiling another 250 metres. That process was repeated until she was confident everyone could shut engines and glide 16 kilometres without panicking. For those that had difficulty at each altitude plateau, she made the entire squadron repeat the exercise until all were equal. Lilia believed training in this manner created a mutual camaraderie. Each supporting the other....emotionally and physically, should the need arise.

From time to time, a squad member complained of exhaustion. Lilia's response was always the same. "Our harassment missions are not the kind of maneuver where you can fetch a fallen comrade. You must be prepared."

To complicate training matters further, Raskova had no official intelligence on what kind of return fire the enemy could muster, or if they had planes that could retaliate once attacked.

On October 30, 1941, the women of the 586th Night Bomber Regiment flew their first combat mission. Galina flew side by side with Lilia.

Chapter 24

Distinctly Russian bunkers weathered the bitter snows and German bombs.

A GERMAN LIEUTENANT, OTTO Deissenroth (Military Post Number 12 827D), sat quietly in his tent, listening to his well-trained, exuberant soldiers drink and sing as they confidently awaited orders to overwhelm their next objective before the bitter Russian winter descended. He decided to write to his wife Gisela.

> "My precious love,
> When we married six years ago, I never
> imagined our family would be in this
> place at this time. I hope Freda and Angelika
> [his daughters, aged four and two] are healthy
> and happy. Tell them Daddy loves them very

much and hopes to be home soon to spend
the rest of our days together in a better world.
I write this letter from the desolation of a
Ukrainian village, 25 miles from Kiev, which
we hope to capture in a few days. The fruitful
land of the Ukraine is all around us, but 20
years of Bolshevist mismanagement have
brought it to ruin. The poverty, misery, and
filth we have seen and experienced in the past
weeks are indescribable. You cannot imagine
the terrible results of Bolshevism in this
fruitful land. Everything that we formerly
read in newspapers and books pales in the
face of the terrible reality. Our eyes look in
vain for some sign of construction, for a trace
of progress, for a bit of culture. We yearn for
the sight of a clean house, an orderly street, a
few tended gardens. Wherever we look, there
is filth, decay, desolation, misery, death, and
suffering!
Hell can be no worse that this 'Soviet
paradise.' Every German who formerly
thought Bolshevism was a worthy idea and
who threatened us National Socialists with
death and bloodshed only because we didn't
believe in this nonsense should be ashamed!
We were right!
When one sees this dismal poverty, one is
reminded that these same Bolshevist animals
wanted to bring culture to us industrious,
clean, and creative Germans. How God has
blessed us! How justified is the Führrer's
claim to European leadership! The poorest
German village is a pearl in comparison to
these ruined Russian villages. We National
Socialist soldiers of Adolf Hitler have

restored the godly order, though some call us
heathens. That is the way life is. And what did
those who spoke about God do? Ask them!
Love forever,
Otto"

His letter finished, the lieutenant decided it was time to
shut down the revelry. It was almost midnight, and the
morning maneuvers would begin promptly after breakfast at
0600 hours. The night was cool and clear. The stars twinkled
brightly, although there was no moonlight to speak of. He
heard a strange unidentifiable sound and imagined shadows
in the sky. Suddenly the sky started raining bombs. The
Russian planes were so close to the ground that he was able
to shoot at them with his pistol. Soldiers scattered
everywhere, some to hide, some to find a location from
which to retaliate. Lt. Deissenroth searched for his platoon
sergeants. He was too late. He found them blown to bits, a
collection of bloody body parts, decks of cards scattered
nearby.

"Man the anti-aircraft guns! Return the fire!" he screamed
as he dashed across the camp to the flak gun embankments.

At that moment, Lilia's plane began to flutter. She
released her last bomb and headed back to the base. Her
bomb exploded less than 20 metres away from the lieutenant.
He died instantly. He was 25 years old.

~

Major Raskova was quite pleased at the debriefing session
the following morning. "Comrades, you performed nobly last
night." (Nine pilots flew with Lilia. All returned unscathed.
They dropped a total of eighteen 227 kilogram bombs.)
"Comrade Litvyak tells me we destroyed a munition depot,

three panzer tanks, a flak gun embankment, and two troop barracks."

The women applauded their accomplishments, apparently oblivious to the destruction they had just caused. At this point, the war seemed more like a distant game. Raskova sensed the sentiment in the room.

"War is not about getting complacent. Last night we owned the element of surprise. They will be expecting us in the future. We need to improve our abilities," urged the major.

"Comrade Major," interrupted Lilia, "Perhaps some-one in the squadron has more ideas. Night combat flying is a new experience for all of us."

Raskova's military instinct was to reprimand Lilia's imprudence, as she had that first week. But she had quickly come to realize that Lilia was wise beyond her years and a respected leader.

"Comrade Litvyak, you are correct," said Raskova, who then paused for what seemed like an eternity.

"I had trouble controlling my plane as I dropped to a low altitude," said Polina. "Did anyone else have that experience?" Three pilots raised their hands.

"Does anyone have a remedial suggestion?"

"I believe that can be repaired," volunteered Galina. "I experienced similar problems at the collective farm when we increased the loads on the crop planes. We discovered by modifying the tension on the cable system, balance was restored."

"And you think that will be useful here?"

"Our bombs are nothing more than increased loads."

"I'm not sure that last night's Germans would agree with that," smiled Lilia wryly.

"Last night was last night. Tonight is tonight," warned Raskova.

"Mechanically, repairs will not be simple," said Nina Onilova.

"Why not?" asked Lilia naively.

"Because each biplane plane was made by hand, so there are differences in wing angle and span lengths. Then there is the weight differential among pilots," laughed Nina, pointing to Galina and Lilia. The pilots roared. "Tension adjustments will have to be customized plane by plane."

"Let us begin immediately then," said the Major.

"I also have a question," said another pilot, Veronika Nikitina. "To your point, Comrade Major, the Germans will be more prepared for our next mission. Is there any way of improving the maneuverability, since our planes do not go very fast?"

"That is a good question," responded Raskova, who noticed Nina Petrova now dozing in the rear of the room. "Comrade Petrova, any thoughts?"

"I'm just an inexperienced private," responded Petrova, assuming her implied humility would make the question go away.

The room snickered. Raskova would not be made a fool of. "Congratulations, Comrade Petrova. You have just volunteered to be part of Airman Onilova's mechanical detail. You will do precisely as she says, when she says it. When

you're finished, you will report to my office for additional evening assignments."

Smiles disappeared.

"Any more ideas? Comments? Suggestions?"

Again Lilia stood up. "Just one. Can mirrors be placed in the cockpits, so we can look our best when defeating the fascists?" This time even Raskova laughed.

~

Later that evening, the Major ordered Lilia to her bunker. She wondered, as she walked, what had she done to raise the major's ire? Lilia saluted upon arrival.

The conversation was short and sweet. "So, how do we think we have performed as a soldier?" asked the major stiffly.

A slightly intimidated Lilia answered from the heart, assuming what would be, would be. "Perhaps there are some things I would do over. Particularly in my first days but, overall, I believe I have performed my job, and acted with good intent to all within our battalion."

The major stood silently. You could hear a pin drop in the room. "Comrade Litvyak, I agree. In fact I wanted to tell you that I am proud to have you in my regiment." The major smiled for the first time and offered Lilia a cup of tea.

~

"We will never again be embarrassed by *peasant men* masquerading as pilots in their rickety old planes," vowed German ace Lieutenant Horst Petzschler, who had replaced the deceased Lieutenant Deissenroth.

"I want night lights added to all gun emplacements immediately, and all Me-109's are to be equipped with radar seekers at the ready 24/7. The skies will be patrolled in two shifts after dark each and every evening until sunrise. I want

177

anything that moves destroyed on sight. Do we understand each other?"

What Petzschler did not understand at the time was that despite the slowness of the Po-2, it had certain advantages over the faster Messerschmitts. The stall speed of the German planes was greater than the top speed of the Po-2s, which made them impossible to attack directly. The Po-2s could maneuver on a dime, while the Me-109s required a much wider turning radius. Lastly, there was the matter of detection. Me-109s equipped with even the latest radar seekers were not designed to detect the miniscule heat stream generated by the Po-2s small 110 horsepower engines. On the ground, Po-2s would often pass undetected because of the mild radar-absorbing nature of the planes' canvas surfaces and the fact that they flew so near the ground.

"There will also be no drinking or singing after dark, and lights must be used with the utmost discretion. We will not again aid the enemy by allowing our overconfidence to identify our positions."

~

Raskova, anticipating greater German resistance, modified the unit's point of entry. She also ordered more planes into combat. "Tonight we will make a 270 degree swing around the German fortifications and surprise them from the southeast. Since 16 planes will fly, I have divided you into four groups, each responsible for a specific geographic quadrant to insure we strike as many different targets within the complex as possible."

"We will attack from the rear where the enemy is probably resting and destroy their munitions dumps, supply depots, and finally the troop barracks. With a little luck, perhaps we can eliminate some fascists from sending worthless mail back home!"

Dangers aside, the 586th was becoming a fun place to be... if you had to participate in a war.

~

Despite the German's increased vigilance, the second raid started out much like the first.

Pilots cut their engines at 2000 metres and glided silently around the encampment before dropping altitude. When they got to about 400 metres, the ground troops started to hear the whistle of the wind against the Po-2s' wings bracing wires. They realized in panic it was too late. They dove for cover wherever they could. All 16 planes began to drop their payloads simultaneously. The explosions and devastation could be seen for miles. For the first time, Lilia was close enough to actually hear the agony of the men she had just maimed. It was a sound she would not soon forget. Lilia's mind searched another time and place. She could see her father tied to a tree. She heard gunshots. She saw him slump.

As the planes headed home, Galina noticed she had been nicked on the wing by a 109. Her plane started to wobble and lose altitude.

"Level," shouted Lilia over the radio, "Level. Do not try to increase altitude. I'll cover your flank." No sooner had Lilia spoken, flak fire from the ground struck Galina's rear.

"I'm going down," screamed Galina. "Chute stuck. Chute stuck."

"Do not concede," screamed Lilia to her friend, "Cut the chute, then bail. We are not far from the ground."

"I have no knife. Impossible." Galina knew she was moments from the end. If she was to die, she wanted to perform one last act for the Motherland. Somehow, using all the force left in her body, she turned the plane and crashed into the German ammo dump, not far from a gun embankment.

As Lilia pulled her plane up to return to base, she could feel a violent explosion that lit up the sky. The group had its first casualty.

~

Out of respect for their fallen comrade, a simple and moving funeral service was held for Galina the next morning. While there was no body to mourn, emotions ran deep. Lilia cried openly. The girls, perhaps for the first time, realized they were in a bloody war. Lilia wrote home.

> "Dear Mummy,
> Today I saw death close-up for the first
> time. It was a difficult experience.
> Training pilots at Taganka was fun.
> Being a pilot in war, while noble, is not.
> I will always remember my new-found
> friend Galina. I also wonder about the
> families of those I killed. Your daughter
> is growing up quickly.
> Take care till we are together again.
> Yours, Lilia"

~

While recovering from the prior evening's carnage, the still shaken German troops came upon a patch of scorched earth where Galina had perished. Charred bits of metal, wood, and canvas lay everywhere. The men could not believe their eyes. They put two and two together.

"Is it possible someone would fly such an ill-equipped aircraft?"

The revelation gave the soldiers cause for hope. "If this is what they fly, last night will not be repeated. The peasant army will be no match for us over time," said one. The others smiled.

At that moment, the lone officer to survive, the company commander, appeared. "What's all the discussion. You find our losses a joking matter?"

"No Lieutenant," said the men, retreating to join the others. The commander inspected the remains with the barrel of his rifle. Amidst the rubble, he found the remains of a flying cap. The size appeared to be rather small. He decided to search the immediate area more thoroughly. He came upon the remnant of a small military boot still warm from the prior evening's activity. The conclusion was unbelievable but unmistakable. The pilot had to be a woman! The plane, an ill-equipped piece of World War I junk. The officer sat quietly on a large rock. He imagined the consequences upon his return. Stories would spread among his peers and superiors of his company's destructive losses to a band of flying witches in old planes, the *Nachthexen*; he would be humiliated, perhaps become the subject of a court-martial, and be hanged as a consequence. And, suppose word of his performance reached Hitler himself? He was certain the humiliation would be too much of a burden. He took his Luger out of his holster, placed it against his temple and pulled the trigger.

~

During the next three months, the *Nachthexen* flew thirty missions, unpredictably spaced to catch the Germans off-guard.

The major's bold plan, Lilia's daring suggestion, and the women pilots' extraordinary valor inflicted a heavy psychological and physical toll on German command centers and on those battalions attempting to push the front lines further into Russian territory.

Official reports indicated *Da Nachthexen* killed 10,000 enemy soldiers, destroyed 25 panzer tanks, and disrupted numerous supply lines during their first two months of existence.

The *Nachthexen* would go on to earn a total of 23 Hero of the Soviet Union medals and dozens of Orders of the Red Banner. Two women bomber pilots–Katya Ryabova and Nadya Popova–in a single evening raided the Germans 18 times. The Po-2 pilots flew more than 24,000 sorties and dropped 23,000 tons of bombs. Most of the women bomber pilots who survived the war in 1945 had racked up nearly 1,000 missions each. Successful American pilots averaged 50.

In the end, General Secretary Stalin rewarded their exemplary achievements throughout the war by giving *The Nachthexin* the honor of participating in the final onslaught on Berlin.

~

Because of the success of the *Nachthexin*, the 586th Regiment was expanded under Raskova's command to include combat fighter and bomber divisions, equipped with the latest equipment and ample munitions. The waiting list of women wanting to join the regiment increased with each story that was published about their exploits. Some wished to fly silently, and some, like burly Katya Budanova, wanted to join the new combat fighter division.

Raskova had seen enough of Lilia's flying skills to know she had the makings of a successful fighter pilot. But Raskova still had certain reservations. It was one thing to slip behind the enemy lines and drop bombs unannounced; it was quite another to participate in direct one-to-one air combat with guns blazing. Could Lilia handle the physical rigors, the pressures? Were her emotions too fragile for such a cathartic experience?

Late one evening, Lilia made her case with the Major. "Have I not proved myself to be a warrior?"

"Yes, Lilia, you have." They debated. Two hours later, Raskova acquiesced. Lilia's tenacity had again won the day.

~

October 1941...

Lilia was promoted to Senior Lieutenant and transferred to the fighter division.

There, she was issued a Yakovlev (Yak-1) fighter, a single-seat, low-wing aircraft with an enclosed cockpit, two small-caliber machine guns, and a liquid-cooled 1100 HP engine that had a top speed of 700 kilometres, more than twice the speed of the Po-2s.

"Training will be intense," warned Raskova. "These aircraft are significantly more powerful than anything you have experienced." Lilia just nodded. She was determined to again let her actions speak for her.

The first week of training was in the classroom and on the runway, where Lilia was briefed on the plane's altitude and maneuver capabilities.

"Now this is a plane," smiled Masha Kuznetsova, a confident junior pilot recently assigned to the 586th. Kuznetsova, who towered over Lilia, smiled confidently as she playfully petted the cannons attached to the fuselage. "I look forward to destroying our enemy face to face."

After what she had already experienced, Lilia was fully aware of the real horrors of war. However, to her reveling in the killing of another human being, no matter how evil, didn't seem right. She realized that, no matter how terrible Hitler's war machine, his evil ideology, his irrational thirst for conquest, she was killing fathers and mothers and children of fathers and mothers. "I see these machines as a means to restore peace to the Motherland, nothing more," responded Lilia, almost nobly.

"You do not sound like the fierce flying partner I could trust if the Messerschmitts made a surprise appearance," mocked Kuznetsova. "I want a killer by my side."

"My master is our Motherland, not your ego," said Lilia, not about to show fear or back down.

Raskova intervened. "Comrades, save your energy for the fascists."

The next few weeks Lilia concentrated on her firing accuracy. At first she missed targets by a substantial margin.

"These cannons are not made for long distance firing. You must get closer," observed Raskova.

By week three, Lilia's firing abilities had improved but still lagged behind her flying skills. She seemed able to place targets in her sights but released the trigger either too quickly or too erratically, which tended to make her bullets stray to the left or right.

Raskova knew the shortfall could probably be corrected with personal tutoring, but she did not have the time, and no one else was so qualified. Raskova decided to do what was best for the battalion. "Lieutenant, I have decided. You will be most valuable by focusing your efforts on training others and flying defensive escort missions, preferably with a skilled wing partner."

Lilia understood the order. While she disagreed, she was now a soldier. She obeyed her orders. Initially she seemed satisfied with that role. After all, she was helping to defend the sky over the town of Saratov, the home of many productive military plants, hospitals, and support services.

By the time she had performed her 35th operational flight patrolling the town and accompanying cargo airplanes, she became bored. She visited Raskova privately. She realized vocal outbursts did nothing for battalion morale.

"I did not join the air force to play nursemaid."

"Patience, Comrade Litvyak, your time will come," assured Raskova.

And come it did.

Chapter 25

Lilia (l) and wingman, Katya Budanova, review flight plan.

December 1916
Smolensk Oblast Region, Russia...

YEKATERINA VASILYEVNA (Katya) Budanova was born on December 7, 1916, to Vasiliy and Nina Budanova, a poor peasant family who lived in the tiny village of Konoplyanka (population 520) 640 kilometres West of Moscow. Her mother died of internal complications at birth, leaving Vasiliy to tend to Katya, her brother Pyotr, and two sisters, Valentina and Olga. She was an unusually hefty child, weighing in at 4 kilograms. By the time she was ten, she was planting and cultivating her father's potato crops. When Katya turned fourteen, her father had a stroke and became physically limited, so her responsibilities expanded to include keeping the fields clear of infestations and carrying the annual harvest on her strong, broad shoulders. In 1936, at the age of twenty, the confident, self-sufficient Katya abandoned the life of a peasant and moved to Moscow with 10 rubles in her pocket and a small bag of personal belongings.

Factory work was plentiful. Stalin's economic plans envisioned Russia as a world-class industrial power with a robust air force to defend the Motherland's vast space. After reading a number of newspaper articles about the growth of aviation, the largely self-educated Katya decided to take a job as a wing assembler at a local aircraft factory producing the single-seat UT-1 and testing the faster, more powerful Yak-1 fighter planes.

Katya, like Lilia, was immediately bitten by the flying bug. She entered the local aero club and received her flight training while still working full-time in the factory. Once licensed, she applied for and obtained a job as a flight instructor. Her manly physique, hearty laugh, and excellent flying instincts made her an immediate student favorite. She also aided the aero club's recruiting efforts by participating in a number of air parades, flying the single seat UT-1. By 1940, she had helped twenty men obtain their flying licenses and was more determined than ever to become a fighter pilot, despite her sex.

After the Germans attacked the USSR in June of 1941 and Stalin's reluctance dissipated she enlisted in military aviation, working in a variety of non-flight operational roles. When the formation of the all-women 586th was announced, Katya had a friend who knew someone in a position to get word of her interests and credentials to Major Raskova.

Katya was summoned for an interview. She came prepared with a petition of endorsement signed by most of the male pilots she had trained. She was also able to discuss the capabilities of the Yak-1, since she had worked on the building and testing of the aircraft.

"Have you actually flown the plane?"

"Many times," said Katya, flatly lying.

"Do you believe you can teach others?"

"Absolutely."

"And what of your combat abilities?"

"I have practiced cannon accuracy, but only on the ground," responded Katya, again bluffing.

"Is there anything you do not know about the aircraft?"

Katya paused. "Nothing, Comrade Major, nothing."

"Then you know all there is to know?"

"Yes, Comrade Major."

Raskova was certain Katya would say anything to join her regiment. "You remind me of another pilot in my squadron. She said whatever I needed to hear."

Katya smiled. "I understand, Comrade Major."

"War is about more than flying."

I understand."

"Are you prepared to die for the Motherland?"

"Yes, Comrade Major."

~

Stalingrad, 1932...

Inna Pasportnikova's physical appearance and family background was different from either Lilia's or Katya's. Her mother and father were elementary school teachers in Stalingrad, having both graduated from the University of Moscow. Their assumption was that their only daughter, Inna, of medium height and build and average appearance, would one day follow in their footsteps. Inna was taught to read and write long before school commenced. By the age of thirteen, she had developed an aptitude for creative problem-solving. As her classmates said, "There doesn't seem to be anything Inna can't determine."

For some reason, her inquisitive mind became interested in automobiles and the workings of the internal combustion engine.

One frigid January morning, Inna's class went on a long-planned excursion to the ancient town of Kostroma on the Volga River with their teacher, Anastasiya Semyonovna. About halfway to their destination, the bus began to malfunction, ultimately shuddering and shaking to a dead stop. After trying to manually restart the engine, the driver was left with no choice but to go fetch help. "Anastasiya Semyonovna," said the driver to Inna's teacher, "do your best to keep your students occupied. I will return as quickly as I can."

The teacher nodded and began to engage the children in the singing of the popular young pioneer song *vzveytes kostrami* (translation:"Light up with Camp-Fires") and the humorous *ah, kartoshka, obyedenye* (translation: "Oh, Potato Yummy") to pass the time. The teacher's efforts were short-lived. Without heat, the children began to shiver. Time seemed to stand still. Finally, Inna took matters into her own hands.

"Where are you going?" asked the teacher as Inna headed toward the driver's seat.

"I am going to get the bus restarted." Inna motioned to Sergei, the strongest of her classmates, "Please come outside and hold up the front hood while I try to restart the engine."

"But, it is cold," protested Sergei.

189

Inna smiled as she appealed to the boy's vanity. "I understand. But I asked you because you are the biggest and strongest in the bus."

Sergei melted. He strained to hold the large hood. Inna tinkered with the starter mechanism then hopped into the bus to start the motor. There was a tiny, small clinking of metal, like something was flapping and tapping. "Is the firing mechanism stuck?" said Inna. Sergei, shrugged his shoulders, he didn't have a clue.

Inna's resourcefulness switched to the next gear. She had a new solution.

"Igor," she said to another boy on the bus, "I am going outside to work with Sergei. You sit behind the wheel, I will signal when I need you to turn on the ignition."

The nervous boy shook his head, "But I've never done such a thing."

"It is easy," responded Inna, pointing. "Just turn this ignition key gently. But remember, turn it too far and you will kill what remains of the battery. And we'll all freeze to death."

The boy had a horrified look on his face.

"Igor, that was a joke."

Inna discovered the carburetor flap opened and closed erratically when Igor turned the key as Sergei again raised the hood. Inna noticed a little excess grease sitting by the battery cable contacts. She took off her gloves and put a dab of grease on her right index finger and held the flap open with her left hand. By the time she finished rubbing the lubricant on the edges of the flap, both hands were almost frozen.

She waved, "Igor, turn the key again." This time the bus started. Inna re-entered the bus to the cheer of her schoolmates. Igor, seeing how raw her hands were, turned on the heater and gently placed her palms against the warm air.

The incident gave Inna an insight into her future. Much to the dismay of her parents, after high school she decided to enroll in a mechanical trade school. Like many young women her age, she became interested in flying after Raskova's twin-engine *Rodina* was forced to land short of fuel. She was convinced that had she been the lead mechanic, no such mistake would have taken place.

Like Lilia and Katya, when word came that Major Raskova was to head the 586th, she immediately applied for enlistment.

"You wish to be a mechanic?" said the incredulous recruiter.

"I have the aptitude."

"But every woman I have met wants to be a fighter pilot."

"I'm not every woman."

~

January 1942...

Katya and Inna arrived at Engels a month after Lilia's promotion.

Lilia was desperate to perform sortie. "Comrade Major, I assure you I can help the other 'free hunters' [fighter pilots assigned to seek and destroy enemy aircraft in Russian air space]."

Raskova realized, perhaps better than Lilia, that Lilia needed two things before she could successfully tackle offensive missions: a "creative" mechanic to insure her plane was more maneuverable than the faster, more powerful Messerschmitt; and a "fearless" wing pilot who possessed an unwavering commitment and passion to crush and annihilate the more experienced German pilots. Lilia grudgingly accepted Raskova's analysis.

~

By the time they completed their first dinner at the mess hall, Katya and Inna had bonded. They sensed each other's commitment to the cause and desire to be assigned to direct combat. Unstated was also the discovery that neither was particularly preoccupied with their physical appearance. Neither had had much luck with the opposite sex.

The sturdy 170 cm, 85 kg Katya was ravenous as she stood in the mess line to receive her bowl of cabbage soup, bread, and a glass of kompot (fruit punch with fruit bits). She looked at her tray. She wanted more. She pointed to the bread. "May I have another piece?"

The mess corporal nodded. Katya reached for two slices.

"I presume you will leave some for the others," teased Lilia, standing directly behind Katya. Inna, two places further back in the line, could see Katya did not find the comment funny. She decided to come to her friend's rescue.

"With all due respect, was that necessary?" asked Inna. Katya nodded her concurrence.

"Is that the way you speak to a senior officer?" said Lilia, turning around so that her rank was now front and center.

Katya and Inna gasped. "We are sorry, Comrade Senior Lieutenant. We didn't realize."

"I hope so. What do you sorry recruits do?"

"I'm a mechanic."

"I wish to be a wingman."

"Are either of you any good?"

"The sergeant is a most resourceful mechanic," said Katya enthusiastically.

"And, Airman Budanova is a fearless pilot."

"Do you always speak for the other?" smiled Lilia. "It just so happens, I need a new wingman and mechanic for my team. Have you been assigned?"

Katya then put her foot in her mouth. "Comrade Senior Lieutenant, thank you for the offer. But I am the best. My desire is to work with the best. I understand that is Senior Lieutenant Litvyak."

"Me too," chimed Inna.

"That is my understanding also," smiled Lilia. "Perhaps another time?"

"Perhaps," responded the girls.

The next morning Raskova was standing in front of Katya and Inna, "I have decided that you will make an excellent flying team with Senior Lieutenant Litvyak." The girls' eyes lit up.

"Senior Lieutenant Litvyak, would you please join us?" Lilia entered. The girls' jaws dropped.

"Comrade Senior Lieutenant, we are so sorry!"

"You'd better be good. Very good," glared Lilia with a twinkle in her eye.

"Comrades, 0600 hours on the runway tomorrow. And sergeant, I expect the planes to be mission-ready."

Chapter 26

*The talented mechanic Inna Pasportnikova is assigned
to support Lilia and Katya.*

MAJOR RASKOVA HAD INFORMED Lilia of Katya's boastfulness. They had made a private agreement. "I will determine if Budanova is as skilled as she suggests," smiled Lilia.

The girls stood on the runway. "Wingman, are you ready to escort and protect your Lieutenant?"

Katya nodded confidently. "It will be my pleasure." Inna sensed otherwise.

Lilia planned to accelerate directly into the clouds, bank sharply to the right, fly sideways at a 90° angle to the earth until she lost Katya, and then return to the base, and wait for her wingman to discover she had lost her Lieutenant.

"Katya, your flight might be more challenging than you anticipate."

"Why so, Inna?"

"The clouds are unusually thick. I would think the lieutenant would not attempt a first-training mission in such weather unless..."

"Stop chatting like two old women," ordered Lilia.

As they roared down the runway, Lilia pulled her yoke back to accelerate straight up into the clouds. She was at 1200 metres and climbing. To her surprise, Katya remained directly parallel. Five seconds later, Lilia's altimeter read 2500 metres and Katya was still at her side. Lilia flipped over and plunged straight down. Again, there was Katya, smiling and waving. Katya had proven herself. Lilia signaled them down.

Once on the runway, Lilia walked over to Inna. "Sergeant, I want my plane modified in the same manner as Airman Budanova."

"What makes you think I have done such things?"

"Nobody outmaneuvers me." (Lilia was correct. Inna had quietly "souped-up" Katya's carburetor settings to increase her friend's ability to respond to sharp turns without losing power.)

"Comrade Senior Lieutenant, consider it done," smiled Inna.

"Comrade Senior Lieutenant," grinned Katya, oblivious to what had just happened, "Does that mean my flight was acceptable?"

"For now, but do not get complacent. Tomorrow is for real." Lilia paused, "And what of your marksmanship? Have we verified that you can you fire accurately?"

"We will find out tomorrow, won't we?" smiled Katya confidently.

~

The next morning, the temperature had plummeted to 29 degrees below. Inna had awoken to start each engine to prevent them from freezing solid. Without warning, a biting north wind suddenly swirled around the airdrome. It was 0500 hours. The engines were again nearly frozen. Inna poured hot water into the cooling systems to melt the ice. She began modifying the plane's performance. Much of the work required some delicacy. Inna stripped her gloves off to complete what needed to be done. Inside the engine, the manifold, which had been running for some time, was now burning hot. She tried to work quickly, but scorched herself because her hands were so cold that she didn't feel the skin on two of her fingers searing on the manifold.

"I think it best, you go to the infirmary. I will assign another," said Lilia.

"Comrade Senior Lieutenant, I am fine, absolutely" responded Inna defiantly. She wrapped her hand in a cloth to stop the bleeding. Her carburetor adjustment was one nut short of completion. She rubbed her numbed fingers to increase blood flow and then cupped her hands, blowing her warm breath into the pocket until some feeling returned. As she carefully set the nut on the screw, the feeling in her fingers quickly dissipated. Ingeniously, she temporarily transformed her fingernail into a screwdriver to twist the nut onto the screw.

"Ready to go," shouted Inna over the roar of the engine.

Lilia nodded. She was proud of Inna's courage, determination, and abilities. Inna was to be her mechanic for the duration of the war.

"I hear the sky may be filled with fascists today," said Katya. "I am ready...Only time will tell if I'm prepared."

~

Katya was ready to go. Lilia insisted on leading their first sortie. Halfway down the runway, she came to a screeching halt and jumped out of the plane.

"What is wrong?" screamed Inna, approaching with her wrench and a few tools.

"I almost forgot," said Lilia, running over to a small crevice by the side of the runway. There sat some frozen thistle and feathergrass. She quickly gathered the colorless weeds. She imagined the lifeless collection were summer bouquet of blue and gold wildflowers.

Lilia motioned to Inna to take her bouquet and carefully place them in the cockpit as she climbed back on the wing. Inna looked at Katya and shrugged her shoulders. Once at the cockpit, Inna couldn't help but notice a postcard filled with red and white roses taped to the control panel. She now realized the "bouquet" of thistle and feather grass was something other than it appeared.

"Out of the way," tapped Lilia. "We have business to complete."

As Lilia climbed in the cockpit, Inna noticed something else that seemed a bit out of place. Lilia was wearing a multi-colored scarf that appeared to have been made with scraps of parachute cloth. Inna thought to herself, *What a crazy lady. All dressed up with no place to go!*

~

The two ladies soared and searched for enemy aircraft for the better part of an hour. They banked left and right, no Germans in sight. They rose above the clouds, still no Germans. Finally, at the edge of Russian air space, they saw in the distance a squadron of eight or perhaps ten Messerschmitts inexplicably returning to their air space.

"Let's attack," shouted Katya.

Lilia's analysis was more sanguine. "Too many. Exiting our space. Return to base."

Katya spun upside down to express her displeasure. "Repeat... return to base... now" ordered Lilia sternly.

After landing they began to argue. "We are soldiers," said Katya. "Our job is to destroy the enemy, not let them fly away."

"Our job is to protect our airspace. We have not been given orders to advance across the front."

"They were easy prey," boasted Katya.

"Not without squadron support."

The next morning Katya, Inna, and Lilia were standing on the runway. It was a cold, but not bitter, a more typical winter day.

"The major must have heard you chattering at dinner or perhaps in the dugout. We have been ordered to 'free hunt' today within a 100 kilometer radius of the airdrome and kill whomever we come into contact with," said Lilia.

"Finally," responded Katya, half boasting, half relieved.

"The aircraft are ready," said Inna.

With map in hand, Lilia and Katya stood by the plane wing to discuss the route they would take. Since the wind was coming strongly from the north, they agreed to head east using the wind to propel them to the agreed cruising altitude of 3000 metres. From there, they would scan the skies for enemy aircraft using the clouds for cover.

The women roared down the runway and banked to the right. Lilia assumed Katya was to her rear as agreed, but as she rose through the clouds, she could not find Katya in the rear mirror. Suddenly she heard Katya screaming and shouting on the radio. Lilia plunged, assuming Katya was in a dogfight. As she dropped below the clouds, Katya's plane was alone but wobbling wildly from side to side. Perhaps the gears had failed, thought Lilia. "Evacuate immediately," shouted Lilia.

Katya screeched as if pierced by a round of ammunition. Lilia again searched the skies. There was not an enemy plane anywhere in sight. Finally, after a long silence, punctuated by scuffling sounds, Katya announced "Regaining control. Returning to base."

As Katya got within 500 metres of the base, there was another sudden jerk of the plane to the right and then the left. Lilia offered a prayer that her comrade would be spared from an all but certain crash landing. Somehow, someway, the plane leveled, Katya bounced along the runway. When the

plane came to a halt, she catapulted out of the cockpit as if she were on fire. Lilia landed moments later and ran to her fallen comrade while Inna inspected the plane. Inna began to laugh as she reached into the cockpit. She stood over Katya holding a tiny mouse by its tail as it squirmed to get free.

"Get the damn thing away from me!" yelled Katya. "First it was inside my uniform; then it was running around the control panel." Inna put the frightened mouse down. It looked at Katya then dashed up the hill on the side of the runway.

From this day on, Katya's nickname became "Mouse Fighter."

~

Despite "the mouse incident," Katya, Inna, and Lilia became the most effective, and perhaps most flamboyant, fighter team in the 586[th.] They flew more than fifty successful missions and continued to ask their commanders for assignment to the Stalingrad front.

As she honed her battle skills, Lilia decided to make two enhancements to her plane. First, she had the number 44 painted on the rear portion of her fuselage. She recalled some of her happiest moments were as a member of the skating team as a child and teenager at school in Moscow. "The number gives me the feeling that I am skating on ice," she explained to Inna, who was rapidly becoming her best friend.

Her second modification was controversial. As a tribute to her mom, she wanted to paint a white lily on each side of the cockpit of her Yak-1. At first, she was rebuffed as foolhardy. But, as usual, she persisted. Eventually, a deal was struck with her commander. If she could find somebody with professional experience to paint the flowers properly, it would be approved.

The next evening, Inna was all smiles. "Lilia, I have found Vladimir Kolesov at the 73rd, and he has agreed."

Lilia and Katya stared blankly. "Kolesov? Agreed?" Inna went on to explain that prior to the war, Vladimir was a sign painter. He had created a number of factory posters as well. "He has agreed to paint your flowers in exchange."

"In exchange for what?"

"That he can share a kiss with Katya."

"I think that is a very fair trade," smiled Lilia.

"What does this Vladimir look like?" asked Katya.

"What does it matter? You have other such offers?" smiled Inna.

"I say we compromise," smiled Lilia. "First Vladimir paints the lilies. If he does acceptable work, Katya shares a kiss when the time is right."

"Do I have any say in the matter?" asked Katya.

~

September 10, 1942...

Lilia, Katya, and Inna's request to be sent to the Stalingrad front was granted. An excited Katya wrote her father.

> "Dear Daddy,
> It is late, so this must be brief. I am going to the front tomorrow. I am not afraid; we are all full of determination to fight to the end and put an end to the fascists. We will win!
> Love, love, love,
> Katya"

~

"Are you asleep?" whispered Inna.

"No," said Lilia.

"Neither am I," responded Katya.

"I think we are all anxious about tomorrow," said Lilia. "Perhaps if we take a walk among the stars, it will calm our senses. It appears to be a beautiful night."

The three women dressed and walked arm in arm around the edge of the camp. They spotted the light on in the major's hut and sneaked a peek in the window. The major was thumbing through their personnel files, sipping a cup of tea. It was clearly a private moment.

"Let's get out of here," whispered Lilia. Unfort-unately, Katya's foot got stuck in an uneven spot of soil. She tripped and crashed into the side of the building. The major dashed to the front door. "Why are you spying in the middle of the night?"

Inna and Katya pushed Lilia to the front. She was the one with the relationship. "Comrade Major, we were not trying to do that. None of us could sleep as we thought about tomorrow. We just saw the light and ...."

Raskova smiled and sighed. "I understand. I was doing the same." She offered them an unusual invitation. "Would you all like to share a cup of tea?"

Raskova spoke from the heart. "I have observed you are an especially close team. The war has made you lifelong friends. "

"Will you miss us?" smiled Lilia.

"You are my children on the way to a noble journey. You represent the hopes and dreams of many women. To defend the Motherland on equal footing with the men."

"I only wish to be equal with respect to a job well done," said Lilia. "In all other matters, I am, and always wish to be respected as a woman."

"That is how I felt before marriage to Sergei. But it is a difficult concept for some men to accept."

"Did he?" asked Lilia.

"Lieutenant, that is too personal," said Katya. "And no one's business."

The major smiled. "It is fine. Perhaps there is a lesson to be learned. Lilia, Sergei wanted an independent woman, which I was, and still am. But he wanted a sensitive wife and caring mother. There I failed. My desire to rally women to our cause took over my life at the expense of my marriage."

"Do you have regrets?" pressed Lilia.

"Lilia!" said a now uncomfortable Inna.

"I ask that question frequently. The true answer is I am not sure. When history is written, I am certain I will be remembered as one who accomplished much. But did I really?"

The women sat quietly for a moment.

"Lieutenant, somewhere, sometime you will meet your one man. My wish is that he provides the respect you crave, and you give the love, affection, and comfort he requires."

Chapter 27

The beautiful officer struggles for her rightful place in the skies.

September 1942
Stalingrad...

THE 473rd AIRFIELD NEAR   Stalingrad was fairly typical of the bases that had been rapidly prepared around the city—an open field some 2000 metres by 500 metres in size, running in the direction of the prevailing east-west wind. It had been leveled and covered with octagonal concrete paving slabs, each about two metres across, in an interlocking honeycomb pattern.

This temporary construction had various advantages: it was very stable; it helped counter the autumn mud; and individual slabs could easily be replaced quickly if damaged during an air attack. The entire project was completed in less than two days and was a good example of a determined Russian citizenry to adapt—crudely but effectively—to the needs of warfare in their own country. The field's single hangar was camouflaged, as were the roofs of the underground bunkers. Ammunition and fuel were also stored in underground dugouts.

~

"Comrade General, I ask for more skilled pilots to fight battles, and you send me three women?" said a disappointed Major Nikolai Baranov, commanding officer of Russia's elite 473rd Fighter Regiment. "Have our actions not proven ourselves? With humility, I say we are the best of the Motherland's pilots."

"I agree," said the voice on the other end of the phone.

"Then why?"

"The ladies have proven themselves brave warriors in battle. Trust me."

"When should they be expected?"

"Tomorrow."

Baranov was a typical male, a confirmed chauvinist. But he was also a loyal soldier, and the latter outweighed the former. He vowed to do his best.

"Have the men prepare a bunker a distance from the others," said Baranov to his station sergeant.

"Who receives such a privileged bunker?" questioned broad shouldered Captain Alexei Solomatin, the regiment's undisputed number one airman in terms of both missions flown and German kills.

Solomatin was born in the forest of Siberia, the son of a logger. At a young age, perhaps twelve, he began to help his father with the logs. He was tall for his age—almost 183 centimetres by some accounts, but quite lean and agile. The strenuous work transformed his body into a powerful and muscular human machine. It wasn't long before he took to boxing. His style was simple and direct. He possessed but one gear... Straight ahead! His attitude was equally one dimensional. No one would ever control him!

At 18, he was unbeaten in 21 fights, roughly classified as the middleweight category, although he fought men much bigger and heavier. He knocked out 18 of his 21 opponents and was never knocked to the canvas. Before long, the local papers carried stories of the "Siberian Stalker," his powerful, undisciplined style, his "strong as bull attitude," and his unblemished record.

The more he won, the grander his dreams. He would defeat everyone in his weight class and one day be proclaimed one of Russia's leading sportsmen. To ensure that end, he moved to Moscow and joined the Moscow Sports Club of Krasnopresnensky District so he could be coached by a local legend, Leonid Fedun. Fedun spent hours trying to teach Alexei to be a less predictable fighter.

"Jab and move, so you are a more difficult target,'" urged Fedun.

But Alexei was so confident in the power of his punches, he saw little reason to box as coached. And the more he won, the more stubborn he became. Despite his technical shortcomings and the constant coach-fighter disputes, a match was made between Alexei and Victor Morozov from Leningrad. Both fighters were undefeated, and the winner was arguably to be considered the finest middleweight of the period.

The fight was never close. Morozov boxed and weaved at will around Alexei, who threw undisciplined punches wildly. Whenever Alexei stopped, Morozov would throw a barrage of his own. After ten rounds, Alexei was bloodied and beaten.

The next day, a humble, contrite Alexei and Fedun met at the sports club. Alexei was now open to suggestions.

"My suggestion," said Fedun, "we have much work to do. Your training routine needs to be more diligent, your workouts more intense. I would also suggest we only schedule fights with the area's tougher fighters, regardless of club affiliation."

Alexei hesitated.

Fedun knew Alexei had the natural talent, he just wasn't sure if he had the commitment, the discipline. He offered him a way out. "Alexei, perhaps, we should even consider another coach or perhaps another club such as the Central Soviet Army Sport Club."

"I may not like it, but I do not run from hard work," responded Alexei.

~

"We have guests."

"Guests?" commented Solomatin as his thick eyebrows rose and black eyes pierced Baranov. "This is a wartime airfield, not a hotel."

"The newest members of the 473rd will be three women. Two pilots and their mechanic."

"How could that be?"

"Captain, I am certain the rigors of fighting over Stalingrad will take its toll, and they will ask to leave."

"How many will have to die before that happens?"

"The team comes with high recommendations from the 586th."

"What do you expect? It is all women."

"I have been advised they have performed admirably, so I require your cooperation."

"What is it that you expect of me?"

"I want you and Lieutenant Litvyak to fly as the lead pair in a sweep over the western approach to the city."

"Major, that area is heavily fortified by the Germans."

"But we must break that stronghold to bring supplies to our soldiers and citizens before the winter settles. It is a mission that requires the utmost flying skills."

"I will do as asked."

~

That first night, the ladies arrived without fanfare and were escorted directly to their bunker, which was a distance away from the rest of the pilots.

To their surprise they were greeted by a stiff, formal Major Baranov.

"Welcome, Comrades. As you know, your arrival is a historic moment in Russian Aviation."

(Lilia, Katya, and Inna had not thought of it in such terms.) "Your bunker is a distance from the rest of the pilots, so I ask you to remain alert in case of a German surprise attack."

"Comrade Major, what are our orders?" asked Lilia.

"Report to the command post at 0600 hours for a mission briefing; then we will see."

Lilia wondered, "See what?" She sensed Baranov was not certain whether the girls would be an asset or a liability to the squadron. She vowed then and there to make it the former.

Moments later, they saluted Baranov and he disappeared into the darkness.

"Welcome to our new home," smiled Katya as she raised her water canteen in a mock toast.

The next morning before the sun rose, Lilia passed the sentry on the way to the command post. He tipped his field cap and performed a casual salute. Lilia, the ranking officer, spoke her mind.

"Soldier, I believe I am owed a proper salute."

"Yes, Comrade Senior Lieutenant," snapped the sentry.

"That will not happen again, will it?"

"No, Comrade Senior Lieutenant."

"Which way is the command bunker?"

"About 400 paces to your right, Comrade Senior Lieutenant." Lilia stared into the darkness and began her trip.

Moments later she was startled by three soldiers with rifles pointed.

"Who goes there?"

"Senior Lieutenant Litvyak," she responded.

"Password."

"I do not know. But I am expected by Major Baranov."

"We will see about that," said the disbelieving sergeant in charge. "Corporal Kislitsa, validate with the command bunker."

Moments later Kislitsa returned. "The Senior Lieutenant is cleared. She is to fly with Captain Solomatin."

By the time Lilia arrived at the bunker, word had spread around the base that the 473rd was being infiltrated by women.

"Good morning, Senior Lieutenant," said Baranov.

"Good morning, Comrade Major," saluted Lilia.

"This is your flying partner, Captain Solomatin."

Solomatin was stunned and smitten. He wondered how someone so small and delicate could possibly handle such a powerful aircraft. At the same time, as he looked into Lilia's sparkling steel-blue eyes, he felt an instant chemistry.

"You have flown Yaks?"

"Yes."

"And for how long?"

"About six months."

"That is not a very long time to master technique."

"I learned that earlier."

"Doing what?"

"Flying Po-2s."

"Po-2s. They belong in a museum."

"I agree," said Lilia. "But it was all we had at the time. Besides, when we shut the engines off to drop our payloads, it was hard for the Germans to identify our exact locations."

Solomatin had heard stories about the brave and effective flyers the Germans had so affectionately named Night Witches. Lilia was the first "witch" he had met in person. Her credentials were now established in his mind.

Minutes later the briefing had concluded. They picked up their maps and parachutes, buckled their pistols, and walked side by side to the aircraft. Solomatin was his usual smiling, confident self. "Senior Lieutenant, I'm sorry."

"About what, Captain?"

"The way I treated you in the bunker."

Lilia was equally smitten. She wondered how someone could so strong and handsome could also be so sensitive and so observant?

Lilia decided to put the Captain at ease. "Comrade Captain, I understand. I assume you have not flown many military missions with a metre and a half blonde partner?"

"That is true," smiled an increasingly relaxed Solomatin.

By the time they reached the planes, they were laughing and joking. Inna, who had made the necessary adjustments so her diminutive boss could reach the pedals, was a bit taken aback. As she explained to Katya later that morning, "The Captain put his hand on her arm and squeezed it and winked at her as she climbed in her cockpit. Then he climbed on the wing and helped Lilia buckle on her parachute. She was bursting with good humor and excitement, like a beautiful little animal, straining at the leash."

Chapter 28

Lilia and Lyosha battle fascists over war torn Stalingrad.

THE 473rd WAS STOCKED WITH the more advanced Yak-9s. The all-metal modified versions of the Yak-1, with a top speed of 550 kilometres per hour, were capable of a fast climb at a steep angle. They housed a 37mm cannon and two 12.7mm machine guns with patented high explosive ammunition the Germans had come to fear. In the opinion of many engineers, the Yak-9 was the best light fighter of the war. Russian factories and workers, under Stalin's direction and support, had made great strides in the design and production of military aircraft since the Germans invaded. In Solomatin's estimation, a Yak-9 in the hands of a skilled and aggressive pilot was a potent killing machine superior to the best Germany could field.

From a height of 3500 metres, Solomatin led Lilia's aircraft on a series of sweeps eastward from the city center,

seeking incoming German formations and then turning back
in the hope of catching a swarm off guard, on its run home.

Lilia slipped the guard off the gun button and fired a
brief burst to test her armament. To her left and several
thousand metres below, a flight of Heinkel 111 bombers
drifted into view through a break in the cloud formations.
"Comrade Captain, three Heinkels below. Three Heinkels
below. Should we not attack?" radioed an excited Lilia.

"I see them," shot back Solomatin. "Did you also see the
three Messerschmitts sitting above them?"

"No."

"Stay your course. We do nothing unless the Germans
spot us."

Solomatin knew after the bombers dropped their loads,
they would change course. It was then that they were most
vulnerable. So Solomatin and Lilia continued to fly parallel, a
distance behind, using the heavy cloud cover to screen
themselves from the Germans.

Lilia was about 600 metres to the right rear of
Solomatin's Yak. Her head constantly swiveled up, right-left,
and to the rear.

"Follow me," boomed Solomatin into her headphones.
The light underbelly of his Yak heeled into view as he rolled
his fighter upside down then turned to the left. Lilia pushed
the throttle to full power, slammed the stick to the left, and
followed him down. They were now above and behind the
German bombers. But where were the Messerschmitts? Lilia's
focus was concentrated straight ahead.

Suddenly the lead bomber spotted the two planes and
changed course. Solomatin fired. The planes scattered. Lilia

saw pieces of a plane wing fly by as smoke gushed from one bomber's port engine. Solomatin kept diving. Lilia followed. They pulled so close to another bomber, its shape filled Lilia's windscreen. "Fire!" screamed Solomatin. "Fire!"

Her hand froze on the cannon trigger. Lilia's killer instinct was not as finely tuned as Solomatin.

Solomatin screamed even louder. "Fire! I say Fire!" The strength of his booming voice flooded her mind. Lilia pressed her gun button and started firing. Her bullets missed their mark. She made a sharp left to avoid the bomber's tail and then pulled hard on her stick and zoomed straight up, searching for her leader.

Lilia had lost Solomatin. She half rolled the Yak out of the climb and back in the direction of the bombers. They had scattered in all directions. The leading Heinkel was spinning out of control, flames and smoke billowing from both engines. Where was the captain? She heard him shout in her headphones: "*Opasnost, Opasnost [danger, danger]*," behind you. Break right." She glanced in her rearview mirror and saw a Messerschmitt flattening out his dive, bobbling in her slip-stream, and firing. There was a hammering of bullets behind her cockpit. She broke hard right, diving and rolling continuously. The German remained on her tail. She could see the flashes of his guns but felt no hits. Suddenly, she saw a ball of orange flame in her rear- view mirror.

As she climbed and turned slightly to the left, there was Solomatin, waiting about 500 metres above her. "Return to battle position 300 metres from my wingtip." The two pilots scanned the sky from horizon to horizon. Just over two minutes had elapsed since their hair-raising dive through the

German formation. The fighters had vanished, as had the Heinkels.

Solomatin motioned downward. Lilia followed through the broken clouds somewhere west of the city.

They spotted an unescorted Heinkel at 1000 metres, retreating at top speed. There was no sign of fighter cover. Solomatin reduced power and dropped behind and slightly below the Heinkel. Lilia knew exactly what he was up to. Solomatin knew from experience that there was a "dead space" to the rear of the German bomber where the defensive machine guns were ineffective. Solomatin waved to Lilia to close in and then attack. "Are you able?" He shouted. "Can I depend on you?"

"Yes," shouted Lilia into the radio.

"Do not, I repeat, do not fire until I give the order!"

When Solomatin gave the order to commence firing, Lilia came so close to her target that she felt she could slide back her cockpit hood and touch the Heinkel. She was swaying in the enemy's slipstream as she further reduced her power to his airspeed. Then she squeezed her finger on the gun button. She held the burst of machine gun and cannon fire for almost ten seconds. She could see her shells tear through the underside of the Heinkel. She then turned the nose of her plane to the left as she kept the spray directed at the port wing and engine.

An explosion and flames erupted from the engine. Suddenly the Heinkel was plummeting downward. Solomatin was not sure if the pilot had been shot or was merely faking an incident, only to slip away. "Continue attack!" screamed Solomatin ruthlessly. "Continue attack!"

"I believe we have a direct hit. The hit is visible, the hit is visible."

Solomatin ignored Lilia's observation. "Attack until I say stop!"

The two alternatively covered and attacked, a sickening spectacle of human target practice. The bomber was completely engulfed in flames from nose to fuselage.

At 1000 metres, Lilia and the Captain pulled up from their dive into a hard left turn. They circled above the doomed bomber until it exploded in the field below. An oily black column of smoke rose from the fierce flames of the wreckage.

When they reached home base, Major Baranov was on the runway, about to enter his aircraft for another mission. Lilia broke right and Solomatin broke left in an acrobatic victory roll not 20 metres above the runway. Inna, standing at the far end of the runway, was certain Baranov would be furious—he had just cautioned his aces about that sort of conduct. "Comrades, playful foolishness in war can make the aircraft break up. Set an example, celebrate on the ground not in the air." But this day, Baranov just looked up, waved his hand and grinned.

Lilia was flushed and delighted, realizing Solomatin was willing to place his fellow pilots—in this case Lilia herself— in the gravest danger in order to destroy the enemy's planes. Her mood was somber. War was a wonton accumulation of individual tragedies, multiplied many times over, that contained no sense or meaning. And Solomatin's last act was unconscionable. Had war totally dulled the captain's sense of morality?

Solomatin's crowing filled the void. "This girl's going to be an ace, I'll bet you anything on that," Solomatin cheerfully declared, loud enough for all to hear. Then he noticed a series of jagged bullet holes behind the cockpit. Suddenly, he realized what had just transpired.

"Are you all right?"

"Perhaps the time to ask was in the air. When lives were at stake."

Solomatin paused. "Under certain circumstances, that is correct. Our mission in wartime is to defeat the enemy for the greater good. By definition that means some of our comrades will not survive. It is my job to determine the odds each time we enter combat."

"Comrade Captain, with all due respect, I believe only God should determine the value of a life." She wanted to discuss the issue further but resisted.

Solomatin knew the discussion was not over as he also realized Lilia was beautiful even in the heat of battle, covered in grime and sweat. "We should discuss the matter at day's end."

"Yes, Comrade Commander."

"If we are going to be a team, I prefer you call me by my real name, Alexei. My friends call me Lyosha."

Lilia looked into his deep, dark eyes. Despite the disagreements, she felt a special connection. "Then I will call you Lyosha."

"What is your peacetime name, Lieutenant?" smiled Alexei.

"Lilia."

"And your good friends call you?"

"Lilia."

The couple laughed warmly.

~

Inna came running. "Are you both okay?"

"Sergeant," said Alexei to Inna. "Prepare the plane for another sortie in about an hour."

"Comrade Captain, with all due respect, I will need longer. I need to check inside the fuselage to see if the hits damaged any of the rudder control cables or rear elevators."

"Perhaps that is enough for one day?" said Alexei. He and Lilia smiled at Inna, then walked briskly across the field to the control bunker to write up their reports.

Reports filed, Lilia returned to chat with Inna. "How is my plane doing?"

"Not flyable today. Too many bullet holes."

"Does Lyosha know?"

"Who is Lyosha?"

"Our Captain."

Lyosha, thought Inna. *One battle, and it's already Lyosha.* "Lyosha is a magnificent fighting machine," sighed Lilia.

In another day and in another place, Alexei and Lilia might have been strolling hand in hand, talking of the future. But the future for them here could be no farther than their next sortie. They spoke privately. Alexei promised that as long as there was a war, "I will teach you how to be a killing machine," and "Every German I kill, I kill for you."

Together that morning, they had already killed eleven Germans.

~

Lilia had always taken pains with her appearance, but she, Katya, and Inna encountered difficulties when it came to keeping themselves fresh and clean in the all-male 473rd.

There were no facilities with running water. When the season allowed, they made do by bathing in a nearby river. During the cooler months, they boiled water on the stoves and gave themselves a thorough wash-down. There was even a crude wooden washing cabin built by the male soldiers.

But the girls loved when the "bath train" came to their part of the front. There was lots of running water, some additional privacy, and, as women, they always received priority. The scene at the 473rd became all too familiar. Scores of pilots and enlisted men patiently lined up outside the train while Lilia, Katya, Inna and the other women luxuriated in the showers and baths, making generous use of the limited hot water. Usually, after the bath train left, Alexei would joke, "You smell more like a woman than I remembered."

~

Hair-washing was a particular problem for the threesome. The grime and dirt of a military existence knotted their hair in spots, requiring longer showers. But this made the men wait even longer, which was unfair and unacceptable.

Consequently, the ever-inventive Lilia created a routine to eliminate the "bothersome hair" issue. At the end of each day's final sortie, Lilia would ask Inna to bring a large bucket and towel and a piece of soap to their bunker. Lilia would open the radiator cap on her Yak, drain the scalding water into the bucket, and then top off the bucket with cold. Then she'd fling off her flying helmet and tuck the towel around her neck. Inna would then pour the hot water over her head and work up lather with the soap. Next, she'd mix more hot water from the radiator and do it again. Finally, she would rinse thoroughly with cold water and walk briskly to her bunker with the towel wrapped around her head. She'd emerge with her hair shiny and bouncy.

At first, the men couldn't believe what they saw. Neither could Katya, who eventually termed the ritual "Lilia's Dance of the Soap." In time, all three women used Lilia's hair-cleansing process. Initially, the men thought Baranov would blow his top at the self-indulgent exercise. But Lilia had clearly won him over. From time to time, he'd observe the routine and then shrug his shoulders and grin.

Inna wrote in her diary many years later,

> "Lilia had proved what a good pilot she was. If she wanted to wash her hair under the Yak's radiator, a bit of hot water was hardly going to break the Soviet Air Force."

Chapter 29

The birch forest where Lilia, Lyosha and friends learned to love

January 1943
Saratov City...

THE BATTLE FOR STALINGRAD WAS coming to an end. The remnants of the German Sixth Army were beginning to retreat in heavy wet snow as the winter sun shone on the shattered remains of this "Great City," as the Russians called it. German air activity over Stalingrad had also ceased.

Lilia and Lyosha decided to make a last sweep across the battleground of the devastated city. They flew in loose formation at a height of only 200 metres, so they could take one last look at the place that had dominated their lives for so many weeks. It turned out to be a sobering experience in which they were confronted with a brief vision of hell shared by the many civilians and soldiers on the ground.

They had never walked these rubble-strewn streets but at this height, the kaleidoscope of scenes racing below their wings gave them a vivid impression of the awesome destruction that had taken place; kilometer after kilometer of flattened buildings had been pulverized into ugly, jagged undulations of brick and stone. They tipped their Yaks as they wheeled around the elevators of the tractor factory which had been a familiar landmark. Neither said much.

Then they peeled off, one after the other, to screech at 550 kilometres an hour around the summit of Mamayev Hill, which had been so bitterly disputed. A burned-out German tank hulk was perched near the summit. On all sides of the hill lay the unburied bodies of the Soviet and German dead. A column of resting Russian soldiers looked up and waved. Lilia and Alexei waggled their wings in salute. That single gesture from the troops below made Lilia feel good about their many difficult missions.

Moments later, they passed directly over what remained of the Stalingrad Grain Silo, where, unbeknownst to Lilia and Alexei, seventeen-year-old Tamara Pamyatnykh, the high school sweetheart of nineteen-year-old Staff Sergeant Ivan Yegorov, had spent her winter working sixteen hours a day and more combining wheat husk fibers, tiny bits of grain, and balls of floor dust into tasteless loaves of bread to sustain the city's citizens who had been cut off from the outside world by the Germans. Tamara carried a picture of Ivan close to her heart. She used to tell her fellow workers, mostly teenagers themselves, "Ivan's love keeps me warm on the coldest, bleakest days."

On the morning of December 11, a German battalion charged the facility and took control after a violent hand-to-hand battle with silo workers brandishing wooden rolling pins, metal baking pans, and kitchen knives. Tamara fought valiantly until a sixteen-inch German bayonet pierced her heart. She died instantly. Ivan did not discover his loss until the spring of the following year.

~

Her flight over Stalingrad completed, a buoyant Lilia felt compelled to write home that evening.

> "My dear Mummy,
> I congratulate you with the Happy New Year!
> I wish you to withstand all the hardships of the war as easily as possible; the main thing is to be healthy, and then everything will restore. Believe in our victory! Believe in forthcoming happiness!
> We celebrate the New Year on the front under the music of war. The front is moving and we are pursuing the enemy. We live in dugouts, the conditions are worse than in huts. It is wet. Of course I feel better in an air battle.
> It has all become rather more habitual than dreadful for me. On the whole everything is good. I am absolutely sure that it is the last New Year that we celebrate apart.
> You must be sure of me. I am always cheerful and healthy. Good bye, kiss you.
> Yours Lilia."

~

Lilia and Katya's bravery, coupled with Lyosha's open support of Lilia and Katya's abilities, had gained the respect and admiration of every man in the 473rd. Every wingman and pilot knew they had supportive comrades when they flew missions and sorties together.

One January evening when the skies were quiet, Lyosha, Daniil Petrov, the close friend of Lilia's sign painter, Vladimir Kolesov, and another pilot, Lt. Maksim Fedoseev, invited themselves to Lilia, Katya, and Inna's bunker.

"We have a toast," said Alexi with a big smile.

"For what occasion?" asked a reluctant Lilia at the entrance to the bunker.

"That we are alive and well."

After a little prodding from Inna and Katya, Lilia agreed to let the men enter. The girls preferred to drink hot tea while the men passed the vodka bottle around. They were sitting boy-girl; Katya next to Daniil, Inna with the handsome dark haired Maksim and Lilia next to Lyosha.

Daniil was the first to notice that the women's bunker seemed considerably warmer than theirs, even though they had the same kerosene heater and the dimensions of the dugout appeared to be the same. "Why is it so much warmer in here than in our bunker?" he questioned.

"Where do you place your kerosene heater?"

"In the middle of the room, of course," responded Daniil thinking privately the question foolish.

"We place ours by the dugout entrance. It helps to warm the air that seeps in." Lyosha laughed. The solution now seemed obvious. "And what about the extra blanket? continued Katya.

"The extra blanket?" stared Daniil.

"And, what have you done with the earth?"

Katya then walked over to the dugout entrance. "You have an extra blanket; tuck it around the entrance. It further insulates the dug-out on cold winter nights."

"And, I thought you were a pilot from peasant surroundings," laughed Daniil. "Who knew you were an engineer from Moscow?"

Lilia couldn't resist a little tease. "Perhaps Katya needs to visit your dugout to assist with the installation?" They all laughed. After finishing the bottle, the men returned to their dugout and made "the suggested improvements." They slept better that evening than they had all winter.

In the morning as Lyosha and Daniil sat in a corner of the mess kitchen, Maksim was describing something with his hands and arms to the supply sergeant. The sergeant nodded agreement. They shook hands. Then Maksim took a handful of makhorka (tobacco) out of a small pouch in his pocket and handed it to the man.

He then entered the mess hall and joined his two comrades. In the course of the conversation, Maksim asked, "Do we agree the woman have treated us well and with respect?"

Lyosha and Daniil nodded.

"Then I propose, when time permits, we treat the ladies to a dance party."

"A grand gesture," laughed Lyosha. "But, have you noticed we are in the middle of a war? Free time may be long in coming, so let us not disappoint by explaining the gift."

"But when that time comes," teased Daniil, "I will write my mama and ask if she please send our family gramophone." Lyosha again laughed at the outrageous suggestion.

To the utter amazement of Lyosha and Daniil, Major Baranov announced at their morning briefing that Comrade Stalin was adding twenty additional pilots, planes, and support staff to the 473rd in recognition of its outstanding record of military achievement.

"Our new staff additions will allow the unheard of during battle... for one day at least. I wish to divide the regiment into groups and give them one day and night of freedom."

In that moment, the possibility of a gathering with the girls morphed from a future dream to a current reality.

Maxim was ready.

"I say we invite Lilia, Inna, and Katya to our dugout for a dance party. Lyosha, will you secure the food and beverages?

I believe I have killed enough Germans to warrant such a favor." Maxim paused.

For whatever reason, Lyosha decided to accept the possibility of a dance party and his suggested role.

"Yes, I agree. Consider the favor done."

"Good," said Maxim. "I will supply the music." He then walked to the sergeant's tent and returned with a somewhat worn gramophone with small built-in speakers, and a record containing the tango *Sparks of Champagne* on one side and the popular *On the Hills of Manchzhuria* on the flip side.

"And, how did you manage that?" asked Lyosha.

"For me to know, and you to discover."

"It appears then the party is planned," said Lyosha. "But who will make the invitation?"

Daniil and Maxim pointed to Lyosha.

"So Daniil, what do you contribute?"

"My presence for Katya."

"That seems not enough."

Daniil paused. "Then I will supply the vodka."

~

"And what do you wish on this visit?" said Lilia, staying at the front of the ladies' bunker.

"We wish that you join us for a dance party in our dugout. The arrangements have been made. Even the dugout is warm."

"Has the war made you crazy?"

"No, that is our gift to you. A thank you for your help with warm sleep. Our bones no longer chatter."

Lyosha stared into Lilia's soul. "We have music and beverage. And, the Major has given us this brief respite from the madness. Please spend the time with us."

She felt the emotion. He was so handsome, so eloquent.

She looked at the girls who smiled and shrugged, as if to say, whatever you decide, but we are truly intrigued.

Lilia nodded reluctantly. Nevertheless, she wished to make it clear their acceptance was contingent. "We will stay as long as you behave like men."

The three men smiled and crossed their hearts

~

Lyosha made certain Baranov placed him, Maxim, Daniil, Lilia, Inna, and Katya into the first group given a respite from the war. The group free time began with a ride to the top of the slope, some five kilometres from base camp. They were surrounded by a patch of tall stately birch trees that had escaped the cannons and the rockets. "I find this spot so beautiful," said Lyosha. "I have walked the paths in my private moments and prayed that God would will help maintain our determination for things to return as they were."

"Perhaps we should all walk together and pray for the same strength," said Lilia. The group nodded and walked for two hours.

"I think we should return to our dugout," said Daniil. "We have a surprise." The men nodded.

Minutes later, the truck came to a halt not far from the dugout. Daniil helped Katya from the truck. Once inside, Maxim revealed the gramophone. He placed a re-cord on the turntable. The music began. His hand reached out to Inna. They began to dance.

Daniil smiled at Katya. She nodded. It was clear to all that Katya had become smitten by his attentive manner. She had never been treated so warmly by a man. She blushed silently.

Lyosha walked slowly toward Lilia. He could not take his eyes off her. He stood in front of her, openly, honestly, his arms outstretched.

"This does not change things," she said.

"Of course."

As they danced, Lilia felt safe and secure. She placed her head on his shoulder. It was hard to imagine they were in the middle of a war.

The music stopped.

Daniil had an announcement. "Let us all celebrate this day and our time together with some vodka!"

The girls became immediately offended. "We will not do such a thing." They headed for the entrance.

"Wait. This is not ordinary run of the mill vodka; this is vodka from cows."

Daniil then removed a pail of milk from the truck with some ladles for sipping. The girls were surprised. Milk at the front was a rare delicacy.

"How were you able to obtain such drink?" asked Katya. Daniil smiled and looked at the other men.

"That is our little secret!"

~

Katya, not known for flights of fancy, offered a most unusual suggestion.

"Now that we are filled with vodka," she smiled wryly as she wiped the milk from her lips, "I would suggest we play *Clouds*." The five stared blankly at each other.

"Tell me you have never played *Clouds*?"

Spontaneously they all replied in unison, "No I have never played *Clouds*!"

Then they all started to giggle like children.

"Then I will explain. Everyone in my village played. First we must return to our hill and look at the heavens."

Five minutes later the group was sitting on tree stumps, eyes toward the blue and white sky.

"Now look at the clouds," instructed Katya. "Imagine what you are seeing. Create a vision. The best vision wins."

Lilia was not sure if Katya was just having a joke at the expense of the others.

"Since you are more experienced at these visions, than we perhaps you should explain first."

"I agree," said Lyosha.

Katya's eyes roamed to the right and left. She saw a large cloud attached to a slightly smaller cloud, followed by two even smaller cloud puffs.

"This is a family of four. Father, followed by mother and their two twin daughters. They are on the way to their grandmother's. See they have a New Year's gift in their hand. The father is turning to tell them to walk faster because they are late."

Daniil was mesmerized by Katya's pleasing gentleness and touching.

Twenty minutes later, each had completed their interpretation. There were dragons in lagoons, ghosts in houses, soldiers in battle, and more.

But all readily agreed, the winning vision belonged to Katya. "It is getting late. I believe we must return," said Lilia dutifully.

"I need persuasion," smiled Lyosha.

"To what kind of persuasion do you refer?"

"A kiss will suffice."

Lilia smiled and walked over to Lyosha. He put her arms around her. They embraced tenderly.

Daniil and Katya, Inna and Maxim applauded.

They were now officially an item.

~

Daniil insisted on driving with Katya by his side as they returned to the base.

Lilia and Lyosha and Maxim and Inna tried to hear what Daniil was saying to Katya. But the trucks engine and the bumpy road made that impossible.

An hour later, the girls had returned to their bunker and were readying for sleep. Finally, Inna asked THE question: "What did you and Daniil talk about for a whole hour?" Katya smiled, put her hand in her pocket and took out the silver and red penknife. "It is very beautiful," said Katya with pride.

"*My* Daniil told me his father gave it to him on his 16th birthday. It belonged to his father and his father before him."

~

Lyosha knew he was beyond smitten.

He sat in their bunker thinking what might be the proper course of action with regard to his feelings for Lilia. He wondered if she felt the same. Little was said as they danced the day away just hours earlier.

He decided he would write a note to explain his feelings. If Lilia did not respond, his heart would be broken, but at least only he would know the outcome.

He found scraps of paper from old flight plans. He decided to write on the backs, so no one would even realize what he was doing. He wrote one letter and then ripped it up; the words were not quite right. He wrote a second and a third with similar results. Finally, on the fourth try, he had achieved the proper balance of guarded emotion, true feelings, and social propriety. He reread the letter, folded it and put it in his pocket.

As events were to unfold, Lyosha would never deliver his letter in person.

Chapter 30

Captain Solomatin (front left) quickly invaded Lieutenant Litvyak's heart.

February 1943...

TODAY HAD BEEN ONE OF the best days of Lilia's life. Inna noticed her distinctive sly smile in the shadows as the two ladies walked toward the end of the airfield after dinner. "Why such a grin?" asked Inna, who was now arguably Lilia's closest friend.

"Today Katya and I agreed with Major Baranov to re-main with the unit till war's end. He said we would be a shining example to those women who follow."

"Since I was not included in your conversation," wondered Inna, "does that mean you and Katya wish me to leave when my time comes?"

"Do not say such silly things. Katya and I spoke for the three of us. We are now family, and our family will defend the Motherland till Hitler ceases to be. And when this war is over, we will remain family because destiny has no boundaries."

The girls stopped to hug each other.

Suddenly out of the shadows, an armed sentry appeared, pointing his gun.

"Halt, who goes there?" said the sentry assigned to protect the antiaircraft gun emplacements. "Password."

"Volga," said Lilia.

The sentry recognized Lilia. "Sorry, but you under-stand."

"Soldier, I have no problems, just do your job."

The sentry smiled. "I am proud to serve under you." Lilia smiled shyly and nodded her head.

"You are a noted celebrity in our war," teased Inna.

Lilia was not sure how to answer, so she simply ig-nored Inna's observation. The ladies continued to walk up a small hill a little past the final defense line and stopped to look at the glow of Stalingrad against the pitch black sky. The dominating sound that night was the whooshing of the multiple Katyusha rockets being launched across the Volga River at the remaining German positions.

"We have prevailed against the odds. The great city remains ours. Do you not feel proud of what we have accomplished, despite all the pain, the suffering?"

Lilia's eyes sparkled in the night's reflections.

"The Major made Katya and me proud today. He informed us that the rest of the men now realized they could place their life in our hands while flying missions," said Lilia with great satisfaction.

"That means my hands will continue to freeze as I make your planes ready for battle," smiled Inna.

Inna noticed Lilia did not respond to her humorous comment. Clearly, her mind was elsewhere.

"Calling Lieutenant Litvyak, over. Repeat. Respond, Lieutenant Litvyak. Over."

Lilia smiled. She was back in the moment.

"Where did your mind travel?"

"Against the odds, I believe I am falling in love with Lyosha."

"Are you mad?" said Inna.

"I do not think so, Inna. I have been fond of others but never like this. My heart beats quickly when he just looks at me. Sometimes it beats quickly when I just imagine his presence."

"You have just recently met. It is a delusion of war."

Lilia paused. "No, this is different. He is like an eagle. My eagle, strong, brave, and beautiful."

"What have we so often discussed? Suppose..."

"I know. I know," smiled Lilia, recanting the decision so many women in the war had previously made. "No commitment to any man until the war is over!"

Lilia stopped and ran her fingers through her hair. "Regardless, it has happened. I need to sort my feelings. Determine how to progress."

Despite the realities, the romantically-inclined Lilia saw her relationship as idyllic. She was flying fighters, which had always been her ambition, and now she was in love with the man who was the best at flying fighters. By her side. To complete the idyll, she was certain he was deeply in love with her.

"Has he told you that..."

"Absolutely not!" responded Lilia almost indignantly, as if some unspoken code of war would be shattered. "He understands the difficulty of commitment."

"Then how can you be so sure? Perhaps you imagine more than reality."

The expression on Lilia's face turned wistful. Inna had never seen such a tender side of Lilia. "The way he looks into my eyes. The way he lifts me onto my wing as I enter my cockpit. The way he smiles when we return. The way..."

Inna waved stop. She was now convinced of her friend's emotions, but Lilia was gushing like a childish teenager, and this was war. She had to stop her before someone else took notice.

"Of course," said the suddenly mature Lilia, "Despite my feelings, I also can make no commitment. How could I?"

"Have you talked of a future? A time after the war?"

"There has not been a private moment to share. He only says, 'Today, only war matters. Tomorrow, I will teach you how to kill more Germans.'"

"Very romantic," chuckled Inna.

~

Through the short winter days, Lilia and Lyosha continued to forge and perfect their partnership.

By February, under Lyosha's tutelage, Lilia had shot down another six German aircraft–three fighters and three transport aircraft attempting to supply the German infantry units who were being surrounded by waves of Russians soldiers gaining strength with each passing day.

When they weren't flying and attacking military targets, they made no secret of their feelings for each other on the ground.

As Inna would later explain in her diary, years after the war ended, "Most of the girls in the women's regiments professed to be in love with someone. It was almost fashionable behavior. In reality, most of the boyfriends were men they had only met briefly while sharing airfields with male regiments. Their romances were almost always conducted at long distance by letter with only the occasional chance meeting, a meeting which rarely, if ever, included sexual relations. There was neither time nor the privacy to consummate matters.

"But for Lilia and Lyosha it was different. And, most of our comrades realized this. The couple flew together most days and in the evenings they were together as much as possible.

"There was nothing undignified about the way they behaved. Lyosha would come and sit and talk to Lilia in the corner of our bunker. They would hold hands and sometimes would just sit together quietly for hours. It wasn't an uncomfortable silence; they just seemed content to be together.

"I think they wondered privately how they would spend their lives together after the war but were afraid to have that discussion publicly for fear that one or the other would not exist after the war."

One day, while Lyosha was resting in his bunker, Katya, Inna, and Lilia were discussing the day's mission.

"It appears to me that the German defenses are most weak at a point about 130 kilometres west of our base."

"Which means?" stared Katya.

"Which means today we should proceed directly to the target rather than take a longer approach by flanking to the left and coming behind the target."

The good-natured Katya decided to tease Lilia. "I guess we are in a hurry to return to our dear Lyosha."

Lilia was insulted by the thought that one of her best friends would consider a dangerous short cut merely to fulfill her own desires.

"Katya, what a terrible thing to say!"

"What? It is not true?"

"I am not ashamed! It is true—I love Lyosha, and I want to spend every possible minute with him, but I would never place my feelings ahead of my mission."

"I am sorry for what I implied," said Katya as she stretched her hand in friendship.

Instead, Lilia hugged Katya warmly. "And, I love you too."

That night Lilia dreamed she and Lyosha were at an officers' club in Moscow, celebrating the end of the war. The band was playing the Andreev Waltz (Day Dreams Waltz). Lyosha held her closely and tenderly as he whispered into her ear, "I have fallen in love with you. Completely and forever." She kissed him tenderly.

~

Sometimes, they found it impossible to hide their feelings, particularly after a tough sortie. One day, upon return to dispersal after such an occurrence, Lyosha noticed Lilia had taken quite a few hits in her fuselage just behind the cockpit. He put his arms under her arms and lifted her slowly down from the wing as if she was a little china doll. Her hair was clinging to her forehead with sweat where she'd taken off her flying helmet. She smiled and rolled her eyes as if to say, "Now that was an intense dogfight." Lyosha lowered her to the ground and, with her face level to his, he whispered something into her ear. She again smiled and whispered something in return. Try as they might, none of the other pilots could hear what they said to each other. They could only speculate.

~

Lilia's love affair with Lyosha was an "open" secret, because virtually everybody in the regiment knew he found any excuse to visit the women's bunker most evenings.

Typically, Lyosha and Lilia would eat in the officers' mess together with others. There would be the occasional laugh, but mostly the talk was of missions and strategies. After dinner, usually around 1800 hours, she would return to her bunker with the girls while he would return to his quarters with the men.

Then, like clockwork, thirty minutes later, he would walk quietly to Lilia's bunker.

"May I come in?" Lyosha would ask.

Inna and Katya would always answer. "And, Captain who do you wish to see?"

Lyosha would always respond in kind. "I wish to discuss changes to tomorrow's mission with the senior officer of the house."

Lyosha would then smile, Inna and Katya would snicker like little girls, and Lilia would appear from a darkened corner, her hair combed, her face glowing, her lips painted red.

~

Most assumed Baranov's close friendship with Lyosha also had something to do with the fact that he seemed to turn a blind eye to Lyosha's passion for the beautiful woman pilot.

The couple recognized they had been given certain freedoms in matters of the heart. They respected those freedoms by never showing displays of affection in public. Lilia never once threw her arms around Lyosha's neck or kissed him before they embarked on a mission. Nor did they stand around the dispersal area holding hands and gazing into each other's eyes as they completed their reports. But they did look at each other with deep concern and obvious love before they flew off together. And, after they landed safe and sound, the relief on Lyosha's face that Lilia had come through the latest dogfight unscathed was quite transparent.

"Mummy," Lilia would write frequently, "sometimes it is so difficult. I am so close to the man I will love forever. I want to hold him tightly. I want him to hold me tightly, yet we both know it is not possible in the heat of battle. Love is crazy, yes? And, war makes no sense, yes?"

As Inna personally explained matters years later, "Circumstances made it almost impossible for people truly in love to be alone for any length of time. But the couple tried their best. Some evenings Lilia and Lyosha would pull their fur-lined helmets over their ears, wrap their heavy coats around themselves and walk across the airfield together, Lilia's slight figure padded out to bulkiness by her heavy clothing and the taller figure of Solomatin walking proudly beside her, his gloved hands thrust deep into his pockets.

"Unfortunately many of these trips of privacy took place in the bitter cold, so even with fur socks and heavy boots they found it necessary to walk briskly to keep their circulation moving.

"Lilia told me that it was agony up there sometimes when she saw her Lyosha being attacked. But, of course it gave them great incentive to fight really well. Far from their love for each other affecting their concentration, I think it helped. Lilia had always showed the sort of aggression you need to be a good pilot from the first day I met her. However, her close relationship with Lyosha brought her battle skills to a new level."

~

An exhausted Lilia was lying in bed with her eyes closed as Lyosha sat in a nearby chair watching and listening to her every breath.

His mind was filled with questions without answers.

Why did they meet here and now rather than on sunny days in fields of splendid flowers?

Why was he chosen to teach this woman, this sweet nectar of the Gods, to maim and kill?

And, what of Hitler? What makes a man crave disruption of the world order, and revel in the untold pain and suffering of so many?

The more Lyosha pondered, the more anxious he became. He could feel moisture on his brow; his heart beat faster and his hand began to quiver. It was time to breathe in deeply the clear crisp evening air. He quietly slipped outside the bunker and removed a pack of cigarettes from his pocket.

A figure approached in the darkness. Lyosha pulled his pistol. "109 circling above the airfield at approximately 2,000 metres. Unable to determine if there are more on the way," screamed a sentry running from bunker to bunker alerting the pilots.

Lyosha ran back into the bunker. He shook Lilia firmly. "Attack, attack," he yelled. "Katya, Inna, [sleeping nearby], up and out. Up and out."

The girls grabbed their equipment, ran outside, and looked toward the clear, star-filled sky.

Sure enough, directly over the field was the unmistakable shape of a single Messerschmitt 109. The four of them tried to protect themselves by identifying the path of the other Messers as they ran to their planes. Suddenly Lyosha stopped. Lilia pulled his arm. "Are you crazy, hurry, please hurry!"

"There are no others," said Lyosha, pointing skyward. Lilia looked up. Lyosha was correct.

The plane circled the base again without firing a single shot. Lyosha wondered about the Messer's purpose. "He makes no sense. Either he is very brave or very foolhardy."

~

Months of constant dogfights with the never-ending stream of Russian fighter planes had taken their toll on the now weary German Luftwaffe. The few remaining pilots around Stalingrad operated most cautiously since they realized air superiority had passed to the Soviets.

Still, this single Messersmitt circled. It could only mean one thing, thought Lyosha. The frustrated pilot was offering an old-fashioned gladiatorial challenge to a single combat pilot.

"Permission to let me take the bastard down," screamed Solomatin to Baranov.

"Permission granted."

Lyosha's Yak was refueled and rearmed.

Lilia was very pale. "Lyosha, why you? There are others. You have just returned."

"Why not me?" asked Lyosha, relishing another kill to his credit.

Lilia squeezed his hand. He pulled away. "I'll be fine."

Minutes later Lyosha was airborne, climbing toward the German. This time, for some inexplicable reason, Lilia could not bear to watch. She turned and went back inside the bunker.

As it turned out, there was little cause for worry. Despite the German having an initial height advantage, it was over in less than five minutes. Lyosha flew toward the Messersmitt's underbelly and climbed straight up, making himself an almost impossible target. Once in range, ammunition blazed from Lyosha's two cannons. Moments later, the fuselage and tail of the Messersmitt was a mass of flames and smoke spiraling to the ground. Either the pilot was hit and unable to eject or there was no parachute. Either way, the plane crashed into a giant ball of red and yellow flames.

Lilia heard the crash and ran from the bunker, a look of terror on her face.

"The Captain's fine. He destroyed the enemy."

A sigh of relief covered Lilia's face as Lyosha's aircraft flew low over the field and pulled up in a victory roll. When he landed, he jumped down from the aircraft and a cheer went up. He grinned with pleasure and winked at Lilia. She blew him a kiss. Inna tapped Katya.

Half an hour later, the couples were again airborne searching for some enemy stragglers.

~

Niko Lataria fell in love with Lilia the first time he saw her covered in perspiration after a particularly difficult sortie. But he knew, as did everyone at the airbase, that Lilia had found the man of her dreams, so the dark-skinned Lataria from Georgia pined for her from afar. He was also a lieutenant, and junior to Solomatin. He knew it would be unwise to create any ill will or dissension within the regiment since Lilia, while fully aware of Lataria' s feelings, did absolutely nothing to encourage him. In fact, there were moments when Katya and Inna both advised Lilia that she was going out of her way to be particularly cruel to Lataria when he offered simple courtesies like letting her refuel before him.

"I neither request nor require favorable treatment," Lilia would comment brusquely.

Lilia also made it abundantly clear she enjoyed the undivided attention of the handsomest, smartest, bravest pilot in the regiment. Solomatin, for his part, never appeared to consider Lataria a serious rival for her affections.

Despite their mutual interest in Lilia, the men appeared to get alone well together. Publicly, the circumstances of Lataria's subsequent death seemed to shock Solomatin deeply, although privately Lyosha wondered if the sensational ending was more pre-meditated suicide than an act of bravery.

~

The act of ramming enemy aircraft was not a standard operational procedure, although it was certainly practiced at stages during the war. Officialdom, which gave high decorations to several pilots who downed enemy aircraft with this desperate technique, did not appear to discourage it as a tactic of last resort.

It was a sunny but bitter cold day. Lataria's eyes followed Lilia to her plane. He had been assigned as wingman for another pair of fighter pilots flying with Lilia and Lyosha, who preferred Katya as their wingman.

The mission was to attack some Junker bombers. Lataria was hit by one of the fighter escorts. The flames reached his cockpit quickly, and the heat twisted the canopy so that he could not eject it to enable himself to parachute clear.

He began to scream in agony. He was a doomed man. He accidentally pressed the radio transmit button, so the dispatcher and those huddled near the radio console heard him talk himself through his last actions in a desperate effort to maintain his concentration as the flames engulfed his body.

"You miserable Hitler Junker, may you rot in hell!" Lilia and others saw his fighter, engulfed in flames along the length of the fuselage, ram the bomber. The two planes locked together and then exploded in mid-air.

"I have heard of others doing what Niko decided, but I have never seen it directly," said Lyosha, shaking his head in disbelief.

Lilia was completely shaken by what she had witnessed. It was bad enough to lose a comrade in combat, but to feel his body sizzling, that was a very different matter.

Lilia was wracked with guilt. Perhaps she should have been more kind to him?

~

That evening, for the second time, and final time, in her military career, Lilia shared a vodka and a tender hug with dear Lyosha.

Her hand shook as she brought the small glass to her lips. "Do you wish children?" said Lyosha, discarding his protective military facade.

Lilia paused. She knew this conversation would be their commitment.

"I would like at least one of each. And after that no matter," responded Lilia, doing likewise.

"Suppose there were only boys?"

"Then I would be the queen of the kingdom," smiled Lilia shyly.

A totally relaxed Lyosha laughed heartily. Lilia had not seen that side of him before.

"And, suppose *we* had all girls?"

"Then I would be their King."

Both knew they had crossed an emotional Rubicon, somewhere in time. There would be no returning.

Ever.

Chapter 31

Lilia's battle skills in the air now equaled her beauty on the ground.

March 1943
Eastern Ukraine...

IT WAS JUST ANOTHER BLOODY day for flying ace Lieutenant Erich Hartmann of *Jagdegeschwader* 52 (JG.52), Germany's most prestigious and vicious killing machine, known as the "Blonde Knight of Germany."

After sweeping victories in North Africa and Eastern Europe, Hitler had ordered the unit to Kharkov airfield in the Eastern Ukraine to provide additional air support to the troops and bombers that invaded Russia during Operation Barbarossa.

JG.52 was a Nazi propaganda dream. Commanded by the noble Major General Manfred von Ricthofen, cousin of Germany's leading WW I ace, the notorious Red Baron, the JG.52 ranks included three of Germany's most decorated flying aces: Ricthofen, Gerald Barkhorn, and Wilhelm Batz. By 1943, the trio had flown an incredible 1100 missions, had 420 aerial victories, and shot down 27, not including 12 parachute bailouts.

The sun rose over Kharkov about 6:00A.M The regiment's inventory of Me-109s lay randomly scattered around the airfield while Hartmann's personal plane, decorated with a large Roman numeral 'I' and the name 'Usch' painted inside a red heart, sat under a cherry tree. (Usch Paetsch was his fiancée. The 21-year-old Hartmann tried to write her daily. After the war, the rich baritone voiced flyer planned to return to Berlin and pursue a career in radio broadcasting).

Hartmann, dressed in a gray shirt, blue-gray trousers, and gray shoes, had just finished washing and shaving in a small nearby stream.

"Two eggs, well done," directed Hartmann to the camp's two captured Russian women.

"Same," echoed Barkhorn and Batz mockingly as they banged their forks on the metal dishes.

"The Major General tells me today we escort the 189s [mid-range bombers] at 0700." (The day's mission was to destroy some mines rich in anthracite (stone coal) deposits near the town of Krasny Luch.)

At 0703, Hartmann strapped himself into his cockpit as he joked with his crew chief, Bimel Merten, "Let's make quick work of the illiterate pigs; I need more time to write Usch. She complains my notes are uninspired. I tell her I am alive and well, at least for another day, while she writes pages to report every detail of her day."

Merten laughed as he cranked the starter and Hartmann set the Messersmitt's flaps and checked the fuel. The plane's twelve cylinders coughed, belched smoke, and then caught smoothly as his two comrades followed him to the take-off spot. He gunned the engine while stomping on the brakes. When he released the brakes, his 109 catapulted forward and quickly reached 200 kilometres per hour. They banked left as they completed their post take-off routines: retracting the landing gear, closing radiator flaps, easing back on the throttle and checking gauges, guns, and gun sight.

They climbed to 2000 metres with the 189s in full view below. The flight proceeded uneventfully. Hartmann's radio crackled with a report from *Adler,* the German forward spotting post, "ten maybe twenty Red planes due west." Hartmann throttled up a bit, gained altitude, and ordered his *schwarm* (flight group) to follow.

"Calling Light Eyes [Hartmann's call sign based on his excellent eyesight and lighting reflexes], screamed Batz over his radio. "Squadron left, squadron left."

Three large Shturmovik (attack plane) II-2 bombers, escorted by a group of Yaks came into view. The armored bombers closed straight on, rear guns blazing. Hartmann unhesitatingly ordered an attack. He dove sharply, picking up airspeed, then came beneath the bombers, aiming for his target's ventral oil radiator.

Now traveling over 600 kilometres an hour, Hartmann streaked into the Shturmovik's blind spot. At 200 metres, its wingspan filled his gun sight ring. He closed to 150 metres, then 100 before firing. He triggered his cannon and two machine guns for about two seconds before his speed carried him in front of the plane. Hartmann glanced back and saw a wall of blue flames and black sooty smoke. He smiled. The young blond ace had notched another Russian kill.

Moments later he spotted a Yak heading directly toward him in his rear view mirror. He swerved side to side to avoid the cannon fire, then dove sharply and looped upward until he was behind the Yak. After two quick burst from his machine guns, he watched a second Yak burst into flames.

Barkhorn and Bartz were equally destructive as they swooped and swerved their 109s, taking three more Yaks with them. Moments later, the outmatched Russian planes fled eastward, returning to their base, mission not accomplished.

Hartmann radioed his group to return to Kharkov.

"Mission incomplete. Repeat, mission incomplete," shouted Ricthofen himself on the radio.

"Out of ammo, out of ammo," responded Hartmann. "Return to base" was the obvious reply.

It was now 0900. As they approached the field, Hartmann waggled his wings twice, indicating his two victories. On landing, Merten and the other ground crew gathered round Hartmann and his two comrades, offering congratulations. Hartmann walked to the operations tent to file his *Gefechtsbericht* (after-action report).

within 100 metres of the enemies' rear, then fired killing bursts from burst cannon and machine guns. Lilia spotted another wounded Comrade, holes in his right wing, battling another Messer about 300 metres below.

Hartmann saw essentially the same thing from another perspective. He also started to come to his comrade's rescue. But it was too late. In a split second, the Russian plane headed straight for Hartmann's comrade. Instinctively the German banked to the left. Lilia had anticipated his move precisely. The Messer literally fell into Lilia's waiting arms. She fired again and again and again. Her bullets riddled the cockpit. She could see only blood splattered windows as the plane fell from the sky.

The confident Hartmann was now on Lilia's tail. She rose through the clouds at some 6000 metres, hoping to shake her pursuer. Hartmann, anticipating Lilia's strategy, disappeared above the clouds. As she passed through the last of the cloud cover, Hartmann started firing. But he had ignored his own philosophy of shooting in tight bursts when near his target. His cannon was empty. His machine guns had missed their mark.

Lilia realized her pursuer was out of ammo. It was now Lilia's turn. He tried to use the 109's superior horsepower to flee. Lilia cut the distance between them by going into a free fall below him, then she looped around. She was now directly in front, some 1000 metres away. She advanced. He swerved to the left and dove straight down. She kept pace stride for stride. He was amazed at the pilot's capabilities. This was not the Russian air force he knew. Lilia started firing. She put half a dozen holes in his right wing. His plane started to wobble. He banked to the right. She fired again. She had placed more holes in his left wing. Hartmann's plane caught fire. He had no alternative but to parachute out of his cockpit.

"Solo, enemy commander floating," advised Lilia.

Lyosha, seeing the other Messers in retreat, signaled three of his planes to land in the vicinity of where they expected the German leader's parachute to settle.

"All other comrades return to base."

Unfortunately for Solomatin's crew, the parachute landed in an open, icy field, a dangerous place for the Yaks to set down. By the time the planes found a suitable landing place, Hartmann had disappeared into the woods less than 2 kilometers away. It was a particularly cold day for March, perhaps 15 degrees. The lightly-clad Hartmann was cold and exhausted. He stopped for a short break and took out his compass to identify the direction back to his front line. He searched his pockets for some gloves. There were none to be found. He began to curse.

He felt a handgun in the back of his head. There was a tap on his shoulder.

"Turn slowly or I will shoot you directly in the skull,' said the armed pilot. "We are going to walk back to the open field. You first."

About halfway, Hartmann decided to feign illness and collapse. The pilot appeared smaller than he, so he figured as the pilot reached for him, he would overpower the Russian, take his pistol, shoot to kill, and flee.

Hartmann collapsed. The pilot was not buying. He started to shoot at Hartmann's feet. "Get up, you fascist."

Hartmann got the message and bounced up immediately. When they got to the open field, the pilot waved to Lyosha to descend and pointed to a spot in the corner where he had landed safely using the winter brush to cushion his stop.

Moments after landing, Lyosha and the other pilots tied Hartmann up and radioed their location to the base.

"Thank you, comrade," smiled Lyosha to the pilot with the handgun.

Chapter 32

German fighter ace discovers he was shot down by a woman.

DURING THE INITIAL interrogation, Hartmann would give only his name, rank, and serial number. "I am Lt. Erich Hartmann, serial number 3468970." Lyosha watch-ed silently.

"And your purpose?"

Hartmann sneered arrogantly. "Pick wildflowers. I am Lt. Erich Hartmann, serial number 3468970."

The Russian interrogator recognized the pilot's name. He took Lyosha aside while the guards watched over Hartmann. "Do you realize, Captain," said the interrogator, "we have captured one of the Ricthofen's most famous aces, 'The Blonde Knight.' Major Baranov will be most pleased."

Lyosha jogged over to Baranov's quarters to break the news. "Hartmann!" said Baranov, "He must have much top-secret information. I want him interrogated until he speaks... even if it takes ten days and nights. We will break the arrogant fascist's spirits."

Lyosha returned with his orders. Minutes turned into hours. Hours turned into one day, then two. But the incessant interrogations yielded nothing. At the end of each session, Hartmann was returned to his cold, barren prison room where he sat in virtual darkness mimicking his interrogators. When he wasn't talking to himself, Hartmann developed his own physical exercise regimen, circling the perimeter of his cell lap after lap after lap. Finally, on the fourth day, he broke his silence. "You want information? Then you give me some first."

"Explain."

"I want to meet the man who shot me down. I want to see him face-to-face. Then maybe, just maybe, I will answer some of your questions."

The interrogator looked at the Captain. Lyosha nodded. "I will inform the pilot." He went over to Lilia's bunker. "Your friend," said Lyosha mockingly, "the one you shot down, wants to meet you."

"Lyosha, you must be joking."

"There is more. Apparently you have downed a fascist fighter ace."

Lilia, the fighter pilot, was suddenly transformed into Lilia the woman. "I am not ready. My hair is a mess, I..."

Katya shook her head. "Lilia you are going to an interrogation, not a ..."

Lilia interrupted. "I know, I know..." The diminutive, delicate-featured Lilia, her blonde hair flowing in the breeze, entered the interrogation quarters.

"Baron Hartmann, meet your captor: this is Lieutenant Litvyak."

Hartmann rose, "You dare to humiliate a war hero by offering a little girl?"

The battalion recorder laughed. Lilia was furious. She walked up to Hartmann and stood right in his face. "Is the truth too difficult for our fascist intruder?"

The rope tied Hartmann tried to intimidate the diminutive Lilia by arrogantly dismissing her, "Child, go away, don't be such a fool."

Lilia began to push Hartmann with her hands. Lyosha pulled them apart. "It is true," he laughed.

"Truth demands proof!"

Lilia obliged. She was determined to put the great Hartmann in his place. "You were flying toward me."

"A lot of planes fly toward me. But few ever leave."

"Perhaps you remember the number 44."

"I have seen lots of numbers; that means nothing," he responded curtly.

"I believe you may also have observed my lilies." Although the image had passed in a split second, Hartmann recalled the flowers quite vividly. They were an unusual artifact of war, not the markings of a true fighter pilot. He wondered, *Could this blonde waif possibly be?*

Hartmann's arrogance turned into a blank stare. She described the course of the fight with her hands. "I swooped down and managed to get behind your plane. I believe you were surprised at my sharp descent because I was able to damage your wing from the rear."

Hartmann's face turned ash white. The Great Ace Hartmann had been brought to earth and captured single-handedly by a woman pilot.

Out of respect for his rank and flight exploits, Lilia saw no need to humiliate him further. Their little walk to the ice field; Hartmann's attempt to feign illness; her bullets dancing around his feet would remain their little secret.

Hartmann offered "selective" cooperation. "Perhaps I will answer your questions tomorrow if you give me some food and drink."

The interrogator looked at the Captain for direction. Lyosha nodded. Surrounded by a room full of guards, the famished Hartmann was eating some bread, potatoes, and water. When he finished he looked at Lilia. "You are quite brave for one so small, so delicate. I commend your courage," said Hartmann. Then Hartman, who had man-aged to hide his handmade Swiss watch in his boot, reached down, pulled it out, and handed it to Lilia. "With compliments. My per-sonal medal."

Lilia looked at the watch, and then threw it to the ground, destroying the face and the mechanism. "I have no need for fascist gifts," she said.

~

That evening, Hartmann was moved to a slightly heated holding area with a light at the far end of the airdrome. The major wanted Hartmann in a pleasant mood to provide greater details.

On the way to the new space, Hartmann passed Lilia's plane. He noticed the number 44 and the white lilies painted on each side of her fuselage.

The next morning when the guards came to fetch Hartmann, the cell was empty. Somehow he had escaped by finding a weak plank that he was able to pry loose with his bare hands. The sentries searched the immediate area. He was nowhere to be found.

~

"Incompetence reigns supreme at our holding areas," shouted Lilia, furious. "Why bother to capture famous killers, if we are to let them escape so easily?"

Lyosha replied, "Be calm. Things happen."

"Alexei, we should not let things be."

"I have a thought. Remember, while the prisoner was being interrogated, the battalion reporter recorded it. I propose we prepare a flyer telling the Germans their ace was captured by a woman."

"And, what will we do with such flyers?"

"We print hundreds, maybe thousands. I will order every pilot to drop them before sorties and during patrols for an entire week. Surely, at least one enemy will find the posters and bring them back to Ricthofen. I would like to be there during Hartmann's embarrassment. He will be a laughing stock."

Lilia smiled. "What kind of mind delivers such a solution?"

~

There was one little detail the major did not reveal to Lyosha or Lilia. He decided to include the drawing of Lilia and Ace Hartmann in the flyer. He thought it would add even more authenticity and embarrassment.

"War hero, congratulations are in order," said Inna and Katya a few days later.

"About what?" asked Lilia.

"You make a very beautiful interrogator," continued Katya. "The photographer captured well."

Again Lilia stared blankly.

"You do not know, do you?" Katya handed Lilia a copy of the flyer. "By now, you are famous across the entire German front!"

~

After escaping, Hartmann walked 50 kilometers in the snow and ice back to his front lines. Major General Ricthofen questioned him about his captivity. Hartmann related all the details save one—that he had been shot down and captured by a woman.

"You are a credit to the cause," said Ricthofen, proud that his ace was able to endure a shoot down, days of torturous interrogation, and a near-death march in the winter elements.

Chapter 33

*Propaganda Ministry transforms Lilia into
a reluctant wartime poster child*

April 1943
Bataisk Airdrome near Rostov...

SOMEHOW, A PRAVDA REPORTER got a copy of the capture story.

The Soviet's chief propaganda officer, Yakov Morozov, quickly realized the morale-boosting possibilities of the story being widely published, and that Lilia's natural beauty and professional efficiency could make her a poster child for Soviet war success.

"With all due respect, Comrade Morozov," said the major over the telephone, "I doubt Comrade Litvyak wants to be interviewed, nor does she wish the story to go further than the flyer."

"Comrade Major, with all due respect," said the foreboding voice on the other end of the telephone, "what kind of military do you run? Soldiers now decide which orders to accept and which to ignore?"

An angered Baranov interrupted. "You still persist? Perhaps you wish to inform Comrade Stalin about our conversation?"

Two days later, reporter Captain Mikhail Sarafanov arrived at Major Baranov's desk. The major called Lilia to his office.

"Comrade Litvyak, this is Captain Sarafanov from the Propaganda Ministry. I am pleased to inform you, Comrade Stalin wishes to do a story on the capture of Hartmann for all to read in Pravda. Congratulations."

Lilia was not sure how to react. Was she being ordered, or was she being given a choice? "I am not sure there is much to tell," said Lilia politely to the reporter.

"That is my business. Let me gather the facts, and I will decide."

~

That evening the three women were huddled in their bunker around the small kerosene stove. It was bitter cold outside. Lyosha stopped by and immediately began his mission.

"The major tells me you rejected the *Pravda* reporter's request?"

"I'm sorry, Lyosha," said Lilia, "I believe my soldier business is soldier business. I did not sign up to be a war pinup. I am here to contribute to the Motherland."

"I understand. But sometimes a soldier must do what she is asked, not what she feels is right."

"Then what about the feelings of the other men? Would that be fair? Do they not make sacrifices every waking moment? Would the press request such stories if I were a man? I have done nothing extraordinary."

"That is incorrect. You have done exemplary work. You are among the very best who represent the Soviet Union."

Lilia blushed. "If I were not Lilia and you were not Lyosha, would you still think so highly?"

"I believe I speak for all the men. It would not offend."

Lyosha challenged her inconsistencies. "Then why the colored scarves?...The flowers on the plane?...The constant attention to your beauty?" She wanted to be noticed for her valor and her beauty and her individualism, yet she was committed to being part of the Motherland's team.

Whenever Lilia disagreed with a matter but did not wish to be confrontational, she used the phrase 'I will think about it.' "I will think about it," said Lilia.

~

"Is she willing?" asked Baranov to Lyosha the following morning.

"She is deciding."

"Captain, clearly your emotions of the heart do not help these matters. It is my turn."

That evening, the Major knocked on the door. "Comrades, you may remember Captain Sarafanov? He has been sent to do a feature story on our female flyers," he announced.

An embarrassed Lilia quickly turned away and tried to pull her leather flying helmet over her curlers, but the bulk was too great. Still with her back to the reporter, she pulled a blue scarf from a bag, put it over her head, and tied it under her chin.

"Captain, you remember Lilia. She is our pride. The one you wanted to interview."

The reporter looked at her and, despite her unflattering headgear, was bedazzled by her natural beauty. He attempted to compliment. "It's unbelievable, a stunning girl like you a fighter pilot."

He could not have chosen worse words to say to Lilia. She felt patronized and clearly offended by the term "girl."

Here was her excuse to refuse the proposed interview.

"You are observant," said Lilia. "You need to interview a real woman."

She disappeared from the bunker, returning dragging Inna by the sleeve. Inna had just finished some work inside a Yak engine, and hadn't even had time to wipe the oil from her hands or face. "This is Inna Pasportnikova," said Lilia, "She's is much older than I [Inna was 21], has had many more experiences. Besides, she knows everything about everyone. That will make your story more interesting." Lilia pulled on her coat and gloves and left the bunker.

"Your friend is either insensitive or rude," commented the annoyed reporter. "The Motherland requires more women to help in the cause. Doesn't she understand that such a story is a good thing?"

"You must forgive our friend. But you caused her to leave."

"What did I say?"

"You called her 'a girl.'"

"And what is so terrible about that?"

"Women who kill or could be killed cannot be girls. But I will help you gather the information you require. Please begin," said Katya.

They spoke for two hours, but he wasn't satisfied. He had done his homework on Lilia. He knew about the boots, her colored scarves, and the wildflowers. He saw Lilia as the focus of his story.

"We cannot divulge such personal information," said Inna.

"Ladies, I have been directed to write this story. I will complete it with or without the lieutenant. Comrades, I understand you are her two best friends. Wouldn't you agree I should include the most accurate information?"

Katya and Inna agreed to answer every question. They discussed Lilia's valor, her killer instinct, her quirky personality, her good looks, and her obsession with her personal appearance. They even gave the reporter a picture taken by the airdrome photographer of a radiant Lilia in full combat gear standing by her plane waving.

"The picture is inspiring," said the reporter.

"Too bad it wasn't her plane," said Katya. "The lily is missing."

"The lily?" said the reporter.

"I thought you had done your homework" teased Katya.

"Lilia's trademark," said Inna. "Did you not know she has a large white lily painted on both sides of her fuselage? 'White Lily' is even her call sign."

A few days later, a big story entitled "Call Sign, White Lily," including the photo, appeared in *Pravda*. News organizations picked up the story and republished it throughout Russia. Lilia became an instant war celebrity. The picture was reproduced as a poster, and on any given day could be found in factories and store windows throughout the land.

"This whole matter is so embarrassing," said Lilia. "How could they have learned all my details?"

"We agree," said Katya and Inna, not daring to tell Lilia that they had been the ultimate source.

~

Prior to the war, the tall, foreboding General Heinrich Aldemar was the Chairman of the Cultural Anthropology Department at the University of Berlin, and a trusted friend of Paul Joseph Goebbels.

Goebbels strongly believed that Nazi intelligence needed to more thoroughly understand the cultural tendencies of the enemy in order to destroy their spirits more quickly and disrupt their strategies upon invasion and occupation.

Although Hitler was initially skeptical, Goebbels convinced him that it was quite ingenious of the superior Aryan intellect to appoint an academician to such a military post. Besides, Aldemar spoke Russian fluently. Aldemar's title, Director of Cultural Affairs, was designed to camouflage his role to all but Hitler's inner circle. At the top of Aldemar's daily activities list was to scan Russian newspapers, press releases, broadcasts—whatever his team could gather. He would sit in his office for hours searching for "cultural kernels" that might provide insights into current and future Russian military weakness.

When he read "Call Sign, White Lily," he realized how differently the Germans and Russians viewed the role of women. Unlike his more chauvinistic Nazi counterparts, Aldemar quickly saw that if a Russian woman could somehow rise to the rank of fighter pilot in a heretofore male-only specialty, she could be a deva-stating propaganda weapon. Wide publication of Lilia's story was his worst military nightmare. Her natural femininity, flamboyant touches, and flower-adorned plane made mockery of German and male air superiority.

"Herr Goebbels," concluded Aldemar, "destruction of 'The White Lily' must be a priority. She represents a class of soldiers that must not contribute to Russia's cause because of their sheer numbers."

Soon all German commands on the Eastern European Front received an unusual communiqué.

BEDARF [urgent]

The Führer directs your attention to a most
dangerous and vicious enemy pilot, call name
"White Lily." Plane identity: number 44 and a
white lily on the fuselage.

Destroy on sight. Repeat, make every effort
to destroy on sight. Validate immediately via
written report to this office upon disposal.

~

Lilia's poster turned Ace Hartmann's version of his
heroism to disgrace.

"Major General, these flyers are everywhere in the fields
behind our emplacements," said the young head of German
sentries. In front of him was the drawing of a rope-bound
Hartmann being interrogated by Lilia. To add insult to injury,
the poster told the story in German of "the foolish fascist
and the little woman who embarrasses the all- powerful
Führer."

Ricthofen was beyond furious.

Hartmann's altercation with Lilia had irreparably
damaged the great ace's reputation among peers and
superiors, even though he was to go on to become the
highest scoring fighter ace in the history of German aerial
combat.

~

Lilia's kill count continued to rise as she flew bravely and
boldly beside her beloved Lyosha. His skill and love were
gradually transforming Lilia from a creative flying machine
into a vicious military machine. In her few private moments,
Lilia continued to write to her mother.

> "Hello, my dear Mummy!
> My greetings and best wishes from the front!
> We are moving ahead. I am fully taken up by
> the battle life.
> It's difficult to find a minute to write you and
> inform you that I am safe and sound, that I

love our Motherland and you, my dear
Mummy, best of all.

I am burning with desire to drive away the
fascist skunks from our land and live quiet
and happy lives again.
I shall come back home and tell you about
everything I have survived during these
difficult days and years when we have been
apart.
Good-bye, I kiss you
Yours, Lilia."

~

The next day, one of Anna's neighbors arrived at the
door waving a copy of *Pravda* with the story of Lilia.

"I had no idea," said the neighbor. "You say so little. You
must be very proud."

Anna had no idea what she was talking about. She read
the story and wondered privately why her daughter had said
Nothing in her letters

Chapter 34

Wait for me me

Poignant thoughts from the front by the poet Simonov

May 1943
Bataisk Airdrome...

INNA WAITED PATIENTLY for Lilia on the parched earth runway, waiting to discuss the modifications she had made to Lilia's plane for the day's training mission.

She assumed Lilia was late because this was not to be a day of combat. It was a day of reconnaissance, of planning aerial strategy.

It was a beautiful early summer day. Lilia had decided to take a walk, cleanse her mind of the madness. Of the killing. Of her father's wasted demise. A few kilometres from base camp, surrounded by a forest of scruffy brush, she came upon a small flowing brook with patches of colorful bluebells, marjorams, and milfoils swaying gently in the soft breeze.

She got down on her hands and knees and began to create a bouquet to accompany her on this day's flights. Before long, she was surrounded by a small squadron of mosquitoes who gently pecked at her face and hands. The more she swatted and shooed, the more persistent they became. Eventually, the parties reached a stalemate. Lilia had enough flowers, and the mosquitoes wished to return to their marshy nest.

As the appearance-conscious Lilia walked back to camp, she could feel the swelling intensify.

Without warning, Lilia snuck up behind Inna and tapped her on the shoulder. It was clear she didn't want to be noticed. Inna quickly learned why! Her friend was covered with mosquito bites.

"What in the world happened to you?"

"Shush," said Lilia, "just get me in the cockpit. I don't want anyone, especially Lyosha, to see me like this."

"Were you attacked by fascist mosquitoes?" giggled Inna.

"I was picking wildflowers," said Lilia, proudly displaying her bouquet.

"There's a war going on," said the grease-covered Inna, "and you're picking flowers?" Inna shook her head. "At least somebody's tending to business."

"What is that supposed to mean?"

"While you've been collecting flowers, I've been making your plane more dangerous."

"How?"

"Follow me."

The girls walked to the front of the plane. "I've modified the forward flaps so you can accelerate faster," said Inna proudly. "If my theory is correct, the adjustment should allow you to outmaneuver the bigger, more powerful Messerschmitts."

"Are you sure?" said Lilia, concerned 'the untested adjustments' could have a negative impact since the margin for error in combat was miniscule.

Inna paused.

"No, I'm not absolutely certain. But that's what training missions are all about."

"Let me ask it another way: If you had to go right this minute, are you sure?"

"I'm pretty sure."

Ironically, moments later the regiment's commanding officer, Major Marina Raskova, was shouting orders over the speakers into every corner of the airdrome.

"Comrades, man your planes. Man your planes, immediately. The Nazis have invaded our airspace. Give them unpleasant memories!"

Lilia scrambled into her Yak-1 as Inna performed a last mechanical check. Lilia started down the runway, a few planes behind Lyosha. Inna waved frantically at Lilia, who came to a screeching halt and opened her cockpit.

"What! What! What!"

"You've forgotten your wildflowers."

Lilia mimicked Inna. "There's a war going on, and you're worried about my wildflowers."

Inna smiled.

"Toss them up," said Lilia, returning the smile.

~

The sounds of a vicious air conflict raged for the next three hours behind the dark cumulus clouds that had suddenly engulfed the majority of the Lugansk and Starobelsk regions. Guns thundered and crackled in the distance, followed by puffs of smoke signaling a downed aircraft.

All at once there was an eerie silence. Every remaining member of the battalion stood silently on the tiny airstrip of the airdrome and looked skyward. Suddenly, Lilia, Lyosha, and their entire battalion were gliding toward the base with their engines shut off, as if to punctuate their success. Moments before landing, Lilia turned her engine back on and playfully swooped to within 20 metres of the commanding officer's roof. The building rattled as blueprints and maps flew off the walls and swirled around the room. Major Raskova was furious.

Lilia then performed her signature 'rollover' communiqué. One roll meant one German kill. Two rolls meant two kills.

Lilia made two rolls that day. Inna knew the flap modification had done its job.

~

The adrenaline rush was gone, but the itchy mosquito bites remained.

Lilia wanted to head straight for her bunker, but she was intercepted by Lyosha.

"Is not a small celebration in order with our comrades?" referring to the day's air dominance.

"I can't," said Lilia, turning her head so Lyosha could not see her face.

"You gave your heart to another in battle," smiled Lyosha. "A German Ace perhaps?"

"That is a terrible thing to say, even in jest."

"Why? They seem to enjoy your interrogations."

"You want to celebrate with this?" asked an embar-rassed Lilia.

It really didn't matter to Lyosha. "You are always beautiful to me." But he was also sensitive to Lilia's obsession about her appearance. "Perhaps a smaller celebration is more appropriate."

"What did you have in mind?"

"Perhaps a walk, a clearing where we can make a fire and watch the sun set. I will even make the tea."

Lilia smiled and nodded. "Let us change."

~

Minutes later the couple were walking through a field and disappeared into the forest among the trees.

"Are they not beautiful?" asked Lilia as she stopped by two small carpets of pink daisies and white camomiles. "So brilliant, so alive."

Lyosha looked into Lilia's radiant blue eyes, "Yes, they are. I hope I am the cause."

Lilia blushed like a little girl then collected a bunch of flowers and handed them to Lyosha. Neither uttered a word.

Eventually the couple came upon a clearing which contained a lake so still, the reflection of the surrounding trees looked like a crisp photograph. The sheer beauty of the surroundings made Lilia feel far away from the war, the suffering, the pain, and the brutality. She raised her arms as if to embrace the whole world and began to recite one of her favorite poems by Pushkin.

> Snow, frost and sunshine... Lovely morning!
> Yet you, dear love, its magic scorning,
> Are still abed... Awake my sweet!
> Cast sleep away, I beg, and rising,
> Yourself a northern star, the blazing
> Aurora, northern beauty, meet.

Lyosha began to laugh. "Lilia, wake up! What frost? It's almost summer!"

Lilia, disappointed by Lyosha's insensitive response, began to defend herself. "What does it matter? It is my favorite verse."

"So you love Pushkin?" asked Lyosha.

"Of course, I always recited his poems at our school concerts." Lilia paused and smiled. "From your initial response, I wasn't sure you even knew Pushkin."

Lyosha responded with another challenge. "If you always recited Pushkin, recite another."

"With pleasure," smiled a confident Lilia.

> I love you-love you, e'en as I
> Rage at myself for this obsession,

> And as I make my shamed confession,
> Despairing at your feet I lie.
> I know, I know-It ill becomes me,
> I am too old, time to be wise...

Lyosha's response was unexpected to say the least. He stood next to Lilia and continued Pushkin's verse with inspiration.

> But how?...This love-it overcomes me,
> A sickness this is passion's guise.
> When you are near I'm filled with sadness,
> When far, I yawn, for life's a bore.
> I must pour out this love, this madness,
> There's nothing that I long for more.

Lilia was delighted at Lyosha's sensitivity. Another reason to love the man of her dreams. "Apparently you know this poem?"

"Why such a surprised look?" asked Lyosha, pretending to be insulted. "Can a man not feel?" He paused for emphasis. "Because I am from Siberia, does that mean I have a heart of ice ...."

Lilia felt terrible. She had accidentally offended. "Please, do not feel that way. I did not mean to imply any such thing."

"Apologies accepted," teased a now smiling Lyosha. "Experts know when to be gracious."

It was now Lilia's turn to play. "If you are such an expert in poetry, guess this poem's creator."

> How superstitiously we love,
> How tenderly towards our days declining...
> Beam brightly, brightly, farewell light of love,
> Of our last love, in evening heavens shining.

Lyosha sat on a fallen tree limb and began to laugh. "That was Tyutchev, Fyodor Tyutchev. Who doesn't know that!"

"Okay, my smart Captain, try to stump your Lieu-tenant."

"And, if I do, what is my prize?" smiled Lyosha with a devilish grin.

"A gentle kiss, from your toughest pilot."

> Oh yes, love, like a bird is free,
> Yes, I'm yours just the same!
> Yes, I shall see your fiery form
> In sweet dream after dream!
> Yes, the fierce strength of lovely arms,
> Eyes sad with treachery,
> Are all my fever of vain passion
> And give no peace to me.

Lilia was embarrassed. She had no answer. "I'm sorry to say, I do not recognize the verse."

"My literary genius, and you do not recognize Blok?"

"That was Blok? I thought I knew all his verses."

"Perhaps, your mind does not work well under pressure?" Lilia gave Lyosha a gentle push.

"No matter. It is time for me to collect my prize."

Lyosha could see his reflection in Lilia's eyes as they gently embraced and then kissed moistly and tenderly. Lilia was filled with emotion she had never experienced before.

"This is madness," she whispered in his ear.

"Hardly," he replied.

~

Hours passed in what seemed like minutes. The clouds began to set behind the sun turning the sky into bold splashes of purple, yellow, and orange.

"There is a chill in the air. Perhaps, we should head back," said Lilia.

"Let us stay till the sun sets and the stars rise. I will make a fire to keep us warm."

Lilia nodded. Lyosha gathered some small branches and placed them in small stone circle. He pulled a small box of wooden matches from his pocket. Moments later the couple sat near a pleasing fire.

Lyosha watched the flames dance in Lilia's steel-gray eyes while she smiled and stared at the handsome pilot, his ruddy complexion, his wavy black hair. Stared quietly at the ground.

"A ruble for your thoughts," smiled Lilia.

"I was just wondering."

"Wondering what?"

"If there had not been a war, would we have met?"

Lilia shrugged. It was a question with no answer.

In the distance, the faint sounds of cannons continued their assault.

"Must we kill to love?"

"Are you saying you love me?" smiled Lilia warmly. "I would prefer your answer first."

"My brave Captain suddenly wants to follow."

"Perhaps he is afraid of being shot down."

"And, what of me?"

Emotions surged while silence descended.

Lilia knew she had never told Lyosha she loved him in so many words. "I would like to read you something," said Lilia who had suddenly turned serious.

Lyosha nodded. Lilia took a folded piece of newspaper out of her pocket.

Wait for me, and I'll come back,
Wait and I'll come.
Wait through autumn's yellow rains And
its tedium.
Steel your heart and do not grieve,
Wait through winter's haze,
Wait through wind and raging storm,
Wait through summer's blaze.
Wait when others wait no more,
When my letters stop,
Wait with hope that never wanes,
Wait and don't give up.

As Lilia continued, and reflections of yellow flames danced upon her face. Lyosha was breathless with emotion.

Wait for me and I'll come back,
Patience, dear one, learn.
Turn away from those who say
That I will not return.
Let my son and mother weep
Tears of sorrow, let
Friends insist that it is time,
That you must forget.
Do not listen to their kind
Words of sympathy,
Do not join them if they drink
To my memory....

Lyosha's eyes swelled with tears. He was shocked, surprised, touched. "It is staggeringly beautiful. Who has written this verse?"

"A young poet named Konstantin Simonov. I read his poem in *Pravda*, and knew I had to keep it close. Although, at the time, I did not know why."

"Then it is about us," said Lyosha. "You and I. About all the people who love each other. About war..."

"No," said Lilia, "It is not about war. It is about love. About faith. About life."

Lyosha finally asked THE question. "Lilia, will you always wait for me?"

Lilia reached for Lyosha's hand. "Yes. And you?"

"Me too. But, we will never die."

"Never?"

"We will always be, if perhaps, somewhere in time. That is my pledge to you."

Chapter 35

The indefatigable Lilia tempts Lady Luck, again and again.

May 1943
Gorlovka, Ukraine...

THE TIDES OF WAR were shifting.

Baranov's 473rd regiment had consistently more than held its own against the faster, more powerful Messerschmitts and their vaunted Aces. Still, privately there had been significant air fatalities. Baranov treated every loss with deep regret. These pilots were more than just soldiers in uniform; they were his extended family. When one fell, fatherly guilt arrived and then magnified. He would challenge himself, what more could I have done to prevent the fatality? How can I reduce future losses?

A plan evolved. "Captain Solomatin, I require your assistance," said Baranov one evening after a particularly difficult day of aerial dogfights.

"Comrade Baranov, whatever you require."

"You lead the men and women well. They unselfishly display their willingness to place themselves in harm's way. But, I believe they fire many more rounds than need be, sometimes they die because they are too obvious. They need to become more difficult targets. More surprising attackers."

"I do not disagree. But the question is how?"

"I would like you to conduct a low-fire practice."

"I am not sure I understand."

"Identify the highest hill in our flying zone. Take our most skilled mechanics and engineers, and construct a target site that approximates the size of a Messerschmitt. Then teach our pilots to hit the target at full throttle."

"Comrade Baranov, I see but one issue," said Lyosha tactfully.

"And, that is?"

"The tallest hills in the area are no more than 1500 metres. To fly that low, hit the targets accurately, and return unscathed will be a difficult task."

"Any more difficult than destroying an enemy that travels 100 kilometres an hour faster at 6000 metres among the clouds?"

~

Katya ran missions for ten months without a break. She felt her success spoke for itself. She didn't need or want any additional target practice.

"What can it hurt?" said Lilia when Solamatin's firing practice program was announced.

"How many missions have we flown together?" said Katya.

"Eighty-seven."

"And, how many times have we been injured or even scarred?"

"None."

"I rest my case," concluded Katya. "If the maneuvers were not under Lyosha's authority, would you volunteer participation?"

Lilia's face scoured. Her answer took Katya by surprise."I say yes because so far, Lady Luck has been on our side. But there will come a difficult time, an outnumbered battle, when every round will count. I wish to be prepared. I have dreams to fulfill after the war."

Katya paused. She thought of fallen Comrades Novikov, Smirov, Lyubimova, and the others—all fine young pilots who had perished in the preceding weeks. "Perhaps they had no Lady Luck?" replied Katya with a confidence that bordered on arrogant.

~

Lilia felt strange standing in front of the man she loved. The sky was a cloudless sapphire blue, and the broad winged hawks circled effortlessly. Yet the talk was not of the feelings they shared or nature's bounty. It was killing and maiming an enemy she would hear and feel but could not see or touch.

"Is it as hard for you as for me?" asked the man who could read her thoughts, feel her feelings.

Lilia's eyes stared toward the dry, dusty earth. Her head shaking in disbelief.

"Our enemy is a worthy adversary. You fly like the wind, but kill like sparrow."

"You know it is not my nature?"

Lyosha stared sternly. Sounding more squadron leader than lover. "Nor is it mine. But fate has placed us in this position at this point in history. We have a job to do. You must become angry when flight bound. Assume each round you fire was meant to annihilate a fascist. Think of each miss as the potential loss of a comrade. Purpose will breed focus."

Lilia's eyes peered deeply into the man standing in front of her. She sighed and took a deep breath. "I understand. Then let us begin. How will you make me a more effective fighter?"

Lyosha explained Baranov's low flying target maneuver then pointed to her plane. "Once air bound, just follow my lead."

Lilia paused on the wing of her plane before entering the cockpit. "Captain, will you need any instruction on how to fly so low at high speeds?"

Lyosha smiled, pursed his lips and blew a kiss.

"White Lily, White Lily, over," radioed Lyosha as they headed toward their target on the hill. "Allow your flying skills to get as close to the target as possible before firing your machine gun and cannons in short concentrated bursts to compensate for their lack of longer range accuracy."

"Into the eye of the storm, over," responded Lilia.

"Our skill and bravery will mask our lack of firepower. We will storm the enemy with surprise," smiled a confident Lyosha. "They also are unaware of our shortcomings. Or the fact that we are sending women to do a man's job."

Lilia glanced at her flying mate and smiled. The confidence in Lyosha's voice, gave Lilia the strength of conviction. "Roger and over, Comrade."

~

Katya's charmed life came to an abrupt halt on 06 June 1943.

The German ground forces near the front were starting to become fractionalized as the prospects of significant air support declined.

Lilia and Katya were cruising side by side at an altitude of some 8000 metres. "White Lily, no krauts at west 90 or 180, over," radioed Katya as she entered a thick cloud formation.

"The same at east 90 and 180."

(The girls incorrectly assumed if there were enemy planes they would be to their right or left at a similar altitude).

Suddenly a half a dozen Messerschmitts dropped through the clouds above, cannons blazing as they headed straight for the girls.

Lilia saw them first. She banked sharply and then began an acrobatic spin downward, making her an almost impossible target.

Katya chose to stay and make a statement. The two-way reign of gunfire was vicious. Katya downed one plane. The other five tried to surround her. She escaped, all but one, by flying up and down like a roller coaster.

The enemy pilot strafed the left side of Katya's plane quite badly. One of her cannons was now inoperative. The German, sensing the end near, kept firing. Katya tried to return the fire from the remaining cannon but missed badly. Suddenly Katya felt a sting in the leg. She had been hit and was bleeding profusely. The rush of blood caused her to become lightheaded. She had no alternative but to descend in the hopes that Lilia was nearby. Lilia watched Katya swoop to some 1500 metres while the enemy paused in disbelief, giving Lilia the opening she needed. Lilia sped to the aid of her friend, viciously strafing the fascist with cannons blazing in short bursts as she had been taught. Seconds later, the enemy was a spiraling, flaming mass.

After they landed, Katya hobbled over to Lilia and gave her a big 'thank you' hug. "I have learned. I will begin my firing practice with Lyosha before I fly another mission."

As Katya was taken to the hospital tent, Lilia stared at the white flowers on her plane. She wondered, had the white flowers become her guardian protectors? After all, she had survived so many sorties where others had been maimed or killed.

That evening Lyosha explained his theory. "It appears to me, the more experience you get, the 'more slices of luck" you receive."

~

The German ace's report was depressing. "We lost but one," said the pilot, trying to put a positive spin on what had just transpired.

"And them?" asked the Major.

"There were only two."

"And them?" said the exasperated Major, repeating the question.

"That lady with the flowers, came from nowhere. Our bad fortune."

"We have battled enough. It's not about fortune," sneered the Major. "The lady is a worthy opponent. But, we must do all within our power to break her string of luck. She provides too much inspiration for Stalin's other peasant flyers."

~

The following day, Lilia was aggressively pursuing a Heinkel 111 bomber with Lyosha acting as wingman to protect her flank from a rogue flyer. Both certain she had just killed the mid-upper gunner in the bomber directly ahead, she descended at a right angle. Her goal? To down the enemy aircraft by destroying the second engine. She pressed her machine trigger firmly. The engine burst into flames. Just before the plane began to nosedive, she was surprised by a sustained burst of gunfire that pierced her engine's cowling. Lilia's engine stopped dead; she began to slowly glide downward, steering her plane away from the nearby descending ball of fire.

Lyosha assumed her plane had stalled briefly. "Call name, White Lily. White Lily," calmly instructed Lyosha "friendly field, 44 kilometres, 80 degrees left. Repeat 80 degrees left."

"Red Mountain [Lyosha's call name], message received. Under control," responded Lilia calmly, realizing there was little Lyosha could do.

Lyosha, unaware of the true danger of her situation, radioed a compliment.

"Nice work, White Lily, the fascists are abandoning aircraft and bailing out."

Lilia did not respond as she braced for an extremely difficult emergency landing. She knew she was losing altitude in a safe zone, somewhere in the Ukraine. She also realized she couldn't reach Lyosha's suggested destination without power. Her only option: a nearby open patch surrounded by tress.

Lyosha noticed Lilia suddenly start to descend. He repeated the target field location.

Lilia had no choice but to reveal the magnitude of her problem.

"Red Mountain, no engine power. Repeat, no power."

Lyosha was horrified but calm. His heart beat wildly. He did not want to lose his lady love in this fashion. He swooped dangerously low to the ground, looking for the flattest, clearest spot for Lilia to land her plane.

"27 degrees right, one mile, best opportunity."

"Thank you, Red Mountain."

The initial shock of the landing situation had worn off. Lilia now realized she had been hit, badly. The pain was appalling. She could feel the blood flowing down her leg, and she wondered if she would land the aircraft before she passed out. Anatoliy's agonizing screams on the airdrome radio reverberated in her ears. She would not do the same to Lyosha; after all, there was absolutely nothing more he could do. She shut down radio transmission.

Fortunately, Lyosha had selected well. The landing field was a long, wide strip of pasture with few trees of substance.

The Yak, with its undercarriage still folded inside the wings, banged and slithered across the field on its belly some 500 metres. It hit a rut and spun around violently before coming to an abrupt halt. Lilia looked around for a split second. She was amazed the plane was still in one piece. Her adrenaline was now full bore as she quickly unfastened her harness, pulled back the canopy over her head, climbed out, and scrambled for an open space. Within seconds, the plane exploded into an orange ball, the force lifting Lilia a metre off the ground.

An exhausted Lilia lay on her back. The blood was pouring out of her leg, and the inside of her boot felt soggy. Lyosha flew low across the field, and she waved her arm vigorously. He had already radioed their position to home base, and continued to circle the crash-landing site to give the ground rescue transport a visual marker.

During the wait, Lilia hobbled to the fallen tree trunk, took her trademark bright red scarf from her neck, and made a tourniquet around her thigh to stop the bleeding; she sat and waited.

Lyosha, running low on fuel, turned for the base, making one more pass over Lilia.

She waved and blew him a kiss as he disappeared behind the tree line.

Minutes later, the transport arrived and a concerned Major Baranov himself jumped out.

Lilia knew Baranov's presence was the ultimate professional complement. Their relationship had come a long way since its rocky beginning.

"Lilia, are you all right?" said the Major.

"Yes Comrade Major," smiled Lilia who stood up to salute and promptly fainted from the significant loss of blood.

~

Anna Litvyak cried as her daughter hobbled into her Novoslobodskaya Street apartment on crutches. "Mummy, there is no need for sympathy; I'm fine."

Lilia explained her version of the truth to her mother. "It was just a freak accident. I didn't see an exposed rivet as I slid off the wing after completing a sortie. It pierced my leg quite deeply. I needed about twenty stitches to close the wound."

The terminology was all foreign to Anna. "What's a sortie? How do rivets become exposed?"

Lilia explained as best she could. But she was careful not to let her mother know she had actually been wounded in combat.

"The doctors gave me time off to recuperate. Let us enjoy ourselves before I return."

Lilia then made an usual request. "Do you still have the sewing machine father bought for my birthday?"

"Certainly. It is in the other room. I still use it from time to time, but arthritis has made the use of machinery more difficult."

"I'm so sorry, Mummy."

"There is nothing to be sorry about. Arthritis is part of the aging process. You will see for yourself when you reach my age."

After lunch and tea, Lilia pulled some strips of colored parachute cloth from the small bag she carried on her shoulder.

"What are you going to do with those scraps, my child?"

"In war time, soldiers learn to make due. I like to fly my plane with a scarf around my neck. It keeps the dampness out. Besides, it is something no one else does in my regiment."

Anna laughed. "My child, you always have had a mind of your own."

They spent the entire week together while Lilia healed and sewed.

"Be careful, my beautiful daughter," pleaded Anna as Lilia made ready to return to the war.

"I have a gift," said Lilia, handing her mother a white scarf. "This is for you to use during the winter. Every time you place it around your neck, you will feel the warmth of my heart and love."

~

During the next two weeks, Lilia and Lyosha performed their missions flawlessly. Without warning, Lyosha became ill with the flu. He could not fly without throwing up. He was ordered to rest.

"Not to worry," said Lilia by his bedside. "You have taught me a great deal. I promise Katya will take good care of me up there."

That very afternoon, word came of a German supply convoy making its way to the front. The 473rd mission was to stop their advance, thereby weakening the Germans front line position.

"Since we are down a number of pilots and planes," said Baranov, "I have made arrangements with the 73rd regiment at Kirov airdrome to fly with us."

The mixed squadron of ten planes rained hell on the convoy for almost twenty minutes. In the end, all that remained was a pile of rubble. As they headed back to their respective bases, four belated Messerschmitts surprised Lilia and a pilot of the 73rd from the rear. She split off and did a sharp turn and a flip to avoid the attackers while the others called for help. One of the Messerschmitts had dropped altitude and was waiting for Lilia as she leveled. His guns ripped through Lilia's cockpit window, wounding her in the arm and shoulder. Blood splattered the windshield. She wasn't sure how badly she was hurt, but she was having trouble controlling her plane with one functioning arm and hand. She decided to land abruptly in an open field and dashed from the plane into the nearby woods.

One of the Messerschmitts spotted the flowers on her fuselage. He knew he had the chance to capture or kill a true war prize. He landed not far from Lilia's plane then headed for the woods, pistol in hand. At that moment, a Russian Yak from the 73rd spotted Lilia's plane, swooped down and destroyed the German plane. The angry pilot became incensed. He then circled and landed. Lilia jumped in the plane and they headed back to her base.

"Comrade, thanks for saving my life," said Lilia, her blonde hair quite visible.

"My pleasure, White Lily. I will have something to tell the grandchildren."

Minutes later, the plane landed in Russian territory. Lilia climbed out of the cockpit. She assumed the pilot would follow. Instead, once she was clear, he waved goodbye and took off. Lilia never learned his name or saw him again. She also wondered how he knew her call sign.

~

Being wounded twice caused Lilia to rethink Lady Luck. Perhaps she was not sitting on Lilia's shoulder.

At the same time, her recent brushes with death made her more determined than ever to pause the German war machine. "Let me shoot down the balloon," pleaded Lilia to Comrade Baranov two days later.

(The German giant hidrogenium-filled balloon fitted with sophisticated intelligence equipment had been a threat to the broad swatches of the Russian front for some time. It was heavily protected by two rings of antiaircraft guns with $360°$ capability.)

Baranov refused the request. Numerous Soviet airmen had lost their lives trying to destroy the target by penetrating the German's heretofore impenetrable wall of fire.

Besides, Lilia was again just out of the hospital and not completely healed from her most recent ordeal. The doctors strongly suggested she regain her strength by again visiting her mother in Moscow. Instead, she would not leave the front area. She merely rested quietly in the bunker until she was strong enough to plead her case with Major Baranov.

"Absolutely not. You have no right to fly."

Lilia responded equally boldly. "If you do not let me do this, I shall go without your permission."

"You cannot disregard orders!"

"I can't?"

Baranov could see the fire in her eyes, the passion in her heart. If it had been anyone but Lilia, he would have had her placed under house arrest for insubordination.

"I presume you have a plan since no one else has been able to penetrate the target."

"I do, Comrade Baranov."

"Then let me hear it, Lieutenant."

After listening, he was convinced her plan contained a worthy strategy that just might work if executed properly.

Four hours later, Lilia sat patiently in her plane on the runway, waiting for the sun to move into a precise position. Suddenly she took off and flew, not straight to the front line, but parallel to it, to the area where there were no troops or artillery. She then crossed the front line and flew to the rear, so that she approached the balloon from the direction of the sun. German troops could see nothing but blinding rays of the sun if they even looked in that direction.

Moments later, Lilia's guns were firing at the target dead ahead. The balloon burst into flames. She could hear the screams of agony from those aboard what was left of the balloon. She headed straight toward the gun emplacements. In that split second, she jammed her rudder stick down and began firing in short concentrated blasts. The human carnage was everywhere. She circled back once more time and emptied what remained in her cannons to insure no one or nothing remained. Then she climbed straight up and headed back to the base.

As she approached the airdrome, she decided to signal a victory. She dropped to less than 200 metres and started doing acrobatics over the field. The activity caused the covers of the aircraft sitting on the runway to flap violently in the Lilia-created wind. Two covers ripped from their rivets and blew up the hill. Baranov was furious at her showboating. "I will destroy her for what she is doing," he shouted. "I will teach her a lesson. She will pay for the repairs."

As she taxied up to Inna she said, "Did our father shout and curse at me?"

"With all his fury."

Baranov ordered her to his office at once. The moment she walked in the door, he threw her flying cap on the table, picked up his chair and slammed it on the floor.

"Comrade Litvyak, what the hell do you think you are doing?"

"Celebrating, Comrade Baranov."

"Celebrating what?"

"The balloon exists no more. Nor do the gun emplacements. Nor the troops guarding."

Baranov's tirade turned into a smile. "Congrat-ulations, Comrade Litvyak."

Two weeks later, Lilia was officially awarded the Order of the Red Banner for her heroic deed

Chapter 36

Hitler's view of women differed considerably from Stalin's.

June 1943
Berlin...

GERMAN BORN AND BRED Millie Brandt, 20, was Lilia's counterpart. She was intelligent, educated, and attractive at 5 '6" with long black hair, light blue eyes, and a fabulous figure. Like most Germans of the time, she was moved by Hitler's hypnotic oratory that over-whelmed the rational mind and left audiences in a fury of indignation coupled with a terrifying sense of impending disaster. At the same time, she rejected Hitler's frequently stated notion of a

296

women that "your world is your husband, your family, your children, and your home."

Millie, like Lilia, saw no reason why she should be excluded from wartime activities. Women had a role. But while the pragmatic Stalin had a growing acceptance of the need for and use of women in the defense of the Motherland, Hitler steadfastly rejected women's emancipation or anything that resembled a feminist movement. That belief system permeated the German military command, making Millie's aspirations more difficult, but in her mind's eye, not impossible.

~

"You want to see who?" said the starched, incredulous sentinel outside the German Chancellery in Berlin.

"The Führer."

"Might I ask what your business is?"

"I would like to discuss how women can be employed in war service."

"Oh, I see," sneered the sentinel. "I'm sure the Führer would like to hear your ideas, but he's just a little preoccupied right now running the country, handling the war, and planning invasions. Could you come back in about five years?"

"That is an ignorant joke." replied Millie.

"Fraulein," said the now agitated soldier taking the rifle from his shoulder. "Go, before I use this for real."

Millie decided to try another approach. She went around to the rear of the Chancellery. She found the laundry area and slipped into a rolling cart. Once in the building, she wandered the halls until she actually found the heavily guarded Führer's office. She approached the guard. "I have an appointment to see the Führer."

"Really. About what?

"Plans for war service."

"Silly Mädchen [girl], leave before I am forced to detain you. And, I guarantee that will be unpleasant."

The guard took her hand. She started to yell. "Take your hands off me you big oaf." At that moment Reichsmarschall Herman Göring surrounded by members of his entourage walked by. Millie recognized him from pictures in the newspaper.

"What is all the commotion about?"

"This little worm says she has an appointment to see the Führer about war crimes."

"War service."

"I beg your pardon."

"Get her out of here," sneered Göring angrily, "through the back stairs. Nobody comes into this building unannounced."

Millie held her ground as the guard tried to pull her away. "Suppose I had you imprisoned for insolence?" said Göring.

"After or before I discuss war service."

The group was horrified. Rarely did anyone tell Göring what they really thought for fear of reprisal. Göring rather liked Millie's passion and resolve, but he also needed to maintain his chain of command. "Young Fraulein, let us go to my office and see what war service ideas you have. But, I warn you in advance there can be consequences."

Moments later Mille explained her idea to create an organization called *Trummerfrauen* ("Women of the Rubble"). These women would perform associated war tasks such as:

bind and guard prisoners, tend the wounded, bury the dead, and salvage belongings.

Göring was intrigued but skeptical. "Do you really think women would volunteer to do such things?"

Millie came well prepared. "I've thought of that, Herr Göring. I think a propaganda campaign of patriotic posters would attract a number of young women to help with the cause."

Trummerfrauen was born two weeks later. Millie would eventually recruit 10,000 women aged 18 to 40, mostly single, who would make significant efforts to the German cause and morale without ever firing a bullet.

Stalin heard the story of Millie Brandt through his intelligence operatives who had infiltrated the Nazi Party. He saw the story as a great opportunity to further galvanize Russian females in support of his regime, and, ultimately, The Great Patriotic War, which he believed was just over the horizon. By the time Stalin's propaganda machine had "retooled" the story for Russian eyes, it was the Germans who owned a peasant's intellect, forcing their women to perform only the most demeaning war time tasks. They were compared to Russian women who were welcomed by Stalin in the Russian Army, according to Stalin.

The modified story deeply touched the Russian populace. Thousands of letters poured into the Kremlin from women of all ages, pledging support of his Communist agenda. Subsequent editions of *Pravda* always included one or two feature stories about the exploits of heroic, determined Russian women who supported the defense of the Motherland.

Chapter 37

Girls will be girls, even during wartime

IT WAS LIKE MANNA from heaven.

A deeply overcast day with massive bulbous dark clouds, sheets of heavy rain, and brisk, swirling winds.

Baranov had no choice but to call off planned missions. As he stood in front of his battalion, he looked straight at Lilia. "You have all flown hard and long. Use this time to rest and heal your physical and emotional wounds." Lilia agreed.

As the pilots left the tent, Lyosha approached Lilia, flanked by Inna, Katya, and a spunky, confident, dark-haired newcomer, Raisa, who had recently joined the 586th after surviving a tour with *Da Nachthexen*. "Shall we share the time?" said her handsome pilot. Lilia stopped, looked at her smiling friends, and then tenderly touched Lyosha's hand.

"Do not take this the wrong way, my love, but I would like some time with the ladies."

Lyosha looked lovingly into her eyes. "I understand." Even though he didn't.

"I know what you are thinking," observed an astute Lilia.

Lyosha smiled and shrugged his shoulders.

"How is it that men can gather, drink, tell stories, and talk about women?"

No more needed to be said. Lyosha tipped his cap and left. Raisa noticed the bath hut empty.

"I propose we treat ourselves to a hot bath, to cleanse the grit and grime of war from our bodies, at least for a few moments," suggested Raisa.

"And, I have our bath towels," said the ever-resourceful Lilia, taking the sheet off her bunk.

Katya went first. She bathed and bathed. "Leave some warm water for the rest," teased Inna.

Finally, some forty minutes later, the refreshed women were wrapped in bed sheets huddled around the warm stove, at peace with the world.

"You have trained Lyosha well," laughed Raisa. "I'm not sure I could get my boyfriend to accept such wishes at such a time."

"Tell us about him," smiled Lilia.

Raisa paused. She was tempted, as so many other female warriors, to imagine a true relationship in her life. "There is nothing to tell."

"Don't be shy," giggled Katya uncharacteristically. "Tell us all about him. We want to know. Don't we, girls?"

Raisa took a small guitar decorated with a red bow from the wall above her bed. "I will let you imagine my Yuri by playing our song." She began to sing and play *Dark Is The Night,* a tender moving war song about love, departure, and hope for a future reconnection.

> The night is dark,
> only bullets are whistling in the field,
> and the wind is moaning, the stars are twinkling.
> You are waiting for me,
> you are not sleeping sitting at the baby's cradle and wiping tears secretly.
> How I love the depth of your tender eyes,
> how I want to press my lips to your eyes.
> The dark night is separating us, my love,
> and the black disturbing steppe lies between us.
> I believe in you, my dear friend,
> this belief saves me from death.
> I am calm in a dangerous battle-
> I know, you will meet me with love whatever happens with me...

As Raisa sang, Lilia imagined a day when all this would be over, when she and Lyosha and their children would spend happy holidays with Mummy and all her friends, new and old.

Inna, ever the joker, imagined a samovar with hot tea and herbs, a jar of currant jam, a jug of honey, a roll of boubliks (bagels), and some good cheer. "Have some tea and fresh baked boubliks while we share the holiday."

When Raisa finished, a dreamy silence entered the room as each girl imagined something near and dear. Lilia walked the wildflowers fields with her Mummy. Raisa recalled family and friends on New Year's Day. The singing, the laughter. Inna remembered her first kiss. The touch. The breath. And,

Katya felt the breeze in her hair as her crop duster hovered over the fields where she grew up.

Some time passed. Katya broke the silence. "Raisa, it is time to play something cheerful. My heart wants to laugh."

Raisa was ready to oblige—with the proper intro-duction. "Take the curtain, make a screen, and introduce me," laughed Raisa.

Katya willingly complied. She stood on a chair, holding the curtain to shield Raisa from the other girls who were now clapping and cheering in anticipation. "Ladies and gentlemen. The 586th musical regiment takes great pleasure in bringing you the beautiful, the talented, Lyubov Orlova, who has taken time from filming *The Merry Guys* [arguably the most acclaimed and popular Russian musical comedy of the time] to join us here this evening."

As Raisa became Orlova, the songs became more joyful, more playful. Katya yanked the dark blanket from her bed, and draped it around herself like a man's suit. "My dear," said Katya in a deep masculine tone, "May I have the pleasure of this dance?"

Inna played along. Her eyes fluttered. "I would be pleased to accept the invitation of such a strong, handsome man."

Raisa began to play *Svetit Mesyats*.

> The moon is shining,
> shining brightly
> The white nightfall is shining too.
> My pathway is eliminated
> All the way to the Sasha's place...

The imaginary party was now in full swing. Lilia, with no partner to speak of, decided to entice Inna's man (Katya) to switch partners. She took a second sheet and quickly constructed a risqué dress with a slit down the side, revealing her shapely leg. "And, who would the man rather dance with?" she said, purring provocatively.

Before long, every sheet, the blanket and the curtain in the hut had found another use. The place was a mess. "Who has seen '*The Merry Guys*'?" asked Raisa.

Everybody raised her hand. "I propose each of you becomes a musical instrument in my jazz band."

The idea sounded like great fun. "I wish to be a bass drum," volunteered Katya.

Inna preferred to be a trumpet and Lilia a piano. Raisa lifted her arm. "Ladies, let us begin."

Lilia decided a little teasing was in order. "Inna, your trumpet sounds like a mechanic is playing." Inna laughed. She decided to respond by picking up a pillow and taking a playful swing at Lilia. Lilia ducked; the pillow hit Katya. She in turn picked up a pillow to respond. Before long, the four girls were banging each other with pillows. Suddenly, one pillow case burst open. Then another. Feathers were everywhere. The exhausted girls fell to the floor and lay side-by-side.

"So Raisa, tell us more about Yuri," said a smiling Lilia who wanted to make small talk.

"There is nothing to tell," responded a suddenly sanguine Raisa. "Yuri died months ago in battle."

The reverie ceased. The room was stone-cold silent. "I understand," said Lilia trying to provide comfort.

Raisa raised her eyebrows and released a deep sigh. "How could you? Your Lyosha mirrors your every step. He wills you to success and safety."

"And I him."

Raisa stepped into her personal abyss. "My Yuri had no such privileges."

"Does your heart blame me for that?"

"That was certainly not my intention."

Katya and Inna tugged on Lilia's arm as if to say, stop before Raisa's sorrow forms dark clouds.

The message was received.

Lilia smiled. "Our struggle is difficult. Private times are few. Let Ms. Lyubov continue to entertain."

Raisa picked up her guitar; once again, the girls began to sing and dance.

Suddenly the door swung open. Major Baranov walked in. He pretended to be furious.

The stunned girls instinctively ranked up, looking ridiculous in their sheets and blankets and such. They tried to be serious, but when they glanced at each other, they began to giggle.

"Ladies, may I remind you we are soldiers at war, not children in kindergarten. I'm certain our enemy does not have time for a pajama party or whatever you were doing to create such a mess."

"Yes, Major," uttered the girls in innocent unison.

Baranov had all he could do to keep a straight face. "I want you in proper uniform and this placed restored before you attend mess! I also want to know the instigator. Perhaps a few days in the guardhouse will restore perspective."

Baranov turned and walked stiffly out the door. The girls looked at each other and burst into laughter.

Baranov, overhearing the burst of gaiety, shrugged his shoulders, shook his head and laughed. The women's girlish behavior reminded him of his own youthful antics. How he loved to show off in gymnastics! A mischievous smile came over his face. He looked around to see if any of his men were in the vicinity. There were none, so he completed a giant cartwheel... twice... and then dashed back to his hut.

~

The women's hut had been restored to its former order, and the girls were in proper military garb when they arrived at mess for dinner. Lilia looked around. She realized some, perhaps many, of the youthful faces in that room would never return home.

The damp chill penetrated her heart as the girls returned to their quarters. Once inside, they again huddled around the stove. Lilia turned wistful.

"Perhaps we can take the chill out of the air by sharing hopes and dreams?"

The other girls had never thought of such an exercise but rather liked the idea.

Katya simply began to speak. "I would like to discover new fertilizers to make the harvests more plentiful, so no one will ever want for food. And then I would like to take the advanced flying skills I have gained to manage a fleet of crop dusters for the state."

"I want to be a test pilot. Try new planes," volunteered Inna.

"But you're a mechanic," said Raisa.

"No," smiled Inna confidently, "I am an aerial artist. My skills make pilots like you fly faster, fly higher."

"Then why not become a pilot now? The war has opened the door."

"I believe I can best serve the cause of the Motherland by doing what I am doing. But when the war is over, I want to play a part in making new planes, new flying machines that will avoid the possibility of future wars."

It was Raisa's turn. She leaned back and laughed. "I have already revealed my wish. I want a strong, gentle, determined yet sensitive man. I also wish him to be handsome, virile, faithful, and fun loving."

Inna rolled her eyes. "That might require some extensive search and discover."

The girls all laughed.

"No problems. The war has made me an expert in search and discover!"

"It is time for our poster child to reveal all,' teased Katya, referring to Lilia's wartime poster which now seemed to be everywhere.

"Can I have more than one wish?"

"Dreams and wishes are not restricted by rules," said Katya.

"My first wish is to be as my mother. I wish a happy family of two, perhaps three children. And, a long life with Lyosha."

"Children of what gender?" asked Raisa.

"It doesn't really matter. So long as they are healthy and loving."

"That seems like a full dream," smiled Inna. "You have more?"

Lilia picked up her cup of tea and looked at each of the girls, one by one.

"I believe when this war is over, planes will fly the heavens regularly carrying civilians, not just soldiers. I wish to fly those planes. Even more importantly, I wish to manage an organization that builds those planes so that people of different languages and cultures will have the opportunity to meet easily and frequently to resolve their differences."

The girls were speechless. Their days were consumed with their survival and the defense of the Motherland against a madman who wanted to dominate the world. They simply had no frame of reference for Lilia's breathtaking dreams. Family. Love. Equality. Peace. Did she dream too big?

•

Chapter 38

Boys will be boys, and girls will be girls, even during wartime.

BARANOV SAT QUIETLY in his quarters, staring into an empty glass, the unopened vodka bottle by its side. There was an eerie silence afoot. No howitzers firing in the distance, no planes circling in the air.

Lyosha entered to ask a question about the morning mission. He noticed the Major's despondent mood. He assumed news from the front was not good. "Comrade Major, are there are unforeseen difficulties with the enemy?"

"Captain, you know things go well," responded Baranov brusquely. "The Fascists are weakening. Do you not see that with each passing day?" Lyosha was confused. Why, then, Baranov's demeanor?

"Captain, do you know what today is?"

"Perhaps not," responded Lyosha, apologetically.

"I am entering the winter of my years. Today I am 50. If the war doesn't take me, old age surely will."

Lyosha wanted to laugh at the Major's vanity, but he dared not. "Comrade Major, you are strong, you are in control. You have many, many good years left. You will outlive us all."

"Unlikely."

~

After deftly retreating from the Major's quarters, Lyosha decided to discuss the issue with Lilia and Baranov's close Non-Commissioned Officer confidant, Sgt. Igor Bulatov. "Comrades, the Major seems deeply depressed."

Lilia became alarmed. "I thought the battle was turning."

"His depression is caused by other matters. Today is his 50th birthday."

"I didn't realize the Major was that old," responded Lilia, now 21 years and 7 months.

"You sound just like him," said Lyosha. "I propose we change his mood with a birthday celebration complete with gifts."

"My clever captain," smiled Lilia, "how do you propose such a celebration in the middle of the war?"

Lyosha had a plan. He suggested he would notify the regiment of a surprise celebration at the mess. Baranov would be told there were some food shortages that he needed to see for himself. There would be three gifts. The Sergeant was charged with finding a pack or two of Comrade Stalin's favorite brand of cigarette, Herzegovina Flor. Lyosha and other volunteers would clean and buff the Major's vehicle, and Lilia would visit a nearby village to gather some scarce provisions to make an unusual tricolor layer birthday cake using potatoes, onions, and beets. All of the other guests would be asked to contribute a shot or two of vodka from their private stashes, so the appropriate toasts could be made.

About three hours later, the preparations were complete. The war had cooperated. There were no military emergencies. The Sergeant summoned the Major. When he entered the tent, the entire regiment raised their tin cups to toast their guest while Lyosha offered the traditional birthday wish for a friend.

> We wish you a long and successful life.
> We wish you excellent health.
> Most importantly, we wish you
> happiness without measure every day!

Baranov looked around the room. It was filled with love and affection. These were his children. He was touched deeply. Despite trying to hide his emotions, a small tear formed in the corner of his eye. "I do not know what to say. For one of the few times in his life, your Major is speechless. Thank you, may God protect all of you."

Lilia then walked into the room with her layered birthday cake. "It never occurred to me, you did woman's work," laughed Baranov, "since you order so many men in battle." Baranov looked at Lyosha affectionately, "This officer will make some man a wonderful wife one day. She exceeds all the requirements of a Russian woman." Baranov then took occasion to remind the men of the traditional definition of a woman. "Through the ages, our women have built a unique self-reliance. They can stop runaway trains with their hands and then enter a burning building to remove those threatened. Now we can add an additional comment to the saying," smiled Baranov at Lilia, "when their work is done, they also make delicious birthday cakes!"

~

"It is now time for the presentation of gifts," said Lyosha. The Sergeant handed the Major a crudely-made cardboard box filled with Herzegovinas elegantly wrapped in gauze pads. "Compliments of Comrade Stalin." The regiment roared their approval as the Major lit one of the cigarettes and blew smoke rings in the air.

"Now Comrade Major, please join us outside," instructed Lyosha. There sat the Major's usual dusty car, shining brightly in the sun. He sat in the front seat and scanned the dashboard.

"The car has features I never realized," laughed the Major. "Who performed such a task?"

Lyosha raised his hand. "Another surprise," said the Major. "The man who flies like a bird, cleans like a monkey."

There was one last matter. Lyosha had arranged with the regiment photographer to take a picture of the Major and his car. The Major decided he should not be alone. "Sergeant, I wish you and Lyosha to join my picture." He paused. "And my daughter too," said Baranov reaching out for Lilia's hand. The photographer then captured the moment in time as Baranov lifted his boot to show the sergeant he missed a spot, while Lilia slinked attractively across the hood of the car like a female ornament, and Lyosha looked on.

Chapter 39

Katya mugs for the camera in a publicity picture.

May 1943...

KATYA RECEIVED WORD FROM home that her
father was quite ill and dying. She decided to write a letter to
cheer his spirits as best she could.

> "Dear Father,
> At this writing, the war effort
> goes well. I have become quite the accomplished
> pilot. Thanks to you for letting me go to the
> factory in Moscow. Without your support, I

might still be leading the life of a peasant farmer.

My work here is noble. I have made two close friends, Inna and Lilia, whom I will bring home for you to meet when we have completed our mission. Your little girl now flies planes at 650 kilometres per hour. And, I have become quite the marksman.

I'm enclosing a recent picture of me taken by a press photographer for a story that ran in *Pravda* about myself and my comrades. Did you see it? Imagine, your little girl, a military action hero for all the country to see.

You are always in my thoughts. Have to go now. More Germans to kill!
Many Hugs,
Katya"

~

Katya's sister, Olga, read the letter to her frail father, Sergei Budanov, the moment it arrived at the house.

She held a picture of her smiling sister entering her cockpit to jog his failing memory. Sergei remembered. He smiled and slowly placed the picture on his chest near his heart. Moments later he passed away peacefully.

~

Daniil had been transferred. The evening he left, he and Katya held hands near the transport tuck. "We will write," he said as he looked in her eyes. "After the war..." Katya put her hand to his lips. She did not want to think of such matters. Lilia pushed Katya into Daniil as if to urge a small kiss before they parted. She refused to budge.

~

The aggressive Katya was building her own combat reputation with each mission. She had twice been awarded the Order of the Red Star and the Order of the Patriotic War.

She had just completed a successful bomber escort mission and was returning to home base. The cloudless skies were bright blue. Few pilots, if any, thoroughly scanned overhead during dogfights. Most locked on 360 degree views at or near eye level.

She decided to identify her maximum flying altitude before her faculties became clouded. She reasoned, with that knowledge that she would know her limits in future dogfights.

She started her climb to 4000 metres. Then 5000, 7000, 8000. And, finally to 10,000 metres, unwittingly drifting far into enemy airspace. She spotted a squadron of 13 Junker Ju 88 bombers flying unescorted thousands of metres below. She decided to attack. Her plane swooped straight down with both machine guns and her cannon blazing. The element of surprise cost the Germans two bombers. The rest formed a wall and began firing from their rear guns. Katya pushed her stick back sharply, causing the plane to rise quickly. She knew the bombers were too slow and lacked the maneuverability to chase her with any effectiveness. "Two is a good full day's work," she laughed to herself in the cockpit.

The German bombers radioed to base for additional support. Moments later the sky was filled with six 109s. The leader searched the skies for the enemy "squadron." All that could be spotted was a solo Yak—Katya. The lead pilot ordered the other five to fly as high as they could behind the emerging cloud formations to the west while he flew at low altitude as a target decoy. His hope was that the solo Yak would take the bait and attack.

Katya obliged. She swooped down for an "easy" kill. Suddenly she found herself surrounded by the other 109s. Katya fought bravely. She downed one plane. Then another. Her plane was finally nicked badly. It became almost impossible to control. During the few moments she struggled to stay air bound and stable, the remaining 109s surrounded her and pummeled her plane again and again in a hail of machine gun fire. Katya's plane was a yellow ball of fire. She struggled to eject. Her battered body landed in thick brush on Russian soil while her plane exploded in an open field on the German side.

"Lyosha," asked Lilia at the command post, "Has there been word from Katya?"

"The bombers have landed. They said they waved goodbye to their escort over two hours ago."

Lilia did not like the sound. "I wish to search."

"I understand," said Lyosha. "I will join you. Two is always better than one. In case..."

The two pilots needed to plan a route to search and explore. There are only two possibilities. She ran out of fuel on her return from the escort mission, which was unlikely. More likely she spotted an enemy plane and decided to free hunt.

They searched for two days at low altitudes in Russian territory. They found neither the plane nor Katya.

About a week later, a Russian patrol was scouring the Lugansk Oblast area, searching for fascist infantry stragglers, surveying damage, and informing the locals that the fascists were beginning to crack. "I am Captain Yakov Egorov," said the officer to those who had gathered in the center of the town of Antracit." I am happy to report our army has made significant progress in pushing the fascists back across the border. But we must continue to be vigilant. Our mission today is to seek and destroy all remaining stragglers. Any assistance you can provide as to sighting would be greatly appreciated."

Egorov saw a human sea of tired, proud faces. A region of mines and miners was the home of the miner's battalions called "Black Death" by the Germans because they always fought to the bitter end. Consequently, there was not a family in the area who had not experienced some tragedy or loss at the hands of the Nazis.

"We have seen and understand your suffering. We too have lost many comrades in this great patriotic struggle for our Motherland. Comrade Stalin, the Father of all Peoples, also extends his sorrow to each and every one of you." When the Captain finished, he was approached by two young girls, about the age of twelve.

"Comrade Commander, we want to report a sighting in the tall brush not far from here."

"Fascist pigs?"

"No. She is one of ours."

Three kilometres from town, Katya lay peacefully in the thick brush. From her clothing and tags, she was identified as a pilot from the 473rd regiment.

~

The trauma of seeing Katya still and dead was too much for the usually stoic Lilia to bear. She burst into tears. Her mind rushed to a time that seemed so long ago. Another Katya, another death. Her spirit was shaken to its core. Was she destined to be a bad luck charm for all those close to her?

"When will all this madness end?" screamed Lilia, pounding Lyosha's chest. He held her shivering body close. The warmth in his heart began to heal her sorrow. "What is to become of us? Suppose one..."

Lyosha gently placed his hand on her lips as if to say, no more. "No matter, we are destined to be together forever."

Lilia's anger subsided. She was at peace for that brief moment. Yesewint's words reverberated.

> Good bye, my friend, goodbye.
> My dear one, you are in my breast.
> A predestined parting
> Promises a reunion ahead.
> Good, my friend,
> without a touch of hand, without a word,
> Don't be sad and do not frown,
> Dying is nothing new in this life.
> And, living, of course, isn't any newer.

~

That evening Lilia wrote Mummy of the day's enormous emotional roller coaster.

> "Mummy Dearest,
> Today I felt your pain most clearly.
> It is one thing to lose a comrade in this war.
> It is quite another to lose a close friend.
> It is with great sadness I inform you about the loss of my good friend Katya, my flying comrade.
> I am angry. Why has that animal done such things?
> I do not know if I could bear another such close loss. I wish you were by my side.
> Mummy, you are always in my thoughts.
> Much love,
> Your Lilia"

In death, Katya was spared one thing. She never learned that her father had died of a massive heart attack just several days before her last flight.

Chapter 40

The beautiful Lieutenant and her handsome Captain
on their wedding day.

EVENTS INVOLVING KATYA, Pankratov, and the others caused Lyosha to rethink his intentions with Lilia. The dream was to marry when the madness ended. A traditional Russian wedding ceremony with family, friends, flowers, and music. But suppose something should happen to one or the other? The dream would be shattered until the hereafter.

Quietly and privately, Lyosha made alternate plans. His closest male friend was mechanic Gennadii Kuzbetsov. "You have saved my life in flight; are you prepared to do the same on the ground?" smiled Lyosha.

"Was that a serious question?" wondered Gennadii.

"Can you keep a secret? I've decided to ask Lilia to become my wife. But I need a proper ring for the ceremony. You are a man full of inventive ideas, so I thought I'd come to you."

Gennadii was pleased that his mechanical abilities had been recognized, but he was more pleased at being the first member of the regiment to know of the wedding plans. He rubbed his chin. He remembered a Messer had been downed not far from the air strip and lay fallow on the side of a hill. "Comrade, like always, Gennadii has solution," smiled the mechanic. He proposed taking a strip of Duralumin from the skin of the enemy plane and forging the material into two rings with the blowtorch he used to repair the regiment planes. "It will not be the stuff of a fine jeweler, but it will serve its purpose."

That evening, Lilia and Lyosha were sitting by a small fire beneath a clear sky full of twinkling stars. Lyosha was nervous, not certain how to broach the subject. "Have you thought of forever?" He asked.

Lilia bright blue eyes twinkled. "Forever is a long, long time."

"Perhaps we should marry now," he asked clumsily. "That will make forever even longer. That's good, no?"

Lilia heart raced. She was pleased but wondered. "Why the urgency? I thought we agreed to...."

Lyosha interrupted, "Sometimes things change. I wish our souls to be joined. So if one part is destined to leave, the other part still remains."

There was no question in Lilia's mind that she loved Lyosha deeply, without reservation. She broke into a broad smile. "Then I say yes. But my Captain, how do you propose to fulfill your marriage proposal?"

"To begin," said Lyosha reaching into his pocket and taking out the two rings. "With these." Crude as they were, to Lilia they were the most beautiful rings she had ever seen. She put her hand out for Lyosha to place the ring on her finger. Lyosha hesitated. Do you not wish a proper wedding day?"

"Every girl wants, but I can live without."

"There is no need," responded Lyosha. Lilia stared. Lyosha continued. ."I will ask the Major to marry us. We will then be more or less official. When the war is over, we can renew our vows in front of friends and family not in attendance."

Lilia smiled at Lyosha's resolve, the same resolve she had witnessed in the air. She was overcome with pride that the man of her forever dreams loved her enough to demand such urgency.

She was also skeptical that the commander would agree to such an unusual request.

Lyosha read the concern in Lilia's eyes. "Remember the Major owes us a favor," chuckled Lyosha. "After all, we gave him a memorable birthday party filled with respect, the sergeant shined his shoes, you pressed his dress uniform, and I polished his car. Remember the picture. Besides, we are his favorites." Lyosha paused. "No, we are like his children."

~

That evening after officer's mess, Lyosha took Baranov aside. To his surprise, the Major not only agreed to perform the ceremony, but also insisted on making a gracious announcement there and then. "Comrades, gather round, I have something important to announce. Something good has finally come of this hellish war. Our Captain and his Lieutenant," said Baranov, wrapping his arms around Lyosha and Lilia, "have decided to marry, and I have been asked to perform the ceremony. You are all invited and will be notified of the particulars."

After the announcement, the couple agreed that when the time came, Lyosha would marry in his dress uniform, and Lilia would wear her favorite brown dress made by her mother, a wreath of white camomiles around her neck.

~

Three days later, the heavens opened and the winds stirred viciously, making flying and air skirmishes with the Nazis impossible.

"Comrades," declared Baranov to the soaked couple, who had been summoned to the Major's quarters, "today is an ideal day for a wedding." Nothing more needed to be said. Two hours later Lyosha's plans came to life. A patch of canvas had been turned into a canopy to shield the couple from the bright sun, and a carpet of parachute cloth had been laid. As the beaming couple readied to walk down the aisle, Gennadii tenderly began to play on his guitar the song personally selected by Lyosha. Halfway down the aisle, the entire regiment chimed in.

> Why do robins sing in December?
> Long before the Springtime is due?
> And even though it's snowing, violets are growing
> I Know Why and so do you
> Why do breezes sigh ev'ry ev'ning
> whispering your name as they do?

And why have I the feeling stars are on my
ceiling?
I Know Why and so do you
When you smile at me
I hear gypsy violins....

Lilia beamed. "What a magnificent bride!" thought
Lyosha as he stood in front of her. Inna, acting as the ring
bearer, handed a circle of Duralumin to each to place on the
other's finger.

When the ceremony ended, the couple kissed, and the
gathering applauded and then disbursed. Lilia hugged the
Major, "Comrade Major, you have made me the happiest
woman in the world."

Baranov smiled. "There is more."

"More?" paused Lilia.

"I have not given my wedding gift," replied Baranov

"There is no need," said Lyosha. "You have done
enough."

"Nonsense," insisted the Major. "This evening my
quarters are your quarters."

Chapter 41

The village of Pavlovka, Russia, subsequently renamed Solomatino in honor of Captain Lyosha Solomatin.

THAT EVENING THE COUPLE exchanged gifts.

Lilia handed her soulmate a small object wrapped in a scrap of cloth. "Here is my gift to you. I am certain he will protect you as he has me."

Lyosha unwrapped the cloth to reveal the tiny statue of Father Frost Lilia had won in the dance contest on New Year's Day some ten years prior.

~

After the couple consummated their marriage, Lilia fell into a deep sleep. Hours later Lilia was awakened by Lyosha, who whispered gently into her ear, "My love, wake yourself. You have been calling in your sleep."

"What was I saying?"

"Do you not remember?"

Lilia stared blankly. "No."

"You were calling out to a plane."

"What was I saying?"

"Only, no, no, nothing else."

Lilia had dreamed the events of the following day.

~

'The latest news is good, very good," said the Major. "I have been told the Germans continue to retreat."

The pilots all cheered in the war bunker.

"The 473rd mission is to now expedite the German retreat by reclaiming all of the Ukrainian air space, to make it easier for our ground forces to drive the fascists further west."

The next morning Lyosha, Lilia, and the rest of a beaming self-confident squadron began to free hunt the skies. The sky was quiet. There were no enemy aircraft to speak of.

Lyosha radioed. "Squadron, return to base. I will explore west to identify future targets."

"I will stay," radioed Lilia.

"No need, White Lily. No contact expected. Return and ready yourself as planned."

She looked over at Lyosha. He smiled and raised his thumb.

As Lilia descended through the clouds to some 3000 metres, a large eagle with wings spread wide whooshed past her cockpit window. *How beautiful!* she thought.

Twenty minutes later as Lyosha cruised at 10,000 metres, dark clouds began to form below. The further Lyosha flew, the darker the clouds became. His visibility was less than three kilometres. He decided to return to base because he would not be able to spot enemy aircraft or troop concentrations.

He dropped to 6000 metres in an attempt to fly below the dark clouds. Suddenly, out of nowhere, three 109s surrounded him. He was struck in the rear before he even aimed his guns. Lyosha's plane began to spin. He fired wildly. The planes stayed in their positions as he attempted to dive. They fired again. His gas tank was pierced. Fuel began leaking profusely. It was certain the plane could not return. He opened his cockpit and parachuted out of the now smoking plane. His hope was that the planes could not see him in the smoke and clouds. Or perhaps, simply show some mercy.

None of those things were to come to pass.

~

Hours had passed and still no sign of Lyosha in the skies.

Lilia knew something was wrong. She suggested a recon mission to search for Lyosha.

"You rest. I will send others," said Baranov, who had his own suspicions.

Lilia would have none of it. Inna insisted on riding with Lilia. She agreed.

Within minutes, the patrol was at the approximate spot where Lyosha had waved to Lilia.

They pushed further west. Lilia's most dreaded fears were realized. There was "her life," dangling from a tree branch in his ripped parachute. It was her worst nightmare. The pilots stood and stared silently.

She sat next to the bloodied mass, screaming and crying for almost 30 minutes. Finally, Inna hugged Lilia's small, shuddering body and began to drag her away. Lilia clung to his jacket. A pocket opened; Father Frost and a small envelope fell out with Lilia's name scribbled across the front.

> "Dearest love,
> Today as we danced among the birches,
> I realized you will be the one true love
> of my love, today, tomorrow and forever.
> I wanted to tell you directly,
> but I was not sure that was the right time
> or place. Besides, suppose you did not feel the same?
> This big tough man was afraid! I have tried to write
> this letter many times. But the words never seem to
> be quite right.
> One day, I hope to share my life with you,
> have children with you, and perhaps one day reach
> heaven together.
> My deepest regret is that I have taught you to kill
> most efficiently.
> I hope that god will forgive me.
> I only want you to be safe and sound.
> My love for eternity,
> Your Lyosha"

~

Two hours later, plans were being made by Major Baranov to bury Lyosha several hundred yards to the right of the runway and hold a small ceremony with the entire regiment in attendance. While Lilia appreciated the gesture, it was not where she wanted her lover's remains to rest.

"Comrade Major," she pleaded, "Lyosha deserves more."

"I understand, Lilia, but we are in the middle of a war. What do you expect of me?"

"I only ask for some time for Inna and me to find a respectful place."

Inna was surprised but willing. She nodded.

"You have twelve hours."

The ladies took a jeep and drove to the nearby village of Pavlovka, Rostov region, where they found a small cemetery with two elderly women praying in the bright sunshine in front of a small, unassuming grave marker. Behind the cemetery sat a small hill filled with yellow, white, and purple wildflowers.

"This is where Lyosha belongs," said Lilia, who then made it her business to find the village's ruling authority, Chairman Yuri Gontar.

"It would be our honor to make our village the resting ground of this brave warrior," said the Chairman, hearing the story and feeling Lilia's sorrow.

~

For six hours on May 2, 1943, the war stopped for the 473rd. The Major instructed all available personnel to climb into every truck, every vehicle, and every personnel carrier to attend the service in the small cemetery.

Baranov gave a fitting tribute to the brave warrior while Lilia gallantly tried to hold back the tears.

"As many of you have sensed, Captain Solomatin was more than just the 473rd's Ace. He was the younger brother I never had. Certainly he was fearless and courageous. But he was more than that." Baranov looked into Lilia's eyes. "He was kind and tender. The kind of man that would have made some woman a loving husband and a wonderful father." Baranov paused to hold back the tears. "It is my hope that one day this place where Alexei rests will become a memorial to the ravages of war. I remember my last conversation with the Captain before that last flight. He asked, 'Why must men make wars?' I had no answer. Today at this hallowed place, I still have no answer."

The grim, solemn faces surrounding the Major spoke volumes. The ceremony was over. Baranov motioned to Lilia to lead the group up the hill to Lyosha's remains in the modest wooden box at the grave site.

Lilia took a deep breath; a single tear formed in each eye and rolled slowly down her cheeks. As she began to walk up the hill, she stopped to pick a few wildflowers and dropped them on the gravesite. Spontaneously, each man and woman present, including the priest and the tiny village's ranking official, Major Viktor Demidov, did likewise.

The Chairman, moved by the tragedy of the handsome pilot, made a pledge to Lilia. "I will make certain this man is never forgotten. We will change the name of our village from Pavlovka." (Today that village is in fact called Solomatino—in the name of the Hero of the Soviet Union, Captain Alexei Solomatin.)

~

The entire regiment then formed a long line and, one by one, silently hugged Lilia. A lifetime of tears were shed. The soldiers left. Lilia was now alone on the small hill. She could feel a gentle breeze and the sound of distant gunfire as she paused one last time by her fallen lover.

Quietly, with heavy head bowed, she recalled their brief moments together. The remarkable power of his tenderness, his sensitivity, his strength, filled her being. Her shaken voice asked, "God, what was the purpose of all this? Why did you provide such a gift then take it away. Please God, why?"

That first day in the woods returned.

> Wait for me, and I'll come back, Wait and I'll come.
> Wait through autumn's yellow rains and its tedium.
> Steel your heart and do not grieve, Wit through winter's haze,
> Wait through wind and raging storm, Wait through summer's blaze.
> Wait when others wait no more.

Inna's hand touched her friend's shoulder.

"I thought you left with the others."

"Then who would be here to support my dear friend in this moment?"

Inna and Lilia knew each other well. They had shared much. Nothing else needed to be said. Inna spread her willing arms. Lilia hugged her friend tightly, tears streaming from her eyes. Inna removed a handkerchief from her pocket and began to dab Lilia's cheeks.

"He promised he'd come back. He deceived me," said a distraught Lilia.

"Harsh thoughts do not become you. Lyosha did not deceive you. Do you not feel his love?"

Lilia nodded.

"Are you not protected by his warmth?"

Lilia's heart released a faint smile.

"He is still here. And, he will love you as long as you honor him."

"Do you think we will meet again?" asked Lilia.

It was Inna's turn to smile softly. "It will simply be in another place. He has merely taken a brief flight."

Lilia looked toward the bright blue sky. There was a single passing cloud. She then took Father Frost from her pocket, shoveled back some of the new earth, and buried the statue by Lyosha's side.

~

That evening Lilia's quivering, unsure hand wrote home.

> "Hello, my dear Mummy!
> Many mournful events have happened which prevented me from writing a letter to you. We have been flying frequently, annihilating the enemy, but we have also had some terrible losses.
> Some people were killed—the navigator of the regiment, my battle friend Katya Budanova, and my friend Lyosha Solomatin. He loved me dearly. We recently buried him in the village of Pavlovka, Rostov Region. The whole regiment and the villagers were in attendance. It was indeed moving.
> I miss him very much—my beloved friend—and I try to fly as much as possible to forget.
> Yours Always,
> Lilia"

~

That evening Lilia cried herself to sleep. She *dreamed a dream* that would touch her soul. A dream that was destined to be placed somewhere in time:

It was a joyous New Year holiday evening after the war, a night of nights on Novoslobodskaya Street.

Anna had spent most of the day decorating the apartment and cooking a splendid feast. She and Vladimir were to meet their son-in-law, decorated military hero Lyosha Solomatin, for the first time. To make the celebration complete, Anna had spent much time finding and inviting many of Lilia's friends from the military. It was to be a surprise celebration on many levels.

Vladimir was resting in his favorite chair reading the newspaper. For the first time since before the war, the railway training and dispatch offices were closed to celebrate the holiday. While the war had been a painful, depressing experience, Anna and Vladimir knew they had much to be thankful about.

Both now had good jobs working for the state. Vladimir's recent promotion to managing supervisor meant there would always be ample "bread and butter" in the cabinet.

Daughter Lilia, a decorated war hero, had married Lyosha, the man of her dreams. They had been blessed with a healthy son, Boris, and Lilia was already expecting a second child.

As Vladimir flipped the pages, he noticed a story about some unique-sounding guitars being made by a small factory in Belarus with the region's spruce and beech wood trees. He smiled.

"Why do you sit and smile so silly?" asked Anna.

"My wife, I was remembering the first time Lilia played my grandfather's guitar. She wanted to pull the strings again and again. She would not take no for an answer."

"Your daughter has always wanted to do more than most," laughed Anna.

"Just like her mother."

Vladimir got up, and walked over to the dresser, opened the drawer, and took out a small red box, tucked inside one of his socks. "For you, woman of my forever dreams."

The box contained a pair of turquoise earrings. "These are my favorite color, my wonderful husband," said Anna Vladimir had always made Anna feel like a princess. She kissed him gently and tenderly.

There was a knock on the door. The guests began to arrive. Anna's little reunion was to be a surprise for Lilia and Lyosha.

"Thank you for inviting me. I am Anatoliy Morozov. I have not seen your daughter since our days at the airdrome. Little did I know when I trained her, she would become famous!"

Next came Katya, husband Daniil, and their twin daughters Viktoriya and Vera.

"I knew from the letters you had a daughter, but I didn't realize two."

"I have finally out-performed your daughter at something," joked Katya.

Shortly thereafter, Sergei Pankratov arrived with his beautiful fiancée, Rada, an up-and-coming actress.

"Rada, you are more beautiful than your pictures."

"Thank you, Anna Mikhailovna. You are most gracious."

"You know I had a terrible crush on your daughter," said Sergei, "before Rada of course."

"Didn't we all?" smiled Anatoliy.

There was another knock. Inna and husband Maxim had arrived. Katya and Inna embraced. A tear formed in both their eyes. "There were times I wondered if we would ever share moments like this again," said Inna sweetly.

"So did I" offered Katya.

Inna turned to the Litvyaks and proudly announced, "This is my husband Maxim."

After everyone reacquainted themselves, there was yet another knock on the door.

Marina Raskova stood in the doorway in a beautiful brown chiffon dress, her long brown hair tied neatly in a bun.

"Anna Mikhailovna and Vladimir Ivanovich, I'm so happy you thought to invite me. This is my good friend Gennadiy Alekseev."

The handsome man kissed Anna's hand. "I now understand where your daughter's beauty comes from."

Marina was a bit surprised by his comment. "You know Lilia?"

"We met just once, briefly, during the war."

"Speaking of Lilia," smiled Inna, "I assume she will be late. She was always late. If it wasn't lipstick, it was her hair. If it wasn't her hair... She used to drive Lyosha crazy while he waited for her during those times we were granted a few spare minutes."

Anna smiled. "From what dear Lyosha tells me in letters, little has changed."

As they all laughed knowingly, the door opened. There stood Lilia, Lyosha, and Boris.

"Surprise!"

They all rushed to hug Lilia and Lyosha.

Lilia blushed. "My goodness, Mummy, what a won-derful surprise!"

There was no need for introductions. Lyosha had already been told much about his new in-laws. And they about him from Lilia's letters. They hugged warmly.

"Welcome to our home and yours," said Vladimir as he shook drive Lyosha's hand while gently embracing little eleven-month-old Boris in his arms. "You have such a beautiful son. Such a strong face. Such beautiful eyes."

"Father," said Lyosha, "May I call you Father?"

"Please."

"Congratulations to you also. Look, he has your daughter's magnificent blue-gray eyes."

"I thought perhaps before dinner, we might sit and talk. Tell us everything," said Anna.

Lilia and Lyosha were delighted to learn Anna and Vladimir were in good health, and that despite the shortages, they lived quite comfortably. That Katya and Inna had married well and were terribly happy. That Anatoliy was studying law, Sergei was studying to be a doctor, and Marina was a professor at a local engineering school.

"The home looks as it was," smiled Lilia as she looked around. In the corner was her old sewing machine and knitting materials.

"Remember, child, how I taught you to make clothes?"

"Certainly, Mother. Believe it or not, those lessons came in handy during the war"

Anna stared quizzically. "How so?"

"Let's just say I learned to make scarves to lift spirits in times of difficulty." Lilia smiled. She wished to go no further. Why worry her parents at this late date about using her scarf to make a tourniquet after being shot from the skies?

Vladimir also had many questions about the war. He knew his daughter had won many medals for bravery, been wounded in flight, and probably seen terrible things. But he also knew tonight there should be no such talk. Lilia, Lyosha, and Boris had traveled quite a distance from their apartment in Leningrad. Besides, there were so many people who wanted to share and celebrate their good fortunes.

"So, Lyosha, what do you do?" asked Vladimir as the family sat around the table.

"I am an engineer at LMZ [Leningradsky Metallichesky Zavod] on the Neva River. We make power turbines for Russian cities. Since the war, there is great need in the rebuilding effort."

"Interesting. But I thought you would have done something with your flying experience?"

The handsome, broad-shouldered Lyosha leaned back and laughed heartily. "The War has cured me of flying. I want to work on land. Your daughter remains the pilot."

"My daughter is a mother," replied Anna in denial.

"And, soon to be another," smiled Lyosha.

"My goodness. That will make us happy. Two little ones will make you a very busy woman."

"But there will still be time," said Lilia.

"Time for what?"

"Time to fly planes."

"Planes?" wondered Vladimir. "What planes?"

"I have applied to be a pilot. I have been accepted by Aeroflot."

"What is Aeroflot?"

"It is a new airline."

"What does it do?"

"Someday people will fly all over Russia to visit family and friends, take jobs, see our Motherland."

"But you can do that now in trains."

"Planes will be faster."

"I don't understand you young people today and your crazy ideas."

"Father, that's what you said when I wanted to be a fighter pilot."

Vladimir turned to Lyosha. "I see you will have your hands full. Marriage has not changed her."

"With respect, Father, I love your daughter the way she is. And, I hope our children are more like her."

Anna smiled proudly. She had done well. Her daughter was her own person and always would be. She had found a man who understood that. A man who was happy for her.

Dinner was over. It was time for some revelry.

Vladimir took out his grandfather's guitar and began to play *Svetit Mesyats* (The Moon is Shining Brightly), a playful folk song that Lilia vividly remembered.

"Father, when you played that song I used to imagine the whole world dancing."

"Perhaps you will remember this one also." He began to play *Moroz Moroz*. While he played, Grandfather Frost and Snegurochka appeared in the center of the room with a bag of gifts.

"Please sit," directed Snegurochka. "There are gifts for all and then some." Family and friends smiled. When Snegurochka had given all the adults a memento of the evening, she walked over to little Boris. There was one gift left in Grandfather Frost's bag. She handed it to Boris—a little green plane with the number 44 and two white lilies painted on the fuselage.

Grandfather Frost and Snegurochka waved to all then disappeared into the night.

~

Lilia realized she had chatted with everyone in the room but Gennadiy, the guest that Marina had brought.

"And, where did you two meet, if you don't mind me asking?"

The man smiled. "Same place we met... in the war." Lilia felt a tug at her soul.

"We have met?"

"Just once."

"I'm sorry, I don't remember."

"You were wandering the fields. I believe you had been shot down. I dropped you off at your base in my plane."

"Now I remember. But why did you not stay so I could thank you properly?"

The man paused and smiled warmly. "I had others to save."

Chapter 42

Lilia's weary eyes now spoke volumes about life on the front.

LILIA WAS NEVER QUITE the same after Lyosha passed.

As her 22nd birthday approached, the innocent, determined teenager, bubbling with vim and vigor, had vanished. She was someone else. Someone she didn't recognize. Someone she didn't know. Her heart had been broken, her soul scorched.

Privately, between missions, she wondered what kind of man was Hitler to have caused the pain and suffering that would ultimately afflict every family in all of Russia for all of history.

And, why would God create such a man? And, what of Stalin, who once captured the ideals of an entire country? Were pilots still his glorious falcons? Had his personal agenda shifted? Were the rumors of debauchery true?

And, why had she been spared? Why not Katya, why not Lyosha? What was her ultimate mission? Why was she granted the gift of flight, against the odds?

Her shy smile became more of a detached stare. She appeared perennially uncomfortable and restless like a caged animal, curled and ready to lurch at its prey. Free hunting in the sky was her pastime; the sky was her home. Her sole mission was the passion Lyosha had instilled: to kill fascists. The war and its miseries had transformed this charming young lady into something else.

Time had become timeless. There were only blurred todays. Tomorrow was an unfathomable labyrinth, difficult to discern, impossible to decipher.

Despite her inner conflicts, outwardly Lilia continued to serve the Motherland with distinction. This petite 150 cm lady turned war machine in her plane. As Inna described her, "the 473rd's guardian angel for challenging enemy sorties." During the 60 days following Lyosha's passing, she completed 38 missions. Not one plane under her wing was lost, not one pilot wounded.

She was promoted to Senior Lieutenant and in the elite 73rd Guards Fighter Regiment, now acknowledged as Russia's leading air combat force.

At Lilia's request, Inna accompanied her.

~

There was nothing particularly unique or memorable about June 11th.

It was a warm, sunny day: cotton-puff clouds dotted the deep blue sky and the bloody, god forsaken war continued to rage.

Lilia, as always, went about her business, free hunting. Efficiently and with a quiet vengeance. Alone.

Two Messers playfully dropped through the clouds. They didn't see her. Lilia locked on the tail of one and shot it down. The other saw the lilies on her fuselage and began to retreat. He made a sharp turn to the right and headed straight up through the clouds, hoping to lose Lilia in the process. She remained on his tail for a few kilometres and then dropped down out of view. He hesitated for a moment to identify her location. In that split second, she slipped under his fuselage and began firing at close range. The Messer was hit. Smoke belched out of its rear. For some curious reason, Lilia was certain the plane's nose dive was a ploy to escape her wrath. She followed the plane straight down.

In her mind, she was flanked on the right by a smiling Lyosha, who gave her a thumbs up. As Lilia smiled back, two more Messers came out of the clouds. Her right wing was nicked badly. She began to lose control but continued to fire as the enemy planes circled. Her hail of bullets caused one of the Messers to burst in midair. She turned to her right to avoid the heat of the explosion. The other Messer was dead ahead, guns blazing. Her left wing was struck. She had no option but to abandon and parachute. Concerned she would be a sitting target, she emptied her guns until the last moment. The plane banked to escape. By then Lilia had parachuted, landed in a field and disappeared, into the nearby woods.

The pilot radioed back to his base. "White Lily in sight. Permission to land."

"Permission granted," said the German commander at his nearby base. "Await assistance. Then search and destroy."

"Finally," thought the commander, "we have the bitch in our grasp! The woman who has humiliated the Fűhrer and his superior soldiers."

Within minutes, three Messers were landing in an open field not far from the parachute.

"I last saw her heading west," said the pilot. "Toward those woods."

As the pilots were to learn quickly, these woods were particularly dense. Night was rapidly approaching. They heard and saw nothing.

"We will camp and wait till morning. Then begin our search anew."

As the men set a campfire and began to eat and drink, Lilia continued to dash through the woods, going as fast and as far as she could. Finally, about midnight, she paused to rest out of sheer exhaustion. She tucked herself under a fallen tree to take a brief nap. The plan was to follow her compass due east back to the Russian front line and her base.

Instead, she fell into a deep sleep. When she awoke, it was morning. She gathered herself and continued east, unaware the compass had slipped out of her pocket during the night. She passed a stream, gathered some water. She also came upon a wild berry patch nestled next to a few white and blue wildflowers laden with pollen. She ate the berries for sustenance and licked the pollen off the flowers for an energy surge, just as Mummy had taught her when she was a little girl.

The air was quiet and still. The sky cloudless. There was a fork in the road. She searched for her compass. She was forced to use the sun as her guide. By the end of the day, she felt no closer to the front line than in the morning. She came upon another small pond, shallow and clear. There she saw a few fish. She chased them into a corner of the pond then reached down with her hat positioned as a fishing net. To her delight, she now had her dinner! She pounded the fish then skinned and boned the fillets, and ate them raw like the Northern Evenks and Chukci men.

When finished, she went to the pond to scoop some water. She saw her reflection. She was a grimy and gritty mess, nothing like the Lilia she knew. It was clear she was not going to reach the front before nightfall, and there did not appear to be a soul nearby. She removed her clothes and took a bath. The pond was cool but refreshing. The sun began to set. Her body quickly chilled. She dressed quickly and began to jump and run through the bushes to increase her body heat. After six or so kilometres, she was exhausted but warm. She made a bed of leaves then fell fast asleep, dreaming dreams of Lyosha. Where he was? What he was doing? When would they be united again?

Chapter 43

The kind Ukrainians, Zina and Ivan Goncharenko,
hid Lilia from the fascist stalkers

May 1943
Chuguyev, Ukraine...

LILIA HAD WANDERED INTO unoccupied Ukrainian territory, about eight kilometres from the tiny peasant town of Chuguyev. As the sun began to rise, Lilia stirred. She saw a figure standing over her. She pulled her gun, only to discover it was a little dark-haired boy with a round face and a broad smile. "You soldier?"

"And what is your name, little boy?" smiled Lilia.

"Anton."

"Do you live here?"

"Where is your rifle?"

Lilia smiled. "I'm a pilot. I fly planes in the sky."

The boy moved backward in fright. "You drop bombs?"

"Only on the fascists."

Anton failed to mention that the German Messers routinely flew over the town and dropped a bomb here and there to make their presence known. Many times he was awakened from his sleep and placed under his mother's sturdy iron sewing machine table. "Down the road behind the trees is our house. Want to see?" As they walked, she kept her hand on her holster and her eyes peeled for a German search party. The boy pointed to a modest stone and plaster structure with a thatched roof. Lilia looked both ways. The coast was clear. They ran to the front door.

~

"Why have you not found the witch?" asked the German commanding officer standing in front of Lilia's fuselage.

"This is her," he continued tapping on the painted flowers. "I donate ten deutschmarks to the one who finds her alive and twenty to the one who brings her back dead."

~

Zina and Ivan Goncharenko were simple folks. They both worked on a nearby collective farm. When Zina wasn't working, she was tending to the house and her two children, Anton and a younger sister, Lidia. The square-jawed Ivan was never happy with his lot in life and frequently drank to forget.

Since the Nazis invaded Russia almost two years earlier, each day was filled with rumors of atrocities beyond description and rumors that the Germans would soon occupy Chuguyev and remove all able-bodied men to concentration camps to make munitions for the German war effort.

"Mama, Papa," Anton said proudly on entering the door with Lilia. "I found this soldier in the field. She is tired and hungry."

Ivan looked at Lilia, "Are we so desperate to place children in the military?"

"Comrade, I'm not a child, I'm 21."

Zina was embarrassed. "My husband does not mean to harm with words. I am Zina Goncharenko. I wish your visit could be better circumstances. Please child, come sit, let us feed you and give you a place to rest. We do not have much, but what we have is yours."

While eating potato soup and a few scraps of some bread, Lilia smiled for the first time in days.

"And so, how did you come to separate from your unit?"

"My plane was shot down somewhere beyond the woods. In the heat of battle I lost my compass and my way."

As Lilia spoke, Ivan noticed her attractive blonde hair and her steel-blue eyes. He recalled an old newspaper article he had seen about a gallant young lady flyer. He wondered.

"You are the lady in the flyer?" questioned Ivan.

"I did not wish it," said an embarrassed Lilia.

"Why? It fills Russian pride at this most difficult moment in history. This young lady is a true war hero. She is White Lily. There are posters. There are words."

"This is so?" asked Zina.

Lilia nodded shyly.

"We are honored," smiled Ivan.

After they ate, Ivan and Zina offered Lilia their bed, their blankets, their pillows.

"That is very kind of you." She looked at Anton, who appeared concerned about something. Zina noticed the same thing. "Anton, my child. Come with mama."

"Mama, I am afraid of the bombs."

Lilia gently interrupted, "Zina, would you mind if Anton and I played a game I learned at his age? It is called *Sea Battle*." Anton's eyes lit up. He was going to play a game with a real soldier.

"Do you have a scrap of paper on which we can write?" asked Lilia. She took the paper, a pencil, and Anton's hand. They sat down at the family table. "First, I draw two large squares, one on each side of the paper. Now I will draw ten lines up and ten lines down in each box. See?"

Anton watched Lilia's every move.

"Now we need to write the letters A to J above the lines and the numbers 1 to 10 down the left. Can you help me?" Slowly Anton wrote the numbers 1 to 10.

"You write well, for one so young."

"Papa taught me," said a smiling Anton.

Lilia outlined ten ships inside the boxes on each and slowly explained how they would then sit at opposite ends of the table with a potato concealing their sheets and try to hit their rival's ships by calling out "D 10," "A-7."

"If you guess correctly, I will declare, 'killed' or 'wounded' and remove the ship from my fleet. Whoever has ships remaining is the winner. Understand?"

Anton again nodded as a slight smile came over his face.

Lilia and Anton played six games of *Sea Battle* that evening. To Lilia's surprise, Anton won four of them, fair and square.

~

The first bomb dropped about midnight. Its fury shook the Goncharenko house. Lilia was tossed out of bed. Anton began to cry. Ivan dashed to their side and dragged them into the cellar. "Zina, grab our daughter and follow. Hurry!"

Suddenly there was a partial hit. The cellar shook as the entire right side of the house disappeared in a cloud of rubble. Then the skies were silent. Ivan dusted himself off and stood up. "The miserable fascists are gone. It is clear to come out," said Ivan. "Wife, let us do our best to clean in the dark. Morning will tell us more. Children, try to get some sleep."

The three adults cleaned a corner of the house as best they could and huddled together, covering themselves with blankets and pieces of cloth from what items remained.

~

Morning came. Zina cried and Ivan stood gloomy and somber. Their home was in ruins. They resolved then and there to start over.

Minutes later, two large German horse-drawn carts arrived. "Go quickly," urged Ivan, "out the back; continue through the woods."

Lilia ran into the woods and hid. A squadron of German foot soldiers, perhaps a hundred strong, appeared. They started dragging men, women and children from the adjoining houses. The tall stern officer in charge shouted orders with disdain. "Women and children in the cart to my right. Able-bodied men to my left." A soldier stood by the cart, separating the men into two groups—some pushed into the cart and others told to stand to the side. Within minutes, the cart was a steaming mass of humanity with barely room to move. The cart's slatted wooden fence was closed. Ivan's eyes searched for Zina.

"My captain, what about the rest?" asked a sergeant, referring to those able-bodied men that could not fit in the cart.

"Put them with the rejected!"

The women were herded and separated similarly. Zina lost track of Anton in the confusion. "Please, my son, please," begged Zina. The soldier picked up his rifle and smashed Zina's face with the butt. Blood streamed out of her mouth as she collapsed. Anton watched the entire scene in horror. It was a scene he would never forget.

Hours later, the processing was complete. 1500 sick and elderly men and women, classified as the rejected, stood in the middle of the field near Ivan's house. "Who is a Jew!" yelled the Captain. No one stepped forward. "And, who is a Communist?" Again no one volunteered. "I see," sneered the Captain. "Then all are worthless." That was the signal. The men lifted their rifles and machine guns and sprayed round after round until no one was left.

"I believe target practice is over. You have done well," mocked the Captain.

~

June 12, 1943
The Russian Front...

When Lilia's petite frame crossed the front line, she was given a hero's welcome by members of the 73rd. Their soulmate had survived. While surprised and pleased about the reception, she was guilt-ridden about her inability to help the Goncharenkos.

"Comrade Litvyak, I believe you should take some days to recover from your ordeal," said the commanding officer.

"Are there not Germans to kill?"

"There are always Germans to kill, until this hell is over."

"Then I must go."

The CO pleaded. Lilia would have none of it.

"Comrade, a small compromise. Begin tomorrow. We need the time to make ready a new number 44 and to paint the lilies."

Lily nodded and returned to her bunker. She decided to write to Mummy.

Chapter 44

Lilia (left) in the last known picture with fellow fighter pilots of the 73rd Regiment.

July 28, 1943
Berlin...

THE WAR WAS NOT GOING as planned for Hitler.

Europe's Allied Forces were showing greater resolve than originally assumed; the weakness of his Axis Powers was stretching his Aryan resources to the breaking point, and then there were those "stupid illiterate Russians with their outdated military machine." How could they not have been occupied and extinguished long ago?

~

Hermann Göring, the Luftwaffe Chief, knew the meeting of the Generals in the Führer's austere war room would not be pleasant.

"What the hell is going on?" demanded the Führer. "We are men against women and children. Still the reports are disappointing. Can you not inspire? Are you less than real soldiers!" shouted the Führer as he pounded the table and his dark brown eyes pierced Göring first, then Heinrich Eberbach, General of Panzer Troops, Karl Eibl, General of Infantry, and finally Karl Eglseer, General of Mountain Troops.

"Our Luftwaffe has made recent success," said Göring, attempting to distance himself from the rest.

"Tell me," sneered the Führer, "your *glowing* report."

The General started to read a summary of recent attacks, kill, targets destroyed, and other statistics meant to impress his Führer.

Hitler interrupted with a report of his own.

"And what of this report, and this," roared Hitler throwing *Pravda* stories of the exploits of one White Lily on the table.

The other generals smirked.

"Wipe those stupid smiles off your faces, not one of you has earned the right."

"You, General Göring, are the most disappointing. You have allowed a woman to make a laughing stock of our entire air force. To make matters worse, that ignorant Stalin uses propaganda to convince his followers there is hope."

Göring foolishly attempted a mild rebuttal which only infuriated Hitler more.

"We are mocked in posters. Called fascist monsters!" shouted Hitler as he threw a poster across the room.

"If I do not see a change in performance quickly, Gallad [29 year-old Adolf Gallad, a general who was admired on both sides of the Channel as a soldier who had not met a foe in the air that he could not vanquish] will be in that seat. Do we understand each other?"

Hitler made two things abundantly clear: The ground forces needed to achieve meaningful advances on the front regardless of the cost of human life. And, he wanted no more stories of a little girl flying planes, killing pilots.

The Machiavellian Hitler understood the value of War Propaganda. "When she has expired, I want her remains in our hands."

The Generals wondered why such a singular directive in a war of many.

Hitler had already decided, once Lilia was dead, he would use his propaganda machine to talk of Lilia's defection, her change of heart, her understanding of German Socialist superiority over Russian Communism.

He would soundly defeat Stalin and his followers by destroying with bullets *and* demoralizing with words.

~

July 31, 1943
Marinovka Village, Ukraine...

Inna wasn't very excited that her application to take the Air Force Academy entrance exam had been approved by her commanders.

"When do you leave?" asked Lilia.

"Tomorrow."

"So soon?"

"I did not ask. I do not wish to study in Moscow," responded Inna defensively.

"Inna, your appointment is a good thing," smiled Lilia empathetically. "The war has taught you much—both good and bad. Who knows? One day you might assist in the development of new planes."

"Is it right that I be safe and sound in Moscow while the war rages elsewhere? Are we not close friends?"

Lilia's mood shifted. Inna felt the change. "We are best friends," uttered Lilia with a tear forming in her eye. "First Lyosha, then Katya, now you."

It was Inna's turn to be supportive. "Lilia, I am not leaving forever; I am leaving to take an exam. I will return in a matter of days."

"I understand. But it will feel like an eternity. My plane has come to depend on you. I have come to depend on you. I look forward to seeing your face when each mission ends."

"Lilia, this is the 73rd. We are the best. I have personally recommended Nikolay Minkov."

"Nikolay. He is so young!" observed the "almost" 22-year-old Lilia.

The difficulties Lilia had been through made her heart old beyond its years. It no longer occurred to her that she was still just a young lady. After more than 170 plus missions, she thought of herself as a battle-hardened veteran.

"He has taken care of the Major's planes without incident. Is that not good enough? I am confident nothing will happen to you in my absence."

"Promise?" smiled Lilia.

Inna hugged her friend. "Promise."

As Inna packed a few clothes, Lilia decided to bare her soul.

"You know, I am not afraid of dying. Such an event will only reunite me with our good friend Katya and permit me to spend eternity with Lyosha." She paused. "Does God allow children in heaven? We talked of one day having children. I would like two."

Inna smiled. "I am sure God will allow children. But this talk..."

Lilia interrupted. She picked up a glove of Katya's she had stored as a memory of her friend. "Do you think she will find Daniil there? He took her heart away, just as Lyosha took mine." Lilia paused again. Inna did not know how to respond. "But, after all this, what if I was to disappear without a trace?"

Chapter 45

Lilia becomes a primary target of Hitler's elite Luftwaffe.

August 1, 1943...

"THERE IS A LEAK IN one of the fuel lines," shouted Nikolay over the roar of the engines on the runway. "You cannot leave until I fix it."

Impatient Lilia looked at her squadron mates disappearing one by one into the clouds. She looked at her mama's postcard of red and white roses. "How bad is it?"

"I would estimate the hole small, but the heat of battle may make it worse.

"I must go, we can fix it later," insisted Lilia.

"I disagree," said Nikolay firmly

Major Baranov overheard the dispute and quickly sided with Nikolay. "Lieutenant, out of the cockpit till the problem is fixed," he shouted. "I don't need a stalling Ace."

~

Lilia's plane was ready to go. Major Baranov put it succinctly: "Our mission is to seek, engage, and destroy enemy aircraft at or near the front until the war ends or we perish, whichever comes first!"

Shortly after takeoff, they hit the jackpot–a convoy of munition-laden bombers.

Lilia was the first to spot and the first to challenge. She strongly believed in the element of surprise. As usual, she assumed her fellow pilots would follow and protect her sides as did Lyosha and Katya. But her new flying partners were unfamiliar with her intent.

Ivan Borisenko, who was flying with Lilia that day, later recalled the incident vividly in a letter to Vera Tilmofeyeva, the Commissar of women's fighter regiments: "Lilia just didn't see the 109s that were hiding in the clouds providing cover for the bombers."

~

As Lilia executed her mission, Stalin planned strategy.

Joseph Stalin had several holiday homes on the Black Sea coast, but the green mansion perched on the hillside at Gagra was his favorite dacha. During the war, he held strategic meetings with approved invitees, surrounded by 3000 security guards assembled in three human rings around the property.

Today was a more private affair. He had only invited his famous Personal Advisor, another Georgian, the notoriously cruel Lavrenty Beria. He was bald, wore thin-rimmed spectacles and well-made suits, and loved attractive women and young girls with equal passion. The Advisor was often seen with Stalin but appeared to play a relatively minor role. Publicly, he was largely silent, whispering to the Premier or providing needed documents. However, he was far more influential and Machiavellian. As Stalin's "right hand" man, he cast horror on people, ordering tens of thousands arrested and executed on a whim or rumor.

When the Advisor arrived at dusk, Stalin was sitting behind his large glass-topped desk. They shook hands, Stalin turned on a pewter lamp with a blue glass shade that sat to the left, and then turned to point at the large glass-covered map of Europe that hung behind his desk. "I am told we are making progress on the ground, here, here, and here. Do you believe?"

"They are mostly true. But the costs are high, and the defections are numerous."

"No matter, we have the necessary population. But the defections must remain quiet. They are a sign of cowardliness and disrespect."

"I understand, Comrade Stalin. There are no defections. Only those who disappear without a trace."

"And, what of our air support?"

"As on the ground, we have lost some talent, but we get stronger everyday against the Messerschmitts and other Nazi aircraft."

Stalin then surprised the Advisor. "What of our poster child? The woman who humiliates Hitler. The one who flies with the flowers."

~

"Solo target at 120 degrees," shouted the German squad leader, Blue Angel, as his bomber traveled below. "Need immediate assistance." With four planes and a dark cloud at his disposal, the leader commanded, "Two flank right, two flank left, 1000 above, 1000 below."

Closing in on the bombers, Lilia suddenly saw the Messers on her tail. "White Lily surrounded. Four Messers. Wing, where are you? Need immediate assistance. All guns blazing." She was sandwiched between four planes. She tried to dive straight down while her flying partners some miles away approached at full speed. The Germans were unable to keep pace. Lilia looked for friendly support. She was still alone.

Executing a perfect summersault, she wound up directly behind one of the planes and opened fire in a concentrated burst. The plane exploded. The three remaining planes banked to avoid residue debris.

"To all in the area, enter Blue Angel space. Solo Yak, dangerous, destroy on sight." Eleven more Messerschmitts entered the battle space.

Lilia was completely surrounded. One pilot, within 50 metres of her fuselage, noticed the white lilies painted on her plane. He knew immediately.

"Achtung, Litvyak. Achtung, Litvyak," he radioed.

"Woman of our bad dreams," Blue Angel radioed. "Keep firing until I say stop."

All of Lyosha's munitions training had not prepared her for this. She couldn't close in on her targets. She tried to use her flying skills to loop over and above the planes to flee. Two of the now fourteen planes surrounding her were destroyed by their own friendly fire. But she knew she could not outrun the dozen that remained.

The Germans formed a straight line as if they were about to distribute a heavy burst of flak cover. Lilia began to level. The sky rained hundreds of 20MM bullets. One pierced Lilia's cockpit; a second shut down her instrument panel, and a third bore a hole in her gas tank, which began to smoke profusely. Best she could surmise, the plane maintained 80% of its functionality, perhaps more, and she had merely been wounded in the leg. She'd been through worse and survived.

She decided to feign a direct hit. She maneuvered the smoking plane through the clouds, spinning, apparently out of control, in the hopes that the Germans would assume she had been hit fatally and would crash.

Late arriving Borisenko heard the gunfire and the roaring of the planes. "White Lily, position. White Lily." Lilia could not respond for fear the Germans would realize she was still alive.

Her plan did not include a burst fuel line. The one Nikolay had repaired burst open from the heat. Lilia's plane was now enveloped in flames. With no instruments and almost no fuel, Lilia tried to evacuate the cockpit, but the window was jammed shut, and she was too small to force it open. She desperately scanned the thickly wooded terrain, hoping there was still time to land. Her only option was a small clearing adjacent to a rocky crevice not far from the tiny Ukrainian village of Kozhevnya. She attempted to glide toward earth and complete a bellyland. Her heart pounded.

Suddenly a beautiful eagle with wings spread wide swooped down from the heavens. He looked into her cockpit. She smiled. She knew it would not be long before she would be reunited with Lyosha. Her body became calm. She began to sing.

> ...Oh song, maiden's song
> Fly towards the clear sun
> And to the warrior on a far away border
> Bring Katyusha's greeting.
> May he remember this simple maiden
> And hear her signing
> May he save our motherland
> And love, Katyusha will save....

The flaming plane skidded through the clearing, crashed into a large boulder, and split in two. The cockpit and aft section of the plane rolled over and slipped into a crevice, while the rear of the fuselage hit the boulder head on and burst into flames. No one would ever know if Lilia died upon impact or was trapped in the burning cockpit.

Borisenko searched frantically for his fallen comrade. He looked everywhere. Unfortunately he never saw the aircraft explode or a pilot jump with a parachute. He radioed back to base, "No trace. No trace." With that, he was ordered back to the airdrome.

Lilia's worse nightmare had been realized. On August 1, 1941, she "disappeared without a trace," a phrase that would find its way into her official documents for the next 36 years.

Chapter 46

In 1942, Valentina Ivanovna Vaschenko was unaware of her fate.

1942

Valentina Vaschenko was eight years old when Hitler invaded her home, the little coal mining town of Krasny Luch, in what today is the Eastern Ukraine. Her parents and grandparents tried to shield her from the ravages of war. Nevertheless she saw things, terrible things.

She witnessed brave foot soldiers of the 383rd Rifle Miners Division, so named because of their prior occupation, who fought bitterly to the very end.

And she heard the sounds of the nearby air battles, which pitted undermanned Russian fighter pilots who performed admirably against the superior Messer-schmitt.

A small battalion of retreating Russian foot soldiers from the 383rd Rifle Miners Division stumbled upon a shattered portion of a Yak fuselage in the Donbass region.

"Sergeant Andreyev, you won't believe this," said a soldier named Taras, searching the cockpit for the downed pilot's identity.

"Flowers? Postcards?" In the cockpit? Strange..." paused Andreyev.

"Quickly, let's bury our comrade before the fascists appear."

As his troops quickly dug a modest grave with the trenching tools, Sergeant Andreyev began to drag the body to the shallow grave site. The body seemed particularly small and light. He removed the pilot's cap. At peace with the world was a beautiful, blonde-haired woman.

"This must be the woman pilot, Lilia. I have heard stories," said Andreyev.

When the men finished burying Lilia, the Sergeant ordered a last salute to honor their fallen comrade. Andreyev called out, "Ready, aim, fire." The men fired three rounds in the honor of the perished heroes, and then headed west. Within a matter of minutes, the battalion was discovered by a low flying Messer. There was a hail of bullets as some of the men dove for cover while others scattered. When the plane was certain it had completed its mission, Andreyev crawled out of a hollow tree trunk where he had been hiding in order to reconnect with his men. He quickly discovered he was the lone survivor. For the remainder of the war and beyond, he was grief-stricken and guilt-laden, con-vinced he should have done more to save his men.

1946

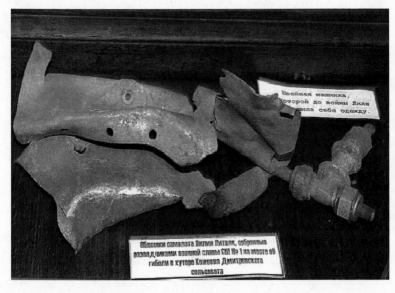

Parts of Lilia's fallen plane.

A partially burnt plane with the number 44 and two charred white lilies painted on its fuselage, along with other downed aircraft, lay unattended in the fields near the village of Kozhevnya. The war now over, the impoverished local citizenry began to search and strip downed war planes–Lilia's included–of its valuable Duralumin skin to make spoons, forks, and cups from which to eat and drink. They also removed many of the engine parts and exchanged them for tractors at a local state factory in order to plant and harvest food.

As the Great Patriotic War survivors in the vicinity of Krasny Luch began to reconstruct their lives, the skeleton of Lilia's plane was left to rust and rot. Lilia's remains lay undiscovered and undisturbed in the make-shift grave created nearby by Sergeant Andreyev and his men.

1961

History teacher Valentina Vaschenko.

After studying at the Pedagogical Institute in Lugansk, Valentina Ivanovna Vaschenko accepted a position as history teacher at School No.1 in Krasny Luch. Her students were teenagers, beginning to spread their wings. She wanted her students to be honorable and patriotic members of the Soviet Society and pass on to their children and children's children the sacrifices of their parents and grandparents in the Great Patriotic War. She began to search for a field research project that would complement their traditional class work.

1963

Valentina is moved by Inna's story of Lilia.

Valentina's patriotic passion took her to Moscow to meet with the Soviet Committee of the Veterans of War. There she was introduced to decorated Aces Porkryshkin and Kozhedub, who explained many pilots perished in Donbass; they remain sadly listed as "unknown, disappeared without a trace." During these meeting, she met Inna Pasportnikova, who recounted the story of her friend, Lilia Litvyak.

Valentina believed she had found the ideal patriotic education project for her current and future students. They would help to find and identify fallen heroes in a radius of the town. It was to become the passion of her life.

Valentina's patriotic passion took her to Moscow to meet with the Soviet Committee of the Veterans of War. There she was introduced to decorated Aces Porkryshkin and Kozhedub, who explained many pilots perished in Donbass; they remain sadly listed as "unknown, dis-appeared without a trace." During this meeting she met Inna Pasportnikova, who recounted the story of her friend, Lilia Litvyak.

Valentina believed she had found the ideal patriotic education project for her current and future students. They would help to find and identify fallen heroes in a radius of the town. It was to become the passion of her life.

1967

The Scouts of Glory is formed in Krasny Luch

Four years and numerous petitions later, Valentina was granted permission by the Ministry of Defense to start a search detachment. The group was named The Scouts of War Glory. Their mission: search the place of battles of the 73rd Guard Pursuit Aviation Regiment in Donbass. That summer, under Valentina's supervision, her students began their hikes and searches.

1969

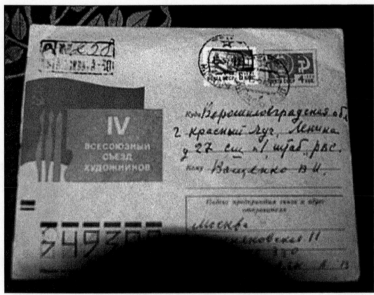

*Lilia's mother writes to Valentina about
her daughter's war missions.*

Unrelated to the Scout searches, local school children on a class outing found bits of a WWII plane and a shallow grave near the tiny village of Dmitrovka, Ukraine. They discovered the grave contained the semi-preserved body of a pilot. Like Sergeant Andreev some 26 years before, the students realized the diminutive pilot was a woman. They also found strands of blonde hair, and a handwritten note folded in her pocket.

Out of respect, the town's elders had the body placed in common grave No.19, reserved for perished heroes, in the center of village some 33 kilometers from Krasny Luch. The pilot's name was listed as "unknown."

1971

The Scouts of Glory grow in size and commitment under Valentina's Leadership

Valentina took members of her now growing Scouts of Glory detachment on a visit to Moscow. There they met In-na, who told them of Lilia's valiant deeds and asked them to keep searching for her remains. She also explained, since her remains were never found, Stalin, Khrushchev and Brezhnev had all refused to posthumously name Lilia a Hero of the Soviet Union, the country's highest military award. Valentina committed to Inna that she and the Scouts of Glory would find Lilia's remains. She also pledged to herself that keeping Lilia's memory alive would be her life's passion.

1974

Inna and Valentina interview a war survivor
who recollects air battles

Inna, her husband, and her grandchildren spent numerous summers with Valentina and her detachment, searching for Lilia, using a metal detector and shovels. They found thirty aircraft but no Lilia. Along the way the ladies interviewed a number of villagers who remembered bits and pieces about local air battles. They would then combine the recollections hoping to better pinpoint where Lilia's plane crashed to earth.

Around the same time, Valentina received gov-ernment approval to open a museum in Krasny Luch in Lilia's honor, although its operations had to be funded by citizen contributions.

One of Valentina's first acts was to create a book of Lilia's memories with all the pictures she had collected. That book, and numerous additions, remains the most complete biography of Lilia's short life. It also contains many pictures never before seen by the general public, some of which have been included in this volume.

The opening page of Lilia's book of memories. Translation: Lilia Forever

Some of the first pieces of memorabilia donated by Anna Litvyak included Lilia's military dress, her first flying book, a copy of the *Pravda* "White Lily" story, and the wartime poster of Lilia interrogating Erich Hartmann.

Family contributions to the Lilia Litvyak Museum—the Hartman poster and one of Lilia's published war stories

1976

The common grave where Lilia's remains sat for more than three decades.

Taras Andreyev, now 57, had been considered the town rebel since he was born in 1926. (Taras is from the Greek word *mutineer... rebel.*)

When his Mother said to do this, he did that. When his teachers suggested a class outing into the woods, he would argue "Why not the lake?" And when his father counseled him to on how to use a plow and spade in the fields, he decided to become a coal miner in nearby Krasny Luch.

To no one's surprise, the day after Hitler invaded Russia, the 15-year-old left school to join the Army. It also came as a surprise that he "adjusted" his birth certificate to indicate he was eighteen, the minimum age necessary to join the military.

He fought gallantly and with distinction (awarded the Order of the Red Star) in the 383rd Rifle Miners' Division, until his leg was shattered by a German bomb as his battalion advanced on the front near war's end in 1945. Consequently, he spent the rest of his adult life doing odd jobs around town, drinking vodka, and telling tales of his military adventures.

~

It was a warm summer day when Valentina and her Scout detachment decided to take a break under a few large cherry trees in a field not far from the village center. While the children rested, Valentina asked the oldest scout in attendance and School No.1's role model, Yevgeniy Krakovsky, to go to the spring in the village and fill the water bags for the others. Yevgeniy obliged.

Yevgeniy, accompanied by two young scout comrades aged 13 and 14, were collecting water when Taras, sunning by the spring, spotted the school children dressed in military attire.

"Boys," laughed Taras, "the war has been over for some time!"

Yevgeniy stared at the gimpy man with the scent of vodka on his breath and replied, "Perhaps for some, but not all." He explained the mission of scouts—to find the remains of the brave woman pilot who defended Donbass.

"Despite her beauty, her small size, and young age, Lt. Litvyak was a ferocious fighter who killed many fascists. We wish her to be recognized and rewarded appropriately."

~

"Who told you this tale?" asked Taras, his mind suddenly flooded with memories of a day in early September some 36 years prior. He and his gallant comrades from 383rd Rifle Miners Division had been engaged in bloody battles for months trying to repel the fascists until they had no alternative but to retreat to Rostov-on-Don through the dense woods, where they found the body of a young female pilot.

"Comrade, are you okay?" said Yevgeniy, noticing the man's eyes blinking and face contorting.

Taras wondered, *Could it be?*

"Who is in charge of your expedition?"

"Comrade Vaschenko, Valentina Ivanovna."

"And, where is this Comrade Vaschenko now?"

"At camp's edge."

The children escorted Taras back to the cherry tree. Taras explained his recollections to Valentina, who was at once elated that her long journey might soon be coming to an end and deeply saddened to think this magnificent war hero lay unattended in a common grave for 36 years.

1977

After 36 years of searching, Lilia's plane is found.

Valentina notified the Military Aviation Expert Group of the War Ministry, which investigated the remains of the plane and established that it was a vintage Yak-1 from the 73rd Regiment, the type of plane Lilia was flying during her last battle. There was also a small skill with two bullet holes, partial remnants of two pelvis bones, and a few strands of blonde hair. The conclusion of local medical experts was that these were the remains of a woman, and these remarks were so noted in correspondence sent to the Aviation Expert Group, who in turn reported their findings to the Ministry of Defense.

1978

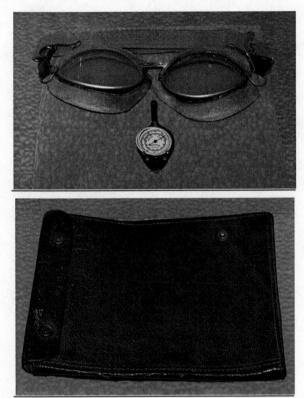

Lilia's flying goggles (top) and leather log case (bottom)

The investigation continued. Official records at the Ministry of Defense revealed there were three women fight-er pilots in the regiment: Lilia, Katya and Masha Kuznetsova. Katya was killed in July 1, 1943, and buried in the village of Novo-Krasnovka, Lugansk region, Masha Kuznetsova was alive. That meant that the pilot in common grave had to be Lilia.

At about the same time, a small display is installed at the Central Army Museum in Moscow. Lilia's flying goggles, compass leather log book, and wool flying cap remain there to this day.

1979

Lilia's monument is created and dedicated in Krasny Luch.

On July 26, 1979, 35 years and 359 days after she perished, the Military Aviation Expert Group of the War Ministry officially declared that the remains were those of Lilia Litvyak, who had disappeared on August 1, 1943.

During the month of August, her personal file was updated by order of the Ministry of Defense of the USSR from "disappeared without a trace" to "perished in the battle on August 1, 1943, near the village of Marinovka, buried in the common grave No.19 in the village of Dmitrovka,

Donetsk region. The facts have been established by the detachment Scouts of War Glory of School No.1, the town of Krasny Luch, Lugansk region."

Lilia's fellow officers, Inna, and the Scouts addressed the government with a petition to award Lilia the title, Hero of the Soviet Union, posthumously.

In September 1979, Valentina received a curt response from then President Brezhnev who wrote, "The Motherland has awarded Lilia Litvyak high enough and all her awards were listed in her records. The best remaining additional reward for Comrade Litvyak would be in your memory."

President Brezhnev's insensitive rejection left Valentina and the Scouts more determined than ever to obtain Lilia's just reward.

She developed a plan. She again visited the veterans' group in Moscow to gain their support to build a monument in Krasny Luch. Thanks to the efforts of the detachment and letters of recommendation for Lilia's flying pilots, the government approved erection of a monument in front of School No.1, although the project was left unfunded. The Scouts took it upon themselves to gather scrap metal (including unnecessary old beds, train rails and water buckets) where they were able to raise the funds to complete the monument.

A former pupil of School No.1, sculptor Nikolay Scherbakov, collaborated with architect Boris Ivanovich Chelombitko on the monument with the assistance of workers from the plants and factories of Krasny Luch, who learned of the project through articles and photos in the local newspaper. It took twelve months to complete. All agreed that space should be left for the words, "Hero of the Soviet Union."

During the emotional installation event, Lilia's best friend and mechanic, Inna, makes an impassioned plea to those in attendance that Lilia deserves her rightful place in history.

Inna Pasportnikova delivers a speech about her friend, Lilia

1981

Valentina spent the next few years actively collecting donations. Her vision, a museum in Lilia's name. She also convinced local Krasny Luch officials to rename school No. 1, the Lilia Litvyak School. A metal sculpture in the shape of a plane is placed at the entrance. Finally, in 1981 the donor fund is large enough to allow Valentina to opens a modest museum in the rear of the Lilia Litvyak School. It includes all the memorabilia collected over the years from family, friends and fellow pilots, including letters to mother Anna from the field. The collection also includes her field writing pad, a small diary with Lilia's innermost thoughts, exhibiting her sense of commitment and personal bond to Katya, Inna and Lyosha.

M.G. Crisci in front of the Litvyak School and Museum.

1988

Largely thanks to the efforts of Valentina, Proletarskaya Street in Krasny Luch was renamed Lilia Litvyak Street, and School No.1 is given the name the Lilia Litvyak School, to honor the legendary pilot and recognize the profound patriotic work of the Scouts of Glory. A memorial plaque is erected on House No. 4 in this street. Valentina lives in Flat 12 of this building to this day.

Lilia street plaque in Krasny Luch

1990

Brezhnev long since gone, the Cold War over, Valentina continues her lifelong mission. Finally, the pertinent facts are presented to now President Mikhail Gorbachev who signs a decree that Lilia is granted the appellation, Hero of the Soviet Union.

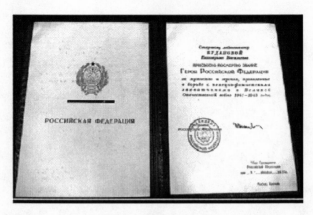

5 May 1990 Lilia President Mikhail Gorbachev officially proclaimed Lilia a Hero of The Soviet Union, the country's highest military award.

1991

One year later, the designation Hero of the Soviet Union" is so inscribed in the blank spot left on Lilia's monument since 1979.

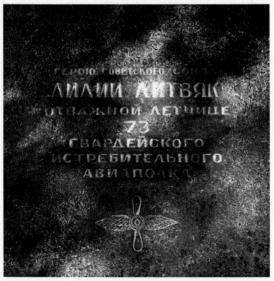

Every journey has secret destinations
of which the traveler is unaware.
                    —Martin Buber

Epilogue

*(f) Friend, advisor, collaborator, and cultural beacon, Yelena Sivolap,
(r) Valentina Vaschenko, founder and curator, Lilia Litvyak Museum*

Valentina and I hope you have enjoyed reading *Call Sign,
White Lily*, a noble collaboration between two cultures with
which we have been proud to be associated.

I am an English teacher from the small Ukrainian town
of Krasny Luch, Lugansk region. Lilia Litvyak, the prototype
of this book, fought for our town during the World War II
and perished not far from it. She was a 21-year-old
Muscovite. Her name is included in the *Guinness Book of World
Records* as the most successful female pilot of World War II.

Valentina is unique in all the world. She, and the children
she trained, searched 36 years to unlock the mystery of Lilia's
death. I myself worked 27 years in the school bearing her
name. In this school there is a Museum of War Glory where
one can see photos, documents, and artifacts belonging to the
heroes of the war; many of them are connected with Lilia
Litvyak. Many generations of children have been brought up

on the heroic past of our country. I am proud to belong to this school.

I think the fact that three persons–an American writer, a Ukrainian teacher, and a Russian museum curator, many thousands of kilometres apart—have gotten connected with one idea—to bring the world this wonderful story—is some new interesting experience that has never occurred before.

We wanted the world to know about the great sacrifices people have paid to save peace on our planet. To know that in America or in Europe—people of good will are alike—they want to live in peace, they want to find the common language, in the wide sense of the word, they want to share their cultural wealth and experience.

We believe this is a story about a beautiful, brave woman about whom the world would want to know. This was not meant to be a narrow trade book about a misunderstood culture. The book is first a celebration of the indomitable spirit of women... all women, everywhere.

The book's honesty also provides insights into how and why our patriotic beliefs, our pride of citizenship, are no different than the average American citizen.

Our wish is that readers the world over will find our literary collaboration informative, entertaining, and insightful. To that end, we have also included some photographs, illustrations, posters, and memorabilia from Lilia' s time that we have reason to believe have never been seen outside Russia. Our hope is that they have enhanced your reading experience.

Afterword

(l to r:) Vera Solovieva, Journalist, Valentin Sapunov, PhD.

We are the Russian text editors. It has been a great pleasure to work with the Russian version of M.G. Crisci's book, *Call Sign, White Lily,* and would certainly recommend it to Russian and American readers. It is very interesting to us that—a respected American writer, Mr. Crisci—who does not have Russian roots and does not speak Russian, took on a difficult mission: to convey to the readers, especially in the United States, the truth about the Second World War and its main component — the Great Patriotic War. The latest estimates are that war cost the country 28 million Soviet dead. If you add the indirect costs—death from deprivation in the evacuation, reduced fertility, and so on, this terrifying figure can be increased to 50 million. These figures are not known to residents of most countries. Recent trends deliberately distort the realities of this most terrible war in history. Training programs, the media in Western Europe and the Americas have consistently pursued two thoughts:

387

1. Fight and win the war: the Americans.

2. Suffered and died: only Jews.

Neither we, nor the author of the book, want in any way to diminish the military victory of the Americans and the suffering of the Jewish people. But that's not the whole story of the Second World War. Matt tries through his story of Lily Litvyak, her family, and friends to show the essence of pre-war Soviet regime with its positive and tragic sides and the actual course of the Great Patriotic War.

To a large extent he succeeded. The talent of an experienced writer was able to penetrate into the history, spirit, and mentality alien to his country and a bygone era. Where there was not enough knowledge, Crisci's intuition completed the picture, which, as a rule, succeeded. Of course, the book is not without some shortcomings. Most of them we tried to fix, such as podredaktirovat details of everyday life in the Soviet Union before the war (which we ourselves know only through the words of the older generation)., and clarified and corrected (perhaps not all) of the technical issues related to the combat aircraft of the period.

This helped us to another member of the project—a veteran of World War II, academic B.V. Sapunov (see the Preface). We agreed, that in some places, it was better to leave certain small inaccuracies. The main thing is that the author undertook the difficult task of creating a large-scale literary work, truthfully describing one of the most tragic periods of world history, and has successfully solved this problem. A low bow to you for that, Mr. Matt Crisci.

Сапунов

THE RUSSIAN CULTURAL CENTRE
IN THE USA

1 February 2013

To All Readers,

In 2011, the Russian Cultural Center in Washington, D.C. hosted a presentation by M.G. Crisci, the American author of "Call Sign, White Lily," a historical novel in collaboration with Russian co-writers Yelena Sivolap and Valentina Vaschenko.

This book centers on real events in the life of a dedicated young woman named Lilia Litvyak, known as Lily. Before even reaching full maturity, she became the first female fighter pilot in the world. During the first two years of World War II, she heroically fought the adversary, commanded a fighter squadron, and shot down 14 enemy planes. She was killed in combat in 1943. After painstaking work, researchers finally found the wreckage of Lilia Litvyak's plane some 37 years after her death. In 1990, President Mikhail Gorbachev posthumously awarded Lilia Litvyak the title "Hero of the Soviet Union."

The book views the life of this young heroine through an artistic lens, exploring Lily's fate and first love. Imbued with many historical facts, the book gives an account of young Russians' lives before and during the war, allowing the reader to become acquainted with the customs and traditions of the time.

Of course, this story is only able to present a small portion of the harsh realities faced by young people during that time. Yet, this book contributes to the important effort to define and evaluate this period of social change, so that new generations of Russians and Americans today may become acquainted with the life and heroic deeds of this modest and brave young Russian woman.

"Call Sign, White Lily" is published in both Russian and English. Through this book, American readers can learn about the character of the Russian people and become aware of Russians' contributions as heroes in world history.

Sincerely,

Yury Zaytsev
The Representative of the
Rossotrudnichestvo in the U.S.,
The Head of the Russian Cultural Centre
1825 Phelps N.W.
Washington, D.C.

Russian Cultural Centre Director Zury Zaitsev and
M.G. Crisci in Washington D.

References

INTERVIEWS

Conversations, interviews and letters. Valentina Vaschenko. Curator, Lilia Litvyak Museum, Krasny Luch, Ukraine. 2007 – 2009.

Conversations, interviews and letters. Yelena Sivolap. School No.1, Krasny Luch, Ukraine. 2007 – 2009.

Interviews with Anthony Goncharenko and Family, San Diego, CA. 2007- 2008.

World War2 through Russian Eyes. Mark Talisman, Exhibit Developer. San Diego, CA. 1999.

Conversations and interviews. Lyudmila Agafejeva. 19 Novoslobodskaya Street, Moscow.

POSTERS, PICTURES AND ARTIFACTS

The Lilia Litvyak Museum, School No 1, Krasny Luch, Ukraine.

Central Armed Forces Museum, Moscow Central.

Zhukovsky Museum of the History of the Conquest of the Sky, outside Moscow.

Anthony Goncharenko Family, San Diego, CA.

Auburn University Library, Auburn AL.

BOOKS

Culture Shock! Russia. Anna Pavlovskaya. Marshall Cavandish Editions 2007.

M.G. Crisci

A Dance with Death. Anne Noggle. Texas A&M University Press. 1994.

Air Aces. Christopher Shonis. Bison Books. 1983.

A History of 20th Century Russia. Robert Service. Harvard University Press. 1997.

Barbarossa – The Air Battle: July – December 1941. Christopher Bergstrom. Classic Publications. 2007

Heroines of the Soviet Union. Henry Sakaida. Osprey Publishing. 2003.

Night Witches. The Untold Story of Soviet Women in Combat. Bruce Myles. Mainstream Press.1981.

Revolution and Civil War in Russia. Elizabeth Ellis, Anthony Esler. Pearson Prentice Hall. 2007.

Russia in the Era of NEP. Shile Fitzgerald. Indian University Press. 1991.

The Soviet Collective Farms. R.W. Davies. MacMillan, London. 1990.

Wings, Women & War. Reina Pennington. University Press of Kansas University. 1997.

Women in Russia. A New Era in Feminism. Edited by Anastasia Posadskaya. Translated by Kate Clark. Centre for Gender Studies. Inter-Verso. London. 1994.

Women in War and Resistance. Selected Biographies of Soviet Woman Soldiers. Kazimiera Cottam. 1998.

Yakovlev Aces of WW2. George Mellinger. Osprey Publishing. 2005.

Young Stalin. Simon Sebag Montefiore. Orion Publishing Group. 2007.

ARTICLES
www.icl-fi.org. From Women and Revolution. Journal of the International Communist League. Issue 12. 1976.

www.vor.ru. Russian Culture Navigator. "The Merry Guys"

www.barynya.com. Russian songs

www.mirpesen.com. Russian songs and lyrics

www.en.wikipedia.org/wiki/lydialitvyak
www.redarmyonline.org.kazimieraJanina, Jean Cottam2006.

www./Sovietawards.com.2002.The memorial to soviet ace Lydia Litvyak.

www.donaldgranger.home.att.net/yak-1 htm

www.123exp-biographies.com/t/00034527358/

(Biography Research Guide).

www.elknet.pl/acestory/litvak.htm

www. ozvarvara.wordpress.com/2008/04/07.

Voices from Russia.

www.experiencefestival.com/lydia
www.encyclo.co.uk/define/zhenotdel

http://pratt.edu/marinaraskova

www.elknet.pl/marinaraskova
www.machair.net/,marinaraskova

http://airports.fai.org/marinaraskova
www.ctie.monash.edu.av/hargrave/soviet_women_pilots.html

www.jewishsightseeing.com/russia/moscow/central_armedfor
ces_museum/1_999021_9-russia_eyes-exhibit.htm

www.6.dw-world.de/en/saa0.phpwww.nationalmuseumafmil
/factsheets. women of rubble www.cmaf.ru. central armed
forces museum of Moscow

www.elknet.pl/acestory/litvak/litvak.htm. WW II Ace. Sto-
ries.Darius Ztyminski.

www.ww2F.com/russia-war/1336-letters-rerman-soldiers.html
Lt. Otto Deissenroth, Military Post No. 12-827D

www.ondirpower.org/docs/litvyak_lidiya_vladirjrovna
www.acepilots.com/german/geraces.html

www.minervacenter.com. Quarterly Report on Women and the
Military 2000.

http://cnc.wikia.com/wiki/stalin'sadvisor

www.emayzine.com/lectures/stalin.html. Stalin's economic
Policy 1930 - 1940